# Some Call it Treason

*Watch out for that [illegible]!*

*Howard Ford*

Howard S. Ford

ISBN: 1-4505-8139-0
ISBN-13: 9781450581394

# Introduction

**Some Call it Treaso**n is a novel in which friends wrestle with which side to be on in the days leading to our American Revolution. It is based on historic facts, but the story of Jamie Claveraque, his life in the English West Country and his adventures when he came to America is pure invention. One might assume, as I did, that historical fiction would not require near as much research as **Sure Signs**, my history of Central New York. But he would be mistaken.

Aside from the serendipity of finding deliciously interesting historical events through browsing bookstores, I owe considerable thanks to historical societies, such as at Walpack Center, librarians, friends and strangers who suggested venues I wouldn't have guessed.

I want to thank John Bausmith, historian at the Maplewood (New Jersey) Historical Society for providing history of my home town including the story of Chief Tuscan. When a child I assumed that my grammar school and Tuscan Road were named after Tuscany since we invested so much time learning about early Rome. John set me strait on pertinent facts regarding Maplewood, called Vaux Hall in Revolutionary War days.

For fun, I planted Jamie's uncle's farm just where Tuscan School was built in the 1920s. Conjecturing how the topography of the tract appeared in the 1770s was exciting. Jack Voorhees, a trumpet player classmate played the trumpet with Chubby Chalker as they do in the book.

The ladies at Skaneateles Library and those at Seymour Library in Auburn also guided me to numerous volumes which advanced my knowledge of the times that helped develop the story.

Then an unfunny thing happened to me when I had written about three fourths of the novel. A scheduled operation to repair an abdominal aortic aneurism was performed, and pronounced a success by the surgeon. Three friends had had the same operation and by the same surgeon; they said it was a piece of cake and that I would be home in three days.

But when I came to after the surgery, I was paralyzed from the waist down. For a few weeks I was literally a basket case and had to be hoisted by a power winch, shoved along a rail on the ceiling, and lowered to use my not-so-private bath. I spent the next three months in rehab learning to use a wheelchair and a walker in a hospital and then, a nursing home.

My wife, Ann, knew I hated the humiliation and lack of privacy in these confines, among other things, and arranged for me to come home. Her care made all the difference. Ann also arranged with our next door neighbor, Robin Debenedetto, an LPN, to line up Tammy Searing and Jackie DeBois, nurses who have been very helpful throughout and have stayed the course with us. And I am on my way to walking again with the help of physical therapists Heath Rush, Ken Rescott, and Susan Dietrich.

Under this greatly improved environment, I was gradually able to resume writing and to pick up the thread of the plot, the main characters and their lives.

My Finger Lakes Writers Group gave suggestions and encouragement as we each read our creations at the bi-weekly meetings. These critiques helped smooth and heighten the narrative, and reminded me that often I did not write what I thought I had. Since I had to discontinue writing for over a year, I know they are anxious to know how the story turned out, as I was.

And I hope you, the reader, will be, too.

# chapter 1

MY BROTHER'S LONG wished-for return home from America was the culmination of our family's education of the troubles in the colonies. He substantiated, or corrected, and added to what we had thought before. Dordy had obtained his commission only a few months before his regiment was ordered to sail to the colonies for the purpose of quelling the irate Bostonians.

He served in the king's army for more than seven years when he was wounded at the Battle of Bunker Hill. I should explain that when a child, I pronounced George, as Dordy, and to our family and among close friends, he has been called Dordy ever since.

His letter told us only that he had suffered a wound and was being shipped to Plymouth for rehabilitation with 170 injured mates. They were to be accompanied by Mrs. Gage, American wife of the governor and military commander, General Thomas Gage, and her entourage. The general was being recalled to London after having been replaced by General William Howe, and would follow his wife to England in a few months.

Dordy also told us that the idea of coming home and retiring to our family farm in the Wye valley now appealed to him mightily. In the same week that his letter arrived we heard more details of Generals Gage and Howe's victory over the rebels at Bunker Hill and Charlestown, a victory seriously tainted with high loss of British officers and men.

My younger brother Jonathan and I had taken the lorry to Plymouth. We arrived at the naval base hospital where Dordy was recovering, just as he and his doctor were finishing the laborious process of determining the final fit for an ankle and foot made of willow wood for his truncated leg. As we entered the reception hall of this old made-over stone fortress, Dordy was straightening up from a bench when he saw us, flinched a bit, recovered, and stepped forward with his arms outstretched to embrace me with welcome.

"Jamie, young lad, you've grown to be a man," he barked as he clasped me around the shoulders.

"It's good to see you after all this time," was all I could muster as I hugged him and realized that he was more of a bony frame than the healthy thick-shouldered young man off the farm when I last saw him. Jonathan greeted Dordy with a hug also but backed away from his older brother whom he hardly knew.

As the doctor straightened up, I offered him my hand and announced, "I'm James Claveraque. Thank you for taking care of our brother. We've come to take him home." We chatted with the doctor for a few minutes but it was obvious to all of us that Dordy was tiring. He quickly sank down on the bench and Jonathan and I appraised the changes that seven years in the army and battling rebels had wrought. He was in full parade uniform; white britches, a fine black leather knee-boot on his good leg and a stocking over his make-do foot, topped off with a scarlet coat crisscrossed with white belting and a silver gorget at his throat.

Of course he wanted to appear his best when returning home to his family after so long a time. He looked splendid in his uniform except for his frailty, his fatigue and his limp.

I started. "What happened to your…?"

"My leg was shattered at the ankle by a rebel musket ball at Breed's Hill though scribblers for the press refer to it as the Battle of Bunker's Hill. I was lucky that I lasted in the fighting as long as I did and that this was all the damage done to me. Almost half of us, of over two thousand men, were either killed or wounded that hot, sweaty, damned afternoon."

Dordy seemed to tire before my eyes during this vigorous, but brief recitation of his trial last June on the hill overlooking Boston Harbor. I came close to feeling guilty that I had not been there on that hill and so tested with him. Jonathan and I assisted him into our lorry, made sure we had all his baggage, and began our trek through the beautiful and bountiful apple country of Devon and Somerset on the way back to our orchards and farm in the beautiful Wye Valley of Herefordshire.

We asked a few more questions about the tensions in Boston and the colonies over the last several years, particularly Lexington, Concord, and Bunker Hill. This was not only to satisfy our curiosity of the happenings that led up to that day, but, as well, to not minimize the suffering and travail he had gone through. Then we realized that the poor man would be asked to relate answers to the many questions all over again when we arrived home. So we stifled our pressing need to go into the details.

"What's that on the axle?" Dordy asked me.

"Those are springs that I made to soften the ride. This lorry rode our Herefordshire roads so roughly, I decided to smooth the jolts by fashioning springs and placing 'em between the axle and the wagon box. When we get off this Devon road and onto Somersetshire country ruts and potholes, see what you think," I said. I knew that we would soon encounter a wretched stretch of road which would put the springs to a real test. As always with Dordy, I hoped that his response to my opinions and projects would be favorable.

We rode the bridge across the Severn and skirted the Forest of Dean which caused us to turn north past Monmouth where the Monnow River joins the River Wye. Then we coursed along the narrow road which refreshingly became paired with the cool breezes and soft purling of the river. It was evident that he wished the questions to cease so that he could focus his full attention to absorb and enjoy the sights and sounds, especially the fragrances peculiar to the apple country in southwestern England this time of year.

The apple harvest was at hand and the different varieties in the orchards we passed were in fruition so that, to one who had been so long removed from his boyhood grounds, the breath of the apples still on the trees and the tang of those beginning to rot on the ground had to be enchanting. Jonathan and I must have sensed his need at the same time and we again resolved ourselves to silence. We rode in unobtrusive quietude as the sun became low enough to throw long tree shadows across the meadows and our silhouettes onto the verge of the red-dusty road.

Fields of red and white clover, buttercups, oxeye daisies, gorse, and crowfoot, punctuated with occasional islands of poppies and cornflowers, alternated with the orchards, separated by red-berried hawthorn hedgerows and coppices of hazel, hardening-off to be made into hurdles. As our lorry proceeded from bright meadows to cool woods undergirded with bracken and out again to orchards heavily hung with maturing pippins, nature orchestrated her beguiling sounds, sights, and mysteries. The sun had lowered to sit on the horizon and flying insects exploded into the light amber air followed by stone chats, crested tits, and meadow pipits.. Skylarks and lapwings warbled excitedly as they feasted on the wing.

"Is that farm on the left still owned by the Bushnells?", Dordy asked as he pointed to the pile of old red sandstone buildings on distant Orange Hill barely visible through the dusk.

"Yes, but things have not gone well for him. Mrs. Bushnell died three years ago. Sally is still there. She has declined as many swains as have come to their door. Helping her father manage the farm and the household is her main concern at the moment. Thank goodness! We still get our hay and oats for our horses from them and they get their cider from us for their field hands. By the way, she knows you're arriving today."

He ignored the answer. " Is your friend Crispin Johnson still here?"

"Yes, but Crispin is not happy working on the farm for his father. Being nursemaid to a herd of cows, as he calls it, is not his idea of the future. He wants to go to America and have a place of his own—an orchard no less.. Sometimes I think all that keeps him here is fishing the pools and riffles of the Wye. He wants to be his own man, independent and adventurous."

I heard a horse and rig catching up with us. "Move over!" was the impatient greeting. Quickly, I veered Nellie to the side of the road, narrowly missing the ditch. The lorry swayed violently, enough I thought, to throw Dordy out onto the road.

"Watch out! You want to get killed?" I called. The driver was too intent on forcing his horse to pass and paid no heed. When I saw who it was, I was not surprised.

"Who'se that?" Dordy shouted.

"That is Wencesles Mochter. I hope we see no more of him. He's nothing but trouble."

We soon arrived at our home situated back from the river a hundred yards. A few pine trees and magnificent copper beeches shelter the house from northwest winds and our orchards, close by the barn, are favored by a northern slope.

Father must have been scanning the road with his glass for he appeared on the porch and hailed us when we were still a furlong off. As we walked up the steps, mother came out on the porch too, tears of joy in her eyes. She and father had thought they would never see Dordy again. To them, he had "gone west." But now, the prodigal son had come home.

The aroma of baked ham, mashed potatoes, coffee and cider, cheese and apple pie, and warm-from-the-oven bread bathed us as we entered the center hall, and conducted us to the dining room where mother had directed the products of her culinary alchemy to be displayed. It was her grand attempt to lure Dordy so that he would never leave home for long again. I'm sure the low-beamed ceiling, the imposing mahogany sideboard and the dining table, garnished with a dooryard bouquet and set with our heirloom silver, reminded Dordy of long-ago delights *de cuisine* and family warmth.

A jumble of three cheerful conversations ensued as we each tried to override the other until one dominated with the dangerous nature of the doings in Boston the previous spring. Dordy had begun the long-awaited recounting of his service in the colonies.

"And it was so stupid of Howe not to let the men unburden themselves of their packs and other gear not necessary to combat. Do you know that each of the men was carrying close to a hundred and twenty-five pounds on his back as he marched up that hill? And, as usual, we were ordered to wear our heavy wool winter uniforms on a hot steamy day—with white crossbelts standing out against the scarlet tunics for near perfect targeting by the rebels. The newer, less faded tunics of the officers signaled us out for the first shots. I'm told it was just as happened with Braddock twenty years ago."

We couldn't believe that the higher officers would not have more compassion for the troops and realize that, unburdened, they would have more strength to carry on their fighting. But we didn't interrupt as Dordy continued.

"General Pigot was with his men on our left flank and I was with Howe on the right. Before the clash of forces, it was a grand sight to see the double lines of troops in their brass-buttoned redcoats and white breaches, close to two thousand men in all, with sunlight glinting on their bayonets held at the ready."

"Realize that Boston is a peninsula a half mile wide and two miles long surrounded by the bay on three sides, and low hills, like Breeds Hill, north, south, and west. Many attractive islands to the east protect it from the sea.

"On that day every hill, every steeple, every eminence of any kind, even the spars of ships in the bay, were crowded with spectators, perhaps as many as twenty thousand partisans of both sides eager to witness this contest of wills; a life-and-death pageantry as in a colossal seaside amphitheater."

"As we proceeded up the hill at the slow drummer's, deliberate pace, we encountered scattered clay pits and kilns, and a series of fences, perhaps as many as ten, which had been obscured by the hip-high grass. We slowed to clamber over these hurdles, and expected to be pummeled with musket balls or grape shot each time. But it was only our own field pieces that were fired at the rebels when we were halted at these detents. They were fired only occasionally since most of the ammunition we had was of the wrong size. Twelve pound balls for six pound guns, for God's sake! And then our field pieces mired in soft ground."

Father snorted in disgust. Dordy didn't let this hinder him.

"Admiral Graves had signaled his warship's guns to stop lobbing shot at the enemy ahead as we closed on the rebel's redoubt on the near hill. But, aside from an occasional hit, the bombardment caused little damage. When the rebels heard a ball coming, they threw themselves to the ground. After the impact, it was safe for them to stand

and resume their mischief. They held their fire as we closed the gap separating us. It became increasingly painful to think what could happen as we hurdled each successive fence."

"How awful!" mother exclaimed. "How could you keep from firing a shot and taking cover?"

"Hush!" said father.

"When we stepped over the last fence within forty yards of the redoubt, we could clearly see the row of muskets leveled at us along the log and dirt wall. Silence still prevailed until their officers belched the command and a blast of smoke, fire, and scud erupted; lead bullets thudded against the bodies of my friends on either side accompanied by a cacophony of screams. Our front row of grenadiers was decimated, but quickly re-formed with fusiliers from behind who were, in turn, shattered by the another deafening discharge from the redoubt wall. Clouds of smoke combined with the blasts of cannon and muskets and yells all around caused us to grope, we became so disoriented. The fallen bodies of my mates hindered any attempt at progress and the remaining men turned away and fled from the raucous pelting from the top of the hill." Father, who had been fascinated with colonial affairs since the beginning of the Seven Years War, had educated himself by subscribing to Mr. Cave's *Gentleman's Magazine* all those years. He was familiar with George Washington's mission to the French Fort Le Boeuf over twenty years ago, his ignominious defeat to a French detachment at Great Meadows and the series of battles culminating with the French surrender of Quebec and Montreal. He had read about Pontiac's Conspiracy and the king's Proclamation Line only three years after the fighting in the French war, and all the government's abusive colonial legislation since, which has so provoked the present conflict with the rebels.

Father also occasionally received letters from uncle Arthur, his brother in New Jersey, with sketchy news of rebellious happenings along with family matters. He read these to the entire family so that we had a better insight of what London policy was doing to the colonists. But he refrained from showing this familiarity now so that Dordy would have unhampered attention, as he deserved.

"Those lads were brave! They reformed under our commands and went up the hill a second time into the face of certain death. And again, we were blasted at twenty or so yards and slaughtered. True, they turned and ran back down the hill. But Howe had them re-form and we went up a third time, with reinforcements which had since crossed the bay from Boston. Howe had finally relented and let us discard our packs to our immense relief. There was less firing from the rebels as we closed on the redoubt and finally overwhelmed them in hand-to-hand fighting. That was when I got shot in the ankle. My, how it hurt for so long. Even after my foot was amputated."

"I have heard that the rebels ran out of gunpowder. That must be when they began to clear the redoubt. In the end, we took the field but in terms of casualties, the rebels won hands down. They lost most of their men during the last fifteen minutes, I'm sure. I read that they had about five hundred dead and wounded. But not near as many as our casualties. We lost well over a thousand out of twenty-three hundred. Among the officers were Colonel Abercromby of the Grenadiers and Major Pitcairn of the Marines.

Jonathan had a question, "How did…?" Father hushed him. "Let Dordy finish," he said.

"Of our squad, my friends Gardiner Colley, Ethelred Barnsby, and Oliver Turnstead were killed at the scene or later died of their wounds. Only David Burns and I, in the squad, were wounded and survived. The idea that the rebels are cowards and won't stand up and fight is now a shattered myth. As General Clinton told us, " It was a dear-bought victory, another such would have ruined us."

Incredulous at what Dordy had said, father asked, "Since those hills are on a peninsula connected to shore by a narrow neck, didn't you try to get behind or flank 'em?" Howe could have easily taken Charlestown Neck which would have left the American contingent to die on the vine."

"Yes, on both sides. On our left was Charlestown; nice homes which the owners were forced to vacate several weeks earlier, now provided perfect cover for rebel snipers to harass us when we tried the flanking attack. So General Gage, from the Copp's Hill battery—that's at the northern tip of the Boston peninsula—and Admiral Graves, from his ships, bombarded the homes with red-hot shot to fire those homes and get relief from the snipers. The weather had been so dry for weeks, those wooden houses were easily ignited by the shot and consumed by flames that rose fifty feet in the air.

"The *Symmetry*, a gun ship near the mouth of the Charles River, was raking Charlestown Neck with grape shot to prevent more rebels from joining the men on Bunker's Hill. Actually the rebel's redoubt was on Breed's Hill, Bunker was at the top of the slope. But never mind, the name has stuck.

"On our right, the rebels had extended a makeshift fence to a drop-off to the shore of the Mystic River and fortified it with sharp-shooters and a field piece. Our men, mostly the Welsh fusiliers, were really piled up there. The wounded and dead I mean."

"The rebels had concentrated their fire at the officers. They knew we were officers by our scarlet tunics which, being new and of higher quality, had not faded like those of the troops. It wasn't long before the men had no one to turn to; all was confusion until Howe ordered the retreat.

"Additional troops had been landed by the transports at Morton's Point by then and Howe brought up the reinforcements, reformed the survivors of the first assaults, and sent us up for another attempt. By nightfall, we commanded all the ground to Charlestown Neck."

Dordy was so carried away by his telling of the battle that he was repeating himself. Father broke in, "How stupid of the government and the generals. London provoked the Bostonians so with taxes and harsh laws, as if they were a defeated people instead of Englishmen. And General Gage so out-generaled himself that he and his army boxed themselves in at Boston.

"The administration in London tried to close the port of Boston and it took thousands of redcoats and their general—- and the Loyalists—to get themselves so crammed in the port that it was choked to death and really closed—to their distress. They caused their own besiegement."

Father added, as an afterthought which turned out to be prescient, "The generals will probably have to vacate the place before long."

As almost always, the value of father's comments and the force of his voice dominated the conversation. "And, in a way, it all started right here with the tax on cider." he said.

The door from the pantry opened, pressed by the ample hip of our cook, Holly, who had a hillock of brown betty on a platter accompanied by a side dish of hard sauce. "Master Dordy!" she cried. "I heard you were coming and I prepared your favorite dessert with our early apples. How grand you look in your officer's uniform and how good it is to see you again."

Dordy rose from the table and gave her a hug as well as he was able. "You're a dish, Holly, and thanks for your consideration. It's glad I am to be home, I can assure you." Holly, a little flushed and flustered, curtsied and returned to the steaming kettles of her kitchen.

Father resumed, "Don't you remember? Right after George the third became king, that ass of an earl, Lord Bute, proposed a tax on cider. Maybe you don't—it was back in '62 and the big-wigs in Whitehall were desperate looking for ways to pay for the French war. And the first thing they thought of to tax was cider, mind you! Four shillings per hogshead! There were riots throughout the West Country for weeks."

"What was so bad about that? That breaks down to be a small amount per tankard at the pub," I volunteered.

"That's right, Jamie, at the pub. So what does the sport in the taproom care, it's not that much out of his pocket. But for the farmer who has to buy a keg for his field hand's cider break every day, that runs into a fair piece of change. And more than that, the collector had the authority—actually, he assumed the authority—- to install himself in our house to verify, to his fussy satisfaction, our cider production and the tax we had to pay."

Father, working himself into an unaccustomed lather, went on, "I think his name was Colvin, a real obnoxious son of a—-. Never had any authority before; tried to make up for it by throwing his weight around here. Accused us of cheating, made passes at your mother, abused the furniture, ate our food like a horse, caused a lot of paperwork. It took several months of complaining to Squire Calloway to get rid of him, and, finally, the cider tax was killed in '64 or '65."

Mother had contributed little to the conversation except to interrupt occasionally with "pass the potatoes to Dordy", 'do you want some gravy", or "cut some more slices of ham, George." But now she added, "It reminds me, George, of what your grandfather told us of conditions in Brittany before he fled the country. You remember, the time of the dragoons, the soldiers mounted on horseback?"

Mother refreshed his memory. "They were dragoons billeted in the houses of Protestants to intentionally, with the sanction of the government—- in other words, the king—- to intentionally harass their reluctant hosts who had no recourse. They could complain to the intendant but he was under orders to do nothing. It went on and on until the victims either left the country or pretended to switch to Catholicism."

"Yes, I had almost forgotten that. It was like the quartering imposed on the colonials in Boston, New York and Albany during the Seven Years war and repeated again now." said Father. "We could have expected the French king to abuse his subjects. But this is England, and we didn't even contemplate such an extremity being practiced here. Or in the colonies."

"Well, the troops have to be housed somewhere." said Dordy.

"Then let the government build barracks for them, feed 'em, grog 'em, and pay for it themselves. I don't blame the colonials'" Father went on, "Who wants to have strangers forced on you, your family, and your larder? Most of the soldiers are coarse, impressed off the street or from taverns, uneducated, no manners, don't know how to think,—- like they're from a different country. They insult your wife and daughters and bludgeon you or your sons if you try to do anything about it."

"Just like grandfather said about the dragoons!" Mother added.

Dordy piped in, "General Loudon tried to do something about getting troops quartered in the last war, but he was too arrogant and tactless, and only rubbed colonial assemblies and governors the wrong way. I'm told it's one of the reasons he was recalled. When William Pitt became first minister, things changed, the generals' arrogance was reigned in. They were directed to use more tact and persuasion, and we noticed that a spirit of cooperation began to take hold with the colonists.

He also gave colonial officers what had formerly been refused and had galled them so, superiority to British regulars below them in rank. The colonists even volunteered to spend some of their own money to build dormitories when there weren't enough public places for the troops. Pitt promised the colonists to reimburse them for their military expenses. In these and other ways, the *Great Commoner* had a magic touch. The colonies then mustered twenty-three thousand troops for the empire within the month."

Dordy had made a half-hearted attempt to defend the army, but it convinced no one. We loved Dordy, respected him, admired his bravery, and were proud of his promotion to Lieutenant, but generally, we thought most of those in the military hierarchy were a bunch of fat heads.

Father considered the conversation about the army finished. "This is very good brown betty, Mother," he said, and we went on to other subjects..

Dordy slept well into the next morning which was as fresh and clear as a glass of Seyval Blanc. I couldn't wait to finish breakfast and see how well the springs for the lorry had survived the rough road home from Plymouth. Even Dordy, who was not given to flip praise, had noticed an improved ride, probably because it favored the sensibilities of his maimed and still-tender leg.

The springs had been weakened and stretched out of shape from the excess strain. So I removed, disassembled, and reheated them over the coals to a yellow heat before re-forging each spring to the desired shape and quenched them in oil. This made the metal stronger, more durable and less brittle. One sees more carriages in use every week as the shire and stage lines improve the roads. But the art of grading and surfacing highways is far from perfection. And the weather undoes any improvement weekly. Having hardware to install and soften the ride should be a profitable enterprise for wainwrights, wagon owners, and people like me.

Crispin Johnson must have heard the hammering on the anvil as I re-made the springs, and he sauntered in sight. "I just delivered the milk to your cistern. How's Dordy?"

I told him of our journey home and Dordy's revelations of the Boston conflict at the dinner table. Crispin was more than pleased that Dordy was not expected to be seriously hindered by his artificial leg after a few weeks of tentative exercise, and recovery was expected soon. He looked forward to when the three of us could go clout shooting again, especially since Dordy was the best shot whether driving an arrow into a straw butt at fifty yards or lobbing a shot into a meadow at three times that. But for now, Crispin wanted to fish.

"Would you like to try casting some this afternoon, James? I think there might be a hatch coming on the river, and the water's cooled from the upriver freshets. The trout could be lively."

Crispin always knew how to lure me away from work. "If we can do it later in the afternoon," I said. "I'll meet you at Wedlich's pool." He continued talking about how good the river conditions had been over the last few days but realized that my attention was engaged in re-installing the reworked springs under the wagon and that I was in no mood to lollygag. He wandered off.

My father came by just as I was finishing up. I jacked the lorry down to the ground. For a man in his fifties and of a few more stone than he should be, his agility surprised me when he jumped in the lorry to test the springiness.

"Let's take it for a spin and see how it rides now", he suggested. "Just what I was going to do," I said as I led gentle Nellie to the traces. By that time Dordy had finished his breakfast and came down the steps. He joined us with little help to climb into the wagon, and when I lightly flicked the reins on Nellie's rump, the three of us began wheeling into the roadway on our way downstream. I steered Nellie over a few mild ruts to get a feel for any improvement. The springs flexed with more response, softening the jolts, and the three of us yelled our "hurrahs!".

"What did you do to improve the springs?", Dordy asked.

"I made them a little longer and more elliptical and in two plies. Then I greased them with tallow so that they would shift against each other and flex more easily. Now, we'll see how well they take the strain", and I steered Nellie to pull us over the "giant's knuckle", a spot where the top of an underground boulder made an unyielding ridge in the red dust of the road. Another series of "hurrahs! Despite this minor victory, I knew I would have to test the ride for a sustained period and examine the springs closely after each sortie. A different way of attaching of the springs to the axle and the wagon box might work better also.

Dordy asked me to stop so that he could get out and see what I had done to the under-carriage. I obliged, but I noticed that we were now within view of Sally Bushnell's home. Dordy climbed down on his own and made a great scene of inspecting the springs, asking again about the changes I had made in them. He also glanced several times in the direction of Bushnell's.

"Whose horse is that tied to the post?" he asked in agitation.

"I think it's Squire Calloway's chestnut," said Father.

"Well, I guess we shouldn't bother them," said Dordy. And with that, he got back in the lorry and asked that we go home.

Just then, the squire came out the front door with Sally lingering on the threshold. We delayed our start for home so as not to give any appearance of furtiveness, and to gain some idea of what was going on. We felt awkward knowing that we must have appeared devious parked so near on the road with no apparent reason.

Though out of earshot, we could see that the conversation had finished, and Sally backed inside and closed the door. The squire mounted his horse and trotted down the drive.

"Good morning, gentlemen.," hailed the squire. " Dordy, good to see you back all in one piece from the troubles in the colonies. What brings all of you by here?"

"We were giving Nellie and the lorry a tryout with some springs James has designed and installed on the lorry," said Father. "We had to stop to make a readjustment."

" I noticed that the wagon bed was higher," said the squire. "James, when you are satisfied that the springs are as marketable as possible, come by my office and we'll register them. Don't forget to emboss them with your name and date for establishing patent rights. "Dordy,

Sally was just saying that she looked forward to seeing you again in the valley. I think she may be expecting you to make a call on her." He lightly flicked the reins on the chestnut's withers. "Gentlemen, I must be on my way. Good day!" The squire surprised us with his economy of words.

Dordy was lifted from his melancholy by the squire's pleasant revelation and, it was obvious, that he was now eager to make good on the squire's suggestion. For myself, I noticed that the sun had been on the downslope and that I should get home to collect my fishing gear and repair to the river to meet Crispin.

Wedlich's pool was wide and deep, and freshets from upstream were roiling the surface so that any presentation of the fly had to be with finesse to have the lure appear to float free with no drag. As always, the sound of the water's crashing and purling stirred a resonance in me as if it was music, and increased my pleasure at being stream side. Ever since my earliest gambols on the river, whether making dams on rivulets, swimming and fishing, or later cavorting with damsels in its dells, an excitement gripped me.

As Crispin predicted, there were a few dimples on the water indicating a mild hatch and flashes of silver briefly glinted as the fish sipped at the surface and turned aside. He was well occupied trying to reach a promising riffle where the pool shallowed, when suddenly, the slack in his line disappeared and the tip of his rod bent sharply down. He set the hook, and cried out to the excitement of the surge of strength at the end of the line.

Alas, Crispin horsed his fish a bit too much and the trout broke free. Probably the hook was not firmly set, or was set, but at the very lip. "Conditions are just right," he shouted, un-daunted, over the rush of the waters. "The freshets have discolored the water just enough so that they can't see that our flies aren't naturals."

He drew his line clear and back from the water without disturbing the surface, and just before the fly reached the end of its travel behind him, he flicked the rod forward. The line snapped like a whip and zipped through the guides with the fly whizzing forward like an arrow, the leader unfolding softly to lower the fly as daintily as milk weed fluff.

It landed on the water upstream of a boulder behind which a pulsing dark shape lay.

Crispin delayed setting the hook a fraction this time to assure a sound set before the trout could spit it out. The fish quickly sounded to the depths of the pool for succor, but to no avail. My friend maintained a tight line so that the quarry had no slack with which to shake free. Suddenly, it moved to the riffle feeding the pool, forcing Crispin to muck his way through hip-deep water and strong current which took his attention for the briefest of moments. The trout seized the opportunity and broke off.

I had my rod set up now despite Crispin's extravagant distraction, but had to pass on the trail around him to reach water where fish had not been spooked by this chaotic activity. A side stream that decanted from a series of small ledges in a shady glen promised a diverse source of natural food for the expectant trout arrayed in wait against the current. Luck had favored me at this delightful moss-carpeted spot which had been fit for a dalliance several times in recent summers, and I stalked my way into position for a favorable cast.

Crispin was far better at fishing than I. If he missed two catches in a row, what could I expect? The hatch seemed a little different here from the main stream and I tied on a fanciful scarlet and black dry fly. Perhaps this feathery creation would be more enticing to these cousins of the trout in the main river. "After all, fishing is like a treasure hunt." I said to myself.

I did not try to out-cast my natural reach as I had so many times, since such a cast usually collapsed in a heap on the water, driving nearby trout to the safety of the deep, and leaving me with no prospect of success for some time afterward. I cast upstream to the far side near a spruce branch overhanging the dark channel. The sparse fly settled on the water as if it had fallen from the branch, and I tweaked it to simulate a fly's frenzied attempt to flee the wet to tantalize any hungry trout in his lair.

Nothing happened. The fly began to drift, then stopped as if the leader had caught on a submerged twig. As the current's pull on the line increased, it startled a large barrel-shaped denizen of the deep so that he set the hook for me and rushed away headlong as would an eager young hunting dog on a leash. I carefully let out hanks of line to lessen the tension and the chance that the hook would be ripped out of his lip. But still I had to follow with cautious strides to protect my bare feet from sliding and being cruelly bashed on the rocky bottom. I could hear Crispin shouting in excitement behind me, unsure of my adventure.

The fish, or was it an otter, rushed about doggedly searching for respite, pulling me along, but did not find safe haven. Up ahead at a sharp bend in the stream, half the roots of a venerable and stately sycamore reached into the shore for anchorage. The remaining roots had been scoured of their soil, a few broken off entirely, and were valiantly, but slowly, losing the battle to keep the thick white-spackled, gnarled trunk upright.

I recognized that this could be the scene of our denouement and the fish seemed to sense the moment, too. He raced deeply into the confusion of underpinnings, ignoring the restraint on the line. Alas, he snarled the leader on numerous root stubs, then surged and broke free to be seen no more. It was heart rending—-he was the largest fish I have ever seen outside of the Bristol fish market.

Crispin was still a considerable distance downstream when I managed my way over to the old tree. The severed leader appeared deep-down, an askew skein messed as by a viciously playful kitten, a cat's cradle gone awry, and impossible to retrieve. The special fly was gone, too. Just then, a breeze waved tree branches so that a ray of sunlight briefly penetrated the depths by the roots and reflected brightly off the corner of a shining yellow hand-sized slab deep against the bottom. As quickly, the breeze died and the depths again became obscure. It was too deep to reach down without submerging entirely and, as I shoved my foot along the bottom in the hopes of relocating the slab, I felt an object that seemed to conform with what I had seen. Whatever it was, it was immoveable, either heavy or firmly wedged between the rocks, or both. The water was too cold and high to crouch down and easily reach for the bottom and, now, Crispin had arrived at the pool below. This was annoying because I wanted privacy to determine what this heavy, bright object might be.

"You should have seen that fish, Crispin, he was more than two feet long. And powerful. It was like trying to hold back your pup setter, once she's spotted a grouse. It was also smart. Wrapped my leader to these roots, and then surged hard enough to break free. That was my last leader, too."

"How big was it?"

"It was about two feet and powerful. It broke the leader. Who knew that I would need one for a fifteen pound fish. Let's go home, I've had enough fishing for one day." I hoped this last would dampen his interest in my curious behavior by the old sycamore and I turned and walked toward him.

I revealed no more interest than that and relied on Crispin's sympathetic accord with my grief to restrain him from further query. Crispin, good friend that he was, honored my tacit request. We left the stream as the sun dropped behind the Welsh mountains. I suspected that the bright object was something of value that had been there a long, long time.

# chapter 2

AFTER DINNER, I asked father more about his grandfather and France. In the past I hadn't paid much attention when talk of family history and relatives was the subject at table—except when it was about cousins that I liked.

He led me to a high shelf in the bookcase and pulled out a leather-bound volume that resisted being moved; so long had it been in the same place, it had stuck to the paint.

"You'll find it all in here. Your great grandfather was so proud of how he managed to cope with a difficult set of conditions and what happened; he wrote everything down as soon as he could. He didn't want to leave out a thing. Read it."

An old ledger book, the first pages of which were filled with figures of cider production, had sufficed to satisfy my great grandfather's love of thrift and, at the same time, his need to perpetuate his memory for the sake of his posterity. He was a man of twenty-five when this turning point in his life happened. He had transcribed the narrative at a later time from hastily-written notes made during his epic adventure to save his family and fortune.

When I opened and turned the thick pages, the spine of the volume cracked in protest and the stale breath of the past suffused the room. I lit another candle and began to read my great grandfather's journal.

*The following is an account of the Claveracque family's harassment and sub-sequent flight from our village in eastern Brittany near the border of Maine province, to England in the year 1695.*

*I had, with the help of my parents, acquired my own thirty- arpent orchard of fine apple trees from which, for generations, our family made a spicy cider and our version of what a good bottle of Calvados should be. Our location on a northern slope (don't ever forget the importance of siting an orchard this way to protect against a late frost) with the windbreak north of the house and barns was very favorable and envied by many neighbors, as was our product.*

*Anne Marie and I were married six years ago and were soon blessed with a son, Etienne. We survived the scourge of smallpox which assaulted our region the fall after our son's birth. But my parents and Anne Marie's aunt were swept away in that period of desperation. For awhile it seemed all we could do was toil to subsist but without gratification or pleasure. We gradually prospered within the limitations imposed by weather and the state.*

*This long-delayed prosperity was not to last. 'Le Roi Soleil', King Louis XIV, had chafed under the common-sense restraints to relieve religious tensions proclaimed by good king Henry a hundred years ago. So Louis revoked the Edict of Nantes as if to legalize years of his harassment of the Huguenots. Then he sent his dragoons our way. Till now his ministers had overlooked our region, not realizing that we had a few Protestant holdouts remaining and still attending church—our church.*

*He gave orders for dragoons to be quartered in the homes of the town's Protestant habitants. The dragoons had no purpose being there other than to harass us so that we either converted to the state religion or were made to flee the region. One or two dragoons were garrisoned in each house to abuse their hard-pressed "hosts" in as many ways as their crude and overbearing manner could fashion. As a consequence, we were as prisoners in our own homes, one could not even walk to the bakery without being molested verbally, sometimes physically.*

*Generations of ignorance, privation, and brutality have conspired to make humans this inhuman. They insulted the master of the house, demanded meals that would be a feast any other time, drank up the family's wine, Calvados, and cider supply, and made lewd passes at mothers and daughters alike. And worse.*

*If the men of the house protested, the dragoons would give them the flat of their sword or gang up and pummel them to un-consciousness. Several peasants in our region were so tormented and brutally treated that they turned on their oppressors but were slain or sent to Marseilles to be bound over to serve on His Majesty's galleys.*

*To be sure, a few habitants, to whom religion was not that important, changed to the Faith and began instructions in the catechism to avoid further devilment. I do not wish to appear hypocritical to my posterity—- organized religion is not that important to me. But ethical and moral values, coupled with living unafraid and out of the reach of rogues whether of the state, the church, or just plain common criminals, are of extreme importance to us.*

*The local constable, Corbier, had been instructed to do nothing about reigning in the perpetrators of these atrocities; there was no recourse, other than ganging up on them, disguised, at night, and unobserved. But this did not serve either because, if caught or recognized when breaking the law, such an infraction meant being broken on the wheel or sent to the galleys.*

*This official blessing on dragoon harassment of Protestants emboldened those who held a grudge to satisfy their need for revenge. So some Catholics sought revenge on Protestant and Catholic acquaintances alike. So too, Protestants obtained vengeance regardless of the religious affiliation of their assumed tormentors. Social conventions were rendered to shreds.*

*The idea of continuing to live under such conditions forecast a terrible destiny, intolerable to anyone who reveres his family and the joys of life. Leaving the region became our paramount goal when we heard that children as young as seven were being taken from their Protestant parents to be raised as Catholics.*

My sister, Ellen, entered the room. "Jamie, I didn't know you and Jonathan would get back with Dordy from Plymouth so soon. Where is Dordy? How is he?"

"He went to bed. He says he still tires easily from his wounds. But he looks alright and it's nice to have him home again after so many years. He says that his leg is less painful and he's learning to manage it now that the last refitting is more comfortable. He'll be up and about tomorrow. You'll be able to see him then. How was the guitar lesson?"

"Dr. Netti is helping me learn to play some Scarlatti piano-forte sonatas transcribed for the guitar. I'm getting the feel of them and they are pleasant to hear. Do you mind if I practice in this room for a bit while what he taught me is fresh in my mind?"

"No, I enjoy hearing you play. Just don't do any finger exercises, please. So go ahead, it won't bother my reading. This is great grandfather's journal."

She sat down, arranged her music on the stand, lit additional candles, and began to pluck the forthright and inventive, but intricate melodies and rhythms of one of Domenico Scarlatti's easier pieces. I went back to my reading.

*Thus, by design, Anne Marie and I, little-by-little, planted signs of neglect and a lack of prosperity about the farm with keen deliberation. Indeed, we weren't the only ones whose industry and prosperity showed signs of decline; the region began to suffer and peasants here and there left their farms, and weavers, carpenters, and other artisans abandoned their trades.*

*When we were out in the open and visible, Anne Marie and I disciplined ourselves to feign ill health for six months or so by slowing our movements as if sickness had been draped on our shoulders. We did not manure the orchards as our huge rotting dunghill testified.*

*This change in our usual activity was to give credence to our story to Corbier, that illness was our reason for selling the farm. Leaving the country was illegal so"removing ourselves to another province" was our story. We made a farewell gift to him of several livres and a few bottles of Calvados in the hopes that this would suppress any suspicions that we might be fleeing from France and the hateful intolerance the king had sewn among the habitants. Or, at least, to incline Corbier to do nothing about it.*

*Giving the farm the appearance of less prosperity reduced the sales proceeds to a disappointing sum, especially with a boundless harvest only a month from fruition. But it was enough to slip away without deprivation. And my good friend and neighbor, Jacques Bosshart, set fire to one of his small out-buildings a league away in order to create a diversion the day we left.*

*With much of our family treasure sewn in our clothes, we drove our wagon loaded with a few necessities, including the chestnut armoire given to us by Anne's parents, in broad daylight in order to allay suspicion. We were instructed by our Catholic friends to seek hospitality only at specified homes known to be friendly to previous emigrés.*

*From our village near Rennes we followed roads leading to Quiberon Bay rather than to St. Malo, though it was a more roundabout way, to make use of these hospices. When we got to sea, we would not have to skirt the Channel Islands where the king's revenue cutters lay in wait to intercept many hapless groups in a similar odyssey.*

*At the coast we had hopes of finding passage in a smuggler's hold as part of his contraband. Avoidance of authorities in both France and England was a smuggler's concern, as much as it would be ours. To be caught by our country-men leaving France with a moderate to large sum of money was another reason to be consigned by Louis' minions to the galleys.*

*We hated to leave our farm and orchards and the region where generations of Claveraques had toiled with foresight and care to develop it into an outstanding model of husbandry. But our friends were leaving, or forced to leave, and there was no charm in being treated like an enemy of the state in your own country. These were our thoughts on that fearful two-day ride.*

*Smuggling was a way of life at Quiberon we had heard, but our highly vouched-for man could not be located; locals protecting him from stranger's prying, perhaps. A few days sampling the clientele of several harbor-side taverns at Quiberon put us in touch with a respectable family of fishermen who supplemented their income by underground activities. They were experienced smugglers whose names I omit should this account fall into unfriendly hands.*

*Once aboard, there were some close moments when we could have been detected by the authorities. As we rounded the Breton coast to enter La Manche, the sea kicked up a chop of waves which threw our small vessel about in a manner similar to driving an empty wagon on frozen wheel ruts. Evening seemed to calm the sea and we coursed in a direction just to the east of the North star as a member of the crew pointed out to me.*

*Several hours later, the smugglers knew at just what point we were off the English coast, even in the dark, and signaled with slit lanterns emitting a narrow beam of light to none other than accomplices on that dark, wooded shore.*

*Years of experience, organization, and success testified to their professionalism. We were well attended. Our fears of the sea and of official intervention were calmed, and they kept us warm and well fed. They also had the consideration, and good business sense, to recognize the need for housing us overnight in obscure surroundings when we reached shore till they could arrange transportation for us to London. My inner voice insisted I make a mental note of this family of smugglers for future use.*

*Within a few weeks of acclimation to English ways of doing things, reviving my ability to speak English fluently, and finding my way around the city, I was able to arrange employment in the financial district. My experience in the French apple and pear market and its effect on the English fruit market. promised my employers opportunities for lucrative arbitrage.*

*After five months, Anne Marie and I felt comfortably ensconced in a new home and the ambience of London when a messenger's knock at the door caused an instant deferral of our plans. For his efforts in creating a diversion to help us leave France, Jacques Bosshart had been jailed, tried, and consigned to the galleys at Marseilles, the message read.*

*My new London associates graciously responded to the task of quickly introducing me to masters in the art of forgery and disguise. They also made suggestions as to how I might gain Jacques' release if the authorities were intransigent, and supplied me with the tools for success. Our precious metals trader was especially helpful. In an afternoon, I emerged a new man, complete with papers en route to Rennes. Even Anne Marie scarcely recognized me.*

*For this trip, I did not need the services of the smugglers of Quiberon and crossed the channel on a regular packet boat in the conventional manner.*

*At my former village, Corbier did not recognize me, not since I was posing as Major Robert Yves Gilbert de Talon, an agent of the government seeking one Jacques Bosshart, "special attaché to deputies of the King". Presenting official-looking stamped-and-sealed papers certifying my authority, I confided to him (in the unctuous manner of one of the king's important officers to another) that we had been expecting sensitive information from Bosshart so that the king could decide a significant matter of state. I informed him that the king was furious at this delay and had directed me to promptly procure Bosshart in person to answer to His Majesty.*

*Corbier's face was its customary bland blank, devoid of interesting features and any suggestion of thought or response. When he spoke it was merely a poor reflection of his superior's mannerisms and officious style. Hearing that I was close to the king was his cue to fawn over me and to grasp for royal favor. He characterized the perfect sycophant so rampant in the king's government. I let Corbier know that if he could be of assistance to me, it wouldn't hurt his career; the king was generous to those who served, and terrifying to those who hindered his wishes.*

*Corbier gave me a start when he said that he recognized me. But his recognition was only of my contrived persona and my "important" post. He insisted that I could count on him for as much assistance as I desired. Bosshart had been detained for "reasons of state", he said, and could be delivered to me upon presentation of Corbier's order to a Captain De Laye at the port of Marseilles. His assistant and scribe (I don't think Corbier could write) began to prepare the necessary papers.*

*Corbier pulled from the bottom of his cabinet two small glasses and a bottle of Calvados. Another shock went through my entire frame, not visible I prayed, when I observed the Claveraque label on the bottle as he poured the libations. We drank on the success of my mission while his clerk wrote out the orders. If ever I drew strength from a glass of Calvados, this was the time.*

*We made small talk, sipped and savored the delicate flavor of the powerful brandy as the afternoon wore on, and the clerk completed the official document for Bosshart's release. I asked Corbier where I could secure a coach, scanned the prepared order, gave him a flamboyant salute as one confident of success, and took my leave of Monsieur Corbier.*

*It occurred to me that Calvados could provide a service to my mission, even if no more than comfort, and I visited Mistur's dram shop to procure several bottles. Jean Mistur did not recognize me either—a good omen for my task.*

*Instead of a coach (which I had mentioned to Corbier to confuse pursuit), I rented a horse. At Tours, I retired the horse at the livery to take a river packet as far upstream as navigation permitted; it was just as fast with no need to stop for room or board. But I eschewed conversation with the few other passengers.*

*To this point, I had been so concerned and concentrated on accomplishing my burlesque with Corbier that I did not notice the countryside through which I was passing. It was as if I had been wearing blinders. But relaxation from the tension of my interview with him opened windows to vistas new to me. The Loire was broad and the valley graced with thriving vineyards and gardens surmounted with chateaux of grand design and copious resources.*

*Of course, I knew the Loire Valley was steeped in history and endowed with magnificent structures, but I could not linger to admire them. I had an obligation to my friend Bosshart to reach Marseilles before they enslaved him on a galley. Thank God he had no kin who depended on him.*

*Examples of vigorous husbandry unfolded for several days as we coursed against the mild Loire current. Even the river islands were planted to grapes, what appeared to be hemp, or were grazing grounds for sleek-looking cattle. Then these bountiful scenes were interrupted by stretches of extreme poverty. Men, women, and children hailed from shore with wretched entreaties for"La Charité! La Charité! au nom de Dieu.".*

*After several days of restful progress up the river, our course, as we passed Orléans, gradually turned from east to south. Wooded hills blanketed by beach and oak that, even in mid-winter, had retained their coppery leaves, gained prominence, and low mountains began to appear in the southern distance. The stream had been narrowing and rapids became common and more vigorous so that our boatmen had to abandon their oars for pikes to pole up the channels.*

*The head boatman pointed out what he called a lock in the near distance of the stream. As we neared, the downstream gates were opened and we berthed inside the first compartment. Men on both sides then levered heavy beams extending from the top of the hinged gates to close them tight against each other behind us.*

*They then twirled a wheel to open a sluice halfway down on the upstream gates allowing water to fill the lock compartment and our boat to rise. In four minutes we were level with the upstream fetch of river, a height of about four feet. Then, the sluices were closed, the upstream gates were swung open and we proceeded up the river. Gramsé, the canal engineer, said that for a boat going downstream the "hydraulics" would simply be reversed.*

Ellen had finished playing, but I had not heard her put down her guitar and leave the room. Her playing must be much better since it was usually the mistakes which interrupted my reading. She soon softly returned and put down a mug of cider in front of me. Thoughtful and considerate, she often did little favors like this. I complimented her on her playing, thanked her for the cider, and wished her a good night. I was eager to read how great-grandfather had engineered Bosshart's release, but Ellen paused to ask me about what he had written. I summarized the main events of his journal for her and returned to my reading.

Great grandfather's new friend, Gramsé, began talking about Marseilles and mentioned that in winter the galleys were in port to refit until the weather improved. When their packet docked at Roanne, Gramsé offered him a ride in the company coach to Marseilles by way of Lyons.

As their carriage rolled down the Rhône valley, his host ladled him full of facts about the Cevennes, the Camisards (hounded and militant Protestants with whom great grandfather could commiserate), until they rounded the base of a mountain and suddenly, they happily were rid of damp, chilly air and dark, dreary chestnut forests for balmy sunshine and hilly olive groves.

Great grandfather wrote that he could not help but enjoy the remaining majestic arches of the famous bridge at Avignon, the other spans of the bridge having "fallen down" as school children have sung for ages. He commented about the chateaux—the schism Pope's palace and fortresses and the many sandstone statues—and the spires of the other cathedrals rising above city clutter. But great-grandfathers and Gramse's need for haste forced him to be content with no more sight-seeing than seen from the coach's window at the ever-changing charm of the valley's forests and fields.

Within hours, Gramsé had dropped him off at a pleasant small inn overlooking the port of Marseilles and the Mediterranean. Here, great grandfather's journal became more serious:

*As I washed the journey's dust off my face and arms and anticipated a pleasant ramekin of lamb served with a dry white wine to compose myself for the next day's performance, I was startled to see that I was wearing my brown and white red-streaked agate ring. I have worn this ring day and night since my father gave it to me when I came of age. Surely Corbier could not have missed noticing this distinctive gem on my hand when I paid my taxes or sought one of the many permits required for this or that. He was not so dim-witted as to not have recognized it when I posed as Major de Talon.*

*One would think that the professional disguise expert would have insisted that I remove it. But I was more guilty than he. After all, it was part of my image—proud son in the Claveraque family—and I should have been more aware of its conspicuous and dangerous presence.*

*Instead of resting mind and body in preparation for the next day's demands, I was in a state of agitation and anxiety all night. If Corbier did notice the ring and recalled where he had seen it before, he might send a guard south to intercept me. Yes, such an act would do much to enhance Corbier's stature in the hierarchy.*

*The ring flawed my disguise, but I decided not to remove it, and conjured up a story to justify sporting this unusual ornament and to refute any accusation.*

*In the morning, the innkeeper pointed out the harbor master's office and the shipyard where I would find Captain De Laye. I screwed up my nerve to act as confidently as I had with Corbier. It had always seemed to me that men in authority, or at least those half-way up the ladder, had a talent for detecting a weakness in courage, unsure poise, or a deviant intent. At the moment, I could have easily been identified with all three.*

I was beginning not only to admire this man who lived long and hard and died ten years before I was born; I enjoyed his style and wished I could have known him. He had a flare for adventure, a talent for telling his story, and the gift of being able to bridge the generations.

*At the shipyard The galleys had been hauled from the water and were attended by many workmen and in a state of repair that would preclude relaunching soon. Bosshart was probably still in port and had not yet been wasted by strain at the oars. If so, this improved the chance to free him and escape to the protective embrace of the mountains.*

*I continued my walk past the yard to the public docks where I paused to admire the beauty of the harbor and talk with some of the boatmen. Becoming somewhat familiar with Marseilles and its shops, I returned to the shipyard with a change of clothes for Bosshart in my portmanteau. My courage was now at the necessary level to enter the building and ask for Captain*

*De Laye, whose office was up a long flight of stairs and commanded a view of the yard.*

*He looked up from his desk as I entered the room and rose to shake my hand. Though clearly busy, he was gracious and showed no annoyance as I had expected from someone referred by Corbier. The coat of his uniform was draped over the chair, epaulettes askew: his shirt sleeves were rolled to the elbows. I introduced myself as I presented the official documents pulled from my portmanteau.*

*Above all, I stressed the importance of my royally-directed mission to procure Bosshart, whom I stated had been accidentally arrested and presumably now under Captain De Laye's control.*

*There was no sign that he recognized either my name or Bosshart's. If Corbier had recognized the ring and sent a guard to intercept me, he hadn't arrived yet.*

*De Laye opened the window and called below, "Bettice, find Pachet and send him to my office." He turned to me, "Please sit down, Major. Pachet will be here in a moment with a list of the new prisoners."*

As I was becoming groggy, this was as good a place as any to close the journal and retire after a long day; I did not want to find myself rereading paragraphs at a crucial part of great grandfather's story. The old gentleman's portrait hung in the hall, and I stopped to peer more closely at the man who had moved our family out of obscurity with his vision, intelligence, and energy. The artist had captured in his portrayal the unmistakable light of intelligence. Myriad facial lines suggested determination as surely as did the lines great grandfather had penned in his journal. I was proud to be one of his descendants.

# chapter 3

THE HARVEST WAS ready to begin subject to father's determination based on the fruit, the weather, and obtaining enough hands. Today was not the day. I retreated to the library and resumed reading great-grandfather's journal

*I did not wish to waste the time of this busy and kind officer, but De Laye and I sat in awkward silence waiting. Pachet did not appear.*

*"On my way down the Rhone yesterday, I traveled with a Mr. Gramsé—do you know him?" I queried.*

*"Yes, he's my younger brother—I should say stepbrother. He was finishing the installation of a lock on the upper Loire." De Laye said. "You must have been in the company coach with him."*

*"Yes, he generously offered me a ride. He was most enthusiastic about the operation of the lock."*

*"Yes, he is going to be a good engineer." De Laye seemed interested in continuing this conversation when his man came breathlessly up the stairs and into the room with an old ledger. "Here's the list of prisoners to arrive over the last three months, sir," he reported as he handed the opened book to De Laye.*

*"The name Bosshart does not appear on these pages. Are you sure it was in the last three months?", De Laye looked me square in the eyes.*

*"Yes, I was informed that he was judged guilty in Rennes, I think in November, and he was supposed to have been sent here."*

*De Laye looked relieved. "Perhaps, because of the lateness of the season when the galleys are returning to this yard for refitting and the crews are sent to the winter compound, your man was sent directly to the yard farm for*

*indoctrination and to work at the compound garden. If so, he's lucky and so are you, sir. Pachet, please get the farm list."*

*As we waited, De Laye mentioned that his firm had studied the locks in the Languedoc Canal and conferred with that canal's operating personnel. "You must see it. It is an engineering marvel completed recently by the famous engineer Riquet. It saves a ship, sailing to the Mediterranean from the Bay of Biscay or to the Atlantic from Marseilles, the time, trouble, and risk of rounding Gibralter," he said as Pachet arrived with the important list.*

*De Laye exclaimed, "Ah, you are in luck! Bosshart—Jacques is it?—- is on the garden list. The compound garden is only a quarter-mile from here. I'm going there, anyway. I'll take you there and you can secure your man." Good fortune, indeed!*

*Captain De Laye led the way to the garden, a large compound of several arpents, most of which had been recently dug, manured, and planted with onions, beans, peas, and lettuce. The dozen men who were scattered in a corner quarter looked up as we entered and I recognized Bosshart's large frame and red hair. He showed no recognition of me, thank God, or the game would have been lost right then if he had called out my real identity.*

*"Jacques Bosshart? You are to get your personal belongings and proceed with Major Talon immediately for discharge! Meet him at my office in five minutes," commanded De Laye. Bosshart straightened and ran to his cell for his few belongings. Never have I seen anyone react so promptly. Just then, the prison concierge appeared at De Laye's office and belligerently expressed serious reservations regarding Bosshart's discharge.*

*I bellowed, "This is not a matter of justice. It is a matter of state security! The king himself demands the presence of Bosshart who is an agent important to His Majesty's intelligence service."*

*I suspected that the concierge's resistance to Bosshart's discharge was an invitation to bribery, but my experience was not sufficient to handle the occasion smoothly and I bungled any chance of a bribe working in my favor. After a half hour of trying to out-bluster the concierge, I retired from the contest. Bosshart's new-found expectations were cruelly deflated.*

*Early the next day, I dressed in coarse and nondescript clothing, secured a map of the region, and rented a horse to ride to the olive-tree-studded limestone foothills where an attractive stream debouched from the mountains into the Durance River. It looked like it might be good habitat for trout. Sure enough, I found a pool where there were slim, dark life shimmering in the depths.*

*A handful of iron pyrites cost next to nothing from Eggleston, my firm's precious-metal specialist. But the sight of its golden excrescence radiating sunlight from the bottom of this and other pools and riffles would stir the reservoir of greed latent in the heart of most men, rich or poor. The poor know the only path to riches for them is through a chance lottery, a scheme offered and administered by an uncaring and exploitive world. Even so, in desperation, the hopeless odds are accepted. I scattered pyrites with abandon up and down the stream.*

*It was necessary to my plan to make sure that I could identify these surroundings when I would subtlety let be known my whereabouts in the foothills. Then I returned some miles to saunter into the suburbs of Aix to buy small items making payment with small, but genuine, gold nuggets thoughtfully provided by Eggleston.*

*It was convenient to buy camp equipment and supplies, including hammers and pry bars, to give the impression that I would be returning to the hills to perform more serious work for a lengthy period. Indeed, I intended to be in the mountains soon with Jacques in hand, but miles to the west. I returned to the inn to await developments.*

*A messenger from De Laye asked me to return to the marine yard where De Laye introduced me with obvious distaste to a uniformed constable.*

*"Mons. Claveraque? Captain Corbier from the Rennes District has directed me to arrest you for impersonating an agent of the king."*

*"Why do you address me as a Mons. Claveraque? I am Major Talon of His Majesty's service and I resent this intrusion in my official affairs."*

*"Major, Captain Corbier noticed your ring, please hold out your hands, yes, the white and brown agate with the red streak. The captain has seen this ring on Mons. Claveraque's right hand many times and is sure that you are Monsieur Claveraque masquerading as Major Talon."*

*"Son, step over here for a moment." I said in sotto voce. "Have you ever added to your income or your possessions by reason of dealing with possible fugitives while employed in the force?"*

*"What do you mean, sir?"*

*I had to tell him the ways of officialdom. "Almost every man who has worked on the force has taken a gratuity. It would be unusual to meet a veteran employee who had not been schooled by his immediate superior that this was the thing to do. To be able to survive, to be one of the men, to not embarrass or, by inference, insult colleagues and your superiors by refusing to participate in the game. It is an honorable way of life in His Majesty's service."*

*He stammered in confusion and I put my hand on his shoulder in what I hoped would pass for avuncular concern. "You can tell me, son, without fear. Every man is tempted and accedes to his temptation. It is natural and nothing to be ashamed of. Even Corbier accepted a bribe from Claveraque, some money and several bottles of Calvados, he told me. And I told Monsieur Claveraque that he could sell his farm without presenting papers when he finally understood he should offer me this ring. I'm not ashamed of this and I expect that you will feel honor-bound not to reveal this to anyone, and thank me in the bargain."*

*It so happened that at this moment, the cry of "Gold" rang out below in the shipyard and there was great clamor for information. The guards flocked together, including the constable, exchanged rumors, and ran off with some of the townspeople to the foothills to search for the yellow metal.*

*I hastened to the garden with my portmanteau, found Bosshart in a cell, spoke softly to him to not yell out when I told him who I really was.*

*He sobbed with gratitude while I removed the small miner's hammer and pry bar from my bag and levered the shackle from his ankles, being careful to spare him any further hurt while doing this. I handed him fresh and modest clothes. He shed his rags, donned this garb, and was anxious, as was I, to leave this oppressive place. I told him that we must stroll from here as if we had every right to come and go even though we were now probably the only ones left except for the prisoners.*

*That is until I heard Captain De Laye call down from his balcony, "Remember the Languedoc Canal! And good luck." Strange and blessed man! He made no attempt to interfere.*

*We hurried to the public docks where a few days before I had befriended a young man, Alex, who assured me that his sloop was one of the fastest in the port of Marseilles. I helped Bosshart step aboard and the mate gave me a hand with the portmanteau crammed with a few days rations.*

*We cast off and drifted free as Guy, the mate, unfurled canvas and set sail for Seté, a day's voyage to the west.*

*We left the cosmopolitan city sheltered by the shallow semicircle of limestone hills gleaming in the late afternoon sun as our sails filled with the steady northern winds of the Mistral.*

*The wind refreshed us and blew away the tension of the prison scene. But Bosshart was weak from months of poor food and fear. I made him comfortable in the cubby, daubed his shins with Calvados, and softly rubbed olive oil on to soothe where the leg irons had chafed. The mate had grabbed several loaves of bread stuffed with onions, olives, pimentos, almonds, and baked cloves of garlic. I tore off a thick chunk for Jacques which he ravenously devoured. When I next looked out above the deck, it was almost dark with not another light visible except myriad stars. The four of us were free and alone. In pairs we managed the boat through the night so that all, especially Jacques, got some rest.*

*As first light crept over us, we could make out the coast which Alex said was our destination. Fortunately, I turned to look out to sea and was startled to see that a felucca with its over-sized lateen sail was bearing down on us, frothing at the bow like a monster's threatening maw about to devour its prey. We had no arms, not even a sword or a dagger and, at most, we had five minutes before our fate would be determined.*

*Jacques had just scratched a small flame to life to warm some coffee. "Quick," I said. "Tear off two rags from your old clothes." Jacques did as he was bid despite the question in his eyes, as I retrieved the two bottles of Calvados from my bag and uncorked them. I grasped the two rags, saturated them with the volatile brandy, and stuffed them into the neck of the bottles.*

*By now I could hear the bow wave of the swiftly approaching felucca over the sound of water washing our lee rail and the rush of wind powering our sails. Our attackers were swarthy, of threatening demeanor, slicing the air with scimitars, eager to get on with the mayhem they had planned when they first sighted us.*

*"Corsairs!" cried Alex. "Five or six of them!"*

*None of them had firearms or bows drawn. They must have planned to board and overwhelm us with threat and fear. We would be worth more alive to be sold as slaves than as dead bodies. The thought solidified my resolve. I quickly explained to the others what we must do. "Let them approach close enough so that they are just short of boarding. Jacques, hand me the bottles and put the stove over here by my side." We were ready. All depended on the accuracy of my throwing arm.*

*When they had come within five meters off our beam, I carefully lit the brandied-rag wick of the first bottle, and tossed it to break in their midst. Quickly, I ignited and hurled the second bottle after the first.*

*"Whoomph!" went the explosive flames and our besiegers jumped into the sea to extinguish their burning clothes. We had little sympathy and left them kicking and splashing to stay afloat. They had secured the main sheet and the tiller for their expectant assault so their boat began to sail in a large arc without them until it became headed by the wind. We caught up with the felucca, dropped the big flapping sail over the side, and doused deck and gear to retrieve a fast and luxurious prize. They had sails on board for a change of wind. A change of wind, indeed.*

*In the distance appeared a sister felucca, so with what little Christian charity we could muster, there was no need to throw flotation to our floundering attackers. Our pursuers could tend to them and ignore us. We would have our prize felucca as well as Alex's boat.*

*After setting fresh sails on the felucca, our passage was swift and we gained Seté by evening that day. Jacques had fallen asleep within minutes of leaving Marseilles and the more than twelve hours of rest, save for the interruption to protect ourselves and gain a felucca, clearly put the blush of life back into his features.*

*We engaged a young man to carry our gear to a nearby inn where we could get our bearings, and paid for our passage and deliverance by making a gift of our share of the felucca to Alex and Guy.*

*The Languedoc Canal was everything Captain De Laye said it was, and then some. The engineering achievement should pay for itself in only a few years, if it hadn't already, and ease the way for travelers anxious to avoid circumnavigating Gibralter and meddling Corsairs.*

*Jacques was able to languish and enjoy the scenery, especially the Pyrenees, from the packet boat as was I. He listened attentively as I told him about my new-found life in London. When we arrived at Bordeaux, he was transformed and eager to depart for England and a new life.*

*During the following fifteen years I was able to become a partner in the London firm, now called Collinson, Burns, and Claveraque.*

*I was appalled by the filth and slovenly poverty so widespread in the city. Nor did I care for those in the desperate quest for status who had financially done well but insisted on trying to live as gloriously as the entrenched men of wealth.*

*I suppose that I could have been so classified as well since the firms profits had climbed considerably. And later I had seen a chance to make some easy money in the silly South Sea investment scheme. Shortly after the scheme began, I could see that it was exploiting the average, and the not so average, man's dreams of avarice, including mine.*

*I subscribed fifty pounds, remembering the effect of scattering fool's gold in the mountain stream near Marseilles years before and how it had played with great benefit to me and freeing Bosshart. Six months of ever-increasing prices and jittery concern was enough of a sojourn with the South Sea folly and I closed out my investment with a tenfold gain only a few weeks before the unbelievable bubble inevitably burst.*

*When the Old Pretender, James Francis Edward Stuart, or James the Third, if you will, made the attempt to regain his father's throne in 1715, his poorly coordinated effort failed and several of his wealthy backers lost their estates by attainder. It became my good fortune to be able to bid on an estate that I had admired ever since I first set eyes on the West Country.*

*This is how the Claveraque family climbed from obscurity, succeeded to the Wye Valley, and gained a foothold on our present state of comfort. So ends this journal.*

# chapter 4

I WAS EAGER to get back to the pool where I lost the large trout but may have found a treasure. Alas, Brian, our foreman, had alerted Father to the ripening of our main harvest. All other desires and considerations had to take second place to plucking apples from the trees when they were at their ripest. The entire family, including Ellen and Jonathan, were expected to rise earlier than normal to go to the orchards with help from what village folk we could muster for a full day of harvesting. And Holly had to arise even earlier, she had so much more cooking to do for the additional hands. We had to work quickly before the fall rains could wet down and likely rot the crop gathered in the wagons and bins.

Each variety was picked at its prime though it was necessary to go back a few days later and pick those fruits that were laggard in maturing. We were so busy, we had no time to do anything but deal with apples as if we were automatons. Throughout, the thought of what might be on the bottom of the river near the old sycamore haunted me.

The weather favored us so that we could gather the harvest in and under cover, secured against the elements. We had begun pressing to extract the juice for our cider when the fall rains commenced as if to make up for the dry season. I kept a close watch on the river as it rose and took on the color of creamed coffee and the demeanor of a mad dragon reaching out to consume its own valley.

What would happen to my find under the roots of the gnarled sycamore—could it possibly wash downstream to some obscure back-water, or remain in place to be covered with silt? Or would it be so scoured of silt by the torrent that it could be seen by anyone who chanced by when the river dropped and the water cleared? There was no way to satisfy my impatience with the prospect of a fortune offered by fate one moment and withdrawn the next. The water was too high and opaque to know the fate of the gold ingot if indeed that's what the shimmering brick-like object was.

With the first cider pressing completed, we began watering the dross in casks so that the remaining must could steep freely before closing it tight for the final fermentation. Next to the perfume of spring bloom and observing bees work the blossoms, the fragrances from different varieties mingling during the press delighted my senses adding to the capricious autumnal tang already tingling the air.

Father and Brian were the only ones sufficiently skilled to determine the precise time and mix of apple varieties, so the rest of the family and hands could now relax to the easy regimen of fixing equipment and planning chores for winter and spring.

Mother resumed attending church with whomever in the family she could coax to endure listening to Reverend Barry. She received inspiration when she saw her occasional friend, Mrs. Johns with her daughter, Esperance, in their family pew. I had almost forgotten about Ancie, what with going to Plymouth to bring Dordy home, making the wagon springs, fishing for trout (or good fortune), and helping to bring the apple harvest in for the press. Four weeks had gone by since our last hike to the quarry, and summer had wheeled into autumn.

Mother seemed more aware of Ancie's and my last meeting than I, and must have been reminded of it by Ancie's mother or Ancie herself—a pleasing thought. I did not wish to alienate Ancie by seeming to ignore her, and cast about for some excuse to ride over to the Johns's now that I had the time.

"Why don't you ride over to the Johns's farm, James?" Mother suggested in her practical way, and inspired by this straight-forward articulation of my thoughts, I saddled Old Nellie.

Ancie lived only two miles away now that her father had purchased one of the barns that had belonged to the monastery. It was one of those estates that had been closed down by Henry the Eighth over two hundred years ago and so had historical significance.

Mr. Johns had examined the barn and decided that it was still sound and worth buying from the owner, desperate for funds to pay his land taxes. As Nellie and I sauntered up the drive, he was restoring the roof on the barn and waggled his hammer in greeting, and to signify that Ancie was in back by the paddock. She was currying her chestnut gelding when I approached.

"The horse looks beautiful", I said and immediately realized that my compliment should have been of Ancie, not her horse. A small yellow ribbon made a pleasant contrast to Ancie's auburn hair glistening in the sun. Her pleasing smile and caring eyes improved this portrait, and her blouse amply hinted of her femininity. She well deserved the praise.

"Is this the first thing that you want to say to me after an absence of more than a month?" Her face flushed.

"Of course, you look very fetching and I've been looking forward to seeing you all this time. How would you would like to make use of this pleasant day by riding to Offa's Dike?"

She softened a bit. "I haven't been there for a while. Do you think Nellie is up to it?"

Ancie often took pot shots at me when she was upset by demeaning Nellie, my clothes, or the way we Claveraques made our living. Not waiting for an answer, she mounted her chestnut and took a shortcut by galloping across their pasture to the narrow trail that wound along a branch of the Wye. Sheepishly, but excited by her natural coquetry, I followed.

Autumn was just short of its climax of color. Saffron chestnuts stood tall with the crimson oaks highlighted by the under-story of hazel trees burdened with nuts; the ground was festooned with bracken ready to turn with the first frost. A few more days and the wind would rend this lace of leaves into drifts of brown and dead red, like a fresh-caught trout losing its life colors. Gray skies and cold would replace this satisfying comfort for four or five months.

We stopped at a spring by the bank of the trail, filled the tin ladle left there for all comers, and drew refreshment from the clear, cold water.

Ancie resumed, "I forgot. I did ride to Offa's Dike only a week ago with Downy Cohan. The Cohans really know how to raise horses. Downy's black is not only fast but a high-riding jumper. We had a spirited ride that day."

"We bought Nellie from the Cohans when I became ten", I replied. " I guess that makes Nellie more than twelve years old, but she's up to it, just the same."

"The Cohans do quite a business with the army. Downey said they were selling the army something like fifty horses this fall and another fifty in the spring to use over in Boston." This was a familiar theme with Ancie. She knew this sort of talk about spending time with other men annoyed me. It seemed the price I had to pay for having upset her.

She changed the subject by turning her horse to go upstream on the trail by the small glen and offered no explanation for this alteration. I had never ventured along this stream; it would have been difficult to fish because of the brush, and it was sure to be too shallow. But I followed.

In a few moments we came to a slender waterfall that plunged fifteen feet or so from a moss and fern-covered rocky precipice into a ten-foot wide crystal pool, deep in the center and evenly shallowing all around to its shore, like the flaring of a trumpet bell. The brassy-bright sand on the bottom glistened. On this warm fall day it was an invitation to dally.

We dismounted from our horses and let them graze on the ample vegetation. Halfway up the side of the falls, there was a small level where a thick patch of grass had grown tall and the seed heads had turned cerise, as if nature had insisted on a second invitation to this colorful bower. I lifted Nellie's saddle, removed the saddle-blanket and spread it where we could view the falls, in the sun and away from the spray.

"It must have been a falls such as this one that inspired my father to build a falls in our house." I said. "He tapped a small spring on the rise behind the house by connecting pipes to sluice the flow to a spigot in the ceiling of a new..."

"My father made those pipes for him." Ancie broke in. " I remember him boring them with an especially long drill that would cut the hole the length of a four-foot log, if he carefully drove it from both ends."

"Yes, that's right. Matching up those holes in the middle of the log must have tried your father's patience to have to be so exacting. Having the falls in the house was wonderful but..."

Ancie seemed shocked. "Wasn't the water awfully cold falling on you like that? A good idea, but too cold for me."

"Yes, the first time we used it, we all hesitated at our turn but finally each of us abandoned caution and instantly became frigid. Father later connected a barrel painted black so that the stored water would absorb the heat from the sun."

"What a smart idea! Did it make much of a difference?"

"In the summer and fall it did. Even Mother took to it. But Father didn't want to give up using the falls in the winter. He had a brass tank made for inside, with several whale-oil lamps to warm it. Even so, the lamps brought the water only to lukewarm and didn't suffice during the worst of winter. So we welcomed our water tub and hot water kettles, but we..."

"Do you know? It never occurred to me to stand under the falls."

"You should try it, Ancie. It isn't too cold when you get used to it. I'll show you."

I took off my outer clothes and waded in. Whenever entering water outdoors, warm or cold, it has always felt shockingly cold at first. Now, I faced away so Ancie could not see me grit my teeth.. Then I waded deeper to the center of the pool and the drenching of the falls from the lip of the rock above.

Ancie stood in awe. Then she belied her hesitancy by stripping to her petticoat. She stepped over to the pool and ventured a toe in the water. She didn't flinch or hesitate but walked in as if it were an every-day occurrence. The bottom was so steep on the sides, it was necessary for us to stand clasped to each other in the pool's center where the falls plunged and splashed. She laughed and we delighted in the deluge.

Soon the sensation of cold diminished, and we could enjoy the embrace of the pool and each other.

As pleasant as having Ancie so close to me was, for warmth as well as her sensuous response, we both realized that we could not endure the cold water for long despite merging our body heat. As we climbed the steep bottom, we stumbled in the sand, pebbles, and stones, and laughed at our clumsy attempt to extract ourselves from the pool. The breeze had freshened and chilled us as we emerged from the water.

I had to search for Ancie's horse for the blanket still draped on her back. Only by lying together on my blanket, covered by hers, were we able to regain normal warmth. The sensuousness that she had previously shared with me returned most agreeably. We were cozier than we had ever been. With great difficulty and reluctance, I decided we must discontinue submission to this delectable temptation as soon as we could without my offending her. A welling of warmth within warned that disengagement had to start soon. We stayed in place.

Gathering courage, I ventured, "I think I heard a noise from over by the trail."

"Just now?"

"Yes, listen closely. It sounds like someone walking in the bracken."

" James, we'd better make ourselves presentable, just in case," as she shuffled the blanket from her and got to her feet.

We quickly garbed ourselves and rounded up our horses. Of course, no one showed on the trail and we left the trysting place reluctantly.

Ancie seemed as relieved as I that we did not permit ourselves the next level of passion and that we could resist the irresistible. That we had allowed ourselves to be so immersed in intimacy and that I rejected going any further was no reflection on my feelings and respect for Ancie. I hoped that she did not suspect that I had broken it off, before she could be the first to claim doing so, and that she was not offended.

But I was not ready to commit to her for a lifetime if that should become necessary. I doubt that she was ready for commitment to me, or anyone else, as well. She would make someone a wonderful, enduring companion, and may hap I would be that someone. But not yet.

The sun had become obscured by clouds for sometime now and, along with the darker shadows for this time of day, I could smell the increased moisture in the air. I was just about to say that it looked like rain when the clouds dropped their burden and we became soaked to the skin for the second time in a few hours. We halted our horses under a grove of dense maples to wait out the rain, but it persisted. The wind picked up and we both began to shiver.

Ancie said she thought we were not far from the Green Bottle Tavern, reputed to be the haunt of rangers and iron mongers from the Forest of Dean nearby. She knew the way.

The Green Bottle had a grungy and rough reputation, but we both needed to dry out quickly by a fire or we were in danger of taking a severe cold or worse. We hastened our horses there when there was a lull in the storm, splattering ourselves with mud in our eager rush for a warm room. The tavern's stone massiveness and chimney smoke promised a welcome reception.

"I have never been in this place, but it has always appeared hospitable," said Ancie.

I wondered how she knew "it appeared to be hospitable" if she had never been inside. We tied our horses to the already crowded rail and entered a dim, smoky glow that immediately offered relief from the chill. The long bar on one side was attended by several men standing in serious conversation. We gravitated to the few remaining empty chairs by the immense fireplace across the room to suffuse ourselves in smokey warmth.

An attractive young barmaid, though slovenly dressed, ambled amiably to our attention, introduced herself, and asked our pleasure. As soon as we had ordered, an officer of the British army brazenly appeared from nowhere and addressed Ancie, "Haven't I seen you here before?"

Ironically, only an hour before I had made a decision that I hoped would protect my and Ancie's future. This gentleman's question had an even more serious outcome.

# chapter 5

"Lieutenant John Brigandi, at your service, M'am." he said to Ancie, ignoring me and gaining my immediate dislike. He was probably ten years older than I, jet black hair turning gray at the temples, boisterous and lusty, and obviously an adventurer.

"I may have met you, sir, in church, in the village or in Bristol or Bath some time in the last year but surely not here at the Green Bottle", parried Ancie. She made it clear that she was tentatively willing to admit meeting the lieutenant but was averse to agreeing that it could have been here at an establishment lacking a genteel reputation.

"My memory of meeting such a beautiful lady is surely more precise than you indicate. But I take pleasure and am flattered that you remember our meeting at all. You are with a different escort this time, are you not?" he purred.

Ancie regained her composure after being caught in a lie not only to Brigandi but to me as well. She was clearly warmed by the compliment, and now politely allowed me to be part of this conversation if not the repartee.

"Lieutenant, may I introduce you to my fiancé, James Claveraque." Was this un-expected announcement of our engagement—news to me—for the purpose of warding off this aggressive character? Or did our warm adventures of the afternoon lead her to think our relationship had more substance than I had thought?

The dashing lieutenant silently bowed forward just enough so that his recognition of my presence was perceptible, but not congenial. Several seconds elapsed until I broke the silence..

"Would you like to join us for a moment?"

Despite his crude intrusion on what was intended to be a cozy afternoon, I felt I had to invite the lieutenant to join us "for a moment". I doubted that he would take the hint that this invitation was conventional only and should be declined, but if accepted, should result only in a brief stay, at most. But he threw himself into a chair with alacrity.

"Are you part of the Claveraque cider family in the valley?"

I volunteered nothing more than a nod.

"I remember hearing about how that family made such a ruckus about the cider tax ten years ago. My unit was detached to separate the tax official and Mr. Claveraque—your father?—before they came to blows or worse. He had his field hands enraged and ready to throw the official and his clerks in the river. He had almost called him out to a duel but neither man looked like they knew anything about the code *duello.* A local lawyer calmed him down or he could have gotten into serious trouble. He was getting rowdy, but I admired him for his spirit."

"You remember well, Lieutenant. That was my father: the lawyer was Squire Calloway."

"Ah yes, I've had some dealings recently with the squire. He has revealed that a client of his in the valley has invented a set of springs for a wagon which makes for a much more comfortable ride over rough roads. Our roads in England could surely benefit from improved grading, but those in America will defy improvement for some time and we need it now." I began to find Brigandi interesting.

"How does a soldier get involved about wagons and roads, Lieutenant?" Ancie brought herself back into the conversation.

"My dear, it is important for the army to be able to get around, to maneuver, to move massive amounts of supplies and ammunition, and most importantly, to not jostle the general's favorite wines, baggage, and mistress in transit." He got up, walked to another table occupied by his soldiers and came back with a half-drained bottle of Chablis.

"We'll get that wench to bring us some glasses and I'll tell you about it." he declared.

"So that's how you met the squire?" I was surprised by his acquaintance with Calloway.

"I'm from this part of the country. I met Calloway when he saved your father. The squire and I have been friends ever since."

The barmaid brought us our mugs of split-pea soup with a floating bit of ham bone. It was just the thing to restore our need for warmth and sustenance and the aroma alone alerted our natures. Brigandi ordered glasses all around. Since he had his Chablis we did not think it rude to enjoy the soup in his presence.

"Getting back to wagons. The army needs to have vehicles that can negotiate the roads of North America or roads that our troops will have to cut through the terrain. Any device that can result in a smoother ride for personnel and their supplies, and stand the abuse will command a premium by the army. We want to meet the inventor of the springs and buy his production or, better yet, offer him a commission in the army."

"Lieutenant, I am the inventor of the spring arrangement that Squire Calloway told you about. I'm flattered that you are interested in the springs and in me, but I have heard about Bunker Hill and I wouldn't care for army life."

"Surely your not afraid, Mr Claveraque?"

His raised eyebrow failed to intimidate me. "Of course I'm afraid. Like all those men who marched up Bunker Hill. And those redcoats who were shot at from behind stone walls while marching back from Concord and Lexington. They were all brave, of course. But they had to have some force or reason that they were brave about. That would be their own fears. And what worse violence is to come since this escalation of friction between the army and the Americans?"

After such provocation and no response from Brigandi, I pursued one of my favorite diatribes. "Besides, I do not like our government treating other Englishmen, even those in the American colonies, or I should say, *especially those in America*, as if they are an inferior and conquered race. From what I hear, they are a smart and energetic people who enjoy a better standard of living than many in this country."

"You've been listening to a lot of balderdash, Mr. Claveraque. Our soldiers are the best in the world, trained to be brave and to know how to fight. They behaved superbly in those actions you cited. Some one who is uninformed has been filling you full of nonsense."

"Tell me why you're interested in the springs?" I did not wish to get into an argument or to involve my brother as the source of my information, and changed the subject.

"What is your first name, sir, if I can be so forward?" Brigandi calmly asked.

"You've already been quite forward. But my name is James."

Ancie added her thoughts on the subject. "James and his father are not in favor of the King's present administration in its conduct with the people of Boston, New York, Philadelphia, and Charleston. They say our government is all wrong and the Americans are all right!" She turned to me, "When my father was asked to make the piping for your waterfall, he admired your father for his inventiveness from that moment. They probably would have become close friends but for your father's taking the American's side on almost everything for the last ten years. He put your father in the same category as Wilkes and Barré, and thinks the King and our English government deserved better than that."

"Well, I'm glad he puts my father in the same category as those members of Parliament—- assuming he has a high opinion of them."

I turned again to Brigandi. "Why are you interested in me and my springs compared to someone else's?"

"Squire Calloway told me of your upbringing and your family. He said your mother and father are well-educated people, that they inquire into the reason for things, subscribe to current reputable journals and so continually re-educate themselves. And they think for themselves."

"The Squire said that this has rubbed off on you. The army needs people who think for themselves and who are self reliant. Let me finish! Yes! Soldiers are taught not to think on their own but to follow orders. This is true of even some of the officers, the younger ones who have not served long or had training to be flexible in battle, strategy, tactics and the rest of it.

"Your spring design shows originality. We need people like you who have open minds to not only develop better springs or other devices, but to assist officers with advice—no, I'll change that—with suggestions to improve the way the army does things."

This flattery emboldened my response. "I've never considered going into the army even though friends have sought commissions or enlisted. My main reason for rejecting the idea is that one's fate is in the hands of many other people who may not be very smart, experienced, or whose agenda may be contrary to mine. And I wouldn't be able to do anything about it. To disagree is to suffer the Army's penalties, which to me always seemed arbitrary and harsh, on mind, body, and career.

"All in all, a not very promising prospect. The very fact that I do not agree at all with the authorities on the treatment of Americans would handicap me from the start and subject me to ridicule, or worse, from those who disagree or wish to toady to their superiors. No thanks, I can't think of a worse direction to aim my career."

"James, one's life is always subject to those with power who may not have experience, wisdom, honesty, or the same objectives you have, no matter what career you elect! But you don't have to join the army. You can be a consultant, something like an adjutant, be well paid, and have more freedom to act. You would have a better venue to build a reputation and, probably, to see America and the Americans you so favor. You could come and go pretty much as you please. Except during a campaign, of course."

He had made some good points. Human nature is much the same all over—no doubt more harshly governed by the army—and I wanted very much to go to America.

Suddenly, the Green Bottle's front door was thrown open wide to crash against the wall and a coat stand, tossing coats and hats to the floor. Ancie was startled, and turned her head away as if to avoid notice by the intruders. Downey Cohan and Strawbur Topping came charging in with a cohort of straggly individuals. Though attired in working clothes, their crude manner gave the impression that they were clad in skins and wielding claymores. They quickly proved their unearned pride, their collective ignorance, and superb ability to be obnoxious in the extreme.

"Drinks for my friends and associates" demanded Downey of the burley man tending bar, who hesitated, but then decided to serve them, and quickly. Downey waited until his eyes adjusted to the dim light in the cavernous corners of the room, and then advanced to the redcoats at the other table.

"My family's steeds carried you men against the Scots at Culloden Moor thirty years ago. Saved your asses they did! You owe me and my men a drink which we graciously accept in the name of the King. Long may he live."

The Green Bottle was used to exuberant revelry every night, but this presumption seemed to be a prelude to mayhem, and the patrons hesitated in silence, as if to shrink from the burden about to be imposed by these intruders.

Lieutenant Brigandi made haste to rise and declare, "By all means, we should stand these men to a drink and raise a toast to their ability and experience in breeding excellent horses. Mr. Hamilton, please serve each of these men with Mr. Cohan a drink of his preference and give the tab to me, if you please."

Brigandi read the situation right and avoided a furor. Even though he was still a stranger to me, I was beginning to see that he was restrained and rational in dealing with nasty situations. I hoped he had some way of gaining recompense for his generosity.

Downey Cohan summoned each of his cohorts, asked their pleasure, and repeated this to the barkeep in an attempt to appropriate Brigandi's generosity. Unfortunately, he succeeded. But Cohan's success obligated him to stand the next round. At the same time, the boisterousness of his men flagged and the various conversations in the Green Bottle resumed.

"That was well done Lieutenant", I said sincerely. "You certainly took command of an uncomfortable situation in the making. How do you know Downey and Strawbur? "It is partly my duty to negotiate for horses with Mr. Cohan, as it is my pleasure to discuss wagons and springs with you. He knows where his bread is buttered."

"I suppose that my opposition to Parliament's treatment of Americans would get around and make my position working with the army untenable? My father and I have been somewhat outspoken about it, but many of our friends agree with us."

"I don't think that would make much difference. Everyone knows that Lord Admiral Howe and his brother, General Howe, are partial to the Americans. As is General Burgoyne. They didn't want to serve in America because of their strong feelings in the matter. The Howes's older brother was killed in one of the beginning skirmishes in the attempt to take Fort Carrillon, now called Ticonderoga, in the French war. Even though General Abercromby was in charge of the campaign, everyone in the brigade deferred to the Viscount as the brains of the operation. Besides, he was well liked by high and low."

"I didn't know that the general and the Lord admiral are brothers, or that they are partial to Americans." Ancie blurted.

Brigandi continued, "Yes, the Howes never forgot that the people of Massachusetts arranged a subscription for a memorial monument to their fallen brother at Westminster Abbey. But getting back to your contention that you'd be at a disadvantage, no, I don't think your leanings for the colonists would be a problem, James. Only, I would advise that you use discretion in discussing your political likes and dislikes. With some, it would be acceptable, with others, you would be bucking the current and court trouble."

Ancie broke in again. "What about me? I don't know whether I want to go to America. I don't know anything about the place!" She had been listening very carefully and took it all in.

"Well, I haven't decided that I'm going to follow the lieutenants advice, however well intentioned. Even if I did, I could not count on the army sending me to America. They might keep me here in some grim manufactory in London or Bristol"

Ancie insisted. "But you haven't even asked me what I think about the army and going to America. It's not fair!"

"We'll talk about it after we've had time to consider such a novel idea, Ancie. And let's find out more about these prospects from the Lieutenant."

Brigandi saw a chance to improve his persuasion and put pressure on me. "Many wives and companions follow the army, James. They are a necessary and expected part of any military unit. They perform many necessary services for us and their mates, and of course, make sure their husbands are in fighting trim."

Did the lieutenant imply that couples were in constant state of intimacy? A glint in his eye added just the inflection to cause me to infer this alternate meaning.

Downey's carousal with his men must have become boring because he swung his liquored-over gaze in our direction and walked across to our table.

"Hello Lieutenant! The last time I saw you was here when I was with Ancie a month ago. I hope you are satisfied with the herd of stallions and would like to increase your order. Can I offer you and your guests a swig of refreshment? Hello Ancie."

Ancie moved slightly closer to me, an action not unnoticed by Downey who then slapped me on the back and grunted, "So, she's yours now, eh, James?"

Ancie did not reply. But her eyes narrowed and her chin lifted a fraction so that there was no doubt in anyone's mind that she certainly was not his.

"Ancie's a good friend, if that's what you mean, Downey." I hoped that this sterile answer would cut off further discussion about Ancie's relationships, and changed the subject. "I hear that you've sold the army several herds of horses."

"Yes, they are going to be used in Boston to replace those wounded and killed by the rabble in their rebellion against the King.

Foolishly, I started to embroil myself in a political argument with him. "There have been problems over there but not to the point that you can call it a rebellion."

"What do you call it when fifteen thousand armed men collect themselves just outside of Boston, and when their so-called congress appoints a former militia colonel to be their commander? It sounds like a rebellion to me. And more important, it does to the King and Parliament." Downey made the first point in this argument.

I didn't drop the subject. "You've got me there. But Gage's aggression at Bunker Hill and, of course, Lexington and Concord, started it. So you can't blame the colonists from protecting themselves from further injury. Who's the commander?"

"He's an officer who was head of the Virginia militia in the Seven Years War. He was with Braddock when the general and many of his men were massacred near the Forks of the Ohio. I think his name is Washington, George Washington."

I remembered my father reading about Washington in *Gentleman's Magazine*, years ago. Washington was my age when he had been sent, with his guide, by the governor of Virginia to the wilderness with a message for the commander of several French forts demanding that the French vacate the upper Ohio Valley since it is British territory.

Over a sumptuous dinner, including fine wines for his trail-weary guest, the French officer listened politely, but firmly rejected the governor's demand. Washington's Indian scouts left them and they had to abandon their lame horses so it was difficult getting back, especially in the severe winter weather in the mountains. They were shot at by Indians and their raft capsized throwing them into a freezing river. Washington wrote a report about it along with a map of his trek from Williamsburg and back. It was published in Virginia and then, in London. A year later, he was made second-in-command to General Braddock.

" He was a brave man. Like General Braddock, he had many horses shot from underneath him yet, unlike Braddock, he survived the massacre without a scratch." I contributed.

"From what I know of Mister Washington, it doesn't sound like we'll have too much trouble from him—- nor from the hordes of ribbon clerks, chicken-hearted farmers, and slave-drivers under his command. One of King George's military aids said, 'with one-thousand Grenadiers I could go through America and geld all the males, partly by force and partly by a little coaxing.' Ha, ha!" Downey insisted on being boorish.

Ancie had been impatient to resume a subject I hoped she would defer until we were alone. "What do you mean, 'We're just good friends'? You were much more than just a good friend a few hours ago. I think..."

In the face of grins and guffaws from our new-found friends, I said firmly, "Let's talk about it when we can talk in private and not bore our friends here with our personal business." "James, you're not being fair or candid with me. Here you're thinking of going to America and..."

Brigandi cut in, "You would see a beautiful and mostly virgin countryside, and a vigorous yeomanry developing an economy where almost anyone who wants to can do very well."

Then Downey pursued his contention. "They're a determined bunch of boneheads. That's what they are. After all, we've had a stamp tax in England for ever since I can, and my father can, remember. It doesn't seem to bother anyone here, so what did they raise such a fuss about in the colonies? It's not as if you need a marriage certificate or a deed or diploma, even a deck of cards, every day of the week. Grenville and Parliament had every right to tax the bastards to help pay for saving their ass against the French and the Indians and to pay for forts to keep the Indians west of the mountains and the colonists east of them."

I wasn't going to stand for misstatements. "The tax has to be paid in sterling. They have very little cash because it's against official policy for the colonists' to have specie, and people of lower income, particularly, would suffer quite a discount converting from paper currency to sterling to pay the tax. It would leave them drained of specie, already in short supply. So it would not only be expensive but throw their economy to the winds." I sensed that I had made a point unknown to the others.

Jamie, I..." Ancie began, but I had momentum that could not be deterred.

" I also think that what they were against is violating the long-held principal that Englishmen can't be taxed except by their lawfully elected representatives in Parliament. They are colonists but, after all, they are Englishmen, too, you know. And have royal charters giving them representation in their own colony, and they do pay taxes there. Parliament should lay off. It has been trying for ten years to dominate them."

"Downey growled "Isn't it enough! Representation in their own colony, I mean."

"Yes! They are content with it as it is. They just don't want Parliament messing in their affairs and screwing things up!" I retorted.

"Well Parliament repealed the stamp tax anyway, so what our we talking about?"

"When they repealed it, they laid down a set of taxes on glass, paint, lead, and several other items. And made a point of insisting that the government had a right to levy taxes of any kind. Oh, and on tea, of course."

"But they repealed that, too. What more do you want?" Downey persisted.

"All, except on tea. One of the insidious ideas was to use the tax moneys they hoped to collect to pay judges and royal governors' salaries. That would remove any influence they had over those officials they had struggled for years to obtain. The King's illegal and devastating reaction to the tea party by shutting down the port of Boston was vicious and shows how right the colonists are. It is not the sign of a king who has affection for his subjects. Unfortunately, the King and Parliament are being run by merchants and manufacturers, and letting them write the laws to suit themselves. I don't blame the rebels for having their tea party."

"See what I mean about him and his family?" said Ancie.

"You sound like a long-winded lawyer, yourself. If you believe all this so much, why don't you go over there?" Downey thought he had triumphed over me.

"I just might, after all. But, you know, it was at least thirty years ago that seeds for all this resentment were planted."

"How so?" said Downey, Brigandi, and Ancie in the same breath

"The French built a massive stone fortress, called Louisbourg, on Cape Breton Island, just off Nova Scotia, around sixty years ago. This fort was a thorn in the side of New Englanders because, in addition to being an enemy fort, it served for years as a haven for French privateers who continually harassed the New England fishing fleet—one of the Yankee's main industries."

"Who cares." said Downey.

"After they could take this humiliation and expense no longer, the New Englanders arranged a siege campaign with the help of the British fleet and the regular army in what was said to be impossible. The fleet and the colonist's militia and the British regulars cooperated to every one's surprise with a minimum of screw-ups. After six weeks of bombarding by both land and naval guns and holding off French relief parties, they took the fortress.

"They were smart about it, too. After taking the fortress, they left the French flag flying and French ships, unaware of the fort's fall, were captured without further shots being fired. Commodore Warren of the Navy and William Pepperel, head of the colonial militia, became household words. Pepperel was made the first colonial baronet and the newly-promoted Admiral Warren walked off with £20,000 in prize money."

"So where is this story going? What does it have to do with the rebellion?"

"Good question, Downey. The cost of the operation was estimated to be over a thousand lives lost and many, many thousands of pounds paid by the colonists of New England. Three years later at the treaty table, at the end of that French war, Louisbourg was given back to the French in return for Britain keeping a large piece of India. New Englanders would have to suffer harassment of their fishing boats again after taxing themselves and losing so many sons and husbands. And London merchants and the East India Company continued making themselves rich. The colonists began to lose faith in the London government right then and there.

"George the third did the same thing in the Treaty of Paris. He gave Cuba back to Spain after several hundreds of Americans gave their lives to capture Havana in '62. Do you begin to understand why they turned sour, now?"

"Well, they had no right to destroy all that tea!" was all Downey could say.

"There are many other incidents that gripe the colonies. The Gaspé affair is an example. And an attempt to take cannon carriages being made in Salem just north of Boston is another. Quartering troops in people's homes and having them endure the insolence of their troops and, in addition, having to pay for part of the troop's grog themselves; closing down the port of Boston and taking their government away from them in reprisal for the tea dumping, the Proclamation line that summarily cut off planning for westward development; all of these inevitably led to mass resentment. I could go on.

"And, oh yes. With your pardon, Lieutenant Brigandi, I understand that the regulars are continually condescending to the colonial militia. We even see a bit of that here, with army officers, present company excepted, acting superior to every body else. Nobody likes that, not even Englishmen! But, of course, the rebels are Englishmen."

Brigandi surprised me. "We see that in the army, yes. Each rank lords it over lower ranks. Its part of the system. In fact it's not just the army—it's embedded in human nature."

I couldn't help myself but to continue with my disgust of the happenings of the last ten years. "I suppose the final outrage is the refusal of the King to even read the most recent petition from the Americans for conciliation. He and the administration seem bent on treating the colonists as a conquered people and subjecting them to as much humiliation as possible.

Ancie chimed in again, "We don't need a long history lesson. How about us? Are you going to take me with you?"

I had to ignore her again. "When Doctor Franklin was expecting an answer to a petition to have the London government withdraw Governor Hutchinson from office over a year ago, the administration ignored the petition and, instead, took this as an opportunity to publicly humiliate Franklin, one of the most admirable men in the world. The paper's account of Wedderburn's clever but savagely stinging attack on Franklin was embarrassing to all Englishmen who believe in civilized discourse. Many of our distinguished statesmen and leaders are appalled at the baseness and corruption in the government. And now we are beginning to reap a harvest of tragedy for such provocation." I was emotionally exhausted after stating my feelings so long kept under wraps.

"You forgot to mention the rebel mob's destruction of Governor Hutchinson's fine house leaving him and his family with nothing but a shambles, and out in the cold." This rebuttal was from Ancie. I had to agree that such inane violence did the patriots no credit.

"Hutchinson was seen as an enemy. He was telling the home government how to curtail the colonists' liberties. That's what was in the letter of Hutchinson's that Franklin came across and the colonists made public. But I agree, the rebels should have restrained themselves. They did their cause and their wiser colleagues a disservice, as well as worsening things with the London government, needlessly." I did not appreciate Ancie checking my arguments and causing me to backwater.

But she continued. "And, as Downey says, we've had a stamp tax on this side of the water for generations with no complaints. If we can stand it, why can't they?" Ancie was beginning to be an annoyance. "After all," she forced, "we spent a lot of money and manpower saving them from the French and the Indians in the French war and again in the Indian conspiracy—what was that Indian chief's name?—Pontiac! That's right! They should pay some of the cost. It's only fair." Ancie chortled

Downey, emboldened by Ancie, ganged up on me. "England planted, nurtured them and built the country for them and now they want us to continue to pay for it. It's not right."

"One of the Lords made that vicious and condescending statement. I think it was Champagne Charlie, otherwise known as Lord Townshend. And he was ably rebutted in Parliament by Colonel Barré." I said.

"Who is he?" Ancie asked..

"He served under Wolfe at Quebec and helped get the troops up on the Plains of Abraham where the French were overwhelmed . And he lived with and fought, side by side, with many Americans. So he knows what he was talking about. "

"What did he say in return?" Downey said. I think he really wanted to know.

"He said that they weren't planted by England. Just the opposite. They fled England's oppression which they thought was worse than chancing the hardships of bringing civilization out of a wilderness and fighting cruel and savage Indians.

"They weren't nourished by England, either. They prospered because they were neglected by England until ten years ago when agents and governors were sent to tell 'em what to do.

"They weren't protected by the army! They took to arms in their and England's defense and sent the products of their economy to enrich the mother country. Barré said something like that. So they flourished not because of England's leaders but despite them."

"What about our going to America, James? You sound so enraged with England maybe you should go to America and start a new life in a new world," Ancie stated what I may have been thinking and tried to say all along.

I looked out the window to see that the storm was over and things had been drying out, including our clothes. "I think we should go home now, Ancie. It'll be getting dark soon."

Brigandi kindly offered to accompany us on the way home which I politely declined, Downey seemed devoid of further argument, and Ancie did not complain, so we took our leave.

# chapter 6

WENCESLAS MOCHTER IS to certain people in our area as a prowling wolf is to a faltering lamb. Most do not realize this to their peril. His appearance and demeanor mark him as a gentleman in all respects until you have the unfortunate occasion to be a rival or own something that he covets.

He looms a few inches over most men and boasts a muscular physique. His serious countenance is crowned by a shiny bald pate, a carefully barbered and abbreviated dark beard, and punctuated by piercing eyes. Mochter couldn't be over thirty but his hairless crown gives him the appearance of a man with many years, each laden with successful experience.

Coupled to these features is a confident mien, perhaps due to having inherited Mochter's Mill from his uncle. Thus he is considered a leader, even at first glance. If you have ever seen a snake gather his coils about a prey, you begin to understand Mochter's acquisitive nature. Indeed, polite intimidation is the first sign of danger to his victims. Whatever his schemes, success can be forecast without fear of contradiction. He is acutely aware of how he appears to most people and knows how to capitalize on this legacy.

Several years ago, when Wenceslas suspected that there would be a revival in the market for wool, he threw a party on his veranda for small freeholders who lived adjacent to the common and pastured their livestock there. To avoid any sign of selectivity, he invited a few others from the country. All were people with whom he would not normally socialize, but no one thought about his choice of guests, especially the guests themselves. Each seemed to think that his invitation acknowledged a certain recognition, almost of kinship.

After an awkward commencement of festivities, everyone became convivial, even garrulous, for the sake of earning the attention and favor of this distinguished man of the community.

He made it a point to converse with every guest, to compliment them, and to inquire of their satisfaction with economic conditions and their personal welfare. He had a knack of finding the nub of each person's dissatisfaction and eking out what they thought could be done about it. In most cases he was gratified to find that money was the essential ingredient that most thought would guarantee the life they fancied. He had counted on it, and invited each guest to call on him at his home for a further conversation about what he could do to help them. Wenceslas bided his time so that his guests would feel as supplicants for his benevolence in case they didn't already.

Through Crispin, whose father had been one of the guests, I found that Mochter offered to loan funds secured by a mortgage on their property or, at least, the rights of common attached to the property. He advanced them funds but, in time, and, as anticipated, most defaulted.

Our benefactor gave them the opportunity of either more time to make payment or, where particularly desirable parcels were at stake, increased the loan to appear more than tolerant of tardy attention. After all, Mr. Mochter was a vestryman of Saint Davids of the Valley.

Of course, deeper debt pushed them over the brink. One by one, except Crispin's father who had declined, he relieved them of the loan by relieving them of their property, or the common rights.

Within weeks, Mochter arranged for a herd of sheep to be pastured on the common. As he had been confident, his operation was perceived by peers as only good business.

In the absence of Dordy in the colonies, he was one of the country gallants who called on Sally Bushnell for her favor. But his timing was unfortunate; Sally's mother was beginning her rapid decline, and neither Doctor Colsch, or Granny Bolster could determine the cause other than use a fancy medical word for dying. Sally's time was more and more taken in caring for her incapacitated and heavily medicated mother. In addition, Mr. Bushnell had his seasonal problem of rounding up enough reapers handy with the scythe to bring in his first hay crop. Sally politely declined Mochter's attentions.

Her mother's illness confined Sally by her concern and ministrations. To Mochter, this was not an acceptable reason for turning away such a desirable swain as Wenceslas considered himself to be. He took Mrs. Bushnell's ailing and Sally's protest as a personal affront, and became disgruntled.

Three weeks later, Wenceslas again sought Sally's attention and again was turned down. This time he did not react in an unseemly manner, but merely mumbled and turned away. In early August, Sally's father came to Mochter's mill with a load of wheat to be ground and was told that they were so busy they could not fit him into their schedule. Nor did they have room to store his grain pending a more opportune time. At great inconvenience, Mr. Bushnell hauled his crop all the way to Monmouth for milling. When he returned home late that evening, he found Sally weeping at his wife's bedside. His wife had died in his absence.

Crispin heard of Mochter's spurning and resulting conduct, and resented the tactics that Mochter had used on his father, and on Sally whom he wished he was old enough to court.

Separate from his house, Wenceslas had his study which had its own necessary close by. Crispin was sure that only Wencesles used the privy and, as well as he was able, he began to keep tabs on Mochter's visitations. When certain that Mochter's schedule would not betray him, he stole into the small structure with his tools to change the seat support in a manner that would not show.

Several of us were in on Crispin's plan and begged him to keep us alert to Mochter's habits, and when he would seek nature's relief. Crispin said it would probably be right after breakfast, but several days in a row Mochter saddled his horse and, without seeming to answer nature's call, rode away for the day. Attention flagged.

When Crispin finally spied Mochter exiting the study and striding to his privy, he could not signal anyone in time for the coup de grâce. Within seconds, the neighborhood's morning serenity was shattered by a crash and Mochter's wails at his introduction to humility.

Several days after Ancie's and my episode at the Green Bottle, the Wye valley was given an early glimpse of winter not expected to reveal its fury for several more weeks. In the early morning, dark gray clouds, that simulated voluminous bladders sagging with moisture, appeared over the Welsh mountains to the northwest. Soon, wet snow, energized by cruel winds, blanketed the valley and felled every weak and hoary branch to mar the pristine scape. Old, weakened trees were wrenched from the earth to lie on their sides or to lean on their neighbors.

By mid-afternoon, this cold fury was replaced by a clear, placid sky and a sun that still had warmth enough to soothe one's exposed skin and to begin the melt. As with the flood of a month ago, I found it fascinating to witness what nature has wrought and what remained after its excesses, so I ventured to one of my favorite places—Wedlich's pool.

The river was full and burbling, the color of gunmetal. A white down had settled and appeared as a comforter sheltering the shore. Legions of small birds, that had dug a retreat in the dead leaves before the storm, reasserted their domain by twittering and imprinting their tracks on the new cottony surface. As I tramped downstream, I was startled to come upon the venerable and stately sycamore lying across the shrubby under-story; its giant roots upthrust at the river bank. The recent floods had loosened the hold of the remaining roots and the sudden force of wind met little resistance to topple her. This paramount landmark of my childhood and recent past, would grace the landscape no more.

Large clods still clung to the matrix of roots torn upwards from the ground. Closer inspection was gratifying. I could just make out a glint of metal still in the grasp of this giant whose riparian roots had given sanctuary to so many fish including the giant trout which, indirectly, had brought me to the spot. I brushed some snow from the recumbent and mottled trunk and sat down to steady my gaze at the object that might have a huge effect on my future. Then I scanned the perimeter of the field to make sure I was alone. This was a secret and sacred moment—a vestige of my past and a tentative view of my future could be seen in this one panorama.

Aside from an occasional flitting finch, all was quiet. There was no motion—no tell-tale exhalation of vapor from a breathing participant to spoil this revealing moment. Small accumulations of snow fell from branches, and rooks called, but this theater had no audience but me. I was to have an experience comparable to pulling Excalibur from the royal stone. Could I recover this prize from the grip of the tree and propel my life to greater prospects?

Fortune had been good to me by this storm. I no longer had to be concerned with wading in frigid waters or deferring retrieval of a precarious prize till spring. Nature had tossed it in full reach only a few feet above my head. I looked about for a straight and sturdy branch long enough to prod the clod of dirt and metal loose from the upended tangle. Alas, I dared not dislodge it for fear of dropping it into the levered-out root cavity now filled with water deeper than before. I could not take a chance with what meager tools I had at hand. This climax to my wild imaginings of the last weeks would have to be delayed so that I could leave here to seek out a basket or bag to suspend from a long pole for retrieval.

'But, hold on. Don't rush off!' I began a soliloquy. 'Stay here a moment and think this out. What is the smartest thing to do? A curious somebody may come by and pluck the prize, if I vacate the scene.'

Contemplating this dilemma, I noticed that, as the sun was melting snow from the old sycamore's bark, gnarls and deep crevasses slowly came into view. These nubs and nooks and the many roots would provide sufficient handholds and 'steps' reminiscent of those our apple trees provided when pruning the orchard. A few more minutes and all would be dry for a secure climb to within easy reach of the long-sought spoil.

As the sun moved west and bore more directly on my intended climb, what I had envisioned evolved. Kicking the impacted snow from my boots, I stepped and pulled myself up. In a trice, I was within reach of the prize. A deep, authoritative voice hailed me. I turned, stunned to see Wenceslas Mochter looking up with a squint and questioning grimace.

"What are you doing in that tree? What are you after?"

I turned away in panic so that the tangle of roots shook a little and, providentially, a glob of snow fell from a clutch of feathers suspended on a fine gut line snared by the broken root. A vision of that marvelous day I caught and lost the trout swept over me and I blurted, "I'm looking for this lure I lost when a huge trout got away from me several months ago. And here it is!"

This answer did not seem to satisfy him. I could hardly believe it myself, but here it was. I cut the lure free, tucked it in my cap, and scrambled down to divert his attention from the uplifted roots. My perch in the tree was beginning to feel like a scaffold under his steely gaze.

"If you fly fish, you'll know how important it is to not lose a lure that works." I said this almost as a question since I didn't know whether my answer would carry weight with him—he had such a reputation for gauging others with disdain. But his gaze fastened on the red and black pinch of feathers.

There was doubt in his voice, "You're very tenacious to chase after something so inconsequential as a fishing lure after so long." Whether he berated or favored me, I was not sure.

"Oh, I didn't come out just to find the lure. I just happened to see it as I was sitting here admiring the view and commiserating over the loss of this old sycamore." I hoped this would satisfy him.

"You act as if you had ownership of the tree, and for a long time."

"Oh, I don't own it. But enjoying something is sort of like owning it. I had hoped nothing would happen to it, that it would continue to grow and cast its shade, and slough old bark to show off a fresh mottled trunk each year. Its been like an old friend ever since I was a child first learning to fish, and now it won't stand here like a grandfather, a comforting guide, anymore."

I was revealing more of my melancholy than I wanted to this unfriendly stranger, but vocalizing my cares seemed to relieve the occasion which would be a memorable day in my life. It was a notable backward glance at a familiar image of my memory, a lovely scene that would never be replicated. Events in my life were moving faster than I cared, and I had a foreboding that there were many scenes that I would no longer be able to enjoy.

He heard me out and we both remained silent. I gradually shifted to one side so that his gaze would likely follow and no reflective glint would catch his eye.

"Do you come out for walks often?" I asked as I sidled.

He coughed and cleared his throat. "Only when I see a trespasser on my property."

"Oh, I'm sorry. I didn't know you owned it."

"Well, you do now. I just bought it—all the way from the glen brook to the common."

"Congratulations!" This seemed the only thing for me to say, but I was aghast. Was he telling the truth? Would he convert it to a sheep pasture? Would all the vegetation, the wood hyacinths, pinks, fox gloves, black-eyed Susans, laurel, michaelmas daisies, mints, jacobs ladder, and other dainty flowers—all these would be cropped by the sheep and the ground trampled?

"Thank you. I may leave it a natural park and give it to the town, including the common, for all to enjoy." Mochter couldn't have surprised me more! He was awfully formal for a conversation alongside a stream bank, as if a statement of his charity should be solemnized.

"Cripin Johnson and I use this field for clout shooting, have for years. Would you let us still use it for such purposes?"

"An excellent usage. But I think the shore of the stream should be preserved for at least fifty yards on both sides. Once this verdure is trampled, it would take a long time to bring it back." Mochter became a far different person from what we had seen and that Crispin described. There would be changes but the general nature of the tract would be preserved..

"Do you fly fish?" I hoped to hear that he did; a dedicated fisherman would insist on keeping the stream and banks beautiful and productive of fish.

"You could say that I never had the opportunity because of lack of time and place. I grew up in London. The Thames and Fleet Brook were not water courses from which to pluck food." He didn't mince words.

"Well, this brook is. You would find it very relaxing and a venue for uninterrupted thinking. The sound of the water is so soothing." To coax him into the sport might guarantee protection of the stream.

"Perhaps you could show me some of the techniques of angling. It might be just the diversion I need. How would I go about beginning?"

"A start might be getting a copy of Isaac Walton's "Compleat Angler" which he wrote a hundred years ago not far from here. But his experience and ideas still apply. You would learn the habits of the trout, how wily he is, tackle to use, flies to tie, how to cast, how to wade, the effect of weather, oh, all sorts of things. And it helps to know an old hand, as well, to tell you the habits of fish, where the best spots in the river are, and to be a fishing companion too, of course." I'd better slack off and let him follow his own inclinations before he throws the hook, I thought.

"Sounds like a lot to learn."

"But you learn at your own rate under excellent conditions and enjoy fishing as you absorb more lore. You might even catch a trout now and then." There I am, trying to sell him. "Several months ago I hooked into a trout the size of a small terrier and he was as rambunctious as a puppy, too. That lure I just cut off the root was the one I caught him with. And that root was the one he used to break the line."

"How did you learn?" he inquired.

"My good friend Crispin Johnson is a natural. He knows more about trout than they know about themselves. And he always catches fish when he goes out. I learned from him." I hoped Mochter didn't know Crispin was the architect of his humiliation last week.

He absorbed this information but said nothing and gave no hint by grimace or shrug that the name meant anything to him.

Mochter squinted at the sun, pulled out his watch, and declared, "I must go. Thank you for your information. Oh! What is your name?" I introduced myself.

"You're George Claveraque's son?" He seemed surprised when I confirmed this. But he did not introduce himself. I guess he assumed everyone knew who he was, being important and all that. I said nothing more, hoping that he would move on so that I could finally retrieve the prize so long agonized over. He turned and walked back whence he came.

As I patiently waited for Mochter to turn the bend and pass behind the screen of beech trees, I could not help but think how different he seemed from Crispin's description. He didn't seem acquisitive even though he had bought my favorite stretch of the stream. But, after all, he may have done it for benevolent reasons, not avarice. He was not arrogant or garrulous or falsely modest. Though smart, sinister scheming didn't seem to be his specialty after all. I rather liked the man.

Crispin must have been jealous of this individual who had so many credentials and could have wooed Sally Bushnell were she not waiting for Dordy's return from America. It was her implied commitment to Dordy that put her out of Crispin's reach, as well as her being four years older.

I again climbed the tree and reached out to grasp the clod that hinted of a brick shape and hid something of value. Maybe it was a box and not an ingot. It was still held firmly in the webbing of roots. I had to wrench it this way and that to dislodge it, and then I came near losing it. I almost dropped it in the water, it was so heavy for its size.

I scanned the perimeter of the meadow. All was clear, and I threw the clod to safe ground. Some of the clay broke away in the fall and the rest I scrubbed off with a fist full of autumn-cered grass. My head throbbed with the excitement of having in hand this relic that might have lain here since Roman times or, at least, from the days of knights in armor, tournaments, and broadswords.

Scratches and gashes, caused by what must have been centuries of spring floods ramming logs, stones, even boulders battering its surface, had severely disfigured this ancient specimen. But there was no sign of corrosion—it was not brass, it was gold!

I realized that I must not remain out there for all to see me ogling this bauble. But how to secrete it safely home? That was the essential question.

Four inches wide by eight inches long by an inch-and-a-half thick, it must have weighed thirty or thirty-five pounds! I had not thought about problems of securing this treasure to safety before coming out.

It took so long for this fulfilling event to unfold that I wasn't prepared for this day to be the day I secured the prize.

When my glance fell on a coppice of hazel, a solution came to mind. I set about to collect a number of inch-thick hazel sticks. My ever-present knife was the only tool at hand but it would be enough to carry out my plan. I deeply scored the hazel sticks to weaken them at the right length. Their exact size was not important; but they all should be about the same length. That way, when I carried a bundle of them enclosing, and I hoped concealing, the yellow ingot, they would appear to be materials for a cabinet-making project or some such. At least, if some busybody inquired, I could say so, I thought.

I scored them again and then, one at a time, inserting the scored part between the crotch of two sturdy upright trunks, firmly grabbing each at the other end of the rod and wrenching hard. Each time it broke off more or less clean. I whittled the uneven ends to some semblance of design. With my undershirt, I wrapped the middle of the bundle, ingot inside, and set about my way home.

Crispin happened by with probably his last catch of the season, but he didn't tarry long. He wanted to show me his trout and hurry them into the ice house or the pan. A few ohs and ahs was all that was necessary before going our separate ways. My bundle was still secure but getting heavier as I continued my way down the road.

Squire Calloway on his chestnut came into view. "I understand you had a good talk with Lieutenant Brigandi. He's a good man. None better. Just the same, I think we should talk about registering your spring gadget and making it exclusively yours so that you realize the royalties. Then you can join the army, act as consultant, or do whatever you wish."

I assured him that I would come by his office soon.

"Working on a new project I see, James? A good man is never idle." He nodded at the bundle in agreement with his own statement, and cantered off to my relief and a "Yes sir!"

A few minutes more after re-hefting my burden, I heard steps catching up to me. Downey Cohan brought himself even and caught my stride. "I got out several copies of the London Rambler to check what you said the other afternoon. You were mostly right. What do you think about the latest? One of the same rebels that took Fort Ticonderoga is now leading an expedition into the wilderness, headed for Canada, perhaps Quebec. Maybe they're going to dig gold out of the deep woods, eh?"

I clung tightly to my 'project', acknowledged his grudging affirmation of my stand last week, and owned I didn't know the latest. "Where did they leave from, and when?" I asked.

"They're working their way up a river in Maine. About a thousand of 'em.

"I think it was mid-September. Kind of late to be going into the north woods on a camp, eh?"

It probably was late for such an excursion, I silently agreed. I had heard that northern New England had severe winters. "What is the date of the paper you got this from?"

"I don't know. Brigandi told me just yesterday. It must be fresh news, this being almost Guy Fawkes day. I assume he got it from the army." Downey opined.

We walked together in silence. I didn't want to be abrupt and disrupt my re-acquaintance with Downey. But I didn't want to encourage conversation that might inquire of my strange bundle. If word got out that I had such a prize, and Downey would be the perfect instrument to herald the news, my life would be changed for the worse. Happily, it happened that he had caught up, not for conversation, but to pass me. He was in a hurry.

Presently, the Bristol stage hove into sight and sound. A true sign of active enterprise, a coach-and-four never ceased to excite me. "Yo, Jamie," yelled Gossett from his perch where he magically handled the team of sweating chargers through the reins. A specter of spinning wheels, jingling harness, fleet hoof beats, and jaded faces, the express raced by in a scud of hoof-hurled mud clods and faded out of sight down the turnpike. One would think I was walking along the Strand in London.

Sally Bushnell and Dordy then appeared. In only a half mile, on this, of all days, I encountered a fair portion of all those I knew well in this world. Had a sinister force arranged for them to parade on the Bristol Pike the very day I wished to smuggle contraband?

Dordy walked with nary a falter—a wish granted by Providence after so many months of grim moments when he suffered pain of limb and spirit. He had feared that his incapacity had irretrievably lost his merit for Sally's hand. Happily, he had misjudged Sally's fidelity and his own healing ability.

Dordy grinned."I think I walk better than I did before Bunker's Hill."

I concurred. "When I finish this project, we'll have to go clout shooting again, just like old times." Dordy was pleased to no longer be considered an invalid. We didn't treat him as being disabled for we all knew that he had considered himself to be inadequate.

"That field is the very place Sally and I are headed. Come join us."

My excuse that I had to unload the hazelwood—a burden which had severely increased as an encumbrance—and could not join them, was readily accepted. They reveled at the news of Mochter's purchase and possible gift of the choice land. Like me, they felt ashamed for thinking Mochter had aggrandized for reasons of commerce. They continued on their way, almost in frolic, they were so happy together.

The remaining eighth of a mile favored me with no more encounters and I finally unloaded my secret burden, as if in sanctuary, on my shop table. When I unwrapped the shirt and swept away the bundle of hazel rods to reveal the gold ingot, the ancient metal glowed even in the dim light of my forge. Closer inspection disclosed the imprint of Roman numerals. Just then, Father unlatched the Dutch door and came into the forge. His bulk cast a shadow on my treasure.

# chapter 7

FATHER LATCHED THE door behind him. "James, in today's post, Parson Barry announced the church is going to have a dance at the parish in celebration of Guy Fawkes Day..." Father broke off and gasped at the small slab of metal. "What have you..., where did you..., how did you acquire this?" He bent over in close inspection. "It looks like gold."

"I think it well may be, Father." I said, proud to have produced such a trove.

He pressed his thick thumbnail against the slab. It made a dent. He picked it up, hefted it and like me, almost dropped it.

"Well, tell me about this." he demanded with arched brows.

I lit the lamp and stoked the coals for more light, as well to dramatize this revelation. "Do you remember a month ago or so when I told you about the large trout that broke off my line by the old sycamore?"

He nodded.

I told him that part of my story that I had kept my own, about the brief moment the sunlight penetrated the water by the old sycamore roots to reveal a yellow form that solidly resisted my foot. Now, the words tumbled out, as if I was emptying a sack of goodies; I had kept them confined in my head all this time. I told him about my wild guess as to what it was, and not letting Crispin get close to seeing it with the pretext that I had no more leaders and wanted to go home. And I revealed to Father my frustration with not being able to verify and get at my find because of the flood, the harvesting, and the severity of the season.

Father put the heavy bar down carefully next to the forge, as if it would break, and sat down in my 'misery' chair, where, whenever I mismanaged a piece, I could relax my anger and begin to rationally reconstruct how I had bungled a job.

"This must be about thirty pounds—almost five hundred ounces. I don't know the price of gold but, this has got to be worth a fortune!" he said.

I nodded agreement.

"Does any one else know or suspect you have this?"

"No one, Father. I have fantasized about what it might be from the moment I was aware of it to the minute I wrenched it from the roots. I thought it might be a gold bar, or maybe it was merely a brass box, or part of a cross, any number of things, or only my imagination. I've told no one. Nor have I hovered over it in trying to retrieve it from the river, afraid someone, like Crispin who frequents the river more than I do, might get curious about such strange antics."

I told him about Mochter seeing me in the field and the providentially downed old sycamore with the upthrust roots obviating the need to grapple in the frigid stream. I hesitated to tell more about Mochter, not wishing to cloud our concern for the gold with Mochter's revelation of prospective benevolence. But then, I blathered all.

He pondered.

"You'll have to give it up to the authorities." he gravely announced.

"To the government?" I was astonished at this possibility.

"They don't know anything about it. They didn't have anything to do with finding it. They don't have a claim to it. I do." I stoutly defended my newfound wealth.

"But, James, the gold was in the river, presumably for a long, long time. At least long enough for the roots of that old tree to thoroughly surround it. So, ownership goes along with the land or according to the riparian rights of the river. It belongs to whoever owns the land. So, it might now belong to Mochter. We'd have to discuss the situation with Squire Calloway. It's a legal question."

"Let's not let anyone else, even Squire Calloway, know about this until we've thought about it more. It has Roman numerals and other marks embossed on it. Maybe a Roman lost it, or the Danes stole it from an ancient monastery, or a coach from the royal treasury was waylaid by highwaymen, and it ended up in the water." To have this wealth pass to a corrupt government would be insane.

I began my remonstrance. "If I drop my purse on a neighbor's property, the purse doesn't then belong to the neighbor. It's still my purse. If he chooses to tell me about it, assuming he knows it is mine, I get it back less a reward. If he doesn't return it to me or doesn't know whom to return it to, then, by right of possession and common sense, it's his.

"In this case, I found it. There is no way to know who the legitimate owner of the ingot is or was. So the gold is mine—or ours, Father."

"James, we'll have to thrash this out. We won't do anything hastily." Father was reassuring.

He continued thinking out loud. "But gold ingots are not usually owned by individuals. They 're held by banks or governments as a banking reserve, to increase and back the coinage, or a financial backlog for war, or to use in exchange with other countries, or for other reasons of state. It has no industrial or practical value like iron, copper, bronze or brass. It's too soft for other than ornamentation." Father was putting his mind to this concern. He always insisted on being honest and fair. I might find myself out of luck if he prevailed..

"I wouldn't want to trust our current government, Father. Officials could easily say it was lost or stolen government property. It's not difficult to surmise that they could counterfeit documents alleging this in a very official manner so that a judge would pass on it in their favor."
"I hate to hear you saying things like that against the crown, James. But I know it could be true, however treasonous it sounds. It's a sad state of affairs."

I countered, "Lord Mansfield has tried to get at critics of the administration, such as Junius, and has charged them with seditious libel. You know, that's why Junius, whoever he is, used a pseudonym as have so many others. When Mansfield couldn't tell who the critics were, he went after the printers and had them tried in Admiralty Court so that a jury wasn't required. Only a judge could try the printers, a judge appointed and paid for by the king.

"You know what happened, Father. You don't read any criticism of the administration any more. They've all gone into anonymity, and the printers are hushed. It was you who pointed out injustices like this to me.

"What I mean to say is that the law is now stacked in favor of the crown. So we would simply be giving a gold bar to the already wealthy and powerful." I rested my case.

"Well, James, suppose you keep the bar. How are you going to realize its value. If you saw off a piece and use it to buy a horse, say, isn't the seller going to want to know where you got the gold. And is it really gold? If you sell a piece of gold to a jeweler, you'll have to trust that he wont say anything about it. Of course, he'll probably want to buy it at a steep discount, knowing you'll have a problem disposing of it. And then, you'll always be hostage to him for what he knows or suspects."

"I suppose I could melt it down and make coins out of it." I was casting in the wind.

"The government wouldn't like that. You would be in competition with them. It's probably illegal. I think we'll have to talk to Squire Calloway," opined Father.

I trusted and liked the squire, but I thought his ethics might require him to report what he knew or be considered a conspirator. And we'd be considered conspirators. There had to be some other way to monetize the gold.

It seemed to me that great grandfather had an unsolvable problem, similar to this, long ago. He knew where to go to solve his problems. First, it was the family of smugglers in Brittany who helped him to safely transport his family out of France. Then it was other men in his business, the ones in London, who fitted his disguise and gave him the gold and fool's gold to implement his strategy when he went back to France. I had to find their modern counterparts.

Sometimes, it is best to put aside a vexing problem; the passage of time, somehow, turns up a solution.

In the meantime, I buried the ingot in the forge coal pile and determined to think of something else for awhile. After all, I had been fretting over the ingot being out of reach and then, without my intervention, the old sycamore blew over and the treasure became readily at hand. I was meant to have it.

Ancie would, no doubt, be stewing about the brash assertions I made at the Green Bottle and my ignoring her pleas to accompany me to America. By now, she has probably simmered-down and relaxed her anxiety.

As often happens in the Wye valley this time of year, the first snow melted so quickly that the landscape resumed its early autumn aspect the following day under a brilliant sun and a south wind. I broke away from mending harness and saddled Old Nellie for a visit to the Jones'. As I approached, Ancie's father was high up on his barn close to the ridgepole nailing shakes to the laths he had put in place the previous week. He waggled his hammer in the direction of the paddock, smiled, and resumed the rhythmic rat-tat that speeded his task.

Again, Ancie was currying her chestnut which gleamed under her care.

"Good morning," I hailed and promptly added, "You look very charming in that hood, Ancie." She responded so sweetly, I don't know why I ever complimented her horse instead of her last time.

"Thank you, Jamie, my handsome prince. I made the hood myself from some of Bushnell's wool Sally gave me. When we go again to the falls, I want to be able to keep warm and stay to enjoy it."

I did not even dismount but took her up on the sly suggestion, "Let's put a heavy blanket on your horse and be on our way."

She quickly produced the blanket, threw on the saddle, and cinched the girth in one smooth motion. Nellie neighed and whinnied, Ancie threw her leg over her chestnut and led the way as we cantered into the soft south wind to the little falls.

The passage of autumn, however slow this year, seemed to have deepened the patina of the foliage along the verge of the narrow trail. Bracken on the small level by the falls had been blackened by frost but had dried and was suitable to spread a blanket for our presumably secret trysting place.

We revealed our anticipation of repeating last week's passion and excitement by a degree of awkwardness uncommon to both of us. We both laughed. As she reclined on the bracken, Ancie asked, "Are you going to join the army or go to America?"

"I don't know, Ancie. Not right away. I have to decide what I want to do with my life before I can answer that question." I hoped that this reply would put a damper on further questions of the sort. Going to America seemed to her the most important consideration since the possibility had come up at the Green Bottle. There, she quickly had found the prospect as agreeable as a parched traveler would at stumbling on a bubbling, clear spring—as if she was in a desperate situation. Of course, I said nothing about the gold ingot.

I spread both blankets on the bracken and lay down next to her. Small talk served well to change the subject of my plans for the future.

"I understand that there's going to be a dance at the parish house next Friday. Would you like to go?" I asked.

"Friday is when my quilting girls plan to meet to decide who will sew what patterns this winter. I don't think I can."

"Chances are that your friends will want to attend the dance. They can always meet some other time to do their quilting."

"I'll have to talk to Sally. She won't be going to the dance. Dordy can't dance with his bad leg and all."

"You'd be surprised. Dordy has been exercising his legs ever since he's been home. I think he'll be anxious to see how well he can shake a leg. He can get up on a horse. He can even climb a ladder. And it will be the first time he's been able to dance with Sally since he went into the army."

Ancie sulked. "I'll think about it."

I was surprised at her hesitation. She gave several weak excuses rather than sticking to one. And none of them made much sense since she liked to dance and enjoyed parties. She must have a reason for her lack of interest, I thought. I said nothing and laid back to listen to the sound of the wind and the falls.

"James, it would be so nice to have a fresh start in life."

Perhaps she thought I would take her to America if she was willing to go to the dance with me. Ancie could think this way at times.

"Ancie, neither of us has made any start to speak of, not to mention a second start."

"Well, I just want to get away. You'll take me someplace wont you?" She threw her arms about me and pressed up close. "I know you will." She began to persuade me without using words and her wiles were more convincing than her vocabulary.

Within a few minutes she started to loosen her hood, blouse and skirt but, as she said, only to allow more freedom of motion. She was enticing and I kissed her longingly as I encircled her in my arms. The air became chill as clouds blanketed the sun and I gathered the other blanket to cover us as in a cozy cave. This courtesy seemed to encourage courtesies on her part and, magically, I found greater facility in slipping my hands beneath her short clothes and caressing her bare torso. She warmed to the mild exertion.

I massaged her slender waist and the gentle flare of her hips first before further discovery of her charms. Ancie shuffled slightly to accommodate more intimate fondling. She cuddled even more as our passions progressed. The warmth of her body against me foreclosed any thought except indulging with abandon. Making love to her was curiously similar to having too much strong cider—I felt capable of anything and was willing to try regardless of predictable and adverse consequences.

As at the falls a week ago, I began to feel in the grasp of forces which I could no longer control. The sensation was being repeated now. She occasionally squirmed, not to free herself, but to press herself so rhythmically and with such strength that my body responded the way nature dictated it should. Ancie sensed this and pressed even more sensuously. An inner voice cautioned, but I made no effort to back away. So far, we had not exceeded proprieties; we both remained clothed, though loosely, and no harm had been done.

It had been evident for several minutes that we could not keep up this pace before a decision had to be mutually accepted. Before this decision could be determined, nature interceded and rendered any decision moot. But no harm was done. Indeed, no harm could now be done. I was spent and we were safe.

"You should not get so impassioned so quickly." Ancie scolded.

I agreed. "You are a seductress of the first order and I love being here with you. I can't resist your charms, Ancie."

She smiled in acknowledgment but remained silent.

Secretly, I felt that destiny had interfered with such a hasty and ill-considered liaison as this with Ancie. She was passionate and marvelous at inciting protracted passion in me. At other times, she could be pleasant to be with only if it fitted with her agenda.

But her conversational range was limited. I reflected that she had not been interested in bettering herself when she attended seminary under Doctor Barry's tutelage. She had been one of that legion which prided itself on rebuking accepted knowledge. Sadly, this was evident when she was in a group; her dexterity at repartee proved barren.

Now, she still was not really interested in bettering herself except, perhaps, if I took her to the colonies with me. Her curiosity about the world around her was non-existent and no amount of prodding to educate her to much of what mankind had discovered, fought over, or invented had any effect.

Her parents were well spoken and interesting but she declined to follow their pattern. She was like a leaf; blown here, then there. Ancie never inquired further about subjects I was talking about or had queries of her own about nature, politics, and philosophy in general. She rarely initiated a sentence unless it had to do with the routine housekeeping of one's life. Besides all this, she lied several times—mostly about being with Downey Cohan.

Downey had taken no pains to treat her well at the Green Bottle. Had she been going with him most of the time? Had they had an argument? I decided to pursue this. Perhaps she had elected me to fill in as paramour pending a re-engagement with Downey

The age we were living in was ripe and replete with fascination: discoveries in science such as Doctor Franklin's experiment's in electricity and his lightning rod, inventions such as Watt's improved steam engine, the politics involved between the colonies and the king and his placemen, or knowledge of new lands such as the vast interior of America. She knew nothing of Swift, Addison, Pope, John Donne, or De Foe. She was not only ignorant of these authors but showed no interest in finding out. There was just no spirit of adventure. Conversation with her was vacuous. I felt sorry for Ancie and her future.

Our relationship had been mainly physical and, as pleasant as that was, I wanted much more in a lifetime companion.

We were still embracing but not with the fervor of a few minutes ago. We released our hold on each other and lay there, each contemplating the implication of this moment for our future. This was not love—only making love.

"James, I think I will go to the dance after all", she declared.

It was clear that Ancie had expected much more. Not just in the sensual act, but in what it might import about our relationship and her prospects to change her life. We both knew then that, except for attending the dance together, we were about to separate as a couple. I was not going to be her husband, the father of her children, or her ticket to America.

# chapter 8

SQUIRE CALLAWAY HAD suggested on two occasions that I should see him to discuss my wagon springs. I did not wish to gain the disfavor of the squire, one of father's favorite friends and advisers, by dithering any longer. Of course, I considered him a respected friend although he firmly belonged to an earlier generation. It was important for me to hear his opinion of the springs and what I should do to secure their value, which he seemed to think was significant.

Unlike the usual professional quarters, his home was an appendage of his office-study, an ivy-strangled ancient pile of stonework, which perhaps had served as one of the early Christian chapels here in the valley. His desk was to the side of the small chancel which had been favorably modified by the addition of a fireplace. A small fire was up to the challenge of chasing the cold from the stonework and its occupants, but just barely.

As I came through the front door, the Squire signaled that he would be with me soon, although two other parties were seated distant from the squire's assemblage of desks and cabinets. He was showing an elderly lady some sort of schedule, perhaps an estate inventory, and explaining each item carefully and with great patience.

The squire's clerk, Algernon Jameson, came over to greet me and to enquire my business. He straightened upon my explanation and grabbed something from his desk for me to review. The squire had written out some questions regarding the spring's design, history, and possible future as well as some thoughts on how to exploit the device. I wrote out answers to the questions and marveled at the expansive thought that he had put into the rest of the survey. It had much more imagination than merely building springs. I began to build on the squire's imagination so that I was prepared when the elderly lady stood up, thanked the squire profusely, and called to her sons that it was time to go.

"Squire Calloway, I thank you for your thoughts on the springs and also for your patience with my impolite lack of response to your kind invitations during the last month." I blurted. He invited me to sit at the side of his desk as I handed the questionnaire back to him. "Jamie, the springs are a good idea and well thought out. I visited your father the other day and he mentioned what an improvement of the ride your springs make on the road. I had a good look at them and can understand why, though I'm no engineer, you understand."

He read my answers to his questions and nodded. "The main value of your springs, as I see it, Jamie, aside from their economic and comfort value, is that they can be a spring board, pardon the pun, to a much more comprehensive and profitable future. Rather than making springs for others to fit to their wagons, why not make the wagons as well. In effect, you would be your own customer and closer commercially to the big money in the burgeoning transport business.

"The big money will be from building the roads and the wagon and coach lines that have to follow. With the turnpikes reaching out from London to Bristol, Bath, Hereford, Gloucester, and Land's End, the prospects are limitless. A few canals have recently been built in the midlands. Markets can be expanded for all sorts of products. Demand is sure to increase."

I could follow his reasoning easily enough, but where would I get the money to buy the supplies, the tools, the space, and to pay the men, skilled men, to bring all this about?

"It makes sense, but the organization, the money it will take…?"

He cut me off. "Of course, it will require significant funds. I have several clients who have large accumulations of capital and are insistently after me to tell them where they can invest in this nascent expansion of our highway system. I, personally, am interested in it. Granted, this will be a great step, nay a leap, for you to take, but I have confidence in you that you can do it."

"Surely, there are companies that can make the wagons in every shire from here to the Wash. How would I enter that market?" I was flabbergasted.

"You are right about that. But there are many canal companies that started in the last ten years, and they and their progeny will most likely grab the bulk cargo business. Bulk items do not have to be transported quickly and so they will be cheaper. What I have in mind is a fine coach for passenger travel. Speed and comfort is what the business traveler is after. Same with the touring family. And, of course the post would be greatly improved by faster service. We think you could design a light weight coach which would be fleet and, with your springs and cushioned seats, would provide a more comfortable ride—a highly desirable commodity." The squire tilted back in his chair to scrutinize my reaction.

I reflected, "I've never even designed a wagon, much less a coach. I"v never seen a coach up close that wasn't moving hellbent for leather. I would be designing a vehicle I know little about."

The squire would not be put off. "That's why we want you to be the one to do this. You aren't paralyzed or burdened with old ideas. You are open to suggestions, willing to try something new, able to learn, and energetic. That combination of talents earns a premium, James. We are enthusiastic about this project and want you to carry through with it.. We have already talked to Amos Dunkholme, a veteran wainwright, who turned us down, but is willing to teach you the basics of design and manufacture. He has many years of experience, but he's old and not interested in the responsibility of a venture such as this. We'll have you talk to him."

I was flattered and flustered. The prospect was daunting but interesting, with a lot of business and professional backup from the squire, my father I'm sure, and their friends as backers who would assist in any way to help the venture succeed. Further reflection brought to mind that this might be the perfect operation to make use of my new-found trove. I must get used to the idea that I now have substantial personal capital.

# chapter 9

Squire Calloway came by in his one-horse cart to pick me up for the purpose of introducing me to the wainwright of whom he had spoken so highly. Thank goodness that the squire was as thin as I am because his cart barely had room for one larger-than-normal man. Even so, it was a tight squeeze for the two of us.

The cart was modestly decorated and would not draw much attention in any setting. Knowing the squire, this was probably intentional. I couldn't help but notice that the springs were of the very rudimentary kind; the jouncing ride to our destination gave proof that the suspension could stand improvement. No doubt his interest in my springs had as much to do with preserving his comfort as with enhancing his investments.

The modest and weathered sign at our destination read "Amos Dunkholme, Wainwright"over the door of the shop. Wagons and lorries of all kinds in various stages of disrepair cluttered the side yard. One ornate cart had a wheel missing, the tongue and double trees of another was off to one side, and a wagon box had been lifted to a high clearance by sturdy jacks.

Off to the side, a large door, like that of a barn, opened so that conveyances could be brought in and serviced during inclement weather. A sluice led to an overshot water wheel which powered the shop. Downstream of the wheel, dead trout and sawdust turned lazily in the eddy. Sawdust covered the edge of the stream and big gobs that had caught on the rocks were gradually being washed away in the rapids.

The squire escorted me into the shop infused with the fragrance of freshly planed timbers of seasoned oak; and the subtleties of the wagon makers trade. Windrows of sawdust covered the floor. In a corner near a window, a grey-haired workman was paring a spoke to final shape with a spoke shave. As the squire and I approached, he straightened up and waited for the squire to make the introduction. Amos Dunkholme offered his hand and firmly shook mine as he deferentially listened to the squire.

"Mister Claveraque has been with his family's cider farm as you probably know. But Jame's skill at ironwork, especially designing and making springs for wagons is what qualifies him for this meeting, Amos. He wants you to teach him the finer points of wagon making with emphasis on the more stylish and weight-saving aspects of the art. In other words, he wants to eventually make fast and luxurious coaches."

"Mr. Dunkholme, I want to be able to personally make each component part of horse-drawn vehicles. I don't have the conceit that I would be able to make them as well as one of your craftsmen, I just want to know, hands on, what's involved. So far, I've only made springs for our own wagon, but I find the prospect of making coaches so fascinating that I have decided to devote my time and energies to your attention if you'll have me as an apprentice."

"Squire Calloway has given me your credentials, young man, and I'd be pleased to show you what I know. Please, just call me Amos, and, if I may, I'll call you James."

"That makes a welcome bit of sense, Amos." I was glad to do away with such formalities. "Where do you think we should start?"

He bent over the spoke he was preparing. "Well, right here. The wheels are the most abused part of the wagon or coach and the spokes are a major part of the wheel. Each spoke has to take its share of the weight of the vehicle plus the load, that is, freight, passengers, and jolts. When the hub is directly over the spoke—are you with me?"—I nodded, he went on—"Each spoke has to be very strong to support all that weight even though it may only be for an instant That's why we make them out of straight-grained oak or ash, some of the strongest of woods. And we let it season for two or more years unless we are going to steam it. In that case, we want green stock, freshly cut, so it will take the steam and bend easily to the shape we want."

"What do you mean by straight-grain?" I had never known precisely what the term meant.

He grimaced ever so slightly, I would have to be taught from the ground up.

Amos continued. "We split the billets rather than saw them out because the split will be along the grain of the wood. The straighter, the better. If the billet is sawed and the grain runs off at an angle to the piece, the wood will be weak at that point. Similarly, a saw cut might cross the grain which, even if at a slight angle, could weaken the spoke. Some wagon drivers spoke their vehicle before going down a grade. That is, they shove a stout billet through the spokes of both rear wheels which fetches up against the underside of the wagon, to brake the speed of the descent; it skids down the hill.

"So you see, the spokes have to be strong to take that kind of treatment. Sawing might be cheaper by cutting down on waste, but it would lower the quality of the work." He waited a bit for me to absorb this or question it. "A vehicle made with inferior spokes might lose this braking power and become a runaway and endanger the lives of the occupants. Such an event would ruin the reputation of the coach builder."

"We also use quarter-sawn stock because it doesn't warp or distort when it gets wet. Warping can tear a jointed piece apart over time." He paused again, then went on. "You can appreciate that we have to select the best timber—which means the most expensive—to use in our work. Not all the parts of a wagon require straight grain or quarter-sawn stock, but most of 'em do." No pause this time.

His intense gaze impelled to agree to the merit of using nothing but quality materials. He nodded approval and went on. "We can get into the details of making spokes later. The same man who makes the spokes also makes the fellies and the hub. Again, we need sturdy timber, especially for the hub because of the torsion and twisting caused by the wheels and the axle. For this, we need cross-grained wood, like elm, gum, and sassafras, so the hub won't split apart. Sometimes a burl will do, but they're hard to turn on the lathe and to get a clean turning." He paused.

"What are the fellies? I asked.

"Those are the outer parts or sections of the rim of the wheel. On the larger wheels there are seven fellies into which two spokes are driven—holes drilled for the spokes, of course—fourteen spokes in all. And then the holes are reamed with a tapered reamer to provide for the tightest of fits." He must have assumed comprehension because he did not pause.

"I suppose the same man who drills the holes for fellies does so for the hub?"

"Not so, James. The hubs are always pierced with rectangular and tapered spoke holes. This requires an expert with the chisel. It is so exacting. And the chisel must be very sharp because the cross grained wood of the hub is so tough. The spoke mortices are cut at a slight outward angle to give the wheel its distinctive flat-cone shape. This requires great care and skill.

The angle permits the wheel to be mounted on the axle so that it tilts outward. But the spokes supporting the weight must be vertical, that is, directly under the hub; those on the top of the wheel angle outwards. Tilting, coupled with toe-in, makes for better steering. The hubs are built with select material to see that it is not prone to split under forces from all angles. A knowledgeable eye and a lot of labor goes into them, so there must be no mistakes made when performing these delicate treatments on them." No pause here either.

"The final component of the wheel is the tire which holds the whole assembly of spokes, fellies, and hub together and takes the abrasion of the road. But that's the wheelwright's job. He fashions just the right length of iron band, always a little smaller than the wheel's circumference, and welds the two ends to make a ringed band. Then, he heats the band red hot so that it expands to just the right diameter. At the right moment, he and his helpers lower it to embrace the fellies. and the whole wheel assembly. With hammering and adjusting he gets it just right. The wheelwright and his helpers have to do it quickly, and it has to be done right the first time. There is no second chance.

"When it's set, they douse the whole with water to cool and shrink the tire on very tight. It also prevents the carefully-made wheel from catching fire. There might be a little charring, but that's all. Charring may even make the wood more durable. Some think so. You can hear the spokes groan and squeal as the shrinkage compresses them deeper into their sockets.

"If it's done right, that wheel will take a lot of punishment and still last a long time. And it won't break down on the road. That's important to our customers. So we have George Giess, our blacksmith and wheelwright, who has sized and applied the tires for years."

Amos paused for a rest. Then he added, "We don't know who invented the idea of the welded band, even though it's recent, but it's a lot stronger, lighter, and reliable than the old method of riveting sections of iron to the fellies."

We moved on to what Amos called the "fifth wheel" and the axletree, the running gear that permits the steering of four-wheeled wagons or carriages.

At that moment, shouting, noisy commotion, dogs barking, accompanied a visitor who stomped into Amos' establishment shouting, "Why is my cart still out in the yard? You promised that I would have it this morning! Damn it, Dunkholme, I'm a busy man." It was Wenceslas Mochter gesticulating wildly with his ever-present ivory-headed blackthorn cane.

He saw me and calmed down a little. "You do business here, Claveraque? I suppose your cart isn't ready yet either." He brazened.

I declined to answer.

I was glad to see that Amos would not be intimidated, and asserted his self-respect by replying quickly, before Mochter could continue. "I sent a boy with a message, Mr. Mochter. He related that no one was home, so he shoved it under your door. We found several serious cracks in the spokes. This requires either a new wheel or careful disassembly of your present wheel and fitting it with replacement spokes. You said you wanted it fixed, so we are fixing it. But it is time consuming. We should have it done by tomorrow afternoon."

"Tomorrow afternoon? I need it now." Mochter yelped.

Amos stood resolute.

"How long does it take to put on a new wheel? And how much more expensive?"

"Probably about fifteen guineas more, sir." said Amos. "But, I can put a new wheel on in a few minutes."

"Well, be quick about it. I don't think I should have to pay extra for it since you've inconvenienced me." That was Mochter; always playing the odds to wangle a lesser price. Mochter, true to form.

All the workmen in the shop had gathered to witness Mochter's blustering arrogance and to enjoy Amos' response.

"Your cart won't move from this shop unless you put coin on the counter now, Mr Mochter. And I require full fee for whichever choice you decide." Amos spoke with authority.

"Fee? Only professionals charge *fees*. Doctors and barristers do, but not wainwrights!" railed Mochter.

"Fee, price, bill, compensation—whatever you wish to call it. Put your money on the counter. I'll put on the wheel and hitch your horse. But never come back, Mr. Mochter."

The workmen applauded and gave a cheer to their straightforward boss.

Mochter took out his fine leather purse, squeezed the nibs to open it, flung the coins on the counter and looked for a chair in which to seethe. There was no chair, only a small empty nail keg. It was beneath his dignity. But Mochter sat. The shop men reluctantly returned to their benches.

Amos asked one of his men to mount the wheel and walked back to the steering gear where we had left off. I followed. He shook his head several times but said nothing about Mochter.

"This device is recently invented, too, James. It's called a fifth wheel in the trade."

The distinctive parts of the gear were two thick metal disks about ten inches in diameter held together by a king bolt in the center so that they could freely rotate against each other in the same plane. The top disk was attached to the underside of the transom which, when the piece was repaired, would be attached to the bottom of the front bolster which would be secured to the front end of the carriage.

The bottom disk was attached to the axletree bed above the axletree which held the wheels and the perch, or tongue, of the vehicle. The disks were well-tallowed so that, as the horses were directed to turn, the lower assembly of wheels and axletree would follow with a minimum of friction, and the carriage would stay stable. At least, most of the time.

Rather than explain all this to me, Amos simply moved the tongue of the wagon left and right. The axle turned; of course, the transom stayed in place. "The main problem here is that the device is not often kept greased. Another is that the whole assembly should be built more sturdily than this is. We'll get into this in more detail in a day or so." Amos sighed.

We moved on to the next section of the shop which had to do with the suspension of the vehicle—my specialty—mechanics I thought I knew something about..

"You'll appreciate this, James. Some wagons have springs, most don't. They all should—to keep the drivers and passengers all in one piece aside from making the ride bearable. Carriages and coaches have either rudimentary springs, or several thicknesses of leather thorough braces, or both. Trouble is, thorough braces cushion the coach but don't do much for the passengers inside. The springs mostly are there to support the leather braces at their ends. And like Mochter there, the sports don't like to shell out coin to repair their toys. But it's either that or they don't ride." He let me climb over and under to see up close how others had handled the problem of suspension and comfort.

I loosened the linch-pin which secured the wheel on the axle, but before I removed the wheel, I raised the axle a bit and supported it with a shop stand. The axle end was a metal fitting which was bolted to the axletree. It had been forged so that it turned down slightly and toed-in a few degrees, as well. I could now see better what Amos was talking about. Amos nodded when I looked at him in understanding. He said, "I forgot to tell you that the hub has a metal sleeve that mates with the forging. Grinding compound is smeared on both parts and the wheel is turned for several minutes so that they become smooth, well-fitting mating surfaces. Then both parts are cleaned of the compound and grindings, and coated with tallow. They are, or should be, constantly greased."

"James, there aren't that many coaches on the road yet and most of them are repaired at the stage line's terminal. Some have to be repaired on the road, that is, brought to a shop such as mine. That's why I have this beauty here today. I built a coach like this, but smaller, for the "Duke" last summer. Let's go take a look at it. Maybe Harrington will be there and we can go for a ride with him or even with the Duke." The Duke, or just plain Duke, was an honorary title for our friend, John Hancock. Though a member of the landed gentry, John was not snobby and aloof like so many of that cadre, but had a reputation for years of conducting himself with geniality and candor with all he met, hence the moniker.

I was all for this and a few minutes later we were driving up the Duke's lane in Amos' chaise, this one, thankfully, was wider and had springs though they were stiff ones. We went around back to the carriage house and sought Harrington, the Duke's coach driver, who was a friend of Amos' and a casual acquaintance of mine.

Harrington was just finishing cleaning mud and horse dung from the running gear of the coach, a nasty job. He brightened at our appearance and a chance to take the coach-and-four for an excursion on Amos' excuse that he wished to compare the springs on the coach to mine.

Amos helped him harness the matched teams of white stallions and the three of us crowded on the driver's bench in front.

Harrington clucked to the teams and lightly flicked the reins. Our assembled coach-and-four team moved out smartly and down the Duke's lane to the Bristol Pike. Harrington clucked a slightly different note, flicked again, and the lead team turned left with the wheel horses in line. Two clucks and the horses changed their gait so that we surged to a speed twice that of a spirited person walking, perhaps seven or eight miles an hour. When I had Nellie on our wagon, she could manage this if the load wasn't much, but not for a sustained period like these two teams could.

I asked Harrington to stop the coach so I could get out and sit inside to test the ride as a passenger. This was my first ride in a coach and the first with four horses providing the power. I noticed that it had thorough braces, thick bands of leather running under both sides of the passenger compartment. These suspended the coach by being attached to springs, which looked more like stanchions, with little give, front and back and at both sides.

We went over that section of the road where I had tested my improved springs, where the top of the in-ground boulder, the "giant's knuckle" gave every vehicle a jolt. There was no question that Harrington had intentionally driven the coach over this ridge for I was thrown off my seat and in the ensuing stretch of rough road, we all had to fumble around to regain our equilibrium.

Harrington cried out, "If you can soften that bump, you will command a handsome market in the carriage trade." Amos, after repositioning himself, agreed.

So, even this magnificently built coach was jarred by an obstacle as if going over cor-du-roy. Fine cabinet work, expertly applied gold leaf, many coats of rubbed varnish and paint, well-cushioned seats, precisely engineered running gear, and the other improvements that went into the design of this expensive coach was for naught if the patron had to endure an uncomfortable ride. Without springs designed like mine, the jolt was unacceptable and I realized, more than ever, that my springs could compete handsomely against this arrangement or, more likely, complement its grandeur with comfort.

Harrington loosened the reins slightly and the horses increased their speed along the pike. A very pleasant sensation, indeed, but one that would be more pleasant with Claveraque springs.

As we drove past the Jones's place, I noticed a roan horse grazing in the paddock. With satisfaction, I remembered Downey Cohan's horse was a roan, and I looked forward to Friday's dance. Would that all complications could unravel as gracefully.

# chapter 10

As I PULLED the lorry in to pick up Ancie for the Guy Fawkes Day dance, darkness came on noticeably earlier than on the previous stretch of clear weather. The venerable black locust tree in the Jones's front lawn was bereft of leaves and its gnarled and twisted limbs were stark and eerie against the fast-receding twilight. Early Celts would have considered this arboreal patriarch a shrine. Despite the fine weather, the tree's bare branches foretold the season's progress.

In contrast, Ancie was warm and alluring in her gown. She had done something to her hair so that it shone even in the diminished light of candles in the Jones' center hallway. I'm sure this careful grooming was made to target and irretrievably capture Downey Cohan even though she accompanied me to the event. My services this evening were understood by both of us to be of an escort and of utilitarian nature only.

The notice of the ball must have appealed to many for the floor of the parish house was crowded with all ages in their best and colorful finery. No doubt the unattached were there at the season's first ball to select a partner not only for the dance but for the duration of winter, or longer. The men were enjoying competing with each other as to what were the cleverest or most humorous pranks done the night before, just so that they were not the victims. Speculating on the perpetrators of the worst and meanest pranks would continue for a week. The day after the traditional Guy Fawkes Day mischief night was always occasion for reviewing the new crop of talented mischief makers to come on the scene. However, their glances betrayed that their main interest lay across the dance floor.

The ladies lined up on their side of the room, excited to have this chance to present themselves in their finest and most attractive raiment. They produced their dance cards with alacrity as the men sought out their partners for the numbered dances of the evening. It was a silent auction.

Ancie was anxious to take her place there and was stunning in her low-cut gown which tastefully accented her slim waste and curvaceous hips, as well. Downey would not be able to resist her.

It has always amazed me that a small country community like ours, can muster the necessary musical talent when the occasion requires. It was so three years ago when a group of our musicians materialized to commemorate the thirtieth anniversary of the first performance of Handel's Messiah in Dublin. I never knew that John Nester played the violin yet there he was with Albert Chalker who was an excellent flautist. Trumpeter Jack Voorhees soon joined them to brandish his horn in the candlelight. As the trio began to sound their "A", to be in tune with Jack's tuning fork, attendee anticipation of the evening's excitement swelled, as did the cacophony of myriad conversations. The overall sounds were not unlike those in a barn when the cows impatiently await milking.

When Downey Cohan saw that Ancie was apparently available and in circulation again, even though I was her escort, he looked to catch my eye to see if this was true. I nodded slightly and Downey quickly walked the few steps to assert his claim. Ancie seemed pleased with this minor triumph and took command right away, as I thought she would.

Some single, aloof men ranged by the punch bowl, probably spiked with stronger spirits by now, in anticipation of the evening's opportunities, noting to each other who was with whom and who was seemingly unattached.

Several announcements were made by Reverend Barry to get them done and out of the way so that the festivities of the ball could proceed unhindered. Then the couples for the first dance took their positions and awaited the introductory notes. Jack started with "The

World Turned Upside Down", and John and Albert added their harmony to the melody. The odd combination of trumpet, violin and flute were surprisingly pleasant sounding. Ancie and Downey cavorted and laughed, and I was thankful for their reconciliation. To be candid, I was unashamedly relieved of an entanglement with Ancie. And this separation did not offend her.

As I turned towards the punch bowl, I stumbled against someone in perfumed silks and started my apologies before even seeing her face. Gracefully, she apologized, too.

We both laughed. I began to stammer, she was so engagingly beautiful. Her coiffure made her raven-black hair appear as if she were facing into a wind. It framed a bright brow, caring eyes, a slightly turned-up nose, a subtle smile, a luminous complexion, and the overall suggestion of a cheerful disposition. Not a provocative beauty such as a stage actress or diva, she possessed beauty that invites discourse, the kind that engages one's interest rather than the frivolous petty- pat that passes for conversation.

Her gown was designed to favor one shoulder but was modest, not as low-cut as Ancies; the decolletage was charming, in good taste, and magnetic. Her clothed shoulder was pinned with a small water-filled phial containing a sprig of dainty, fragrant flowers like small twisted yellow ribbons, which took me a moment to recognize.

"Why, that's witch hazel!" I said.

She nodded and smiled. "Yes, I cut the blossoms from a tree in our yard just before we left to come here."

This evening was destined to be delightful. I told her my name and asked hers.

"I am Olivia Farrell. We live near Ross. I heard about this ball and asked my brother to bring me. Here he is. Alan, please come here, I want you to meet James Claveraque."

We shook hands and made small talk. I thought it would be rude to ask Olivia to dance and leave Alan abandoned in a crowd of what I assumed were strangers to him. I suggested that the three of us gravitate to the table where apples, cookies, cider, and slices of cheese and cold meats were at hand. I could not take my eyes off Olivia, she was so attractive. Her soft voice would certainly turn away wrath. I guessed she gardened, played some instrument, sang, and was sharp at whist.

Before I could ask if this was so, she declared, "Actually, the Duke invited Alan and me to join in his hunt to ride to hounds. That's why we are here. But when we heard of this dance, we decided to attend. The Duke was returning a favor from last year. Are you going to participate, Mr Claveraque?" Olivia asked.

I never thought about joining in the fox hunts that crowded the autumn calendar of those who had the time, although everyone in the area, from the Duke to deacon to farrier, could join the fun if he chose. Now, it seemed like an excellent idea. "I think I would like to ride this year." I said, as if it were a choice to which I was accustomed. "When is it to be?" I think she knew I was putting on airs and why, but she was gracious in not letting on.

"Two days after tomorrow at the Duke's stables—at ten of the morning." she said. I was elated. This seemed an invitation to join them, as if she found me interesting. Alan wandered away and mingled in the crowd to greet old friends. He appeared to know everyone. I needed not to worry about our abandoning him.

"I will spruce up Nellie and be there to join you. Several of my friends enjoy the hunt and it must be exciting, but autumn is the busiest season for my family. When I am not enmeshed in the harvest and related work, I am usually fishing the Wye and other streams nearby for trout or salmon. Have you tried fly fishing?" I changed the subject to something I knew about.

"What a delightful thing to do. When I was growing up my father and brothers took me fishing every spring and I became fairly good at casting, but not at catching fish. I haven't had a rod in my hands for years and would like to take it up again. The fall must be a beautiful time to do it. You must take me soon before winter sets in. What harvest engages so much of your time?"

I told her about our orchards, a little family history and tradition, and the different varieties of apples, pears, cider, perry, and Calvados.

"Calvados! That's the first alcoholic beverage my family ever let me try. If I remember, it was very strong. I think they let me try it to discourage me from drinking. And they succeeded. If you spilled any on your hands, it evaporated right away, like it was nothing but alcohol. Do you make that?" she cried.

"It's one of our specialties, probably what our family is most known for. I hope you didn't gulp it down. It is so strong, a small glass downed in a short time can make you sick."

"That's exactly what happened, but it was at home so I didn't embarrass the family or myself too badly. It took me a long time to accept a drink after that and I have become very careful what I imbibe and how I drink it."

"Yes, Calvados must be sipped and savored. Some prefer it with water," I told her. "What does your family do?"

"Have you ever heard of Farrells Nursery? We have greenhouses in which we cultivate trees, shrubs, and flowers, especially those specimens from the American Colonies."

"I've heard of your family business and seen the greenhouses from a distance. I thought you merely grew flowers to grace milady's table and corsages for the gentry's dancing partners."

"Well, we do all of that, but the most interesting part of it, and what I specialize in, is the propagation of seeds and small plants that our agent obtains for us from his sources in America." She warmed to her story.

"One of our suppliers is John Bartram, in Philadelphia, who for many years has been venturing into the wilderness looking for exotic specimens. When he sees something of interest or a plant species others are ordering for a patron, he digs it and prepares it for carrying back to his nursery just across the Schuylkill River from Philadelphia. If the season is right, he collects the seeds as well. Have you ever heard of mountain laurel, blue-eyed grass, sassafras, or Oswego tea? Bartram has collected all of these and made them known to his agents and to scientists such as Mr. Linnaeus and Peter Kalm."

"Very interesting. How far does he go into the country? I think I've read about him. If I'm not mistaken, it was an article by Peter Kalm who visited him at his nursery after Kalm made his famous trip to Niagara Falls." I was thrilled to hear of these people first hand.

"Carl Linnaeus is the one who devised a classification system for identifying species and their varieties. He's given plants binomial names in Latin so that there is no question in any language about what plant is being discussed. For example, there are many plants called mayflowers. Linnaeus' system makes it definite as to which one of them is meant." Surely, Olivia loved her work. And I could see why.

I encouraged her to continue. "Bartram sent Linnaeus a specimen of mountain laurel and described its habitat and its flowering period and Linnaeus named it Kalmia latifolia after Peter Kalm, who was one of his students and disciples. Latifolia describes the plant's structure."

"So, discovering merits fame to the deserving.'

"I suppose so. The man who first brings a plant to the public's attention usually gets the credit." Olivia replied. She proved to be a trove of information on a subject I knew little about.

"What do you do to propagate these plants? Are they in a condition so that all one has to do is stick them in the ground?"

"It's a little more complicated than that. First, we read the information sheets that are sent us and decide what we can and can't grow here, even in our greenhouse's artificial climate, and sound out what our clients find of interest. Then we place our order and wait hoping that we'll receive the seeds or plants within a year and pray that the ship going either there or back doesn't go down in the Atlantic with our order."

"But how do you propagate them? What do you do differently from what the average gardener might do?

"Some seeds we have to scarify, or abrade, the seed capsule for better water absorption to accelerate the growing process. Even then, we may have to soak the seed before placing it in the soil so germination will begin. Other seeds, like delphinium, have to be frozen for several months, as would happen in their native environs, before they will germinate.

"Some have to have light, others shade, some planted deep, others on top of the soil, some need dry, some need wet soil. A number of them, such as laurel, require sour soil while others, like elm trees, do best in a soil rich in limestone. To many plants and trees, it makes no difference. But each plant will do better if attention is given to the conditions it was growing under in the wild.

"So, we're guided by what nature requires for that plant. Much of what we do is trial and error, mostly error. Propagation is one of nature's phenomenons that make our work interesting. I'm sorry for running on so." she said. She brimmed over with enthusiasm for her subject.

"I suppose that since you have to go to all this trouble merely ordering the plants, aside from the hazzards of growing them, that you can charge a premium for them." I asked

"Oh yes" said Olivia. "Our patrons and Collinson's patrons are well-heeled, and when they want something to be a part of their landscaping plans, they're willing to pay for it. Except for the few who habitually growl and hesitate, of course."

"Of course." I agreed. "Once you get the seeds or the plants growing, what then?"

Alan wandered back to our table and declared, "Why aren't you dancing? The music is easy to dance to if you don't mind a quadrille once in a while."

"You are right, Alan, a good suggestion. Olivia, how about it, shall we join the throng? But I want you to tell me more about propagation when we return to the table."

We waited on the sidelines until the beginning of the next dance which was a slow waltz .Dancing made a wonderful excuse for holding her even though at arm's length. We turned and circled the floor despite my clumsiness. After a few minutes, what I had learned in dancing school long ago came back to me, and the exercise became more enjoyable for the both of us.

"I forgot to ask you where Bartram goes for these specimens." I declared.

"All over the northeastern colonies and in the south several times. Perhaps his most famous trip was made thirty years ago. He traveled to Onondaga and Oswego, on Lake Ontario, leaving Philadelphia with Lewis Evans, a surveyor and map maker. You may have seen Evan's famous map of the middle colonies. They say his map was printed just in time for General Braddock to use it on his infamous attempt to take Fort Duquesne.

"Near Reading, perhaps fifty miles west of Philadelphia, Bartram and Evans picked up Conrad Weiser, an agent and translator for the colony of Pennsylvania who had extensive experience with the Iroquois. Later, when they reached the Susquehanna, Shickelamy joined them. He was a half-king, so called, or an ambassador of the Iroquois who presided over the tributary Delaware and Shawnee Indians and dealt with Weiser, his counterpart for the province of Pennsylvania. I'm sorry, I'm making too long a story of this. May I call you Jamie?"

"Of course, I meant to ask you to. Please go on." I urged.

"Bartram kept a journal of all they encountered—Indian villages, groves of laurel, oaks, swamps, clearings in the forest, or whatever took his fancy, and, of course, rivers and mountains. His description was so detailed, I think that someone could follow the same route along the Indian trails just by reading his observations, and get to Onondaga with no trouble.

"At the Onondagas' village, Weiser and Schikelamy attended a conference with the League's tribal chiefs while Evans and Bartram explored the region, particularly around the salt spring. The water was so salty that it could float a potato, they said. They boiled a gallon of it and got a pound of salt! Then they went north down the outlet of the Onondaga's lake to Oswego.

"That's where he came across a peculiar mint plant three feet high—mint stems are four-sided, you know—which was blooming, a beautiful demitasse saucer-sized red inflorescence. The Indians dried the leaves and made a tea of it to treat chills and fevers. He'd seen it in the wild before but never so that he had time or space to bring it back. He decided it was too spectacular not to add to his collection.

"When he returned to Philadelphia, he would plant the specimens and the seeds in his nursery beds. When he had enough plants for further propagation, he sent a few specimens to Peter Collinson who named it "Oswego tea" after Bartram's description of its locale. Some call it bee balm. The generic name, Monarda, was given to it in honor of a Spanish doctor, Nicholas Monardes, who catalogued the plant in the sixteenth century."

"How do you know all this?" I almost had to shout, we were so close and directly in front of messrs. Voorhees, Chalker, and Nester playing their hearts out.

"Oh, I read Bartram's journal of the trip which was finally published in the early fifties, ten years after he made the trip. I read it thoroughly several times, in fact. I've also had a chance to talk to Peter Kalm when he visited this country several years ago."

"He is a botanist from Finland who worked for Linnaeas. He was looking for plants and other forms of life that grow in chilly climes in America and could be grown for food for the Scandinavians. You should see a copy of his letter describing Niagara Falls that he wrote twenty-some years ago. I felt like I had been there seeing the torrent of the river plunging the chasm, hearing the vast sound of the surge, and seeing the rainbows as the mist rises from the gorge, disappearing and recurring as the vapor is blown about by the wind."

"Have you ever met Bartram?"

"No, he's never come here, nor have I gone there. I would like to someday. But Mr Bartram is in his late seventies. If I'm going to go to America to visit him, I'd better do it soon."

Olivia and I had common ground in so many ways already within an hour of meeting.

"Yes. I've been thinking of going to America, too." I volunteered. "I have an uncle who has a farm in New Jersey not far from New York City. But he's not that far from Philadelphia, either, which I would like to visit. The prospect of sailing to America is even more attractive now that you've told me about Mr. Bartram. It seems Boston is to be avoided and maybe New York, too, if the turmoil there gets out of hand."

"I feel sorry for those people in Boston. It seems to me that General Gage could be a little more accommodating. Instead, the army is treating the Bostonians as if they are a conquered people rather than Englishmen." I was delighted to hear that Olivia was in sympathy with my and my father's opinion.

As Alan returned, he overheard the last part of our conversation. " I think you may have both forgotten that King George is reported to have contemptuously ignored the so-called Olive Branch Petition for conciliation. His response was to declare a state of war between the

Americans and Great Britain" he said as he pulled up his chair ."The king has also hired over twenty thousand Hessian soldiers to supplement the regular army. So, I'm sorry to say, the rebels will soon suffer more than turmoil. Boston and New York won't be pleasant places to visit in the foreseeable future."

Olivia and I were surprised that we'd missed this news, and shocked at what it foreshadowed for England and the colonies. She changed the subject. "I've talked too much, Jamie. Tell me what else you are interested in."

"Well, I've had a forge ever since I can remember. When I was very young, I used to scavenge lumps of coal that spilled on our road from the wagons hauling it from the mines in the Forest of Dean to Bristol. My father would give me a pence for each peck I was able to collect. Then he helped me build a forge and I became able to repair utensils from the kitchen and then farm implements. It was fun and practical. I learned by trial and error, much as you learned about propagation. And I frequently had some help from the village smith.

"Recently, I began thinking that there must be a way to cushion the jolts and bumps of the roadway. Something could be built to lessen the shock to passengers, and to the wagon itself.

"I thought using long lengths of rope roved back and forth to cradle the wagon might do it. It did, a little bit, but that arrangement wasn't satisfactory and the rope stretched and wore excessively from the constant pulling and abrasion even when using line such as used on the running rigging of a ship.

"Then I thought of using metal springs to cushion the shock between the wheel and the wagon box. The idea came to me while looking at the works of our hallway clock. Metal springs flexed with the shock and worked much better than the ropes. This put me on the right course and I began perfecting the scheme."

Olivia listened attentively which encouraged me to tell her more. So I mentioned meeting Brigandi and the army's interest, Squire Callaway and his support, being introduced to Amos Dunkholme and his shop full of expert wainwrights, and finally, the ride in the Duke's coach. Of course, I said nothing of finding the gold ingot. It would stay safe in the coal pile by the forge until I could determine how to monetize it.

"That sounds like a great idea, James. I would enjoy going for a ride were it not for the constant unpleasant bumps and agitation. Of course, the roads could be smoothed, too. But, even so, they would be rutted again in a short time by the express coaches and those heavy coal wagons, especially during the rainy season. Our wagon vibrates so much that occasionally the dirt is shaken from the roots of our larger specimens even when the dirt ball is moistened, tightly bagged and tied. I'd like to try your inventive springs on our wagons."

Our dance had finished and the intermission began as we were still talking on the dance floor after most others had resumed their seats. We flushed in embarrassment and returned to Alan who was amused by our mutual attraction and intense conversation.

Olivia and I laughed, too, and she briefly recounted our conversation to her brother.

Alan was a good listener and was also interested in the wagon springs. But he sighed and told me some bad news. "The colonies have stopped exporting their iron to England again in protest of the administration's policy toward Boston and New York. And they turn out as much of the metal as we do. You might be able to get a small supply from the foundries at the forest unless the government has shut off sales to all but defense contractors. For that matter, you might present yourself, your operation, as a defense contractor."

Startled by this thought, I said, "But I couldn't do that. I've only made a few springs and never attempted to even sell them. Not yet, anyway. I haven't perfected them to my satisfaction. To present myself as a defense contractor would be a sham that I couldn't live with or back up. My word would have no value or authority any more if I did that. I would rather try making the springs with wood!"

These words came into my head and tumbled out my mouth without much thought. The idea of making springs with wood, say with hickory or white oak, perhaps backed up with a piece of steel, might not be a bad idea. I'll have to experiment with it, I thought.

"It would not be a new practice, James. You would be surprised how many "defense contractors" have materialized since Lexington and Concord. Once they smell money, some business men, mostly the well-connected, claim they can manufacture or procure anything." Alan revealed. "They usually make sure they have a buyer before they start production. Having a friend at court helps. And the friend at court is usually encouraged by getting a cut in on the deal."

"Procure is probably an apt word, I suppose. They sound like they might be procurers of an other sort." I snorted.

"Now James, Alan's right. As the need arises, good business men come forth to meet it. I see nothing wrong with someone going into the defense business. Being new in the industry doesn't mean that he's not genuine or honest. Just so long as he delivers a reliable product at a reasonable price. That's just common sense. Besides, that is the way this country works, like it or not." Olivia made the practice seem acceptable, even honorable.

Again, I calmed down and began to consider...If the country is to have the amount of material it needs to carry out a war with the colonies and to supply the troops and move all three thousand miles across the Atlantic, of course more people have to augment the industries to make this possible. After all, this is what Downey Cohan has been doing, selling horses to the army through Brigandi. I don't consider Downey an outstanding example of ethical behavior but I wouldn't say he's guilty of profiteering. I found it easy to rationalize siding with Olivia.

"What you say makes good sense. You're both probably right. I just don't like the idea of the government commandeering my supply of iron just at the time I need it any more than I like judges putting people in jail because they criticize self-serving policies of bought-and-paid-for officials. I don't like Parliament passing abusive laws such as closing the port of Boston or taking away their right to run their own government. If the king's men can do it to them, then they can do the same to us. Our policies now seem to be against all the principals that Englishmen have been proud of, and no better than those of France."

Alan corrected me. "The government hasn't shut off civilian use of iron yet, to my knowledge, but if it makes sense for them to do that. They probably will."

"I should probably increase my stock of iron and whatever else I'll need, what with war to be raging soon. Neither the rebels or the government is likely to back off." I added.

"Olivia, It would make sense to stock up on war materials that many would not think of as coming into short supply." Alan suggested.

"Yes, if prices haven't already been bid up too high, like they have for coal. I've been too busy getting ready for next season's garden market to follow the commodities market." Olivia volunteered. She added. "We're getting too serious for this occasion. This is a dance and I hear the musicians preparing for the next round."

As if reporting to a superior officer, Wenceslas Mochter appeared at attention before Olivia. He showed no notice of Alan and me, but spoke directly to her. "I believe I have the honor of this dance, Miss Farrell."

Coming from him, it was not a question but a command. Olivia winced slightly but backed her chair, stood up, and offered her hand to Mochter, "It's true. I am yours for the next dance, Wenceslas", she smiled.

She whirled away holding on to Mochter but winked as she disappeared among the maelstrom of frolicking couples.

Alan commented, "She wasn't too happy to let Mochter have even one dance, but she gets a lot of inside information from him regarding markets and who would be an up-and-coming estate owner to sell a raft of exotic plants to. When she returns, she'll have a laundry list of commodities that we should consider purchasing. She'll also likely know what the government is going to do next. She's the brains of our business. Do you know Mochter?"

"Yes, but you wouldn't know it from the way he snubbed both of us. I met him, by chance, a week ago, and again also by chance, only a few days ago. He didn't seem to be as forbidding as I was led to believe. When he told me that he was thinking of donating some land along my favorite stream as well as the common to the village, I had a much higher opinion of him. And he was pleasant to carry on a conversation with. Frankly, I liked him. I hope he follows through as he indicated. What do you think Alan?"

"Oh, he's likeable enough and he's smart and useful to us. But he's an odd duck. Difficult to warm up to. He had been referred to us because he wished to do some additional landscaping on his property. When we delivered the plants he selected, he informed us of his business and government contacts and said he could be serviceable to us in several capacities. In the year we have known him, he's proven himself so."

"Well, that's nice of him. What a friendly thing to do." I commented.

"It was friendly, but not that friendly. We pay him a fee, each time."

"What does he do to afford living with the top of society? The milling business couldn't be that lucrative. He seems to be on his own, has an office next to his home. He must be an investor as well as a broker." I said. Alan agreed but could add no more information on Mochter.

"Are you and Olivia alone in your business? Outside of your help, of course." I was curious mainly because I thought Alan would be anxious to tell of himself, as Olivia had been.

"Oh yes, we have only three helpers. Our grandfather started the business out of his hobby of gardening and he became more active in his later years. He had the means to obtain several acres surrounding us. He bought the tract for privacy and wanted to put a pond on it by damning the spring-fed stream. After the pond was in, he decided to landscape the entire tract. That's when he met Peter Collinson. Howda, we called him, liked doing this so much that he spent all his time reading the literature Collinson gave him and ordered more and varied plants to place along a serpentine tanbark trail that he'd designed.

"Some of his well-to-do friends saw what he had accomplished and wanted him to do the same thing for them. This gave Grandpa the material to work with, without spending any money of his own. That alone was worth it, Howda said. He became a disciple of Eveyln by reading his book. Evelyn is the man who fostered the reforestation of much of England during the Restoration after the industrial exploitation of the last century. Howda loved growing and landscaping gardens so much that I think it added years to his life. He lived to be eighty-three. Active and healthy to the last day, he was.

"Father took over when Howda died and turned it into a paying enterprise. Olivia and I helped out as soon as we were old enough, and father knew how to make it interesting to us. But then, father died two years ago. Mother died of small pox when she visited her aunt in London four years ago. Auntie convinced mother to be inoculated for small pox but something went wrong and she died of it. Ironically, father died of it because he declined to be inoculated.

".Despite our parents dying at a young age, in their forties, we had a good start with the knowledge, the reputation and quality customers they had built up. Of course, we have our estate grounds from which we can work. Besides that, we love the work and the people who supply us. I would love to show you our place sometime, Jamie. I think you'd like it. I know you would—- Olivia would be there!"

"You're right about that, Alan. Olivia is very charming. I was lucky to stumble on her, literally. But I would like to see how you do all this." I delightedly anticipated the prospect..

The dance came to an end leaving Olivia and Mochter on the far side of the dance floor. Olivia chatted politely with him but not engagingly, I was glad to observe.

Alan noticed this too, and said. "She's probably learned of what commodities are likely to come into short supply and the names of several lords to solicit for their landscaping plans. Plans they won't know they have until she starts to persuade them.."

"Your grandfather and father certainly gave you both a good grounding in business and dealing with people. Was your mother active in the nursery business, too?"

"Mother primarily ran the house, arranged for our schooling, socialized with those she liked, and fended off those she didn't—- in a nice way, of course. But she stayed away from the business, except to occasionally suggest certain likely persons as prospective customers."

Lieutenant Brigandi appeared on the far edge of the floor and apparently wanted to cut in on Mochter. He bowed gracefully to Olivia, as he had bowed weeks ago to Ancie. Olivia smiled and made a pleasant-appearing response, but Mochter brushed him aside. The music resumed. Mochter took his stance and Olivia prepared for her ordeal.

"She must be getting some good leads to give him a second dance." Alan said.

"I suppose you have met many interesting people in your business dealings?" I suggested. It pained me to watch Olivia in Mochter's arms.

"Yes. Many were introduced to me by Peter Collinson. Plant collection and landscaping was a hobby with him, and he was so enthusiastic, that he told others of our operation and they sought us out. Poor Peter died seven or eight years ago, and I miss him. But those customers referred us to others: judges, doctors, generals, MPs, wool merchants, and those of the landed gentry who wished to enliven the appearance of their estates."

"Do you ever find yourself involved in political discussions with customers?"

"Oh yes. But it's not good business. Particularly now, what with the king's men being so abusive. There, you see. I'm involving my self politically with you. And I don't even know where you stand between Whigs and Tories, although I know your father's reputation for fairness and moderation. Some people get livid talking about the rebels. They shout and remonstrate as if the rebels are wayward, ungrateful children and should be thrashed within an inch of their lives.

"As much as I detest the government's determination to assert its will with the colonies, I don't wish to find myself on the wrong side of government or community favor or gain a customer's animosity. Best for business to just stay neutral—hard as it may be at times." Alan got a bit worked up himself, but I understood his position.

"Has Olivia told you about the fox hunt? We'd be pleased if you would join us."

"Yes, I must ready Nellie and search out my riding clothes so as to be ready by ten Saturday morning. Before I leave, I'll wait for Olivia to return so I can say my goodbyes to her." Coincidentally, Olivia and Mochter stopped their dance abruptly. Olivia turned and resolutely strode for our table followed by a startled Mochter. Their dance was obviously over.

She looked at Alan and me. "Please, take me home." demanded Olivia.

We exited the parish hall promptly to foreclose any attempt of Mochter's to catch up to us.

As we approached Alan's chaise, it was plain there was no reason for me to linger since they were going to the Duke's where they were guests. Nor would the situation, whatever it was, be anything but awkward if I included my self any longer. I bid my goodnight to them despite an intense desire to be with Olivia on into the night wherever fortune might take us.

Like the euphoria experienced in the presence of a forest stream or anticipating the strike of a trout, I was stricken by her good looks and personal charm. Being with her, the time passed quickly but was well spent. Something useful had transpired, a tonic had enlivened my blood, life was worth living more than ever before. In my joy, I did handstands, flips, and other gymnastics impossible for me to achieve under normal circumstances.

It was just as well that the evening with them was over and the rest of my night was private for I could not contain my joy.

Nellie was busy grazing the verdant and dewy grass at the back of the parish yard. At my two "clucks", Nellie straightened and I hitched her to the lorry in the dim light of a waning moon and drove home.

# chapter 11

RIDING TO HOUNDS would be a new experience for me and I approached father for guidance in how to prepare Nellie and myself for the occasion. He dug into an old trunk from under the eaves for a jacket and trousers that would serve. Since a novice was a "ratcatcher"and father had progressed in the social sport no farther than that, and at about my age, the costume had retained its color in storage, and fit remarkably well. All it needed was a brushing and to be hung for the wrinkles of twenty-five years to fall out.

Nellie's tack, especially the saddle, and my black leather knee-boots had to be soaped so that they gleamed and were brought back to their original supple softness.. Nellie stood patiently for scrubbing, but I think she knew something was up when I wielded the currycomb with more than usual vigor. She was reassured that the morrow would be different and exciting when I presented her with a larger than customary chunk of sugar and a bucket of oats

During these preparations, father told me of as many protocols as he could remember from his brief sojourn in the hunt years ago. Progressing from "ratcatcher" to master and captain was, in his mind, too much of an expense of time and concern for proprieties that seemed artificial and too intricate to learn. As he reflected on it now, Father said he probably should have spent the time and effort, if not for the sheer excitement of it, for the comradery and social capital he would have gained.

His main advice was to watch carefully what the others did, to be deferential but not servile (this last advice I thought unnecessary) and to try to stay with the main group, neither getting ahead nor lagging. The latter, for a novice, would suggest sloth and be unacceptable, and to be in the lead would be considered immature exhibitionism. With those suggestions delivered, he was sure I would behave as one new to the game should. His parting comment was to congratulate me on gaining an invitation from the Farrells, whose parents he knew casually but had enjoyed their enthusiasm for attractive activity, and respected their industry.

The next day, Nellie and I, both caparisoned suitably for the affair, made our way down the drive and to the Dukes' who was hosting the event this week. During the last half-mile my pulse quickened in anticipation of again being in the presence of Olivia. I prayed that I would not embarrass myself. As we neared the commotion of people, horses, and milling hounds, Nellie became more alert and held her head in a dignified manner. Her ears became upright, alert to each fresh excitement. I made a mental note to loosen the martingale when I was able to dismount to assist her in her attempt at decorum.

Abruptly, I realized that for years I had shut myself out of an exciting activity which the broad spectrum of people from our shire, from shoemaker and chimney sweeps to barristers and reverends, from six-year old youngsters to grizzled veterans of Culloden, gathered to enjoy, some to participate; many more to spectate.

Squire Calloway, Crispin, whom I hadn't seen for weeks, Harrison, Amos Dunkeholm, Sally Bushnell, Mochter, Captain Brigandi, and even Ancie's father, who was familiarly introduced by Downey Cohan as Monty (for Montgomery, I suppose), were in attendance.

Olivia and Alan assumed different personae in their attire on horseback, and in this crowd.

"Oh, there you are, Jamie. You know the Duke and his wife, Elizabeth, I believe." she said.

We all shook hands, but the formality of the traditional event stilted the conversation so that the easy banter of the other evening at the dance was missing. Being distant neighbors, Alan and Olivia, no-doubt wanted, and were honor-bound, to re-acquaint themselves with numerous personages they had not seen socially during the press of their busy season.

Hounds were all about in aimless confusion and underfoot of as many horses until the master, Colonel Masterson, looking splendid in his master's costume, blew several blasts on his horn. As these calls resounded through the valley, hounds, horses, and riders began to organize themselves to the awaited excitement.

The Colonel greeted everyone, participants and spectators alike, and read the field bounds of the hunt course. When the fox was brought to ground or at dusk, the hunt was over and the hunters were welcome to the Dukes' main barn for refreshments. The Colonel again sounded his horn and he and his coterie moved out down the swale towards Millburn Run.

I followed father's advice and, with Nellie's forbearance, stayed in the middle of the horde. This excitement of galloping full-out over strange but beautiful country must be similar to a rookie in his first cavalry charge. Alan and Olivia stayed together until the field became more open and then Olivia turned her head to survey the array. My heart warmed with encouragement as she turned her horse in my direction.

"You look like you've been in the hunt for years," she hailed, brightening my outlook. I nudged Nellie to intercept her. "You look like a veteran yourself," I countered.

The hound pack ran ahead of the riders and reached the run. Without hesitation they splashed through the water, shuffling spray from their pelts as they emerged. Then, noses to the ground, they began yelping wildly as they turned abruptly to the right. They had scented the fox!

The Colonel blew a tattoo on his horn to signal that the fox trail had been found, and the increased pitch of cries from the pack of hounds converging on the trail confirmed his signal. The pace of the horde intensified. Rather than take a short cut to catch up with the hounds, the horde insisted on following the trail the hounds had made. Farther down this trail, I could see that the hounds had chosen the sole shallow place in the stream and herd and riders had foreseen this. So it was not an arbitrary rule that the hunt must follow the trail of the hounds as I had thought. It was simply experience and common sense jointly exercised by man and beast. This sense, seemingly shared by hounds, horses, and riders, was a large part of the fun.

Try as I might, I could not see the fox. His coat must blend perfectly with the landscape, a Joseph's coat, at this time of the year. The sight of many hounds, determinedly on the trail of one sly creature who ably outpaced them through brush and covert, was energizing. Even though I value all forms of life, an irrepressible blood-lust of the chase rose within me and I yelled and spurred Nellie in pursuit even more.

As the throng rushed up a hill from the stream, a stone wall, obscured by shrubs and the brow of the hill, suddenly appeared in the path. The foremost riders girded their mounts and easily scaled the pile, but Nellie and I have always ignored challenges of this sort and we looked left and right for an alternate course. Olivia, who had pulled ahead of us by fifty yards, sat her horse beautifully and adroitly maneuvered her mount over the fence with extreme exhilaration to my admiration and dismay.

Other riders were coming up on either side which channeled our course so that we had no choice but to jump or be trounced. We jumped but I was jettisoned anyway, as if I was some unessential burden in this endeavor. Nellie kept her feet and slowed to the left, free of further interference, but I crashed to the ground, somewhat cushioned in my fall by a drift of leaves banked by a yew. Nothing broke except my fragile dignity.

A blurred figure appeared and quickly gathered me up and out of the pathway of the clattering stampede. I was set down free from harm next to the wall and asked if I was hurt. Still dazed, I took inventory and nodded that I was not. I mumbled my thanks profusely for getting me out from the onslaught.

His huge frame gave the illusion of a Highland chieftain; his tangled hair and grisly beard framed a florid weather-washed face. He grinned down at me, but upon taking my thanks, he scowled and curtly called, "I'm glad to get you out'en the way. My friends and their mounts could get serious hurt comin' o'er that wall with you in their path!" My savior threw this humiliation for me to wear and was gone whence he came.

I rested a moment to get my wind and to verify my good fortune of falling, if I had to fall, into the cushioned embrace of an ancient yew bush, and having been saved from further danger in such quick succession. I hadn't fallen from Nellie since the first day I rode her. When thrown, I should get back on the horse as soon as possible, I'd always been told. Besides, I thought, I would probably be more comfortable in the saddle than suffering my aches on damp, stony ground.

Nellie was only twenty feet away and appeared anxious to regain her new-found glory. My foot finally found the stirrup and I flung myself into the saddle. We were off again, but this time, cautiously to the side and behind the crowd.

With muscles flexing in time to Nellie's trot, I began to feel free of the distressful aching. The pack had rounded a copse flanked by a huge boulder and continued across a field to a wide path in the edge of the woods on the other side, but without enthusiasm. They must have lost the scent of the fox.

The horde slowed to a walk and conversations among huntsmen began anew. Crispin came over my way.

"Your coat is torn in back. Did you scoop a branch, or did you miss a fence?" he smiled. I owned up to my distressful jump and the countryman who moved me out of the way at the crucial time.

"That was probably my uncle, Banjo. He looks fierce, like a tribal chieftain with a claymore, but he has a heart of gold, a real softy. Ten years ago, he hurt himself jumping a rail fence. A rail broke and a piece of it spun around and pierced his chest. He near died but for Doctor Bolster removing the splinter. Ever since, he has stationed himself at one of the fences to watch the hunt and to help anyone who gets in trouble. I imagine he's helped several dozen over the years. You're lucky he was there to move you; you could have been seriously trampled. "

"Or even unseriously," I countered. It was too flip an answer to throw at a close friend and, to soften the sarcasm, I asked. "Have you been fishing any, Crispin?"

"Only once since you and I last gave it a try—the day you caught and lost the big one." he murmured. He hesitated, then said, "You won't believe this, James. But I've decided to join the army. Brigandi convinced me it was the thing to do if I want to get to America. He gave me what he called the King's shilling. I'll finally get to see America and its big rivers, full of fish, and the mountains. Before you know it, the war will be over and the king will give me land over there. And Brigandi said I won't have to pay for it. I'll have my own greenwood." He was in rapture.

I was startled that Crispin would give up his independence and put himself under such regimentation as the army, and that he was so gullible. But I congratulated him. No sense in telling him what I thought. It was a done deal and nothing could reverse it. No point in pointing out a poor bargain. "When do you go in and where are you going to do your training?"

He was very excited. "I'm to be indoctrinated sometime soon, at a new camp someplace near Plymouth. Brigandi will tell me when he knows for sure. I may even become a non-com if I learn fast enough to suit them. I'm supposed to be training with Hessian officers as sort of a go-between our and their forces. My mother's parents were from Hesse and I naturally learned the language growing up. I can still speak it. In a couple of years, I'm going to own an orchard near the Hudson River. I understand there are many Dutch there. You may doubt this, about getting land, I mean. Just you wait and see."

"You'll get out in only a few years?"

"The war shouldn't last long against those ribbon clerks, and the government won't want to spend any more money when its over. So, it looks awfully good to me. We'll teach those rebels as fast as it takes to bring this fox to ground." Crispin said.

"I hope you get a chance to go fishing before you go. It might be the last time for some time, Crispin."

If they send me to a post along the Hudson or the Susquehanna, I should get plenty of fishing in. But I'll get on a stream anyway, just in case they don't."

The pack began to howl, the Colonel blew his horn and the hunt began anew as the horde of huntsmen and hounds moved in a crescendo along a ditch through the wood. I wished Crispin well and hoped it wasn't the last time I would ever see him.

A few over-dressed people (from Hereford, perhaps) mixed with the farmers in their more rugged clothes to watch the progress of the hunt. They clustered by the stone wall near Banjo. I judged it to be the place where a lot of excitement, like my fall from Nellie, would occur. They seemed disappointed that I had recovered from my fall so soon.

Olivia had turned her horse to the side and back in my direction. The rouge of her cheeks showed that she thrived under this rigorous regimen. It made an exciting offset to her mild labors at the nursery.

"What happened, James? I thought you were right behind me. Are you alright?"

I briefly told her of my mishap and assured her that nothing was broken, just a few bruises, scratches, and my nose 'out of joint'. I wished to make nothing of the fall so that she wouldn't decide that I should be excluded from this sport, one of her favorite pleasures. I told her about Crispin and his joining the army by taking the King's shilling and that Crispin and I had wandered through this patch of wooded hills and large meadows during our bow hunts and clout shooting.

Olivia patted her horse on the neck to steady him. "He sounds like a desperate person to want to get away so badly. Doesn't he know how brutal life in the army can be, even when they are only on garrison duty? A cousin of mine hated it so much that he escaped camp, intending to desert. When they caught him a few days later, they gave him five hundred lashes with the cat-o-nine tails. It practically killed him and he shrieked with pain for months. His back was shredded like he had been dragged by horses. The pain and mutilation made it very difficult for him to carry out his duties. He was shunned and given the most dirty and obnoxious chores so that he lost all his humanity. Death was his only release. He died within the year, poor man. I feel so sorry for your Crispin."

"Yes", I agreed, "Crispin is so independent-minded that he resents having to milk and feed the cows, and fork the manure on his family's dairy. He loves nature and the freedom of roaming at will. He so wants to be his own boss. If he can endure the army and come safely through combat, perhaps he can. But, I can't think of anything worse than being in the army, particularly for a free spirit like him. Even if he becomes an officer, he'll still have to do the bidding of the man above him no matter how unreasonable he may be. There is no alternative except the unthinkable. I wish him well."

The master blared the tattoo on his horn quickly halting our conversation and signaling that the fox had been sighted again, this time not far from where we were. So we were in the van. Remembering my father's advise, I hung back to avoid leading the leaders, and Olivia picked up the pace and followed the hounds, their quick-wagging tails testifying to their eagerness to join in the hunt's climax.

Quickly, the hounds increased their yelping and congregated in a melée surrounding the fox who must have become woefully inattentive to have come to this sorry impasse. I arrived just in time to see this beautiful and cunning creature being torn and clawed by the throng of senseless canines contending for the trophy of that which quickly was no longer a creature of lithe beauty. The master shouted "Halt", startling the hounds to a silent dead stop. He bent over to retrieve the cruelly rent limp remains. As he held the fox high for all to see, the fox uttered one last barely audible plaint, shuddered and went limp.

The scene made both Olivia and me feel grim despite the clamor of the kill. We spurred our mounts and retired from the field.

# chapter 12

Father became excited when he heard from Squire Calloway that a letter from his brother, was waiting for him at Wedlich's store. We were all anxious to hear what he had to say from his side of the water, both personal and of the tense political situation there. I hastened to jump on Nellie's back for the short ride to the post.

There was a line at the clerk's window which gave me a few minutes to overhear that the army was possibly going to build a training camp and recruiting station nearby. As important as this might be to us, I put it as rumor only. It was of secondary importance at the moment to what might be contained in uncle Arthur's letter, considering the absence of word from him.

There were no other letters for us except the November issue of *The Gentleman's Magazine*, and I hastened home to the family who had seated themselves at the dining room table to hear father read the news from New Jersey. Father began to read as Mother poured cold cider for each of us.

*Dear George,*

*As of late September, we are more than halfway through the harvest and I am happy to say that this should be a good year judging by the number of bushels of apples and pears we have harvested since mid-August. We had a good spring with plentiful rain as well as perfect weather for the peregrinations of the bees from the hive you sent. They have helped set more than our usual run of fruit, and we thank you for your kindness.*

*Despite the flight of city residents due to the naval bombardment as well as the shipping out last June of the last army regulars from New York, the market there for our cider and perry has picked up. The city has always favored "Jersey Lightning". We hope the Sons of Liberty will concentrate on their normal trades now that tensions in the city are eased.*

*King George and his ministers persist on treating the colonists as if we are secondary citizens, instead of Englishmen like you and the rest of the mother country. The most recent outrage, you've probably heard, is the passage of the Quebec Act, which, in one fell swoop, dashes the financial hopes of many who have been counting on a return from investments made in the Ohio Valley. The king has declared that all lands north of the Ohio River and east of the Mississippi are now part of the province of Quebec and are reserved for the Indians, and that no whites except the army, certified English traders, and thousands of indigenous Frenchmen are to be permitted to live there.*

*This slams the door on a host of people who are investors in land companies and have been patiently waiting for as much as twenty-five years for the westward migration to fulfill their expectations. One of the more candid ministry explanations for the act is that it will make it easier for the government to "govern" us if we are contained not too far from the seaboard. Since Boston and environs is largely delineated by seaboard, this does not seem to have helped the government control the Yankees these last ten years.*

*Including lands north of the Ohio as part of Canada is especially resented because many businessmen, such as Washington and Doctor Franklin, I'm told, have used their influence and connections to inveigle high government officials to participate in, till now, what should be profitable ventures. In this way our investors feel more secure in their efforts to obtain land grants from the crown. So this piece of mischief has to have come from the very highest circles of government, that is, the king himself.*

*Some of our more pompous and high-minded Presbyterians and Baptists are affronted by another provision that permits the French Canadians to practice their Roman Catholic religion without the restraints enforced in England. As you would guess, this doesn't upset Arabella and me but some of the local churchmen and their parishioners in Newark, Elizabethtown, and New York are all upset by it. They don't seem to remember when Protestants were prohibited from worshiping in their own manner in England and France, and the attendant atrocities as witnessed by great grandfather in his journal. It seems vicious and at odds with the tenets of our Christian Faith to want re-*

*venge. They don't seem to be aware that intolerance is not only un-Christian but it is very costly for the expense of putting down riots and wars for the resentment caused.*

*And, after all, Canadian Catholics were not, as a practical matter, restricted from the overt practice of their religion after Quebec fell to the success of General Wolfe. It seems that ridiculous positions are being taken by those who do not really understand the humanity of the Christian religion regardless of their ecclesiastical degrees. Someday, perhaps soon, they will regret their loud, abusive statements.*

*The law also says that the Canadians can live under French civil laws and will be ruled by an appointed governor and council as they were under the French colonial regime. The Ministry hopes that this legislation will cause the French Canadians to cleave more closely to England in the event of war between the colonies and the mother country. They fear the patriots will try to annex Canada. The Act has been the source of uproarious objection around here.*

*We have so many legitimate and important gripes to be acted upon, it is foolish to dilute their importance with petty complaints and intolerance such as this.*

*Enough about politics. How I hate to discuss and carp about what is going on here and in the mother country.*

*Tuscan Road, which runs right by our orchards, is being widened and graded from the Valley road to Springfield Avenue. This should invite more traffic from both roads favoring us, Pearson's mill, Houseman's Tavern and the village of Vaux Hall. We are planting shrubs and perennials about the house, even the barn, at Arabella's suggestion. It looks better already, not to mention how it will look as they mature.*

*Arabella wants some Asian rhododendron to plant in a small oak grove near Tuscan Brook but we can't locate any, even from Bartram's in Philadelphia. They are a brilliant red and bloom about two weeks later than the Catawba in this climate. They are supposed to come originally from the foothills of the Himalayas and are hardy here. Do you know where we can acquire some?*

*Since in England many young gentlemen take the Grand Tour of Europe following their formal education, we think that James might want to travel the Colonies. It would be a wonderful opportunity to broaden his outlook of where we think the future is for the forward-thinking and adventurous. Despite the last decade's ill-advised legislation for controlling the Colonies (and governor Franklin's eager agreement with it) and the riots that have ensued, we think there is remarkable opportunity to make one's fortune, and keep it, in North Jersey. There are ample natural resources, the climate is favorable, and we practically straddle the main highway between New York, Philadelphia and beyond.*

*We will host and sponsor you Jamie. This deserves serious consideration as your entire future may be influenced by it, so we hope that you all will give the idea careful thought and with your parent's blessing.*

*As George Arcularious, the stage driver, has finished the drink we promised him if he would delay his departure so we could finish this letter for his pouch, we have to conclude with our best wishes for you and your family's good fortune and health. Your loving brother, and his wife.*

*Arthur and Arabella*

# chapter 13

WHAT SEEMED LIKE an relentlessly long week trying to improve the suspension on our lorry ended agreeably by receiving a note from Olivia inviting me to visit her and her brother. I was thrilled that my week-long longing for her company may have been mutual. I arrived late Saturday in time for a sumptuous and delicious meal prepared by Olivia and the accompanying conversation in which we scrupulously avoided politics. I knew I could count upon it to be informative and interesting.

Alan and Olivia had invited their minister, the Reverend Alphonse Diamonde, to a dinner the previous week, which had been their annual custom when their parents were living. Their attendance at church had been sporadic which the reverend made sure to emphasize his censure when enjoying their hospitality. They promised to mend their ways, in keeping with the demands of the nursery business, at least in the near future since the seasonal business had dwindled to near dormancy.

The following Sunday was when they had determined to demonstrate their conformity and 'remission of sins', and as their house guest, I was invited to join them. The weather had turned cold enough to freeze the pond and winter had further asserted itself with a cold fog that threatened snow and clutched the inner body even though I had chosen a sweater and heavy coat.

As we approached the church, the music of Handel lured us up the steps.

I turned to Olivia, "My younger sister, Ellen, has been practicing this music on her guitar for weeks. I think it's Handel's *Water Music*."

We crossed the threshold where I was introduced to the reverend. He had a confident, round and florid face surmounted with white tufts on either side of a shiny pate. One could easily see the reflection of the candelabra on the stretched-tight expanse of skin on the crown of his head. His raiment proclaimed his academic and theological credentials as did his warm greeting and handshake testify to his years behind the altar.

He was cordial but I was grateful that I did not have to disclose my denomination. We Claveraques are not Anglican, although part of the taxes we pay, as with all other denominations in England, supports the state-established church.

I must admit that beholding the marvelous design and accessories of this small country church, reveling in the music, and participating in the ceremony, even if somewhat foreign to my own experience, has a consecrating effect on one's soul. One feels separate and secure from the secular world.

After the preliminary part of the service, the reverend stepped over to behind the large carved oak pulpit and launched into his sermon. He spoke of the good Samaritan and of the letters of Saint Paul. Having heard harangues along these lines many times, my attention wandered to the varying lengths of the organ pipes, the figures in the stained-glass windows, the large cross in the chancel, and the number of squares made on the ceiling by crossbeams and the arched timbers. The church must have been favored at one time by a cunning carver. The bench ends were chiseled to show such depictions as an abbot with miter and crozier, his dignity surmounted with an ass's head. I was amused by another, a manacled monkey sitting with his feet clamped in the stocks. Imagine—a church that can laugh at itself.

Occasionally, an emphasized word would catch my attention and arrest my count of ceiling squares. I began to muse over the beginnings of the Anglican Church that took place well over two hundred years ago. After twenty years of wedded bliss, Henry VIII wished to discard his queen, Catherine of Aragon, in favor of Anne Boleyn, a daughter of the proud and noble Howard family. She was a generation younger, attractive, skilled in court flirtation, and the lady whom Henry hoped would give him a male heir.

Largely because the Pope would not allow the divorce, Henry separated from the Church of Rome, discarded Catherine, made Anne his queen, and forced all English communicants to adhere to a church presided over by him and his dictates. His new queen gave birth, but to a female heir, Elizabeth. He considered this unacceptable and began to concoct unfaithful behavior on Anne's part as reason for abandoning her. Within three years, he directed that Anne be executed by beheading.

So the Anglican Church owes its existence to either Henry's sexual urges, his need for a regal heir, his stubbornness, his massive ego, or all of these traits.

Then the king took over the monasteries and gave these self-contained and money-making estates to his sycophants and those he desired as supporters, at the expense of the monks who had, over the centuries, made the monasteries a prosperous English institution.

Thus the Church of England was founded by a monster who did not hesitate to have beheaded some of England's finest men and women, or anyone who disagreed with him—a man whose life was the antithesis of Jesus' teachings. Henry's actions also caused England much strife, not only in his reign but that of his son, Edward, his daughters, Mary and Elizabeth, and over the span of the ensuing hundred years of the Stuarts. What a legacy! Henry was as bad as Louis XIV. They both exploited religion for political and personal gains. Of what stuff are kings!

I did not wish to be a practicing non-conformist, and I have never revealed my religious stance to others except to my father and mother. Indeed, to do so could expose me to the neighborhood citizenry whom, I assumed, might consider me a heretic and traitorous. Perhaps they would even ostracize me and my family. Or worse, I could be questioned by the church or the state and be subject to jail and other abuse. One wit said, "The Popes Bull tied the king's balls." Henry went to the trouble of finding the miscreant and having him strangled in the Tower.

My main hope was that religion, regardless of denomination, would fulfill its mission to improve the moral beliefs and actions of civilization the world round. Peace and order had to be established in the face of different opinions. The important thing was for people to act decently to others; whatever theocracy they believed, or professed to believe, was not important, just so long as it motivated benign and fraternal results.

I became so absorbed in this concentration that Olivia had to nudge me that the service was over. I stopped my revery and looked up as people were chatting and standing up to shuffle, haltingly, out of their pews..

At the church door, I again shook hands with the reverend and assured him of my attention and concentration on church matters and his well-chosen words. Then Olivia and I went straight away to her home to change clothes for skating on their pond.

The ice was not firm enough, so we brought out Olivia's new cart to try another pond in the woods several miles distant, after first fortifying ourselves against the damp and the cold, which bit to the bone, with several cups of hot tea.

We had to drive carefully, the road being narrowed by deep ditches on either side and the fog more dense and on the brink of turning to snow. I told her of my uncle Arthur's letter offering me a Grand Tour of the American Colonies and how excited I and the whole family was over this prospect. I also asked her if she had any red-flowered rhododendron that I could take with me and present to aunt Arabella..

"We do have a variety of dark red which will soon go into dormancy and would travel well in ball and burlap this time of the year. The ball of earth would have to be protected from freezing solid. But, if horses or cattle are aboard, their manure could be used as a mulch." She was both informative and resourceful which emboldened me.

I asked her if she would like to accompany me to America since she expressed such an interest at the Guy Fawkes ball in seeing where so many of their plants from America had originated, and in meeting John Bartram in Philadelphia.

She was startled at the idea of making such a trip. "I have never traveled far from home or thought traveling out of the country was a possibility for me—having to pay constant attention to the business, you know."

I let her think about it as our horse clopped along on the frozen roadway.

She looked up at me as she mused out loud, "I'll have to talk to my brother about it, of course. This would be a good time to make the trip what with sales in their seasonal doldrums. But my brother would be counting on my help next spring and, of course, if I go, we would be there for...How long do you think we would be there?"

I was greatly encouraged by her positive questions and trying to find ways to go rather than the opposite. "Better to count on a year." I answered.

"He probably knows someone who could fill in for me for a season or two. Oh! I would love to go. And to go there with you. I'll ask Alan when we get home this afternoon. It will be so much fun making plans of where to go and what to do!"

Not once did she hesitate or question the propriety of traveling to America with me and for such a long duration that could inconvenience her brother.. I told her of my extraordinary adventure of finding the gold ingot (and almost being apprehended by Mochter), and that I would pay all her expenses, of course. But I wanted to find some way of monetizing the gold and how to carry it safely to America where it could be put to good use.

"Saw the ingot into as many thin pieces as you carry rhododendron and put each piece into the ball of earth that will be wrapped with burlap around the roots of the plants. And we'll take the rhododendron with us to present them, personally, to aunt Arabella as a house gift." She answered so confidently, as if questions of this sort were posed to her every day.

"What an innocent way to carry gold." I marveled.

Olivia was in an enthusiastic mood when suddenly she bid me stop the cart,

"Jamie, I have to go round the back of the cart. Please see to my horse for a minute, will you? Perhaps, if you look carefully you can see the skating pond from here."

She moved with haste to behind the cart, shuffled her clothes, and then remained silent.

Presently, she called. "Jamie, I have a problem. Can you come here. Never mind the horse."

I took in the situation when I rounded the cart but she explained in the hopes I could quickly remedy her problem.

"I had to go, and I made the mistake of easing myself on the metal fitting at the edge of the cart. It's very cold and, well, I froze to it and now I cant get off. Can you do something?"

I concentrated hard on not laughing as I recalled to myself that every kid learned early on that he should never stick his tongue to frozen metal. Olivia, in her haste, had forgotten this principle perhaps because it wasn't her tongue.

I suggested, "I can get you free with some hot water, but it will take a while to get it."

"You already have some. You had tea the same time I did. Mine has gotten me into trouble. Yours can get me free!"

I did not comprehend her meaning of what sounded like a riddle right off, but then I had to admire her ingenuity despite her so-personal distress. And standing in the cold had made me increasingly discomfitted from foolishly drinking that hot tea just before going outside.

Skating was forgotten as I delicately, and with abject discretion, freed the distressed lady for whom I was quickly coming to have a strong affection and to admire.

This sensitive operation had required our complete concentration and, particularly, precision of execution on my part to avoid further complication. We had the privacy of being ensconced in a dense fog and did not see or hear anyone coming along the road until he was right upon us. Of all people, though the encounter was such an embarrassment it didn't really make any difference who it might be, our witness was the Reverend Diamonde whose service and sermon we had attended but an hour before.

As he approached and could see what was being done, but not the reason for it, he looked aghast but withheld judgment.

He hesitated and asked, "Can I be of any assistance?"

Olivia exploded with laughter as did I. When the reverend realized Olivia's plight and our solution, and the context of his offer, he affected restraint to his utmost, then roared and guffawed, almost falling from his horse, till he ran out of breath. He made his apologies, expressed his sympathy, threw us a blanket, negotiated his horse around us to continue on his way, and resumed laughing.

We were sure of his confidentiality; the most he might do, in future, was wink.

I nudged her horse forward to a place where we could turn around, and made our way back to her place in silence.

I didn't want the day's excursion to end without conversation. I said, "I think your solution to the problem was quite keen."—no comment—"And the Reverend Diamonde, I'm sure, is an understanding and discrete gentleman, an honor to his profession. We were lucky it was he who apprehended us instead of some narrow-minded wag who would tell the story at every last back fence and tavern."

Still, silence.

After five minutes, Olivia burst into laughter. I kept my composure.

She put her hand on mine holding the reins and said, "Jamie, you are a gentleman, and I'm getting to like you very much."

We rode on in silence.

# chapter 14

THE WEEK AFTER I returned home from Olivia's saw a rapid succession of events that were not expected or welcome.

Squire Calloway had returned from London and dropped by our house to inform me that he had made inquiry at the patent office. It was almost noon and Mother invited him to dinner. All the family was there including father, Ellen, Jonathan, and Dordy. We enjoyed the Squire's company but I'm sure mother thought that such an invitation would have a modifying effect on his attorney's fee. The Squire cracked a smile and sat down to several slices of roast beef. After complimenting the hostess, the Squire said that by studying the records carefully, he found that a doctor Erasmus Darwin from Birmingham had registered a device for suspension of a vehicle using springs that were virtually the same as mine.

I was devastated. "It is strange how so many inventions that are alike or try to fulfill the same need, though from different and remote sections of the country, often occur within weeks of each other." I wailed.

The Squire went on to say, "As well as the suspension, Darwin has an arrangement so that on turning a wagon, the forward wheel on the turn does not throw the vehicle out of balance endangering the passengers and the cargo."

"I suspect he has built something into the turning plate, the fifth wheel, perhaps a gradual bulge that, during the turn, raises the carriage slightly on the outside of the turn. Is that right, Squire?"

The Squire cocked his wizened head to the side in surprise. "I believe it was something like that. How did you know?" he said.

"I was thinking of doing something like that next week to see if it would work. Now, I guess I know that it does."

It was flattering to know that I had been on the same course of solving a problem which has vexed carriage makers and hobbyists of repute for some time. Mr. Darwin is a famous doctor of medicine over in Lichfield, near Birmingham, who meets monthly with other enlightened men such as James Watt, who has invented a more efficient steam engine to drain the mines, Josiah Wedgewood, the Queen's potter, the Reverend Joseph Priestly, who has discovered oxygen which is replacing the phlogiston theory, and Matthew Boulton, the toy and notion magnate, among others. Benjamin Franklin has met with them several times, I understand.

It was inevitable that someone would think out the suspension problem and come up with a decent answer. I was just a bit too late.

"When did he get the patent?" I asked the Squire.

"About five years ago, Jamie. But don't be discouraged. You're on the right track." he answered.

This double-edged news laid me low for a while. I say double-edged because of the pleasure of knowing that I was in the same thinking pattern as other inventors but at the same time, I was distressed to realize that I had been so negligent in registering my ideas.

A few days later, the Squire came by a second time, again just as we were sitting down to dinner. Mother invited him to join us at table after greetings were said all around. The Squire sat down and was passed bowls and platters of food from which he pleasurably filled his plate. Small talk prevailed over an obligato of knives, forks, and spoons making a gentle tatoo on the china as we stuffed ourselves with lamb stew and washed it down with drafts of cider.

Then the Squire cleared his throat and drained a cup of coffee before declaiming, "Wencesles Mochter has grossly fooled and disappointed us by either selling or leasing his new-bought land to the army to be used as a recruiting and basic training camp. Construction is to begin tomorrow."

We all registered shock. Members of our family and many others had enjoyed the stretch of river, meadow, and woods for generations.

Mother said what we all thought. "That beautiful tract, with its many delightful glades, will now be despoiled and forever lost to us. How sad that objects of natural beauty that take millenia for formation and can't be duplicated by man are exploited for the wrong reasons and for paltry sums compared to the pleasure thousands take from their enjoyment."

We were dumfounded by Mochter's duplicity. Crispin had been right about him after all. I was one of those who had been persuaded by his charm and guile to think that he was charitably inclined and valued nature's treasures.

This depressing news lowered a pall on the entire family. Jonathan would not be able to enjoy youthful adventure within its dales any more. Ellen and any future swain will have to find other grounds for romance. Dordy and Sally will be denied a parkland for their children to frolic in and learn of nature's treasures. I would certainly miss it. I began to think of the shock to Crispin.

Strange, Mochter had, with seeming regret, declared to me that clean, leafy environs were unavailable to him in London when he was growing up. He had offered this as the reason he had never gone fishing. Perhaps that is why he has no real appreciation of the area's essential value.

The Squire hesitated as he was about to eat a bite of mince pie, and volunteered, "I might as well inform you of something else depressing. Crispin entered the army two weeks ago and is at that army base. He and other recruits are going to start their basic training by digging latrines, begging your pardon, Edith, and building barracks just where Jamie and he do their fishing and hunting. And what Mochter did, though despicable, is completely legal, its part of the laws with respect to enclosure. We can't do anything about it."

Spoons clattered on plates, aghs were sighed by all. The world was turned upside down. Crispin's identity was almost synonymous with Wedlich's pool, he spent so much of his time there. We were all speechless with the irony of it. Crispin, poor fellow, will have to participate in the greenwood's destruction. How ironic. What a tragedy for him. And for all the community.

After dinner, I repaired to my forge where I could be alone in the quiet of the dim light. I accomplished nothing but sat in my misery chair brooding over this sad news. As the evening darkened, the wind rose so that several bushes next to the forge scratched and knocked at the walls.

But, it was not the wind. It was Crispin in the darkness clandestinely trying to get my attention. He was not in uniform.

"My God! Crispin! What are you doing here? And where is your uniform?"

"I just couldn't stand it, Jamie. Everybody telling me what to do on threat of being flogged. All of us recruits are scared to death of sergeants and officers yelling at us to march all day, back and forth, to no end that we could see. And when they told us to pull down those trees and dig up those flowers and to damn the brook, why I just took it as a personal insult, an attack on the greenwood and everything I hold dear. I took it for two weeks, I did, before I split. Can you help me?"

"I'll do what I can. Come in here and we'll think about what to do." I said, with authority as if I knew what to do. Then I closed the shutter and brightened the forge with a pull or two on the bellows.

"How did you get away? When?"

"When the sergeant relieved us from the field we'd cleared, and said we could go to mess, that is to eat, I dashed for the bushes as if to relieve myself. I tore off my jacket, stuffed it in a hedgehog hole, and ran to follow the brook so as to not leave a print or scent. When I came to a sturdy branch over the stream, I thrust myself up and climbed through the trees for about fifty feet from the bank to avoid leaving any trace. I think it may have thrown them off the track. I haven't heard anyone, or dogs, following me, anyway. That was several hours ago."

My eyes fell on some work clothes hanging on a peg that I used for smithing. "Here, put these on and give me those army breeches and I'll burn them in the forge. Rip off any metal buttons first.' I sat down in my misery chair for some serious thinking.

"Do you still want to go to America?" I asked.

Crispin was startled and nodded a vigorous yes. "How would you manage that?" he said.

I told him about uncle Arthur's offer of a tour to America and my invitation to Olivia to join me. "I don't know if Olivia will be able to come with me but I'm certain she wants to. I'm hoping to get word of her decision soon." I wanted to tell Crispin of how well things had gone with Olivia and me, that ours was a serious romance, but time was of the essence.

"Would you like to join us going to New York?"

Crispin glowed in gratitude, but raised his hand in protest while he thought how to answer. "This would be the time to go, if I'm ever going to, and I'd like to go with you. I appreciate your offer, but I'm now a fugitive, guilty of a serious offense. You shouldn't expose yourself and Olivia to danger of this sort on my account. Thanks, anyway, but I should go separately."

He spoke so forcefully, I knew that he would not allow us to take him with us. I was pleased by his show of common sense under stress which was wiser than my hasty decision to needlessly endanger Olivia. I was sure that he would prefer to go it alone, but I wanted to make the offer, anyway.

"You're right, Crispin. But, as it happens, I think that Olivia and I are going to sail from Bristol, hopefully within a fortnight. You might want to be on the same ship but travel to Bristol separately. Once we're underway at sea we will probably be out of danger of your being caught."

"But I have no means to get to Bristol, much less New York, my savings are nil and I spent the king's shilling. I can't use your horse if you will excuse my presumption. They'll think I stole her or, more likely, that you gave me the use of her which would make you guilty of aiding a fugitive, or something like that."

"That's true, Crispin, but I could have you drive a hogshead of cider we're due to deliver to the *Silver Swan* at dockside, Bristol. The army won't be looking for a teamster in a sack coat and denims. Father can have someone pick up the rig some other time. Or better yet, Jonathan and Dordy can ride with Olivia and me several hours after you leave and bring both rigs back."

"That makes sense. How do I pay my fare on board and what ship?" he queried.

I was surprised that I had a ready answer for this. "When they pay you for the cider at the *Silver Swan, the owner*—Beauchamp Tudor—we call him Beau—has been our customer for years—you keep the money. It ought to be more than enough to pay your fare. When we get to New York, we'll think more about what to do. Right now, I've got to think of a safe place around here to put you up for the night. Would you mind sleeping in a hogshead before we fill it up tomorrow? We'll drain the dregs, wipe it dry, and put some straw in it to make it comfortable."

"Sure. Just don't fill it up while I'm still inside." Crispin quipped. With that I took him to the barn and the hogshead wagon where, after we cleaned his hidey-hole, he soon collapsed as if in a coma. The large barrel was perfect for his small frame. I returned to my misery chair.

The next day, I told father and mother about Crispin and what my plans were. They were shocked by this turn of events, and agreed that it was an awkward way to start the Grand Tour. I had already arranged to be accompanied by a young lady who seemed inevitably, and soon, to become my intended, and compounded this engagement by inviting my best friend to accompany us because he has become a fugitive from the British army. My parents were concerned for our welfare but thought that we had designed a reasonable plan to cope with the danger.

Father suggested that I try the *Borealis*, manned by Captain John Chamberlain, or the *Gray Goose*, captained by Erasmus Haege. Both ships were packets to New York and one of them ought to be in Bristol. They agreed to my gift of the cider proceeds to Crispin in view of his possible capture and a sure, swift and brutal punishment if we didn't help him. We examined my plan all day looking for flaws and ways to avoid being apprehended. As I fell asleep, I was praying for a quick and positive outcome to these dire complications.

At breakfast, one of Olivia's workers arrived with a note. I tore open the wax seal.

*Wednesday, November 29th*

*Dear Jamie,*

*Alan is astonished at how quickly our romance has progressed—he hoped not too far—- but he is pleased, and gives us his blessing . He is agreeable to my sojourn to America with you provided you do not put me in a compromising position and that I agree to return by January one, 1777.*

*I have tentatively agreed to the second requirement and hope that you will, at least tentatively, accept the first.*

*When I finish putting my wardrobe together and preparing eight rhododendron, balled-and-burlapped for your aunt, and for your other purposes, I will be on my way to your place. I should arrive Saturday afternoon, December second. I hope you haven't changed your mind.*

*Here's to a happy New Year.*

*All my Love,*

*Olivia*

Dordy was eager to help me in preparing for this very Grand Tour to America. I sent him to Bristol to verify that either the *Gray Goose* or the *Borealis* was in port or expected shortly and when they would leave port. Happy to have an excuse to break away from his rural isolation, he invited a more-than-willing Sally to accompany him on the excursion..

I had checked on Crispin in the hogshead. He was still tired from the rigors of his army ordeal and the tension and exhaustion of his fugitive role the previous evening. He asked me to let him sleep several more hours which I was more than pleased to do. Father had gone to Ross on Wye on some business.

The distractions of others and Father's absence afforded me the opportunity to make use of the forge and to have the privacy to dig the ingot out of the coal bin so I could saw it into pieces as suggested by Olivia. Each piece would be about an inch wide and weigh about four pounds, about the size of a serving of fruit cake and weighing about the same as Gramma used to make. It was not that much more weight to add to a forty or fifty-pound ball of earth, required for a four-year shrub, to cause reason for suspicion.

My hack saw was reasonably sharp allowing it to quickly work its way through the soft metal. I had prepared a page from an old newspaper to receive the gold sawdust so as to leave no trace. When I finished sawing I thought it would be a nice touch to melt the leavings into a nugget to give to Olivia to wear on a necklace. On second thought, I decided that one nugget would be too large and conspicuous. Better to make three smaller nuggets, two of them about a quarter-inch in diameter for a pair of earrings and a slightly larger, flatter one for a pendant.

The three pieces would still attract too much attention for comfort so I daubed them with some russet paint which made the baubles less conspicuous. I had just finished doing all this, including hiding the nuggets and gold slices back into the depths of the coal bin when it occurred to me that, in a pinch, the nuggets would be handy money. But I wanted Olivia to have these rather than our having to spend them.

I was so relieved to have this clandestine chore accomplished. A guardian angel must have been looking over me that night. I sat down in my misery chair to reflect that problems were being solved and solutions falling nicely into place. I was on the brink of traveling to America to a welcoming aunt and uncle and I would be accompanied by the most charming and beautiful woman I knew. As it turned out, I should not have even *thought* such a smug and piquant opinion of fortune's favor.

# chapter 15

MY REVERIE WAS interrupted by the sound of a ruckus being made at the front porch. Wencesles Mochter was exercising his most hectoring manner by banging on the door with his blackthorn ivory-headed cane and demanding the attention of the Claveraque family. Holly had answered the door and Mochter verbally abused her until mother intervened whereupon he shifted his abuse to her.

"I wish to question James Claveraque whom I believe is your son." he blustered as if he were an actor giving a performance at Covent Garden. The veins of his bald scalp were distended in his anger and his temples were surging. He was bent on inflicting us with his presence and strode into the center hall uninvited. My initial reaction was to whisk him outside by the collar, but I was six inches short of his bulk and thought better of it. I controlled my anger and girded myself for a sensible response to deflect his wrath, whatever it was about.

"Mother, this is Wencesles Mochter. He is the gentleman I met a month ago by Wedlich's pool the day after the storm blew the old sycamore down. He is also the man who bought the commons and the greenwood and then tuned around and sold it to the army. How can I help you, Mr. Mochter?" I said. Mother coldly nodded but said nothing.

"Mr. Claveraque, I demand to know what you took from my property just after I left you that day!"

"Why certainly. I cut the feather lure that had snagged on the roots of the sycamore that had fallen in the storm. Do you wish to see it?"

"You climbed the trunk to get whatever it was and spent quite a bit of time at it. What were you about?"

"That is true, Mr. Mochter. After you left, the snow had melted off several other objects that turned out to be lures, so I cut them down, and added them to my collection." I was truthful, albeit not fully truthful. "I shouldn't have, they were not mine to take. Do you want them? Have you decided to take up fishing?" I dusted off my hands, as if I had just finished a dirty bit of work. Which indeed I had. It would not do for him to detect specks of gold dust on my person—particularly at this juncture.

"Would you like some tea and scones, Mr. Mochter? Holly, our cook, has just made some. They are cooling in the pantry. Perhaps you smell their delicious flavor. Please join Mother and me for tea and perhaps we can satisfy your questions."

Mother hastened to beg off. She claimed to have sewing repairs to finish and strode from the room with decorum.

Mochter coughed into his neckerchief as if this gesture would help him determine his next turn. "I have not taken up fishing. Nor is this discussion about feathers." he scolded.

It became difficult to conceal my exasperation. "Do you wish advice on teaching the army how to fish? Or drilling the troops without trampling the posies, eh? Nice piece of work, Mr. Mochter. You must have made a killing on our park land."

He was about to protest but I overrode his bluster with my own. "And you think *I* was looking for money in the roots of a felled sycamore on your land?" I thought he would regard this as a preposterous statement, but this is what he had been thinking all along. I had only increased the fervor of his suspicions. I was bungling my argument. And Mochter refused to be out-blustered.

"What is it about, Mr. Mochter?" I insisted.

"You know what it's about. Now what were you doing up in the roots of that tree?" he was adamant. His scalp was bald and taut like a drum, and white, as if it had never seen sunshine. Yet his face was contorted beet-red with fury.

"I have told you just now as I told you then. Don't you remember? I had caught a large trout that had snagged the line in the roots of the sycamore several months previous. So the trout got off. And I thought I would never see that lure again. But the tree later upended in the storm and there it was. I spotted it as I was walking by. Any fisherman would have been glad to retrieve such a successful lure, Mr. Mochter, as well as the other lures there for the taking."

He was about to answer. I parried, "I'll be glad to give you the lures, if that's what you want." He was flustered and glared at me. Then he turned and stomped out.

No doubt he would be back. I realized that the sooner Olivia and I left the country, the better off we would be. I went upstairs to begin packing.

Mochter returned the next morning, anxious to put into operation whatever coercion he had planned, I supposed. He repeated yesterday's rapping on the door, but much more gently. I opened the door to a plaintiff in contrition..

"Mr. Claveraque. I'm here to apologize for my actions yesterday. If you have a moment, I must explain." Such an introduction warranted my courtesy and gained my curiosity, but put me on my guard.

I welcomed him. Once seated in the kitchen with a proffered mug of coffee, he launched into a detailed story. "When I bought the commons, I was in hopes of tearing down those wretched hovels that must have been rotting there since the days of Richard Plantagenet and replacing them with modern and fashionable cottages that would make our residents proud.

"I had been told that each of those small buildings had been part of a monastery that was taken over by Henry VIII well over two hundred years ago.

"Over the years I have heard stories about the place and its people from various sources in Herefordshire. Each story had no particular significance except for its charm and illumination of what life must have been like around this part of England during the early years.

"When all these stories are pieced together, the aggregate comes into focus as a startling chronicle. The monks had been very successful over a long period selling their excess produce such as green goods, wheat flour, poultry, saddles of mutton, baskets, target butts, tin work, and wine. Their white wine was so scintillating that they sold it not only locally but in pubs all over the West Country and halfway to London..

"The monks used the revenue to maintain the buildings and equipment in excellent condition and to enable them to live not only an appropriate spiritual life, but a very comfortable, almost luxurious, one.

"Even so, it is said that they had plenty of funds left over. They had the good sense to put the excess aside for a rainy day or for a commune project. They also kept this financial success private which precluded them from having to make forced loans to the nobility and local entrepreneurs, and made them less likely to be a target for other thieves."

I found this interesting but the story was lengthening with no end in sight. I interrupted Mochter whose story was so well delivered without faltering that I could not help think that he had recited it before.

"I don't have much time available this morning, Mochter. Can you conclude this soon?" .

"Of course." He replied. Then, without missing a beat, he continued. "Many transactions were bartered and they consumed the received goods or traded them. When they were paid in gold or silver coins, they fashioned vases, crosses, reliquaries, and other items as needed in their ceremonies and melted the rest into ingots.

"Like any prudent investor, they kept these ingots as a reserve and separated them into small caches under lock and key. There were many of them, so that if one cache was found, the remaining might still be safe from discovery. When word leaked out that Henry was going to take over the monasteries, it has been said by many sources that the monks collected all the keys to these small vaults, secured them in a small lockbox and, in the dark of night, lowered it to the bottom of the deepest pool in the river, so the story goes.

"Some say they deposited the box with the keys directly under the mill's water wheel for easy retrieval. But the mill was destroyed during the civil war. Some of the stories have it that the ingots were thrown in as well."

While I was intensely interested, I did not wish to show it. With feigned indifference I insisted, "I will give you a few more minutes to finish the story, but then you must leave. I have much to do."

"But don't you see? The box with the keys or some of the gold ingots may still be in the river. When these different stories are coordinated, they make sense. My property is a little downstream from where the monastery was located. I planned to drag the river next summer when the current slows and the water is warm enough to work in." he pleaded.

I interrupted. "If you do that, everybody in the shire will soon be out there combing the bottom with you. But, boxes of keys or any gold in the water would, after all these years, have been washed away. It could be a hundred yards downstream or all he way to the Severn River maybe even to the Bristol Channel. It's been something like two-hundred and forty years. You can't expect to find any of that now. For that matter, it would have been difficult for the monks to find it a few day after they put it in the river. One heavy rain or snow melt would have been able to dislodge the keys in the box, even the gold."

I was warming up with negative reasons for him to drop the matter.

"Also, King Henry and his men probably wheedled the location of this concealment from the poor monks. Your chances of reaping anything from this are so slight, I wouldn't waste my time on it if I were you."

Mochter was deflated. "Well, I guess you're right. The story intrigued me and it seemed worth mentioning. I thought you might have found something in the roots of that tree. I'm sorry to have troubled you." This last mumble was drowned in disappointment..

"How can you drag the river when you no longer own it? It belongs to the army now. Remember?" I flung at him. I loved to throw salt in the wound. "It's an interesting story, anyway. And thank you for sharing it with me."

He rose from the chair. As he went out the door, I thought bitterly, *Though you didn't find any gold bars, you made a nice pile of money selling the greenwood to the army. Saved yourself a lot of effort, too. But ruined for succeeding generations a beautiful piece of land.*

Of course, Mochter only had to smash the caches in the hovels, once he found them, for easier access to the gold ingots than dragging the bottom of the river, if there's any credit to his story. But, he would have thought of that. I didn't want to suggest it and increase his ardor for such an enterprise. I sighed with relief that I had satisfied his dogged need for an audience. I could put this haunting concern behind me. Or could I?

Once he left, mother returned without the slightest interest in what occurred during Mochter's visit. Instead she suggested, nay insisted, that before Olivia accompany me to America, that we should be married. The travel arrangements lent too much opportunity for temptation, she said. It was only fair to Olivia. Besides, what would people think, she added

Mother was right, of course. Olivia and I hadn't even talked about marriage. But Olivia's willingness to go to America with me for over a year, our mutual interests, and her passion convinced me that she would agree to a lifelong liaison cemented with a small ceremony before leaving for Bristol.

I didn't have to wait long. Olivia arrived the next afternoon, as promised, with her wardrobe and her brother. My parents were clearly pleased with her charm when I introduced Olivia and Alan.. Mother turned to me and subtly nodded confirmation of my discriminating selection of a bride. Olivia watched me closely as she introduced her favorite helper, Priscilla, as her chaperone. Dutifully, I welcomed Priscilla, but felt suitably chastened. I helped them carry their trunks to their rooms.

When Priscilla was excused, I told Olivia about Crispin, how we were going to assist his flight from the army and from England, preparing the gold slices for insertion in the root balls, and Mochter's two visits. She accepted this information with confidence that we could cope with whatever may present itself.

Then I told her of mother's encouragement that we have a small marriage ceremony before embarking on our Grand Tour honeymoon, a la fugitive.

"But you haven't proposed to me." she invited.

I dropped to bended knee and proposed. She laughed and helped me to my feet. "I think it's been implicit that I would say yes. But, of course, I hoped you would propose before we became shipboard. I can't think of a better honeymoon than a year-long excursion to America. And after the wedding, Priscilla can return home with Alan."

I sighed in wonderment that we had surmounted what so easily could have been a snarl in our plans. "We'll tell my family and your brother, and arrange a date with Squire Calloway to officiate here at home." I said.

"No, Jamie, this is the bride's choice." Olivia declared. "I prefer Reverend Diamonde, a small gathering of friends at our church, and a simple ceremony. I should think that your mother will agree."

There was a clattering in the yard which was Dordy and Sally returning from Bristol. God hope we can be off in a week, I prayed.

Dordy and Sally looked so refreshed and enthralled with each other, it was obvious that they would soon follow Olivia's and my lead. I wondered if their trip to Bristol was the occasion for a proposal to her.

"You made good time." I yelled. "What did you find out about a packet to New York?"

Dordy paused to get his breath as he dismounted Nellie. "Neither the *Borealis* or the *Gray Goose* is in port or expected for a month. But there is a handsome-looking American schooner out of Perth Amboy leaving in a week—the *Raritan*—built there only two years ago. I went aboard and talked to the skipper, a Captain Glass, who was just finishing unloading the cargo, and about to take on fresh lading.

"He showed me the hold and the passenger berths—commodious accommodations and room on deck to move about. The ship can take six passengers. He sails by way of Saint Eustatius in the West Indies so most of the trip should be in warm weather. I took the liberty of engaging a cabin for you."

"That sounds excellent." I said as I patted Dordy on the back. Then, in a more private tone of voice, in case of inquisitive ears, I revealed to Dordy, "Crispin will be on the same ship but should make his own arrangements so as to not appear to be connected to us."

I turned to Olivia, "If we hurry we'll have just enough time to have the ceremony and arrive at Bristol to get aboard. We'd better notify our guests.

To Dordy I said, "Did anything else happen at Bristol?

"No. Except that Beau at the Silver Swan said he was looking forward to seeing you and that hogshead of cider. He had heard that a regiment of troops are to arrive and leave port in a few weeks and your cider would be the last they would have before their crossing to the colonies." If Dordy proposed to Sally, he wasn't ready to announce it.

To account for Crispen's presence in our house, I loaned him some of my old, but still presentable, clothes that we were saving for Jonathan to grow into. They fit Crispen reasonably well so that, if it became necessary, we could present him as an itinerant portrait artist, given a few cosmetic changes. This new identity enabled him to eat with the family and stay in the back room, where we usually put up the tailor and the tinker when they come by, rather than Crispin having to live a fugitive's reclusive existence, however temporary.

I knew that Crispen was a good artist, at least in painting fish in the creel and bucks on the run from the longbow. We had him begin a portrait of Ellen and soon her likeness appeared so well executed that we wondered that we had not commissioned him to sketch us all before this. This talent would serve well to validate his pose as an itinerant portraitist. But the army had exhausted its pursuit for Crispen locally and we began to breathe more easily.

I made a circuit to the Reverend Diamonde's parsonage to ask him to preside at our wedding; he was available and pleased to. To clear any dark suspicions that he may have gathered from our chance meeting on the road several weeks past, coupled with a hasty wedding, I explained the awkward circumstances of our embarrassment to the marveling cleric, who had the good sense to realize it was just one of those things.

Next on the circuit was a visit to Squire Calloway to ask him to honor us with his presence. He was delighted at the news of the wedding and our forthcoming trip to America. He had some friends in the colonies he wanted us to call on. The Squire also offered to pick up Sally Bushnell and some of Olivia's friends.

Over tea, I told the Squire of Mochter's two threatening visits and what Mochter intimated, but not about the gold in my possession.

The Squire's many years of listening to client's one-sided stories of their innocence or victimization must have alerted him to the veracity of my partial revelation. He did not, out-and-out, reveal that he understood that there were more facts than I presented in my story, but indirectly, he mentioned that he had heard that gold and sterling carried a premium in America, and items could be purchased more readily for less in this medium. He said the problem was how to transport bullion or specie there, it being against the law to export gold and silver except as worn items of jewelry.

At that, the Squire stopped giving subtle, under-the-counter advice except to say that Mochter had done well enough on his purchase and sale of the greenwood, and should expect no more emolument therefrom.

As he waved goodbye, the Squire re-confirmed his attendance at the wedding. My parents would ask a few other close friends and Alan would ask friends of the Farrells, so my task was completed. I returned home and got out the Atlas which included a map of the Carribean to locate the Dutch island of St. Eustatius.

# chapter 16

AFTER THE WEDDING, Olivia and I basked in the good wishes of our families and friends. The Reverend Diamonde had performed a simple but graceful ceremony at the church that we would remember for a long time. I have never seen Olivia look lovelier. So did Sally Bushnell whom Olivia graciously chose as her maid of honor. Dordy was my best man. Olivia threw her bride's bouquet, of rhododendron, spruce, and witch hazel sprigs, to Sally which was applauded by all. After I gave Olivia the first kiss of our marriage, the reverend conferred on us the Lord's blessing followed by a subtle wink.

When we returned to my parent's home, we inspected the table of wedding gifts. The most prominent was a set of pewter cups and plates for our household wherever that future abode may be. The set was jointly from my parents and Olivia's brother. From Dordy and Sally Bushnell, a warm red wool coat with fur trim was given to Olivia and a fine green one for me, similarly trimmed, to keep us warm in the New World. We considered these wedding presents as sufficient armament of good wishes for many years. Squire Calloway gave us each a leather sheath enclosing a fine knife, fork, and spoon for managing whatever fare came our way.

Mssrs. Chalker, Nester, and Voorhees were asked to perform for our reception and their set up in the dining room still left space for cold cuts, small cakes, and a punch bowl on our dining room table after two leaves were removed. They played various minuets and gigues, including what Jack called a Virginia reel. The music of Handel and Purcell, and a few ancient folk tunes pervaded the Claveraque household, perhaps the entire neighborhood, it was so loud. Everyone had fun as they frolicked to the music.

And Ellen, now well practiced, played her favorite Scarlatti sonata, transcribed for the guitar, as a musical centerpiece for the occasion Dancing, lively as it was, was confined by not only the limitations of our parlor, but by the heat thrown off from the yule log, and the punch bowl which, as was the custom, had been mildly spiked. Could this be Crispen's doing?, I speculated.

It seemed every one at the party had a friend in America or in the West Indies, and much scribbling of names and addresses ensued with promises of writing their friends to expect our visit. Chances were, their letters would be on our packet or arrive coincident with our landing expected to be two or three months from departure.

In the gaiety and excitement, Olivia and I stole away to our room, where the last thing we remembered before falling off to sleep in each other's arms, was the faint, but persistent music and hubbub made by the hard core of our stalwart friends.

The next morning I stole into the barn before dawn light to implant the gold slices into the root balls. I wrapped them in small wads of brown cloth first to make them difficult to spy should a root ball separate for some reason. We could take few chances with this fortune.

I woke Crispin, gave him a clean pair of breeches and a sack coat, pressed a few rolls and some coins into his hand and started him on the way to Bristol driving the hogshead wagon. This early departure would give him a good head start so that no one encountered on the road should link him with us.

After breakfast, I hitched Nellie in the traces and added Olivia's wardrobe and what there was of mine to the bank of rhododendron plants on the lorry. At the last moment, I ran back into the house and returned with two bottles of Claveraque Calvados. This epic parting reminded me of great grandfather's journal and how useful the liquor had been to him on his odyssey eighty years ago. Olivia arched an eyebrow in question and laughed. "There is no need to get me intoxicated, you know." she said as would a coquette. I told her I would explain the Calvados later.

At this, Mother threw up her arms, exclaimed "oh!", and ran back into the house. She soon returned with a basket full of apples, a ham, preserves, and crackers. "You'll need this before the day is out." she declared. She ran back into the house again for only a moment before she came back with two heavy stones which she had heated by the fireplace all night as foot warmers for Olivia and Jonathan. Olivia was overcome with appreciation for her consideration. "Thank you, Mama!" At that exclaimed sentiment, I know mother felt well repaid. Both of them had tears in their eyes.

We finally said goodbye to my parents and Ellen, and to Alan and the Squire. Dordy and Jonathan accompanied us to bring back both the lorry and the hogshead wagon Crispin was driving. The last sentiment I heard was mother's. "Don't forget to write."

We hated to leave the embrace of those dear to us, and the comfortable ambiance of the farm and valley. But we were thrilled at the thought of this adventure that could—would—change our lives. Augmented by the excitement that accompanies any trip, we were exhilarated.

The sun glistened on the hoar frost that encapsulated trees and grass alike. Its brightness began to thaw the frozen road but the melt evaporated under the more direct beams as the day progressed and there was no threat of miring down. What with a heavy load in the wagon, Nellie strained mightily at our urging and we slowly moved forward, spokes creaking under the strain. Once under way, we jogged along easily, the going was easier on her as it was a gentle downhill drive all the way. I felt guilty nonetheless and stopped after an hour to give Nellie a rest of a few minutes with a chunk of sugar and a bag of oats. Indeed, we had to go into the woods ourselves.

When we resumed, Olivia asked Dordy about his part in the battle of Lexington and Concord, and then about Bunker Hill and his wound. Time had healed his ankle, but the overwhelming loss of his comrades and his feeling of guilt that he had survived and they had not lingered like the aftertaste of cod liver oil. I was surprised that he so freely told her of those grim events.

"I was with Colonel Percy's relief force at Lexington," he said. "It was the first combat I was to experience. When we caught up with the main force, we could see that they were outnumbered by the rebels and suffering for it. The rebels also had the advantage of cover compared to our being on the open road. New England soil is so full of rocks that for well over a hundred years of clearing fields the American generations had made many stone walls which now the rebels found convenient to crouch behind to take pot shots at us. Percy finally decided there was no reason that we should stay on the road in such an exposed column formation, so he directed us to break ranks to file along about seventy-five yards off both sides of the road."

"In this way, we continually flanked them and kept them on the move so there were far fewer casualties on the return to Cambridge. Percy is fat, which slowed him down, but he was not without wit. His management under fire was firm and cool and very few of my mates were wounded as a result."

Dordy stopped talking. I thought because he was in sorrow for them. But then, he continued, "Some of the rebels fired from houses along the way and the lieutenant directed fire against them. He demanded that they surrender. And when they didn't, he directed that we set fire to the house and told us to shoot those trying to escape. Even though they were rebels, and had fired at us, I thought that forcing them to be burned alive or shot in this way was intolerably cruel."

"Did you shoot at any of them?" Olivia asked.

"Yes, they were shooting at us. I must admit I thought it was fun, at first, like hunting rabbits. But when we came closer to them and I saw the blood and wounds as they happened and the flames rising from their coats, and the screaming, and realized all this mayhem and pain was because we had provoked it by marching out to Concord, it became a different matter. By afternoon, I still fired my musket but didn't aim at anyone—just a tree or a rock.

"At the time, it seemed to take forever for us to return since we had been on the march since early morning with little chance to eat except for nipping a chunk of cheese. We were all exhausted.

"But looking back now, it's as if it were a dream, a sequence that took only a minute or less. I should be thankful for that." he said. It was the most I had heard Dordy speak of the war in months.

We heard hoof beats and a jingling of harnesses approaching and turned to see who was in such a hurry in pursuit of whom. A squad of a dozen soldiers rounded a glade of trees and slowed to surround us as if we were their quarry. It was Lieutenant Brigandi, whom I last saw months ago at the Green Bottle. He was evidently in charge.

"Ho! It's Mr. Claveraque! What brings you this way, Jamie?" He seemed cold and officious.

"We, my two brothers and my wife are on our way to Bristol. But we are not in as much of a hurry as you seem to be. Who are you chasing?"

"Your wife? This isn't the same lady as you were with at the Green Bottle." This is the same kind of provocative statement he made to embarrass Ancie at the Green Bottle. His tone demanded an answer.

"No. That lady is restored to her former lover, Downey Mohan. Lieutenant Brigandi, let me introduce you to my bride of a few days, Olivia Farrell, now Olivia Claveraque. And these are my brothers, George and Jonathan."

Brigandi mumbled an embarassed, "Congratulations."

One of the cavalrymen caught Brigandi's attention, and whispered in his ear. The Lieutenant turned to me. "My sergeant says he knew the fugitive and says that the younger one looks like him, looking at Jonathan. Can you vouch for him?"

I was flabbergasted. "I just said that he was my brother, Lieutenant. We don't find it necessary to carry papers for a fifteen year old. My older brother here, George, was a lieutenant and was at Lexington and Concord and was wounded at Bunker Hill. Will you accept his word?"

Brigandi then remembered hearing about Lieutenant George Claveraque at Bunker Hill and immediately made an apology and dropped his questioning. I asked where he and his men were going.

"A recruit deserted from Camp Mochter. We've been looking for him for a week. Someone said they saw a lone hiker down this way yesterday morning. Have you seen a young man, about twenty, on the road? We don't know what he's wearing. He's probably discarded his uniform and is wearing someone else's clothes by now. He's a smart one, I'll tell you."

I was about to answer when Jonathan spoke up, "I saw a young man take a rabbit from a snare about a half hour ago. He was a few hundred yards off the road at the edge of the Forest of Dean." Jonathan told him. I was astonished that my younger brother could render such a story with a straight face.

"What was he wearing?" Brigandi bore in.

"He had a fur cap. Maybe rabbit, and a faded red jacket with gray breeches. He looked kind of cold." said Jonathan solemnly. I thought he sounded convincing. Evidently, so did Brigandi.

"Thanks, young man. Sorry for the misidentification but we dare not overlook any possibility. There's a reward to anyone providing information that leads to the fugitive's capture. We'll let you know if that's our man. Good to see you , Jamie, 'Mam." Brigandi saluted and wheeled his horse and his squad, all anxious to be off and resume the chase. They raced back the way they came.

Olivia spoke, "Jamie, I didn't see that young man!

"Neither did I." said Jonathan triumphantly.

"Crispen will be proud of you, Jonathan. You threw Brigandi off the track but I hope the lieutenant doesn't suspect that you fibbed." I patted him on the back.

"How would he find out that I didn't see a young man dressed that way?" Jonathan replied, happy to have thwarted an adult of authority, and saved Crispin.

We all laughed and pondered Jonathan's ingenious master stroke.

Olivia brought the conversation back to Dordy's travails and encouraged him to talk more about his combat, partly out of curiosity and more, I believe, to help him expunge the memory of horror from his system.

"How did you get your wound?" she asked.

"We had made two disastrous marches up the slope at Bunker Hill with General Howe leading us on. Each attempt was decimated by rebel fire as we made our final approach to the redoubt at Breed's Hill which was the first and lower of the two hills. We fell back both times with severe losses.

"Meanwhile, the rebels had sharpshooters taking shots at us from the abandoned homes of Charlestown on our left flank. So, our war ships, Lively and Somerset, lobbed hot shot which set the buildings on fire. The flames shot up fifty feet and we could feel the heat all the way on the right flank.

"We all needed to rest and refresh ourselves. It was a very hot day, especially with those huge flames that lasted for over an hour, and we had on wool uniforms and heavy packs. Then, reinforcements had been sent over and Howe had us re-form for a third charge. This final time, Howe had enough mercy to let us drop our packs, it was so hot and steaming. We did not need three days rations to get us up that hill.

No one interrupted Dordy. Jonathan and I had heard him recount the battle before but each time he added something we had not heard.

"So we again marched up the hill through the hip-high grass with bayonets at the ready to intimidate the rebels. General Howe kept saying, "steady lads", as we came closer to them. We did not fire at the them and they mostly held off firing at us, even when, again, we had to stop in order to step high over the many fences crossing the field. It later turned out that the rebels were low on ammunition but we didn't know that at the time.

"When we had gotten to about twenty yards from the redoubt, their officers yelled "fire", and they let loose a heavy volley at us. I had been talking quietly with Jim Henley when a bullet cut him down, just like that. Jim said no more, he was dead in an instant. I could hear bullets splat against my mates and whistling through the air. I remember thinking that it was incredible that none had hit me.

"Up ahead, a cannonball suddenly decapitated a rebel and I was horrified at seeing his severed neck gush a fountain of red over everyone nearby. Within a second, a bullet hit me just above my ankle. It hurt like the devil and I collapsed and passed out just short of the redoubt. I didn't come to until the following morning when a doctor began to examine my leg at the dispensary at Castle William.

"Grisly events happened so quickly in the last minute before I was wounded that it was as if they had compressed in my mind into a hard aggregate of horror that was slow to dissolve. That continuing dissolution has been the pain of the last few months."

Olivia had been listening carefully as Dordy relived his ordeal. She especially sympathized with the revelation of the very gory part about the rebel decapitation.

"You and your mates had a terrible time of it but you gained the field and were an honor to your country." she said with tears in her eyes..

Dordy looked up with a wry grin and declared to us. "I understand one wag said that any more victories like that and there wouldn't be anyone left to carry the news of victory home." Olivia and I chuckled, but Dordy became reserved and no more was said. Conversation had relieved the monotony of a charming landscape made dreary by winter and the rigors of travel. Soon, we crossed the Severn River and could see from the bridge the spires of Bristol and the milieu of masts in the far distance. The sky seemed to become brighter as we neared the estuary, and the air became pleasantly infused with the salt smell from the sea..

"I haven't seen that view since I was a child," said Olivia.

"It's beautiful. Because it is our beginning path by sea to America." I joined in. Nellie kept moving at an easy lope since we had been coming down out of the low hills all day and now the ground was almost level.

Flurries began to fall with varied intensity: one moment we could see the opposite shore of the estuary, the next, all became opaque. Then, a wind off the channel wafted this white screen aside and we were in a maritime world at the edge of England and Wales.

An hour later, as we neared Avonsmouth, the large half-timbered Silver Swan came into view through the fading gray-gold light of a winter sunset. Among the many wagons and horses in the yard, I was glad to see that our wagon with its hogshead was pulled up near the service entrance. I knocked on the hogshead staves. It was empty, Crispin had made his delivery. The cider-filled hogshead had been taken indoors and replaced by an empty one for return home.

The sight of a knot of soldiers lingering about the entrance of a nearby tavern alerted me to possible danger, so that I quickly shunted

Olivia, Dordy, and Jonathan out of sight and sought out Beau to see what was going on.

Beau said it was a press gang. They had already scoured his place of a few poor souls to augment the under-manned ships of his Majesty's fleet. What irony it would be if Crispin had successfully eluded the army's search for him, only to be impressed to the dangerous and cruel life at sea as an unwilling 'guest' of the navy.

Olivia and Dordy were famished, and tired of the jolts of the ruts and the incessant sway of the wagon from six this morning. The wagon ride had not discomfitted Jonathan, he said, but he admitted that he was famished despite the snacks we had munched on, mainly to endure the tedium, and looked forward to a hot dinner. We all knew that he was not old enough to get tired.

Beau invited us to sit at a table by the window overlooking the tavern next door so I could watch through the dim light of dusk to see if I should be concerned by the presence of the regulars.

Beau also reminded me that this was sheep country and we all took the suggestion and had lamb stew to be washed down by mugs of fresh Claveraque cider.

The second swallow was made unpalatable by the unmistakable sight of a tall, bald headed man, brandishing an ivory-headed blackthorn cane entering the tavern next door. It was Mochter! I began to fear for Crispin as well as for the four of us.

But Beau confirmed that Crispin had earlier delivered the cider, had been paid for it, and then had asked where the *Raritan* was berthed. Beau had watched him go on board to deal with Captain Glass.

It was just after that, Beau said, that the press gang of army toughs descended upon his establishment and harshly rounded up the young men that had the misfortune to be there, and hauled them off bound, yelling and screaming. He pointed out the *Raritan* in the dimness at dockside, and I thanked him but kept mum about our doings until I had a better chance to gauge the situation. I suggested to Dordy and Olivia that we would be safer spending the night on the *Raritan* than at the Tavern. I wanted to be close to the rhododendron and their precious root balls.

Dordy drove the wagon in dusk relieved only by torchlight down to the dock while I went on board the schooner and halloed for Captain Glass who answered "Down here," from the hold. I went down the companionway and introduced myself to a short, graying, muscular man in his thirties whose swarthy and benign face bespoke of many years spent at sea. He was surrounded by crates loaded with muskets, and kegs of gunpowder, as well as clutches of uniforms and cartons of shoes.

There were also bales of hay for fodder and straw for bedding on one side and what looked like an improvised barn stall. Evidently, we were going to have a horse or fresh milk on the trip. Later on, I found that it was Glass' patrons in France who were shipping arms, ammunition, and clothing to the rebels. Glass referred to it as bombastic ballast. The cow was his idea; he had a life-long craving for milk.

"I've been looking forward to your appearance, Mr. Claveraque. Your friend preceded you by an hour and just missed being made a part of His Majesty's Navy. Unfortunately, several of my crew were languishing in the Silver Swan at the wrong time and, against their wishes, will be rounding out the crew on one of His Majesty's royal ships.

"I'm sorry to say, we may be delayed in making sail until I can regain a full crew to sail this ship." he said matter-of-factly. His speech was hearty and very clear, unburdened of dialect to fuzz or confound his meaning. His use of words suggested that he was largely self taught, to me, a sign of high intelligence and ambition. And he was the first American I had ever met.

"I'm sorry to hear that, sir. Is there any way of getting your crewmen back? May I be of service?" I offered.

"I don't know of anything you could do. The Navy is a law unto itself. Naval officers will brook no interference in their affairs."

"Well, my brother in the wagon is an army officer, a wounded hero of Bunker Hill. And my lawyer is Squire Calloway of Herefordshire. They may be persuasive."

A drop had formed at the end of the captains nose. As well, he had to cough. "That sounds interesting, Mr. Claveraque. But first, I have a few things I must do here and now. You and your folks must be cold, out in the weather all day. There's no sense you're getting colder standing here in this hold. My first mate, Estrich, will assist you with your baggage and show you your berths. I will meet you in my cabin in half an hour to further discuss any interesting course of action you can suggest."

Estrich was very helpful in bringing aboard our baggage and in placing the rhododendron in the hold away from any possible traffic except to accommodate our access. When deep in the hold, I noticed that the captain had arranged kegs of salt in front of the gunpowder kegs, and that the musket were well hidden behind crates of yellow Dutch bricks and Delft tiles. Olivia, Dordy, and Jonathan came on board and tidied up in our cabin which was the mid-ships deck house and comprised two two-foot wide bunks in a eight-foot square room, cozy but confining for what could be a two-month cruise. It was clear that newly weds were not in mind when the ship was designed. The usual accessories for hygiene were prominent, except modified to not slop in high seas.

When we were all satisfactorily dusted, washed, and relieved, Olivia and my brothers accompanied me to Captain Glass' cabin—the aft deck house. It was a bit of a squeeze what with his wider bunk and a small fold-up desk dedicated to charts and equipment for navigating our course. This brought me face-to-face with the maritime necessity that every square inch of space on a ship had to pay its way. This requirement did not preclude several shelves of books.

Crispin had at first found his way to the least cold quarter of the ship but had bargained with Glass to do his portrait to pay his fare. So Crispin had the forward cabin all to himself. As the five of us filed into the captain's cabin, the captain gasped.

"Are all these people going to New York?"

"No sir. Only my wife and I, and Crispin, are making the voyage. My two brothers are returning to the Wye when we weigh anchor." I assured him.

"Well, if they could handle sail, they'd be welcome on this cruise. Not to say they are not welcome in my cabin. Would you all care for coffee to take off the chill?" he offered.

The hospitality was too tempting to turn down, the evening having turned frigid.

After Estrich brought us coffee, I explained. "Captain, we might begin by toting up any bargaining chips that could be used with the captain in charge of the naval squadron. For example, I suppose you carry mail to the colonies?"

The captain nodded.

"Suppose the officers have some mail, personal or official, that they consider important to arrive in New York, Boston, or Philadelphia. Might an agreement be arranged? Say, something like...that you will be glad to provide every act possible to guarantee safe delivery, and that the release of your crew would be considered a gentlemanly exchange for this favor." I saw that this honest appearing man was immediately interested in the benefits of guile.

"That sounds like an intriguing game, Mr Claveraque. We have carried the post for some years. Just this morning, I received a parcel of letters from London and another from Captain Chickerton of His Majesty's Ship, *Poseidon,* in the channel. We might study the addressees to see how important their safe delivery may be."

"Captain, I'll wager that we may sail on the next ebb tide."

The following morning, I went on deck and could see the reason for the phrase "in Bristol fashion". *Raritan* was a two-masted schooner with the two masts, spars, and the rail done bright, that is, oiled or varnished. While the hull was painted a dark blue, the deck houses were painted oyster shell white to blend with the usual visage of the horizon at sea. The tall masts and long booms assured large gobs of wind could be manipulated to move us quickly. Some of the spars had been tied with lines to serve as a hoist to bring cargo onboard. I was pleased to see that a cow and her calf were being lowered into the hold.

To a landlubber like me, the rigging and sails looked like they were ready for action as I fervently hoped they were. All lines and equipment were stowed and secured in an orderly and businesslike fashion to function smoothly. Glass ran a handsome and tight ship.

Myriad seagulls were gliding in large arcs over the sea, screeching as they hovered to inspect what might be a morsel on the surface of the slate-green marine surge. The wind was steady out of the northwest and gave the water farther out in the channel a dark blue cast with just a few waves breaking into low white curls of foam, or white caps, as Glass referred to them.

He also informed me that we would have to sail first in a northerly direction, and then directly westward for the wind to bear properly on our sails to clear Bristol Channel. He pointed to the west across the estuary to clumps of buildings clustered around church spires. "That's Cardiff and Glamorgan in Wales." For a farm boy, it was a beautiful day to have one's first sail at sea.

Olivia had checked the rhododendron to see that the root balls were intact and not frozen, and watered them with fresh water that she had insisted be brought aboard and dedicated to watering the plants. She asked that the hatch be kept open in fair weather to let in light for the plants. She promised to close it should the weather change.

Olivia asked Captain Adam's further indulgence to shift the cargo slightly so that the plants had more light to which he agreed. A spot next to the improvised stall made it easier to shovel fresh manure and its warmth on the rootballs should the weather remain cold, she had explained. She bribed Estrich with the coin of charm to round up a detail to do the shoveling.

Crispin had finished his pen-and-ink portrait of the captain who was very pleased with his likeness. "When we reach 'Statia', perhaps you'll do one in oils for me. My wife would like that. All we have is one of those silhouettes that they do at fairs. I'm at sea so much, she says she forgets what I look like." Perhaps Crispin had found his trade.

Mid-morning saw the captain return from the *Poseidon* with his wayward, but happy, crew members in tow. We said our goodbyes to Dordy and Jonathan who wanted to leave for home as soon as possible to take advantage of the remaining daylight and fair weather.

With sorrow I thought of the happy events to come that I would not be able to witness. Dordy and Sally would surely marry soon, and could even have a child before we returned. And Jonathan would grow into manhood in the next year or so. I hope he kept an adequate distance from the military; the family didn't need to have two sons bruised by war.

Perhaps it was foolish, but my parting words were, "Take care of Nellie and say goodbye to her for me."

Captain Glass was anxious to set sail and weigh anchor. He was mindful that a higher command could rescind the local commander's decision to release his crewmen just as Mother Nature could quickly change the weather. Ebb tide began at mid-afternoon and all was made secure and ready to spread sail and cast off the lines as soon as the tide reversed. Glass was at the wheel as he supervised the exacting exertions leading up to getting under way.

At the critical moment, the captain gave the command and the hands hoisted the large fore-and-aft sail on the mainmast and freed the lines to shore at the same time. We moved away from the dock on a steady course to the north, picking up speed and heeling to leeward as more sails were set and spanked hard by a stronger wind off shore than at dockside.

An accelerating tattoo of the waves on the hull and the wave patterns made by the ship told the captain that we were close to maximum speed for the ship, which he said was twelve knots—about fourteen miles per hour. We were quickly approaching the far shore. Except for hooking a large trout, it was the most exhilarating experience one could wish for. Well, almost.

After twenty minutes on this course, the captain hailed the hands to tack and come about, so that he could bring the ship to a heading of 240 degrees on the compass. We turned into the wind, the ship righted, the sails luffed and slatted and the spars creaked as the strain eased. The momentum of the ship brought us around until the wind again filled the sails on the starboard tack, and we were then comfortably heeled over and on course—southwest by west—just west of the afternoon sun.

Glass said that the tide was running at five knots so that in six hours, when the tide reverses again, we would be about thirty-five miles down the channel even if we hadn't hoisted sail. "By then, the effect of the tide on the ship will have greatly diminished", he added. The forces of nature, the wind and the tide, had been handily harnessed by the inventiveness of man.

The captain obviously was proud of his ship for its ease of handling and speed, and of his crew for their competence and timely execution of orders. He turned my way, sensible that a landsman like myself was curious about all that was going on.

"We'll probably stay on this tack for a few hours, provided the wind doesn't shift much. Then we'll tack again to exit Bristol Channel and clear Lands End. After that, we will set a course south by southwest to stay well off the coast of Spain and Africa to avoid being preyed upon by Barbary pirates, and to eventually catch the northeast trade winds."

He pulled out a chart and sketched the course with his thick thumb nail. "When we approach the Azores, about a week from now, the weather should be warm and the trades will begin to kick in and propel us on a broad reach all the way to the West Indies.

"Changes in the weather, unexpected rendezvous with ships at sea, friendly or unfriendly, the horse latitudes where one can sometimes languish for weeks without wind, all can delay our expected time of arrival. At least, the hurricane season is over and will be of no concern crossing the Atlantic to the Carribean. Absent such hindrances, we should hail Statia in three or four weeks."

"Why not sail directly across to New York instead of sailing south like this," I asked him.

"Several reasons, Jamie. Sailing straight across to New York would put us up against the eastward current of the Gulf Stream. It's like a river of warm water that flows out of the Gulf of Mexico up along the coast of America as far north as Newfoundland where it crosses to the British Isles. Fighting that current would take us longer, maybe twice as long, to get there. So it makes sense to avoid the stream and sail south and west to catch the trade winds to the islands. Even if I didn't want to sail to Statia. Bristol is about six hundred miles north of New York, so we would have to sail south anyway.

"But I have reasons to go to Statia so it really isn't out of our way. Besides, it's a warmer, more comfortable voyage heading south at the outset." He secured a spoke of the wheel with a loop of line and walked to the fife rail at the mainmast to examine a line held by a marlinspike.

I thanked the captain for his considerate, careful explanations and walked fifty feet forward along the canted narrow deck on the windward side of the deckhouses to the bowsprit. The water had become progressively clearer of discoloration from the Severn and the stains of humanity as we moved smartly down the ever-widening estuary guarded by the Cambrian Mountains of Wales on one side and the hills of Somerset on the other.

Some very large fish, eight or ten feet long that Glass said were porpoises, appeared off the bow cavorting and frisking for the lead as if to escort us by continually leaping clear of the water. I called to Olivia to come up and see this exhibition.

My lungs filled more than usual with the unsullied salt air. It had been purified by crossing three thousand miles of Atlantic Ocean. I felt invigorated and immensely encouraged by our decision to make the Grand Tour to America—and to bring Crispin with us.

From what I could read and hear, the Americans felt they could do very well without England. For over a hundred and fifty years, the colonies had prospered, mostly on their own. Now, England was actually a hindrance. Americans were beginning to realize, after all this protestation, rancor, and violence, that they should break away and form their own nation; a nation that will reconsider the basic but outmoded conventions of Europe regarding class, power and privilege.

Olivia and I were going to witness this revolutionary cataclysm that had never been enacted before. God hope that they make the change and that it will work.

Just then, Olivia came on deck and slipped her arm around my waist. Despite the cold breeze, we were enchanted with the sea, the adventure, and each other, and satisfied to stay at the bow till after a serene sun set on an accommodating sea.

# chapter 17

ON THIS BRISK day near the end of November of '75, Trevor Shaw leaned back in his captain's chair to survey his surroundings and status on this, his thirty-fifth birthday. His fireplace threw glowing warmth and the fragrance of burning oak as cold winds swept across the Hudson and along Greenwich Street. The arrangement of desk, lighting, visitor's chairs, files and shelves in his office was designed as much for impressing buyers, bankers, and customers as well as for his own convenience.

The solid mahogany testified to his success and taste. He had been assured by the auctioneer that the black walnut grandfather's clock would signify his firm's stability. The room was his lair and provided him with a cozy den where he could think out his plans so long as his clerk, Jordan, was judicious in who he allowed in. His visitors felt flattered and privileged to share this sanctum.

With pleasure he counted such as Jemmy Rivington, publisher of *Rivington's Gazette*, as one of a long list of interesting and impressive friends. So was Marinus Willet, an experienced and competitive merchant, but one who did not deny him sensible advice, just the same. Gouverneur Morris came by to chat, tell jokes, and revile Cadwallader Colden, General Gage, and the London Ministry. Gage himself traded here before he was transferred to Boston.

Trevor was grateful to have young Alex Hamilton advise him on financial matters. The man, though fifteen years younger and a student at King's College, had convincing retail experience in the West Indies and kept him from making mistakes that saved him considerable cash.

Captain John Mygatt often came in to buy supplies for his many parties in his efforts to cater to British brass.

Up until last June, it seemed every fifth person walking by his window was in the British army, which made sense since they had been garrisoned nearby. Despite their rowdy behavior at times, Trevor had been pleased with the increased number of troops in the city and their seemingly insatiable need for all sorts of items provided by his store. Now they were gone, shipped out to Boston.

Knives, fishing gear, hand tools of all kinds, bottle openers, cider, biscuits, blankets, candles, tea, nail clippers, sharpening stones, neat's foot oil, razors, metal flasks were there for the haggling. Even a few buffalo hides from upstate, which were becoming increasingly difficult to obtain, and anything else which would ease the life of a soldier on garrison duty, were piled high on the counters and shelves. These items had all sold well along with his usual inventory of household articles as varied as candies, fruits in season, and notions for the ladies.

All this could be found in the cavernous and formerly musty cellar of the stone building alleged to have been owned by Peter Stuyvesant when he was governor of New York over a hundred years before. Trevor had had the walls whitewashed to brighten up the place and highlight the sturdy and rugged beams that buttressed the ceiling and the first floor.

The whole gave off a subtle and heady fragrance that made customers feel at home and in a mood to buy.

Trevor's chair creaked in protest of his solid weight and reminded him that his success was partly attributable to dining well with commissary officers at his expense. He brushed crumbs of the morning's toast off his scarlet vest and tugged on the gold chain of his watch to see just how many minutes his next visitor was late.

It would be just as well if he didn't show up at all, he thought, since he had just heard of another building coming on the market on Greenwich Street just two blocks north of St. Paul's Chapel in the section of town where he was accumulating properties. The place probably was worth more to him than to others because of his plan to renovate the entire block. Indeed, he was sure the owner would prefer his offer of Spanish dollars to the usual paper money.

Jordan opened the door. "Colonel Lanier is here to see you, sir." he announced.

The smiling gray-haired Colonel strode in. His short stature and quick step was suggestive of a gymnast. "I was on my way to City Hall when I saw that Isaac Sears and his rebels have demolished Rivington's press. It was bound to happen."

"I'm sorry to hear that, Lamar, but I'm afraid you're right. Jemmy tried to show both sides of the argument of rebels versus the King and Parliament, and the mob couldn't tolerate that." said Trevor.

"I know you carry everything at your store but what are these? They look like a larger version of children's jacks." The Colonel held up a fist-sized object of four iron spikes radiating from a small ball in the center.

"These are caltrops, some call them crow's feet, that my trader at Fort Stanwix sent to me. It's his way of being sarcastic about the safety from the Indians they have there. Pretty medieval, eh?""

"What are they for?

"Numbers of them are scattered on the ground a distance from an encampment or fort to serve as an alarm of an attack. Notice that however way they lay, there is always a spike pointing upwards. If an intruder steps on one of those, he can't help but be discouraged in his attack or, at least, reveal his presence. The trader is implying that we need them to protect us from the rebels."

"Well, it was only about twenty-five years or so ago that the city built the palisade across the island at Chambers Street in a frenzy to keep out the French and Indians. As many predicted, it was never needed for the stated purpose." said Lamar. "The city had outgrown palisades such as the old one at Wall Street."

Lamar dropped four of the caltrops on the rug. He laughed. "These are so simple! But they look wicked. Just the same, I hope we have better defenses than that! I have to run. I wanted to let you know about Jemmy." He let himself out without further adieu.

Trevor sat down to continue his reflections.

Yes, life had been good to him despite the occasional riot made in protest to His Majesty's Ministers and their incompetent handling of the rebels in New York as well as Boston. But, were it not for the riots the city would not have had as many soldiers to boost the economy, in which he so well participated, so he had nothing to complain about. If war was to finally break out, he would profit even more.

Trevor remembered vividly when he had started out at age twelve working as a kitchen helper at the ferry tavern in Paulus Hook across the Hudson. As he washed the pots and tableware, he had scavenged meals from the leavings in the pans and slept near the hearth which enabled him to put aside most of his meager pay.

Sometimes, he was asked to wait on table when Josiah or Molly were sick or, for what-ever reason, could not show for work. Mr. Bellona insisted that he have on hand clean trousers and a decent waistcoat for waiting on table so as to not offend the local businessmen and travelers taking the ferry to or from New York.

His practice had been to hold himself in readiness near the table with the most astute-sounding conversation, not only to deserve a generous tip for being attentive, but to overhear any opportunities to invest his small but ever-increasing hoard.

His first investment was a hunch on a horse in the Hempstead race on the island; he tripled his money. Within six months, he learned that hearsay, luck, and un-researched investments could give him a false sense of confidence which, more often than not, lead to losses exceeding his gains. Pride *does* go before a fall, he mused.

Thereafter, he sorted out what he had heard and tried to verify the likelihood of success balanced against the risk. He avoided horse races and pie-in-the-sky deals, and sought out additional information concerning each prospective investment, including what political or economic event could help or hamper its success.

After six years he had amassed enough funds to enable him to leave Bellona. The benign tavern owner had begged him to stay with promises of promotion, even to a share of the business, but Trevor was enthusiastic about his success so far, and began full-time to sell wares door-to-door by catering to needs that other merchants had overlooked.

Acquiring a coterie of satisfied customers had been his goal coupled with accumulating sufficient capital for a down payment on this building to house his wares and establish a presence in the city. He had furnished his first office with a squat upended log for a chair and boxes for the counters and his desk.

Ten years ago, Trevor had read about the objections to the imposition of a stamp tax. It was one of the first of a series of foolish attempts to generate revenue for the mother country to help pay for the French and Indian War. The end of the war caused the withdrawal of British troops, and businesses suffered; many good people became unemployed. It was not an easy time for Trevor, only a few years in the business on his own. Nor was it timely for Parliament, rarely in touch with the colonial populace, to impose a tax on Americans.

Many made a fuss about not merely the tax itself, but the precedent it would establish if Parliament could impose taxes, however small, on the colonies. Only provincial assemblies could do that. Objections to the stamp tax were voiced in colonial assemblies in Boston, New York, and Williamsburg as well as by agitators such as Sam Adams on the streets and James Otis in the courts of Boston, and Isaac Sears and Alexander McDougall in New York. Partisan newspapers added their two-cents to the fray which quickly led to riots and bodily threats, and worse, to cronies appointed to collect the tax.

Trevor remembered reading about mobs burning effigies of proposed officials (even governor Hutchinson of Massachuses, who had appointed his two sons as tax collectors), and trashed their homes and equipage. Here in New York, Lieutenant Governor Cadwallader Colvin's elaborate carriage and his sleigh were hauled out and burned as well as his effigy. Does a protest have to be so ruinous to officials? Trevor pondered.

Trevor didn't understand what the complaint was all about because the mother country had had a stamp tax for near eighty years and no one in England had complained about it—not that he knew of. Even Doctor Franklin did not make any objection to this method of raising revenue, at first. Franklin had even recommended a friend to be appointed a tax collector until a threatening crowd helped him decide that the tax was ill-conceived.

Besides, Trevor had heard that an average Briton pays overall taxes of twenty-six shillings for every shilling paid by a Bostonian and even less for a New Yorker. And it is said that Britons do not earn as much as Americans do.

Pressure had cleverly been put on the English merchants by the rebel leaders by enlisting an agreement among merchants to refuse to import English goods. The cry went out from mother country merchants that business would suffer and people would lose their jobs; the rebels knew such complaints would follow as planned. The stamp tax was repealed. In Trevor's view, that showed an intelligent and responsive Parliament.

But then, two years later, members of Parliament tried to impose taxes on glass, lead, paint, paper, and tea, by passing the Townshend Acts, and again accused us Americans of not paying our share of the cost of the last war. This was doubly resented, with good reason, Trevor thought. The colonies bordering the French and Indian menace financed militia to fight along with the regulars in defending the frontier and payed for horses, wagons, and arms and supplies to provision them. And those people on the frontier never knew when they were going to be attacked, their house and barns burned down, and their families maimed, killed, or captured.

Trevor thought that Parliament showed an unusual degree of common sense by backing down in the face of lost business and jobs in an already depressed economy. Again, the English system allowed for the curbing of excess and foolish legislation. He was proud to be a subject of the British Empire. Besides, American merchants, including Trevor, lost money by agreeing to not import and sell English goods. Even certain fashionable ladies in New York were wearing homespun to express their outrage. Princeton students put aside their Saville Row attire in favor of homespun to assert their patriotic stance at graduation exercises.

But then Parliament insisted that it had the right to tax Americans "in all cases whatsoever" by retaining the tax on tea. Trevor hadn't liked this arrogant assertion nor did he favor the government's later giving the financially embarrassed East India Company a monopoly on tea, effectively canceling the right of merchants such as himself to sell tea. He understood the resentment of the Sons of Liberty, masquerading as Mohawks when they dumped the tea in Boston Harbor. And local chapters of Sons followed suit by preventing its sale in New York, Philadelphia, and Charleston by intimidating the favored agents. But dammit! They were trashing somebody's property! Even if it did belong to the all-powerful East India Company.

Trevor was now prospering as a merchant himself and enjoying friendships with other businessmen, some of them influential and well-to-do, as well as army officers on both sides from whom favors could be expected if he played his hand right. The following spring, news came from Britain of the series of acts passed by an infuriated Parliament bent on punishing the Bostonians, collectively called the Coercive Acts.

He'd never forget the Port of Boston being closed down tight to starve the port of supplies and trade as revenge for the dumping of the tea and to teach the Bay Province that England was boss. Ferries couldn't even cross the bay! General Gage was transferred from New York to Boston to take over as royal governor in place of Thomas Hutchinson, who had been recalled to England. As directed, Gage imposed military government to replace provincial legislatures, and had the sole right to appoint sheriffs and determine if colonists would be permitted to assemble. London sent four additional regiments to Boston and, throwing salt in the wound, many of the troops were arbitrarily quartered in the homes of private families.

In the face of expected reprisals, New York's own Sons of Liberty sequestered tea and kept it off the market three months later. Trevor chuckled a little at their impudence.

When General Gage sent a detachment of troops out to Lexington and Concord to commandeer hidden arms and take into custody noted smuggler John Hancock and rabble-rouser Sam Adams, the operation blew up in Gage's face. The Yankees removed the arms to new hiding places, spirited Adams and Hancock out of harm's way, and fought the regulars to a humiliating impasse. Much blood was spilled, mostly by the British troops. George III got a black eye from this. Now, everyone had to fish or cut bait as to what their sympathies were or the worst would be surmised and acted upon by neighbors.

Though Trevor had prospered from all the troops sent here due to the agitation, he did not like the severe and unfair actions of the ministry in response to the protests. The dilemma annoyed his conscience. He still had not decided with whom to side.

He cut short his reverie and prepared to leave by summoning Jordan.

"I'm going over to the Royal Gazette, Roland. I'll be back in an hour or two. I'm expecting a visit from Arthur Claveraque around eleven thirty. Serve him some coffee, make him comfortable, and ask him to please wait. Thanks."

As he stepped from his office and into his emporium, Trevor stopped as he always did, to pet black long-haired Marty Mittens. She was all feline but her appearance was much like that of a small border collie. Marty had presided over the store from this pile of blankets since she ceased the tough life working the back alleys for mice and selected Trevor's store as her new home. Were it not for her four white paws, and her white whiskered face, her reposed body could easily be mistaken for a jumbled blanket.

An unaccountable white patch of fur to the left of her nose gave the appearance that she had confused vision, but at night she focused with deadly accuracy on her squealing quarries and paid her way by keeping the mice and rats down.

Marty also had the ability to hear far-distant thunder that was inaudible to Trevor, Jordan, and the sales clerks. She quailed and sought haven in the depths of the cellar among the bales of hides. Nothing could entice her to return until she was satisfied that all danger had passed.

At Trevor's hesitation, Marty stood up, stretched full length, and thrust her head into Trevor's outstretched palm, expecting repeated caresses in compensation for interrupting her morning nap. She was comforted by his petting as was Trevor to feel her silky fur.

Trevor walked up Greenwich street to survey his next property purchase. It was near the Holy Ground, a local euphemism for the red light district, which was within the tract owned by Trinity Church. Students from Kings College vied with sailors from South Street and troops from the nearby barracks for the risky adventures that could be had there. He shuddered at the thought of satisfying one's romantic hunger under such circumstances, and hastened his pace.

Ah. Here it was. The building's location was near the only side of the town that could be expanded. The southern tip of Manhattan was solidly built up with Fort George, fine homes, shipping firms, rope walks, naval suppliers, small shops, taverns and coffee houses. Future development had no choice but to move north. Future families would likely cluster around St Paul's Chapel for not only religious but secular ceremonies such as the graduation exercises for King's College held there since the chapel's completion about ten years ago. It was bound to be the center of social activities what with prominent families such as the DeLanceys, the Bayards, the Livingstons, and the Lispenards living in the vicinity.

It had taken New York city one hundred and fifty years to cover the lower mile of Manhattan Island, from the fort to Chambers Street. He was sure it would take far less than that to develop the next mile north; he was determined to be one of the developers to do just that.

Several of his friends complained of their personal and professional accommodations elsewhere. Trevor planned on wooing them to move into his building by custom-fashioning the rooms to their satisfaction at reasonable rates. His immediate plans were to modify the old apartments and stores anyway, it might as well be to attract preferential patrons right at the start.

Every time he looked at the old building, a new idea came to mind. He would plant fast-growing honey locust trees on the south side to throw shade on the ground floor of that side: a minimum expense to keep the place cool and look trendy—and draw tenants.

He turned right to walk the slight incline to Broadway and felt relieved that the sharp wind was now behind him. At the corner of Broadway, if he looked north, there was still some farm land amidst the estates of the well-to-do. As the city grew and moved farther north they would gladly sell at a profit and re-establish the center of the social and business activity. Trevor was convinced that this inevitable progression was to make his fortune if he kept attuned to business and social trends and played his cards right.

One of the De Lancey's old residences was now the Province Tavern. Indeed, James De Lancy was born in the building which has evolved into the Queen's Head Tavern on Pearl Street. Certainly, these moves foretell the pattern of continued progress, Trevor thought.

Trevor laughed to himself. The same day that Washington was celebrated by the city, Governor Tryon's ship landed on his return from England. City officials had a dilemma but successfully organized two welcoming ceremonies without conflict or incident, he thought. Washington was honored and celebrated in the morning and Governor Tryon was given the same welcoming parade in the evening, attended by mostly the same crowd as hailed the general. It could have been just another pretext for the Sons of Liberty to raise hell.

Across Broadway, the Fields, with the Collect Pond nearby, made a pleasant expanse to relax as did the graveyards at Trinity Church and St Pauls.. Trevor hoped that a future syndicate would not convince the royal governor to develop it by cutting the gov in on the deal, he mused.

Trevor always enjoyed walking down Broadway to Bowling Green. For one thing, the road was usually clear of hogs and chickens. It was also paved with flagstones so that, whatever the season, there was a minimum of dust or mud. For him, it was the heart of New York. He could count on unexpectedly meeting a friend or being introduced to someone interesting in this cosmopolitan complex. Indeed, it's how he had met Gouverneur Morris last summer, through John Morin Scott, when General Washington, rode down Broadway flanked by Generals Schuyler and Charles Lee. It was quite a parade consisting of liveried aides and servants but a beautifully uniformed company of Pennsylvania Horse together with the local militia which fell out to honor the "Hero of the Monongahela" on his way to Boston to take command of the Continental Army.

Washington sat his horse as if he and the horse were one. Despite many mounted British regulars he had seen in the city over the years, Trevor had never seen a more magnificent display of horsemanship. He surmised that Washington must have grown up with a great deal of ambition and self esteem to still be able to hold himself so erect with such a natural, dignified demeanor. His old red and blue uniform from the French wars, despite looking a little tight, only enhanced this image. It's encouraging to know that we have a commander who, at least, looks like a commander, Trevor thought.

The morning parade had proceeded no more than several hundred yards from the ferry landing at Canal Street to the elegant Lispenard mansion where a local committeeman handed the new general an express from the Massachusetts Provincial Congress. The dispatch was addressed to John Hancock, but Washington was urged to open it since it was assumed to be a factual account of the fighting on Charlestown Neck which would verify unconfirmed bits of information passing through the grape vine.

It was the first official account of the Battle of Bunker Hill. Although the patriots lost the field, they considered it a victory because of the horrific British casualties compared to their own. The yahoos thought that patriotism alone was sufficient for farmers, artisans, and farmers to overcome a trained professional army. 'God', thought Trevor, 'One half-assed victory and reason flies out the window.'

Trevor had read that, ever since Lexington and Concord, Cambridge had been the lodestone that drew recruits from all New England and several other states to dislodge the British from their hold on Boston.

Despite the cold, people were active and about this day. The tea-water wagon had attracted numerous customers with kegs and large pails to resupply their drinking water, the old wells being unsafe what with all kinds of waste draining underground.

Down the street, the usual crowd was drawn by the sweet warm fragrance wafting from the push cart to purchase roasted chestnuts made more welcome by the cold day. As was his habit, Trevor bought a bag and told Charlie—never knew his last name—to "keep the change."

A grizzled old man, trudging with a portable grindstone, followed the chestnut cart to cage what business he could from Charlie's crowd. Trevor handed him his penknife. The old man rapidly treadled the spinning stone as he bent over, a perpetual drop at the end of his nose. He carefully applied the blade at the desired angle by slightly deflecting the sparks up or down.

Trevor threw a scattering of corn kernels to the pigeons. The knife was handed back to him after the final step of being honed smooth on an ancient pad of thick leather. He pricked the bulge of his thumb to test the edge, and drew blood. "Worth 'tupence," he said, paid the old man, and resumed his stroll.

He was hailed at Maiden Lane by his old drinking pal, Bill Farrell.

"Trevor. How good to see you. Let's go over to The Indian Queen and see what you're doing these days."

Trevor hesitated, he had spent enough time ambling on his way to Rivington's. But, he always learned something from Bill, and was truly glad to see him for the sheer enjoyment of the Irishman's conversation and good humor.

"I see you're managing to keep busy, Bill. Sure, I'll join you for a few minutes." Trevor swung in step to catch up with him. They entered the "Queen".

When they ordered coffee, Trevor realized what a boon the ruckus over tea must have meant to the coffeehouses. No one of sound mind would still insist on tea in this political climate, even if any were available.

Trevor asked, "And how is the book-selling business, Bill? Any new books of interest?"

"Several! *Wealth of Nations* by Adam Smith just came in on the last ship. Another you might find interesting is by that old curmudgeon, member of the literati, and pensioner of King George, Samuel Johnson. *A Journey to the Western Islands of Scotland*, his newest. It's about his travels in the Hebrides two years ago with his friend and biographer, James Boswell. Its main value has been to perk up sales of his dictionary that he came out with twenty years ago."

"What is a dictionary?" Trevor asked.

"It's two hefty intimidating volumes in which you can look up a word not only for its meaning and spelling, but even its genesis and usage. It costs a pretty penny, too. But Johnson uses quotes from Shakespeare, Swift, and Defoe to explain the words and their various usages so one gets a smattering of literature in the bargain. One would need it to look up the meaning of most of the words he uses in his travel book. But in the last month I've sold sixteen of them."

"You mean the new book?"

"No, the travel book hasn't sold well. I mean the dictionary. What's new with you?"

"I find myself trying to decide what side to be on. I can see why people want to remain loyal to the crown. And yet the ministry seems to want to provoke us in every conceivable way. Each successive office holder is bellicose and wants to insist on Parliament's mastery over us. Their arrogance and meanness gets my dander up as does their mercantile policy.

"But, if we are to go to war, I don't see how the colonists could possibly hold their own. We have no money to pay for it and no army or navy to fight it save what Washington has in Massachusetts. The regulars would have to make a lot of stupid moves for us to win."

"You might have the answer right there, Trevor."

"What do you mean, 'have the answer'?"

"Well, consider some of the stupid moves the ministry and the army made. Thirty years ago they soured a lot of New Englanders when they gave back Louisbourg to the French. New Englanders paid a lot to support that campaign. And a thousand men died to take that fortress the experts thought was impregnable. Then the government negotiated it back to the frogs a few years later by treaty. New Englanders began to think that London was playing stupid games by squandering their hard-earned money and being awfully casual with the lives of their men."

"That's true. But, you're going back a long ways. Be more current." Trevor insisted.

"All right. Ten years later, General Braddock could have been smarter fighting the French and Indians, but he was too ignorant of colonial conditions and too sure of himself to pay any attention to our people about how to fight Indians. He was simply an incompetent crony of the Duke of Cumberland. Like many regular army officers, Braddock was arrogant, and browbeat the colonial assemblies demanding that the colonists put up the money to support his regiments.

"He acted so superior. I'm told that he was so brusque to our Indian scouts that they abandoned the expedition early on leaving Braddock with no scouts to detect the ambush. Braddock antagonized so many that he had to rely on Franklin's persuasion to rent teams and wagons to carry his baggage and provisions and haul his field pieces. So he went all that distance to take Fort Duquesne only to be waylaid and lose many of his troops and his own life..

"Another example was General Abercromby and the fiasco of his attempt to take Fort Carillon two years later. He had sixteen thousand troops, the largest ever mustered in North America, and eighteen siege guns. Forced his men to charge, over and over again, into a mess of tree trunks and sharpened branches where they got hung up and were mercilessly shot to pieces.

"This ran up over two thousand casualties in the fight against three thousand Frenchmen. Abercromby himself stayed back from the fighting, and didn't even order into action the artillery he had brought all the way from Albany. He could have easily blasted down a wall of the fort so they could take the place. It would have saved the lives of many men. Another Cumberland crony. If that's the kind of generals we have to fight, we couldn't be any luckier." Bill paused to get his breath but was so worked up about the subject, he couldn't stop.

"Too bad Lord Viscount Howe was shot in one of the first skirmishes and didn't survive long enough so that common sense, and the guns, could have been brought to bear. It was the worst military disaster in more than a decade, and that's going some. They should have shot Abercromby for stupidity. But the Brits seem to award medals for that! We put too much credit in the competence of the regulars, Trevor."

"That was still twenty years ago. Not all their generals are stupid." Trevor insisted.

Bill had an answer for that. "Well, look at General Howe in Boston. He's got himself boxed in on that peninsula so that he's short on rations for his men, and the rebels ships are capturing his supply boats. All Washington has to do is fortify the heights surrounding Boston and the harbor, and Howe has had it. How smart is that?"

"Well, that was largely Gage's fault when his men attack Lexington and Concord. But the British beat the French and Indians and won Canada. They can't be too bad." Trevor said meekly.

"I'm just saying that we shouldn't conclude that the British can win against us, despite their size and reputation." Bill had an open mind, thought Trevor. Knew his history, too.

"Well," said Trevor, "I've adopted an idea proposed by one of the ministry."

"What's that."

"I'm going to have a new food item. It seems that the Earl of Sandwich is determined to gamble so incessantly, all night till dawn, that he refuses to leave the gaming table, even to eat. So he ordered a slice of meat, fish, or cheese to be put between two slices of bread and served to him at the gaming table. Try it, Bill. It's delicious and particularly convenient to have on hand on a trip or when hunting or fishing."

Trevor then called out, "Waiter! Please bring me a slice of ham, with mustard, inserted between two slices of rye bread." Then to Bill, "It's called a sandwich after the old bastard. They do some things right—these Englishmen."

Bill noted the curious story, but continued. "Lord North was sensible when he said the Townshend Acts were preposterous. After Townshend died and North succeeded him as Chancellor of the Exchequer, he pointed out that the revenue from taxing glass, paint, tea and whatever else would amount to no more than about one tenth of the cost of collecting the tax. He rightly thought that the act stirred up the American 'bees without getting the honey', as he expressed it. So Parliament was persuaded to repeal the act."

Trevor jumped on this statement. "It was our non-importation policy that got Parliament to repeal that. I know. I had to give up handling some well-selling English woolens and silver service because of that. All the merchants did—we had to or be accused of being unpatriotic—and it cost us quite a bit of badly needed revenue. But our refusal to import hurt the manufacturers, the merchants, and the working man over there and they all pressured Parliament. It's the old 'politics of the pocketbook', Bill, that carried the day."

"Yes, and a lot of dunces think it was King George who repealed it. Just like they did with the stamp tax. You remember the local assembly voted a thousand pounds to have that statue of the King on his horse erected at Bowling Green as a memorial to express 'its deep sense of the eminent and singular benefits received from him.' That's the essence of the inscription—as if he is the one that repealed the tax. The public doesn't even know who is hurting them. It's good old George, that's who!" Bill declared.

"Trevor, all these stupid and greedy power plays are just what England and the Whigs did to Ireland. They started out just this way. The folks wouldn't stand for it, fought and lost, and the English then laid it on even worse. I think that's why so many of the American rich are against the ministry. They don't want to lose their status, their good way of life, their ability to control what's going to happen to them and their children and, yes, to the rest of us, too.

Trevor responded, "The De Lancey's are noted Tories and so are so many other well-to-do. They must have their reasons!"

"Well, I'm against the king, the ministry, and Parliament because of what they did to Ireland and what they're doing to Boston and to us. They are a bunch of mean-spirited bastards. A country like Ireland, that used to be the equal of England and Wales in industry, farming, the arts and literature, statesmanship, and just being decent, caring folk. It's all changed. That's why I came over here fifteen years ago.

"Do you know, Trevor, that Irish Catholics can't own any land, can't hold leases for more than thirty-one years, and they can't make a profit on their crops greater than a third of their rent. The English own all the land. When my father died, none of us Catholic children could inherit because my brother, Jerome, was Protestant. (He was always contrary). So all the estate had to go to him. By English law!

"Your not supposed to teach your children, nor can you send them out of the country to be educated. You can't even own a horse, or a fire arm worth more than five pounds! They have hammered us all into being peasants. By passing laws enriching themselves." And we're supposed to tithe to the Anglican Church!

Trevor winced. "I knew the Irish were poor but I didn't know why. I suppose it could happen here."

"The language used in the Declaratory Act after they repealed the Townshend Acts is the same that was used to intimidate the Irish back in 1719. Just as with Ireland, they reserved the right to tax Americans *in all cases whatsoever*! In other words, they are announcing that they can be as harsh with Americans as they treated the Irish." Bill narrowed his eyes and hunched his shoulders. "If they continue to get away with these practices and add additional burdens and insults, there's no question that impoverishment, as in Ireland, could happen here, too."

Both men then relaxed and pondered what each had said. After a few minutes, Bill poured out more of his troubling deliberations. "This country should not be forced by a long out-dated law to send our raw materials to England so that only they can process them and send the manufactured goods back to us at much higher prices. Such a practice defies common sense. "I've heard that some plantation owners have found that they can manufacture items they and their neighbors need far more cheaply than it costs to send to England for them. If America developed a group of manufacturers, all vying for the public acceptance of their goods, such competition would lower the price every one has to pay, probably improve the product, too."

"Trevor, no one should be locked in to selling his crop to an agent in England, receive only credit, never cash, and so have to buy goods from him only. He's got you both ways. Any excess money or credit balance should stay here rather than end up in England, and payment would be in hard money. As it is now, your agent has a monopoly on your purchasing options.

"You can see many places in the marketing chain where savings would result and the prices would be reduced considerably. This would widen the market and create further price reduction. We've just got to get England off our back."

"It all makes sense, Bill. But, you know, I think there's more to all this tension and rioting than just what we've been talking about. Ten years ago, I overheard some young bucks griping about how the red-coats were taking their girl friends out.

"They were sore as hell and started picking fights with off-duty soldiers because of it. Some of them had lost out on jobs, too, because the soldiers had time to kill when the French war was over and, on their off-time, took the jobs that these fellows used to have. Riots were started over things like this. I'll bet that the Golden Hill riots had some of this rivalry behind it."

"The same thing happened in Boston a couple of years ago. The redcoats were taking jobs from the locals in a rope walk and it rankled those affected as well as some of the men down by the wharves who were out of work. The soldiers were probably taking out their girl friends, too. "Several regiments of troops had been brought down from Halifax to reduce the tension, but, of course, their very presence increased it. A small group of malcontents began to razz a guard at the Customs House but, being a good soldier, the poor fellow did not allow it to faze him.. This goaded them even more. They got a local gang of brawlers to join in the harassment the next day. They started to throw sticks and snow balls, some with stones packed in them, and even though the soldiers tolerated this abuse for a while, things soon got to be kind of nasty." Trevor warmed to telling the story and spoke faster as the story progressed..

"More redcoats were posted outside the Customs House and the heckling and pelting increased to the point that a gun fired, whether a soldier's or a brawler's, no one knows. Then the soldiers fired and five of the rowdy's fell dead, and a few others were wounded. Sam Adams drummed it up as the 'Boston Massacre' and tried to make heros out of the victims. It was mostly just a street fight built up to have political consequences. Adams exploited it as propaganda.

"You remember, his cousin, John Adams, and his partner took the redcoat's case but delayed their defense until fall so everyone, especially those selected for the jury, would have a chance to cool down. Adams defended the soldiers successfully except for one who was only slapped on the wrist. Made a name for John Adams, it did, because it was such an unpopular case. It took courage and determination to see that the mob didn't determine court cases. But no other lawyers would take it on."

"Well, my point is, at the time, I didn't want to find us in a war all because some toughs' girlfriends were being taken over by the redcoat. I know, there's a lot more to these protests than that, but I think we should cool off some. Let cooler heads decide what to do."

"If the problem was just local friction, Trevor, I would agree with you. But these laws and taxes which provoke us so much are a long-continued official policy from London and all part and parcel to exploit our economy and reduce our ability to fight back. We have to do something about it before we lose any remaining clout, and it's too late to do anything about it—as happened in Ireland."

Bill looked at the clock on the wall. "Trevor, I've got to get back to the store. I see some one walking around in there unattended. *Non carborundum illegitami*—don't let the bastards grind you down. See you soon."

# chapter 18

TREVOR WAS SURPRISED that the time was getting ahead of him. He didn't really want to miss seeing Claveraque or cause him inconvenience. He paid for the two coffees and departed with a quickened pace that took him back to his office in five minutes.

He entered his store, hastened past Jordan's desk and Marty Mittens, and held out his hand to his old friend who was deeply absorbed in reading a magazine.

"Arthur! It's good to see you. I apologize for being late and hope that I have not caused any serious delay. How have you and Arabella been?"

Arthur put down the magazine, resolving to come back after lunch to finish the article. He stood to his full height, towering over Trevor by six inches as if to assert his right to punctuality.

"We've been fine. Had a good crop and the cider this year is especially ample and high quality. I'll arrange for a hogshead to be shipped to you as soon as I get back."

"Send me some of that Calvados, too. Though we could probably stop the riots if I didn't sell any. Come into my office and we'll talk a bit before having lunch." Trevor offered.

"Trevor, you've heard me talk about my brother in Herefordshire. One of his sons is probably coming here to take a tour of the colonies. The oldest son is a redcoat and was badly wounded at Bunker Hill. The poor man's lower leg was amputated and he now has a wooden leg and is back home with his parents."

"I'm sorry to hear that," said Trevor.

"Yes, it's a shame but I'm told he is walking and able to get around on the farm. My brother has always been curious as to what's going on, not only in England, but over here, and goes to great pains to educate himself. His wife is the same way. The son who is coming here, the second son, Jamie, is a chip off the old block, and I want to make his tour as interesting for him as possible. That's why I'm here this morning."

"You want me, an uneducated store keeper, to suggest what he ought to see?"

"You old fox, you know more than many men I know who have had a formal education. I would appreciate any suggestions you have. You have so many contacts that I wonder if you would write letters of introduction to ease Jamie's way to those interesting people and places he should visit. Otherwise he may not see what he ought to and with the right perspective. Know what I mean?"

"How extensive is his trip going to be? What does he want to see?"

"He's going to be here, if indeed he comes at all—the violence may scare him off—for about a year. He knows the orchard business and has always fashioned the farm's tools and hardware at his forge. Like his father, he reads a lot and loves to fly fish for trout and salmon.

"Through his father, who opposes almost everything King George and Parliament have done, he has learned something about the colonies and our concerns. George, his father, says that Jamie sees the overall picture, not just the petty jealousies and rivalry, and wants to see how the coming military and political events will play out, first hand. Does that give you a better idea as to who and what he should see?"

"A number of people immediately come to mind, Arthur. Most of 'em are here in New York. I know some influential people in Albany, Philadelphia and I even know Governor Franklin of New Jersey. In these times, I don't know whether he is in Burlington or Perth Amboy. Your nephew may want to go to Fort Stanwix and German Flats and Boston. Another friend has a large tract in the Kittatinny mountains of northern New Jersey with a trout stream he's always bragging about. How's that for starters?"

"That's the idea. I think they ought to see the Jersey beaches, too, in season, of course, but I can take him there. And I'll bring him to New

York now that the redcoats are mostly in Boston. You could introduce him to those you think best.

"Maybe he will want to see Charleston, but that's another sailing excursion and, by the time he gets here, he might not want to be at sea again for some time. It starts to get hot in Charleston in May and he may not arrive here until then. A good time to see the Catskills, maybe even the Adirondacks, would be sometime in July or August when the black fly and midge season is ov..."

Trevor cut him short. "Let's go to lunch. How about the Queen's Head Tavern?"

"Sounds good to me. I haven't been there in a long time. You can tell me what's new. Pressing cider in the country doesn't keep me well informed."

Arthur had prepared for the damp cold and the severe winds he knew would be whipping across city streets by wearing his shaggy buffalo-robe coat and a racoon hat. This attire branded him as an outsider from the boondocks, but he would rather be comfortable despite the stares.

"There seems to be fewer people on the streets. Has there been something going around?" Arthur was always concerned about sickness where many people gathered. "I'll tell you about it when we sit down." said Trevor as he opened the door to the warmth of the tavern. As they took their seats, Arthur looked up and exclaimed. "What happened to the roof? It looks like a cannonball must have hit it."

"That's exactly what happened, Arthur. Last summer, the patriots decided to fortify the Hudson River Highlands near West Point to prevent the British navy from passing up river and making mischief. Isaac Sears, one of the more aggressive Sons of Liberty, suggested that the twenty-one guns in front of Fort George were idle and could fill the bill. His resolution was approved by the Provincial Congress and so these heavy cannon were to be moved for the purpose.

"These were naval guns; their gun carriages have small wheels which allows them to roll from the recoil on a ship's deck, but they were not designed for overland travel. Just the same, one night last August, many of the militia attempted to haul them from the ramparts of the fort up Broadway. They weren't having much luck because of the small wheels which dug in, and they had to stop several times in their struggle to move these monsters.

"Word about plans to remove the cannon had reached Governor Tryon who left standing orders for Captain Vandeput, commander of HMS *Asia*, to take a boat of sailors to stop them if they tried anything..."

A waiter came over to wait on them. Trevor was annoyed at this interruption of his story, waved him off, and continued.

"Well, anyway, taking a gunboat, Vandeput caught up with them, pulled close to shore and fired some shots at the militia. They shot back and a sailor was killed and others wounded, so Vandeput took his boat out of range. Then he went back aboard the *Asia*, which—it was midnight by then—lobbed a few shots ashore from the East River, near the foot of Wall Street. No one was hit but many people panicked and fled their homes, some with their valuables, headed toward the ferries to Jersey and Brooklyn."

Arthur hated to interrupt but he was getting hungry. "Let's order, Trevor," he demanded. Trevor nodded, but continued.

" As I say, no more were hurt and soon all quieted down. About three in the morning, the *Asia* fired a full broadside—that's thirty-two guns at once—which some said felt like an earth-quake and scared the city out of its wits. For five days people were fleeing the city. An eighteen pound cannonball hit the roof here at Fraunces' place and some damage was done to Roger Morris' roof as well as to other houses near the battery."

Held spellbound by this revelation, Arthur exclaimed, "So, the violence is getting close to home? Each incident leads us inevitably towards war with the mother country."

"Well, yes and no. Quite a few of the young men signed up and left town with General Schuyler and Montgomery to try to persuade the Canadians, by diplomacy or military means, to become our fourteenth state. Schuyler started his march to Ticonderoga just about the time the *Asia* bombardment occurred. It was reported that, ten days later, he and his men invested the Fort at St. Johns. Only a week after that, Schuyler took sick and was taken to the rear and General Montgomery assumed command.

"Just the other day, we heard that the siege ended successfully, after fifty-five days, with six hundred British and Canadian troops taken prisoner. That's good, and, bad news, Arthur. Good, because we are closer to finishing the business, and bad, because the delay of almost two months means the campaign for Quebec will extend deep into winter. You know how cold and snowy their winters are.

"By the way, don't look now but the lady at the table by the window is Judge Livingston's daughter and the wife of General Montgomery.

Black Sam Fraunces came out from the kitchen and waited on them personally. "Glad to see you here on this blustery day, Mr. Shaw. What can I get you and your friend?"

"Sam, I would like some onion soup and then, some toast only. I'm really not hungry. I had a sandwich with a friend only an hour or so ago."

"What's a sandwich, Mr. Shaw?" asked Sam. Trevor repeated the story he had told Bill Farrell.

"That sounds like a great idea. I'll tell the chef about it and we'll put sandwiches on the menu. Thanks for the idea, Mr. Shaw. Your lunch is on me, today."

Sam turned to Arthur for his order. But Trevor interrupted, "Sam, I'd like you to meet a long-time friend and supplier of mine, Arthur Claveraque, of Vaux Hall in Jersey. He makes a tart cider you might like to carry. Sam Fraunces is the owner of this establishment, Arthur. I remember when he bought it about a dozen years ago. Everybody calls Black Sam, Sam."

Sam nodded with a smile in greeting.

"Nice to meet you, Sam." Arthur smiled back. "I'll try one of those sandwiches with a slice of ham and some onion soup."

"As the first recipient of a sandwich from the Queen's Head, Mr. Claveraque, you are entitled to have your lunch on the house, too, sir." Sam turned and went to the kitchen, happy to have a new and unique item to add to the menu.

"Well, thank you kindly, Sam." Arthur called to the departing Sam, and picked up the conversation where they were interrupted. "The army's gotten off to a good start then. What else?"

"Then, that damn fool, Ethan Allen, decides, with no coordination with any higher command, to try to take Montreal with less than three hundred men. Can you believe it? Only three hundred men! But it became worse than that. Talk about vainglory!

"He and another officer had agreed to take their positions, and then rush the city. But when the other captain failed to get into place in time, Allen became impatient and attacked without him. He and forty men were promptly captured. Kind of ruined his reputation less than four months after becoming a hero at Ticonderoga. The Brits sent him in chains to England to be tried for treason. That's the last I've heard."

"Trevor, all that happened way north of New York. What happened here?"

"Well, I meant to say that after the naval bombardment, people in the city have become jittery of what may happen. Many fled to Long Island or Jersey. Shortly after the *Asia* affair, another British warship bombarded Stonington, Connecticut, in retribution because the residents had repulsed a foraging expedition. Homes were damaged and a few people were injured, but they used only cold shot so, at least, there was no fire.

"Bristol was also bombarded for well over an hour only a few days later. The captain had demanded two hundred sheep and thirty cattle for God's sake! The townsmen resisted, which caused the firing, but the captain finally settled for forty sheep.

"Hearing continually about all this doesn't make people in New York feel any more comfortable. We're an island. The navy can send broadsides at us from three sides and we can't do much about it.

Arthur spoke up. "Those guns from the fort would have helped, wouldn't they?"

"Well the island would have to have batteries of guns like that every mile of shoreline, and even then, the British would easily be able to match us, naval broadside to battery fire."

"There must have been orders out to intimidate coastal towns this fall because Falmouth was bombarded and burned by two Royal Navy ships. At least the Brits warned the residents of the shelling so no one was hurt. I've heard it was an attempt to stop privateering on the high seas. If that's true, they must have been intent on ruining the boatyards there. What a mean-spirited thing to do—to completely burn a town just before the onset of winter."

"You've probably heard that Governor Tryon has moved aboard a navy frigate in the harbor. He's on the *Duchess of Gordon* and is conducting business as if he was on shore. That was in late October. Another royal governor, Dunmore of Virginia, has fled from Williamsburg to Newport. He's another hero whose star has fallen. He started a war against the Shawnees and Delawares and beat them a year ago at Point Pleasant, on the Ohio. But it looks like royal authority is being subdued. And lines are being drawn, Arthur."

"Oh! I meant to tell you the outcome of the *Asia* affair." Trevor interrupted himself. "When Tryon came back from Long Island where he had been overnight visiting friends, he arranged a meeting with members of the Provincial Congress and the New York City Committee. They weren't supposed to have any authority according to the governor's own reckoning. I give Tryon credit for not making a big issue out of it, and for cooling down both sides. That's *ad hoc* diplomacy for you!

"Tryon permitted the guns to remain where the patriots had taken them on the Common, provided no further attempt would be made to move them. In return, our people allowed the navy ships, including the *Asia* and the *Kingfisher,* to continue to buy fresh provisions from city suppliers—things like bread, butter, eggs, meat, cheeses, ale, rum, and beer—to be paid for on the spot. New York needs the specie to strengthen its economy."

Arthur brightened. "You mean that common sense crept back, along with money concerns, to bring the two parties together? Too bad that the King and Parliament don't act as reasonably as the governor. A lot of grief could have been avoided in other situations."

"Yes. But I think too many insults, recriminations and acts of violence have taken us past that. We're past the point of no return. Some people are thinking that complete separation from the mother country is the only sensible choice now. And I'm beginning to agree. Talking with you and others has helped clear the air for me, finally. I've lost faith in the sincerity and honesty of the King and his ministers, as well as the toadies in Parliament. We should seek independence and that means war!" Trevor had, after months of painful inner struggle, made up his mind. 'What a relief', he thought.

Trevor remembered he hadn't answered Arthur's main question. "I'm sorry. I got off on this political talk. You want introductions to interesting people for your nephew to see America. Another man I know could show you the Hudson and the Mohawk valleys. He's from around here but he's gone with Montgomery to take Montreal. I'm talking about Marinus Willett, a merchant, a fine cabinet maker, and an active Liberty Boy in town..

"Not as voluble as Isaac Sears or Alex McDougall, but just as noteworthy. Now thirty-five years old, he was a Lieutenant with Oliver DeLancey's regiment under Abercromby at that disastrous attempt on Ticonderoga and with Bradstreet on that great raid on Fort Frontenac.

"Last summer, Major Hamilton's Royal Irish Regiment, much hated by the Liberty Boys, was being transferred to Boston. Willett and a half-dozen Sons heard that they were taking several cartloads of spare arms with them. On the bright sunny morning of June sixth, Willett and friends alarmed customers in nearby coffee houses in order to build an agitated crowd. When he had a fair-sized crowd behind him, Willett intercepted the regiment at Broad Street as they were marching to the wharf.

"They saw five carts, loaded with arms and guarded by only a few redcoats, leading the procession. Suddenly, Willett grabbed the bridle of the first horse which halted the march. Major Hamilton rode up to see what the trouble was and Willett advised him that the regiment was permitted to take only arms they carried with them as agreed by the Committee of One Hundred.

"At this, Mayor Hicks, a loud, head-strong Tory, hurried to add his two cents to the argument, and Willett waved many of the gathering crowd to join in. Then Gouverneur Morris, who happened by, intervened and, to Willetts amazement, took the mayor's side. John Marin Scott, a well respected lawyer who helped found the local chapter of Liberty Boys, was drawn to the uproar and helped Willet to change Morris' mind.

"The arguments and the angry crowd, and confusion, enabled Willett to somehow make off with the five carts loaded with arms and take them to John Street off Broadway where a loyal patriot had a large yard to hide them.

"As he rode off with the carts, Willett, knowing the regiment was infamous for its high rate of desertions, challenged the redcoats, if they were ready, to 'join the bloody business being transacted at Boston', and he and his comrades were ready to meet them on the battlefield. 'But if they felt a repugnance to the unnatural work of shedding the blood of their countrymen,' they could keep their arms and join him with the protection of the crowd. The crowd roared its approval.

"An old man in the crowd had a flute with him and played several choruses of *Yankee Doodle*. The entire multitude joined in, clapping and stamping their feet in time with the music and singing many refrains.

"A few of the redcoats took advantage of this confusion to desert and were swallowed up by the crowd eager to hide them. The rest of the regiment marched off, accompanied by hisses, to go aboard the *Asia* and await being transported to Boston."

Arthur was impressed. "I'm sure my nephew would enjoy being shown the Hudson and Mohawk valleys by such as Mr. Willett. Indeed, I would, too."

"That's not all, Arthur. Three weeks after he was made captain, Willet and a group of Sons obtained a sloop at Greenwich, Connecticut, and sailed it past Hell Gate to Turtle Bay, four miles up the east shore of Manhattan. They scaled the bluff there, overwhelmed a guard at the British arsenal and took all the arms. The raids Willett made provided most of the arms for McDougall's Battalion in the North Country. He showed a great deal of daring and enterprise. We're lucky to have men like him. Unfortunately, he's up north and it's hard to say when he'll be back."

"I'll wager that Jamie would go up north just to meet him. I haven't seen Jamie since he was a child, but from what I've heard from his parents, prejudiced in his favor, of course, he would do his best to make an adventure out of the trip and make a friend of Willett, too," Arthur offered.

Trevor thought about this favorable comment regarding Jamie, but added, "I'm sorry to say that several Loyalists, who would be interesting for your nephew to talk to, have left town. They're fearful that some of our more vigorous patriots would rough them up, even tar-and-feather them, as has been done to several worthy but wrong-headed men lately.

"Even John DeLancey, former judge, Lieutenant Governor, and patriarch of the DeLancey faction, left the area last spring. Among other things, he was accused of engineering the defeat of Philip Schuyler's motion for the Provincial Assembly to approve the proceedings of the Congress. He was continually undercutting everything the Assembly wanted to do. He annoyed us the most when he took it upon himself to write a resolution, in our name, to the king and Parliament saying the Assembly recognized its subordination to Parliament's authority.

"He left his wife and children behind, as well as a fortune in real estate. No one that I know has heard from him since."

"Where is his home, Trevor? I hear it's quite a place."

"It's a sumptuous mansion on Bowery Lane just south of the old Peter Stuyvesant farm.

"Tell me of some others, preferably Whigs, who could be of interest to Jamie."

"The most interesting of all is Benjamin Franklin in Philadelphia. But you will have to be quick. He just got back from England last spring and rumor says that he'll be off to France soon. Also in Philadelphia is Robert Morris, one of the most savvy financial men in the country. He has a very successful trading business with many contacts. I might be seeing him myself soon about a financial matter. I'm sorry, Arthur, for going on so. Everybody is worked up about the positions and actions of both sides and how things are escalating out of control."

"Trevor, we have the same problem in New Jersey. I dare not open my mouth to voice an opinion. Most people don't even know that it's the king and his placemen who are behind all this taxation, closing of ports, and doing away with assemblies and councils that won't do the king's bidding. They don't seem to be able to detect bad character, especially in a king. They blindly believe in Parliament, that the courts are just, that the ministry has the country's best interest at heart, when most of what the government does is in the interest of money and power for them-selves and their friends. The present government corruption…"

Trevor cut in, nervously aware that, for the second time today, he had overstayed his time. "That reminds me. I was going to see Jemmy Rivington this morning. His shop was raided yesterday by Isaac Sears and his Connecticut mob. Rivington's a friend of mine despite what some people think about him." Trevor was worked up and he had become louder.

"I think he's trying to be fair and show both sides. Just because he's the king's official printer doesn't mean he's a Loyalist! He prints pamphlets and letters for both sides. The public must like him, he sells more copies of his Gazetteer than any other paper in the city.

"He's smart, considerate, an interesting conversationalist, a lot of fun at a party, and honest. What more could you want in a friend?"

Just then, a chair was noisily pushed back at the nearest table and a bearded hulk of a man rose to a bullying height made more so by an unbrushed beaver top hat. "Sir! Your taste in friends should be remedied!"

He closed the short distance and repeated his tirade directly in Trevor's face. "Rivington is a liar even though he's in the pay of King George. He ought to be tarred and feathered. And so should you if you think such a rotter should be printing lies and slander!

"And Marinus Willett is nothing more than a highway thief. He had no right to those guns. He and his cronies just up and stole them."

Black Sam shot out of the kitchen and confronted this customer whose face liquor had contorted to look like a beefsteak pierced by bleary, bloodshot eyes. "Mr. Cunningham! Please restrain yourself. Let me help you sit down.."

Cunningham violently shoved Sam to a chair, "You nigger! Get back in the kitchen where you belong." He outraged everyone in the Long Room.

Trevor held out a restraining hand. "You shouldn't talk to Sam, that way. He's a respected and beloved citizen of New York who carries his own weight in service to this community. You should hold yourself in contempt, as I do."

Other diners had left their tables and gathered around Trevor.

"Quite the contrary! You should be thrashed for not being loyal to your king and country!" With this insulting declaration, Cunningham slapped Trevor hard on the face with his gloves. The room became stark silent. No one stirred; hardly anyone breathed.

Trevor did not blanche. He measured his words carefully to leave no doubt of his contempt for Cunningham, "If that means you wish me to demand satisfaction on the so-called field of honor, forget it. I have never met you before, and if I had, would pay you no mind. So what should I care what you think? There's no reason that, just because you're drunk and quarrelsome, that I should take arms against you and risk getting run through or shot.

"You're a coward. You're afraid to die. I demand satisfaction!" Cried Cunningham.

"I'll forget that you've called me a coward this time, but no more, and you'll not get satisfaction. I should be demanding satisfaction from you."

Trevor went on, "Yes, I'm afraid of the possibility of death. But I won't throw my life away because of a frivolous attack by a drunken ass. I value my life and would rather use it by saving someone from harm or in the service of my country. In fact, I insist on it. So, go to hell!"

Cunningham winced. "I repeat, sir, you are a coward! I will cudgel and berate you until you agree to meet me on the field of honor. Choose your weapon, and select a second. Any man of repute would not shrink from such service."

Cunningham then razed his arm to strike and Trevor startled himself as well as onlookers by lashing out with lightning speed, landing a well-placed fist to Cunningham's protruding stomach, surfeited with rum and roast.

Cunningham's face erupted in astonishment and pain, and he began to fall sideways. Quickly, fellow diners arrested his fall, lowered him to a chair, and held him upright, though his head wobbled to the side.

Trevor's response was not what Cunningham had expected. As onlookers held him steady in the chair, Cunningham's face turned white, as if drained of blood, and he began to drool. Someone fetched a glass of water, and when Cunningham feebly brushed it aside, splashed his face to bring him around.

Trevor looked down on Cunningham with disgust and, at the same time, with satisfaction. But he sensed that this was not the last time he would encounter this man.

He turned to Sam. "Are you alright? I'm sorry that this erratic had to take it out on you."

"I'm alright, Mr. Shaw. Cunningham's acted badly before. I should have never let him in my place. He's hounded others in here when he gets in his cups. How are you, sir?"

Trevor was daubing his face with a dampened napkin. "I've never felt better, Sam. This incident has helped me make up my mind."

# chapter 19

CAPTAIN GLASS AND his crew were not only excellent sailors, but they made a point of explaining what they were doing, and why. Only a few days after clearing Bristol Channel, Captain Glass became Captain Adam Glass, then Adam Glass, and finally, I felt comfortable to follow the crew's manner and call him just Adam, or Captain Adam. This familiarity did not lessen his authority with us nor had it done so with his crew. His skill and consideration for them had earned his crew's respect and affection.

Our meals were served in the captain's cabin on a clever table-arrangement in which the table top folded upward to secure his books in the bookcase in a blow and to be out of the way in any event. Captain Adam presided, provided weather conditions permitted him the luxury of coming to table. He also scheduled two of his crew to take meals with us, a different pair each day. This certainly made for a more varied conversation. The mates went out of their way to tell us of their lives, and their likes and dislikes ashore and at sea.

With a crew of nine besides the captain, we had different members as company six days a week—the cook participated on the run as he served every day, week by week. On Sundays, the captain's cabin was reserved for us passengers and Captain Adam. By the crossing's end, all on board had become a formidably cohesive group of shipmates.

We must have looked formidable, too. We had all grown beards since sea water does not allow our soap to lather well. Shaving was painful and made us look worse with nicks and cuts and manes that resisted the sharpest scissors. Crispin, especially, looked bizarre. His normally youthful appearance was obscured by a lusterless auburn mat and his mouth became minced and mean like an annoyed Pekingese about to bite. As his beard grew, he fancied this change and tweaked an errant whisker every few days to shape and refine this accelerated appearance of maturity. He was almost a different character and later, this distinguishment saved his life.

We crowded in the small cabin during meals, but such close quarters made for more convivial conversation. Sea stories, opinions of the best Atlantic ports, and politics were prominent. Sometimes the conversation became heated but mostly because of a misuse of words, or a misunderstanding. Like many arguments, what appears to be disagreement between adversaries is often because of the wrong choice of words or inability to articulate what one really means.

Fortunately, we were mostly of the similar opinion about the corruption and stupidities perpetuated by great Britain. I was astonished at the depth of political thought and philosophies of the supposedly non-philosophical were expressed. Adam said that being host to both passengers and crew took the loneliness out of being captain.

The first day of this procedure required some prodding on the part of Captain Adam. Mink, a dark-haired swarthy man of middle age, spoke up first. "I come from the upper Delaware Valley near Minisink Ford. In fact, I am a Minisink Lenni-Lenape, what you call a Delaware Indian.

"My father used to scout for the British in the French war, and I learned the trade from him. But the war came to an end after Pontiac, an Ottawa chief, decided there was no point in fighting further. The French had surrendered Canada three years before and he discovered that he would be able to get guns and powder only from the British. With the war over and Pontiac's confederation collapsed, there was less need for scouts. My father went west to the Illinois country, but I stayed in New Jersey.

"I did some farming on the Brotherton reservation in the pine barrens but that became very boring and the agent there kept a high part of the crop for himself and his squaw. I drifted to the great water and did some odd jobs around the ship yards there when I met Captain Adam at Tom's River. I've been with him ever since."

Captain Adam added, "Mink is an expert rigger and carpenter. Whenever we spring a leak or have trouble with the rigging, I can count on him to repair the trouble fast." He turned to the farm-fresh youngster across the table. "Ross, tell them what you do and where you're from."

Ross had a fat-dripping drumstick from our very last chicken at the threshold of his mouth when called upon. Rather than hesitate, he indelicately bit off a large chunk and began chewing until his adams apple finally convulsed.

Only then did he announce, "I'm from Chatham, in the Passaic valley just west of the first ridge of the Watchungs where my father has a wheat farm. I've worked on the farm ever since I was a youngster. Last Spring, when I became fifteen, I wanted to go to Cambridge and join the Continental Army, but my Daddy wouldn't let me. He said he needed me on the farm.

"I'd taken the family rifle off the chimney front when he grabbed it out of my hand and whacked me on the ear. Not hard. But I thought I was old enough to do what I want with my life and didn't deserve being hit like that.

"We argued, and both of us got heated and said a few things we shouldn't have.

I grabbed the rest of my dinner off the table and stuffed it into a ditty bag with a change of clothes and ran off. Almost everybody I asked for a job thought I was a runaway and wanted to look at the tavern boards or the paper to see if there was a reward. So I kept running and walking towards the Raritan River and Perth Amboy.

"When I saw the mouth of the river and the shipyard where they were building ships, I watched the workers for a while and they thought I was a runaway, too. But I told 'em what happened with my Dad, so they laid off. They asked me, could I sharpen knives, and spokeshave and plane irons. I said 'hell yes I could' so they handed me some chisels and said to show 'em. I did. When they found that they could dry-shave their whiskers, they hired me." Ross stopped abruptly. He then drank half his milk in one gulp.

Olivia was genuinely curious, "How did you get to be part of the crew on the *Raritan,* Ross?"

Ross licked the milk off his upper lip fuzz.. "Captain Adam asked me what a wheat farmer's son could do on a ship. As I said, I could keep all the carpenter mate's tools sharp. Also, I'm not afraid of being underwater, even in a strong storm, so captain was glad to have someone to repair leaks or the pumps in bad weather. I'm also good at doin' other chores that nobody else wants to do, like loading and movin' cargo, swabbin' decks, learning how to cook. I'm a fast learner." A second wrenching bite finished the drum stick.

"Ross is a good apprentice and, as he says, quick to learn many jobs. He's a damned good shot, too. On our next cruise we can really use such a man. He'll be one of the best by the time his first cruise is over. I'm proud of him," said Captain Adam.

Estrich had grown up in the Short Hills, nestled like a saddle in the ridge of the Watchungs, near Springfield, in East Jersey. He worked at his father's paper mill and had hated the work, the stench, and the domination of an over-bearing parent. But he didn't know what else to do for a living and he was secretly engaged to a young lady from a well-to-do family..

She was almost twenty-one and about to come into the remainder of a substantial trust left by her grandfather who had founded the family firm. She was crossing the turnpike one day when the wheel came off a stagecoach barreling into the village. The stage careened in her direction and killed her. Grant was distraught for months. He said that he had come close to suicide but couldn't think of any acceptably painless way to do it. He chose going to sea instead.

When the rest of the crew , who were more reticent than the others, had each told their brief stories over the course of the week, I prompted Captain Adam to tell his.

"I started my career at sea on a privateer under Captain Alex McDougall in the French war. We were stopped at sea one day by a British frigate and I and two others were pressed on board her. A week later, one of my mates didn't respond fast enough to an order by a lieutenant and was given forty lashes for it. I spoke up in protest and was given fifty.

"When the frigate sailed into Portsmouth for repairs, they wouldn't let us go ashore. They were afraid of desertions which on a British Navy ship was like a wound that wouldn't stop bleeding whenever one of their ships came in to port. I was determined to get off this hell ship and this was the time to make my try. If my plan miscarried, I would be flogged near to death and it would probably be a long time before I would have another chance in American waters.

"It was dark as a coal mine at midnight that night and there was a blow so there was plenty of noise and distraction. I had curled up by the breeching of one of the twenty-fours 'cause it was a hot night and I could be near a gun port, ready for the chance. On the second dog watch, I pushed open the gun port and slithered over the side. The water was fearful cold but it told me I had to swim for it before the cold got me. A quarter of a mile of swimming hard against those waves and the cold and I was ashore under a pier and away from the open. The wind seemed colder than the water despite it being a warm night.

"I made my way to an out-of-the-way tavern where I knew the owner. He gave me a large towel, some fresh clothes, and fed me some hot onion soup. We heard about the search detail but I was never threatened by it. I laid low for several days until the ship had been repaired and went back on station. I had a few Spanish dollars and did odd jobs as I made my way back to Tom's River.

"Then I joined another privateer that had a smart captain. He took several good prizes and was generous with his crews. I saved my share—- hell, there was no place to spend it—- and with some merchant friends bought the *Raritan*.

"The war was over by then but I did well in the coastal trade until I managed to become a trans-Atlantic packet carrying the mail. That's when I met Doctor Franklin. He's the one who gave me the mail contract.. So, here I am." He had lived up to the kindness and skill exemplified by his first captain.

I'm also pleased to say that Captain Adam didn't take on any one who smoked. Not because he thought it immoral or anything like that, but because of the fire hazard. He explained that the mates are sure to get into the rum, either the ship's or some they smuggle on board. If they get drunk and light a pipe, a cinder could ignite something, perhaps the gunpowder. Besides he hates the stench of the smoke and it carries a long way down wind.

Crispin occupied his time by fishing off the stern when the opportunity arose. When the ship cruised under light breezes at a more leisurely speed, he threw a line over the side and tried his luck. He said it was a different technique from fly fishing and it took him quite a while to catch on. He admitted that a bit of luck helped, too. He caught several sharks and was about to throw the first one back when Cookie said, "No. The skins can be sold to cabinet makers for a fair price. The dried skins are abrasive and can be used to rub down and smooth furniture pieces before applying the final finish."

After members of the crew saw Crispin's portrait of the captain, each of them wanted him to do a portrait of themselves. Olivia and I realized that Crispin would be able to step off the ship in New York a well-heeled professional.

Serene sailing had been our lot for the first few days when Adam pointed to the long swell that he said had been gradually building before us. The swell underlay the usual waves and reoccurred about every five deep breaths if one took the trouble to time the cycle.. It countered the waves coming abaft our starboard quarter and made a slight chop on the crests. But neither Olivia, Crispin, or I had any reason to give it any concern.

A large bird with a wide wingspan became attracted to our ship and continually hovered over our wake as if to shepherd our way across the seas. Adam said it was the same albatross. I marveled that it hardly lifted a wing to maintain its graceful flight, nor did it rest on the sea or anyplace else that I could see.

Adam said the swell was coming from a storm a few hours ahead of us and that soon the wind would increase, and swing around to come from the southwest. Then, we would have to shorten sail using the reef points, several rows of short lines pierced through the lower part of the mainsail, to tie the unwanted sail area back to the boom. Another job for Mink..

A thin but unmistakable haze began to obscure the ceiling of blue sky, and Adam broke out his sextant to take several sightings of the sun to establish our current position. He said that soon the sky would be clouded over and we wouldn't have such an opportunity for a day or more and the storm, depending upon its severity, could easily throw us off course. Best to know exactly where we were, now. He told me to read off the time on the chronometer in his cabin the exact moment he said, "now".

He took several readings to pin-point our position and marked it on his chart with the exact time. At the end of each day, he religiously wrote in his journal, or log as he called it, of unusual events as well as the progress of the voyage. He treated this as sacred information since it enabled him to detect such things as currents and weather patterns as well as providing a memorandum of his navigation.

As Adam had foreseen, the wind soon swung around to the south-west bringing much cooler air as it freshened. *Raritan* heeled over a bit more and the ship pitched so that the dolphin striker often nipped a wave. The ship seemed more determined and sliced her way through the sea with a fluid 'swish' on the hull, and foam trailed from her quarter.

Ross and a mate took two reefs in the mainsail which brought the heel back to its customary angle but less sail hardly diminished our rush through the tumultuous waves. Adam braced himself at the wheel and surveyed the set of the sails, the efforts of the crew to lessen the strain, the fast-darkening sky, and the ship's course buffeted by mount-ing hillocks of foam-flecked ocean. "Get out the slickers, Jamie!" he shouted. "Rain is going to batter us soon!"

We three landlubbers held on tightly to anything within reach, fascinated by this mad ride into the depths of a cold, dark, deluge. Fascination soon gave way to wariness and Olivia went below to our cabin. I went below to the hold to check on the rhododendron and our carefully wrapped fortune. All the shrubs were in place and well secured with expert shoring.

The kegs of gunpowder and of salt, as well as the Dutch bricks were still well stowed as a wall confining the shrubs with not much danger of them shifting and coming loose. I hastened to secure the hatch to protect the cargo and not betray Captain Adam's confidence in Olivia's pledge. The cow and its calf had sensibly lain down in the straw bedding, seemingly oblivious to the hectic rise and fall of the deck and shrill of the tempest.

We found out the hard way that one learned to endure *mal de mer* on his own. Olivia must have had a more delicate sensitivity than Crispin and I because she suddenly bolted from the cabin to the lee rail just in time to throw her breakfast. She gasped several times in her misery and I ran to her aid and to see that she did not make matters worse for herself by throwing up in the face of the wind.

"I think that's all of it." she howled and then doubled over with her second set of convulsions. This time, her efforts were more miserable because she had nothing to erupt. For fear she may fall over the side in her sickened state, I conducted her back to the cabin and put her to bed with a chamber pot handy, just in case her system became 'recharged'. I stayed with her hoping to provide a calming effect in the face of this dizzying torment.

Crispin and I both felt relieved that we had not succumbed to what we surmised was a woman's natural vulnerability, but this was just another case of fat-headedness that must have a reckoning. Within minutes, we both ran to the rail, as if in competition, and upchucked what had been a superbly delicious breakfast now turned to bitter corruption. Our indisposition turned worse when our convulsions reached the bottom of the barrel and continually failed to produce anything. We retired to the cabin to commiserate with Olivia.

We all felt heartened when Captain Adam looked in on us, despite his concerns about the storm. We knew all was alright, or soon would be, if he felt he could take himself away from the wheel to show us compassion. He assured us that ours were normal reactions for those who never before had been subject to the tumult of the sea. We should lay quiet and accept it, that's all one could do, anyway. It would soon pass, he said, and went back on deck.

The initial violence of the storm was over, too, he had said. Just then, a thunder clap jarred our world and gave emphasis to his statement. It turned away any other thoughts. The next I knew, I awoke rested but weak. Olivia and Crispin were already stirring. Wind and wave had returned to normal; only the drone of a pelting rain on the cabin roof remained. We were all ready for something to eat to fill a most noticeable void.

After her bout with mal de mer, Olivia stepped into Cookie's galley, if one could call it that, to ask for something to nibble on and restore her vigor. Cookie suggested toast and they began discussing food preparation, something Olivia had learned from her mother, I'm glad to say.

Like Sheherazade, Olivia revealed to Cookie another recipe each day in order to have continuing access to his "kitchen". Cookie realized that he could learn how to make a variety of dishes from Olivia that would please us all and heighten Cookie's image with his mates. The resulting variety of food along with the more diverse conversation brought to table by the crew heightened the enjoyment of the voyage for all of us.

As Adam had predicted, once we picked up the south-east trade winds, the weather cooperated to provide us with smooth sailing. We found ourselves accompanied by a large graceful bird with a nine-foot wingspan. Adam said it was an albatross and that it might be with us for weeks. I was delighted that he proved to be right, it was so fascinating to watch it effortlessly glide and cavort over the waves. Sometimes porpoises acted in counterpoint to the albatross by gamboling in the waves as if to direct us on our true heading.

Our dining routine became more certain and the six of us, which varied as determined by the day of the week, enjoyed an interesting and enjoyable table. The mates soon warmed up to us, hesitantly at first, and we to them, as everyone revealed their contribution on board, backgrounds, interests, and aspirations to the others.

Word must have gotten around that Olivia, Cispin, and I were just plain country people, though new to the sea. Captain Adam nudged the conversation along in the beginning until natural conviviality prevailed, and we came to characterize our collective selves as the 'Round Table'. No one but the cook could prepare meals, so he had to enjoy the table conversation, catch-as-catch-can.

During the first two weeks, as blue-water neophytes, Olivia, Crispin, and I learned from our messmates the basics of sailing, how the wind propelled the ship (more often the ship was pulled forward), the basics of navigation, setting the sails just so, and aphorisms that helped forecast the weather. *Red sky at morning, sailors take warning; Red sky at night, sailor's delight,* made sense for the first time when explained to us by sailors whose existence intimately depended upon reasonably correct forecasts. It is so much easier, and fun, to learn from a hands-on expert *in situ* rather than from a book or in the classroom.

The air became balmy, as on an April day when the sun appears after a shower. It became increasingly warm with the wind so steady on our starboard quarter, we were on the same tack for weeks at a time. We encountered schools of flying fish that actually flew using extra large ribbed fins to propel them, albeit haphazardly and low, through the air. Several landed on deck each day and Cookie fried and served them until we tired of the novelty.

The hold actually became hot. Olivia and I both frequently checked on the rhododendron. We knew that if the roots were allowed to dry, and the plants died, over the side they would go with our fortune wrapped in the roots. Aunt Arabella would be disappointed if we appeared without her plants. But we would be mortified and destitute. Never was a duty more attended to.

One evening when Adam was at the wheel, I asked him how far he estimated we had sailed. He was able to answer off the top of his head. "Not quiet three thousand miles, Jamie. This is according to my shot of the sun at noon today. We don't have far to go to Statia. We are now at latitude twenty degrees North. Statia is but a hundred miles to the southwest. Perhaps you've noticed that the water has turned from a slate blue to more of a turquoise. That means were coming on to shallower water. We could arrive there by tomorrow noon. But we won't."

"Why not, if we can?"

"Statia is a focal point for shipping contraband from Europe to the colonies. The Royal navy and British privateers will be thick on station in these waters looking for ships like ours, smugglers of contraband. They own the island of St. Kitts only a few miles away. That's why you'll notice I have four lookouts on watch now. If the navy or a British privateer spy us, we'll want to get out of range of their guns and have a head start."

"I know things are testy, but we aren't formally at war yet, are we? I didn't know you were a smuggler." I said.

"Well, I don't have a sign saying that I am. But I do have a cargo of arms consigned for the patriots at New York. Ordered and paid for by an American diplomat and some Frenchmen friends of his. The Brits, if you'll pardon the derision, don't like ships favoring us patriots, you know. What with Lexington, Concord, and Bunker Hill, we're close enough to war that I don't think a formal declaration is necessary. At any rate, I don't think either Britain or America has declared war.

"Who are the Frenchmen?" I asked.

"Well, there are two of them. One is Caron de Beaumarchaise, a well-to-do playwright, musician, councilor and personal friend of King Louis, who has set up a trading company as a cover for the purpose of smuggling arms to us Americans. The other is another councilor of the king, also very rich, who is paying for the arms. He is an admirer of Benjamin Franklin and of the American cause. But that's all I know. It's all very hush-hush. The French don't want to risk war with Britain just now but they are happy to harass the Brits any way they can. Franklin is a friend of the anonymous Frenchman in Paris."

"You seem to know quite a bit about them." I said.

"That's a long story but I did have a letter of introduction to the Frenchman."

"How do we avoid the British navy and privateers?"

"We have a fast ship but no armament except a pair of swivel guns that I can mount on the bow rail, Jamie. We'll sail closer in to Statia tonight with all lights out. At first light tomorrow, we'll be close enough to see the island and determine if we can make a run for it to get under the protection of the guns of Fort Orange there. That's what I'm counting on, anyway."

"Sounds pretty risky to me. But, it must be lucrative." I volunteered.

"It is Jamie. Next cruise, I plan to get letters of marque to go privateering. Congress is close to adopting the idea. We have no navy or money to build one. But we have many good ships like this one on the Atlantic which can be armed and fitted out for hit and run attacks or taking merchant ships as prizes. I look at it as a great way to harass and damage the enemy, or at least cause them to tie up part of their fleet, and make a handsome profit at the same time."

"Aren't you afraid of the British Navy? The largest in the world."

"It was, and maybe still is, but the admiralty let it decline. When the Seven Years War finished, they wanted to save money, the war had been so expensive. So the admiralty didn't build any new ships or maintain the ones they had. These ships cost a lot of money to build, to maintain, and to provision with an adequate crew. Particularly ships of the line."

It was now entirely dark and the rim of the sea grew smaller. Adam continued. "You saw the Brits impress some of my crew. They treat the sailors so poorly—horrible discipline, stale, rotten food bought from corrupt suppliers by corrupt commissaries, awful living conditions, poor pay when they deign to pay it—they have very few volunteers and a high rate of desertion.

"Many deserters go aboard our merchant fleet. The pay is better, and the discipline is more relaxed; not non-existent, just more reasonable. A high percentage of the men aren't really sailors—they are mostly farmers, artisans, or ne'er-do-wells, and they've been rounded up off the streets and out of the taverns as you saw back in Avonsmouth.

"Also, the British upper crust has a talent for making stupid regulations and rules that are inflexible and not related to reality. Sending a child of eleven to the colonies for stealing a loaf of bread, for example. Or hanging adults for grabbing a snip of cloth! The hangings at Tyburn are notorious for attracting cutpurses who thrive on picking the pockets of the spectators! The establisment's way of dealing with crime only breeds more crime."

It was getting dark now. I was surprised how brief twilight is in the tropics, and I noticed an unfamiliar pattern of stars and that the north star was low above the northern horizon. Adam said that if you could view the north star with the sextant you could determine your exact latitude. All the stars were so clear, it was as if you could reach out and grab them

In moments like this, listening to Adam, and where there is little distraction, I didn't want to interrupt, even to ask a question. He knew so much and was willing to share it with me. But, I was afraid I would forget to ask a question or what had prompted my query. Adam was constantly on the lookout, even with four men on watch, but he continued his explanation, not wishing to lose the point of his theme.

"In the case of the Royal Navy, they penalize an officer for using common sense and taking the initiative. Their *Fighting Instructions,* a handbook of rigid rules, forces decisions to be made on the timid side, to be safe and not suffer a fate such as happened to Admiral Byng less than twenty years ago. He was made a scapegoat, charged with neglect of duty at Minorca and shot by a firing squad, because of using his own initiative when the situation demanded nothing less. Even Voltaire commented about it when he said the British have to execute an admiral occasionally "to encourage the others".

"The rule makers, whether it be the Admiralty or Parliament, insist that their way is the only way. Even when common sense unites with human nature to show another way may be better. The rule, and its enforcement, seems mainly to permit one man, or one man's bureau or government to dominate another or a whole navy or even country, as the case may be."

Adam paused a minute to look around the horizon. It was now almost entirely dark. Stars were at their brightest. The rim of the sea seemed closer. Adam resumed his discourse.

"King George is a perfect example. He is obsessed with being a king and intimidating his ministers and his subjects to the point of generating an impossibly stupid war. Because Britain has such a debt as a result of the Seven Years War, he wants to risk another one by intimidating us to pay for the last one. How's that for being a leader?

"There are other factors—jobbery or profiteering and graft. It's so rampant in the Royal Navy, probably the army, too, that ships are unseaworthy, they're under equipped and under provisioned, undermanned, and not maintained. That's why we have a chance of outrunning any of their ships that choose to give chase. For that matter, a schooner, much like this one, the *Hannah*, overtook a British supply ship last September on Long Island Sound. It's not the same as taking a well-armed ship, but it was a victory. The first naval one publicized.

"In these warm waters, particularly, any ship will grow a garden of weeds on the under side of the hull that will slow it down like a giant restraining hand. So the ships on station down here in warm water for months on end have such a heavy growth that they lose their smooth surface and speed. They can't move swiftly through the water anymore unless they have copper sheathing on their bottoms to restrain seaweed and worms or are properly maintained and cleaned. So I'm not really worried about being overtaken and boarded by one of them.

"Anyway, I want to fight back and prosper at the same time. The crew is agreeable, too. Now, if we can just manage to reach port." He raised his mug, drained it, asked the mate to take the wheel, and prepared to go forward. "Nice talking with you, Jamie, goodnight." he said.

I remained there at the rail fascinated by the luminescence of our wake burbling behind us. It was the only light to distinguish the velvet-black sea.

# chapter 20

AT FIRST LIGHT we began to see palm branches in the water. We even saw a wayward flock of pigeons flying north. When we saw a sawn board, clearly we were approaching land still beyond our gaze. Soon the fragrance of orange blossoms confirmed this and refreshed our salt-laden nostrils. The sea turned from dark blue to lighter shades of green and Adam, a veteran of making this successful landfall, was relieved, and proud of his navigation.

Soon, we saw sail far to the southwest but we had the weather gage on them and Adam thought we would have no problem making Fort Orange without incident. He brought the ship into the roadstead where there were many merchantmen, and dropped the anchor on good holding ground only two hundred yards off the great dock. Olivia stayed on board, but Crispin and I went ashore with Captain Adam as he had spare room in the captain's gig. It was January 2, 1776.

We headed to the governor's palace overlooking the harbor. The alabaster mansion was situated on an eminence amidst several clumps of coconut palms bordered by a rainbow palette of exotic flowers. Several orange trees were blooming with a lovely fresh fragrance yet, unlike apples, peaches, and pears, had full-sized fruit on them at the same time . The view alone was so refreshing after a winter scene devoid of color from cramped quarters seventy by eighteen feet. My sea-legs still ached to be able to run, at least to walk. The fragrance, bird songs, and dappled green shade was so welcome and refreshing, it brought life to a body long denied nature's gifts. .

Captain Adam twisted the bell ringer and the imposing portal was immediately opened by an elderly liveried servant. "Who should I say is calling, sir?"

"Good afternoon. Will you tell Governor de Windt that Captain Adam Glass is here for a brief visit with him, if you please." Captain Adam could be formal as well as anyone.

"His excellency Governor de Windt is deceased, just this fall, captain. Mr. Heyliger is Governor now. Would you wish to see him?" said the servant as he opened the door wider and backed inside with a welcome smile.

As we tiptoed across the deeply-soft oriental carpet, we were impressed by the furnishings and, especially, the cool atmosphere. It quickly cleaned the sweat from our brows incurred in climbing the stairs leading to the entrance of this epitome of empire. Wide ceiling fans turned slowly. The richness of the place, however overwhelming, cried out to be softened by warm hospitality. It was.

A man in uniform with a military bearing yelled "Adam!" as he arose from his desk, in the depth of the room, and marched quickly forward. "How good to see you here. What brings you to our small island?" Bushy eyebrows over deeply recessed twinkling eyes and an aquiline nose suggested years of competent management, probably in the military.

"A favorable wind and a desire for riches, your Excellency," parried our Captain Adam.

"Have you a nice big cargo of salt for us and arms for the Americans?"

"Abe, we have all that and every thing you want including some French white wine and several wheels of cheddar cheese."

"You're just in time. I was beginning to run out. But sit down an make yourselves comfortable. Howland will serve what you want."

Adam was anxious to know what was advisable and available. "But we need more cannon, muskets and powder. Where do you suggest I obtain these? I also want to arm my schooner in preparation for obtaining letters of marque as soon as I reach the colonies. When I left, they were talking about helping support a navy by issuing letters.

I'm thinking of say, eight six-pounders and two carronades, perhaps four-pounders, in brass, to save weight.

"I'm sorry for running on like this. Congratulations on becoming Governor, by the way, but you were practically governor last time I saw you."

I was aghast that Adam would consider arming his ship and putting us three passengers at risk. I didn't say anything, not wishing to interrupt this camaraderie between long-time friends.

Heyliger lowered his head reverently, and said, "I was sorry to see the old boy go. I was his assistant for several yearss before he died. I think the diplomatic pressure put on him by the British over our letting the Americans use our port had something to do with his passing."

Looking up, he said "But he was seventy-nine, you know? I'm just a temporary gov; I have too many other things of my own to manage. I'm recommending that my son-in-law—you remember—Johannes de Graaff—take the job."

He paused, then, "How long are you going to be here? You and your friends must have dinner with me tonight."

"We'd love to. Governor, I want you to meet my passengers and friends, Jamie Claveraque, and his friend, Crispin Johnson, both from Herefordshire. Mrs. Claveraque is still on board *the Raritan*, but I'm sure Olivia would welcome a shoreside dinner, eh Jamie?"

We all shook hands with the amiable gentleman. Before I could answer to the governor's generous hospitality, Adam said he wanted to see the arms dealer at his warehouse before he closed for the day, scribbled the name and address, and we turned after farewells and left.

It was not far to Jan Hoogs & Sons, and the brisk walk helped us limber up and shake out our sea-legs on solid land. Captain Adam had had slight acquaintance with Hoogs several years back but, warming to business, they both claimed close friendship and proceeded to dealing.

Hoogs had had military service at sea and advised Adam that all ten guns should be the new-fashioned carronades and in the four pounder caliber to save weight. "Any-thing larger would be too heavy for the ship," he said, looking out to the harbor. "Carronades would weigh about a third as much as a cannon of the same caliber and use a fifth of the powder. They would also take up much less space. It is crucial to a schooner the size of yours. Brass would be a step up in quality and would save a little more weight." Hoogs asserted all this with confidence.

I had found that economies of any kind whether space, weight, or cost had a telling effect on Adam, especially when he saw the difference between carronades and cannon side by side at the yard. The difference in pounds sterling clinched the deal.

The carronades were made by a famous foundry in Scotland and had been taken off a British snow captured by an American privateer. Hoogs had bought the lot recently at auction. Hoogs had plenty of the right-caliber shot, too, another reason for acquiring the carronades.. Adam didn't forget to order five dozen barrels of gunpowder and more muskets for trade with the New York militia or whoever was willing to pay his price. All this would sell for more than twice as much in New York, Adam whispered in my ear. "Don't forget flints," said Hoogs.

Hoogs said he could have the guns, tackle, powder and shot dockside by tomorrow noon. Adam haggled some on the price, got it down enough to salve his bargaining pride, (I was sure it was well allowed for by Hoogs) and shook hands on the deal. He also bought some tools and hardware for cutting through the bulwarks to mount the gun ports and tackle. All this took place within an hour, leaving us plenty of time to get back out to the ship to freshen up for dinner with His Excellency, the Governor.

Back on board the *Raritan* , I took issue with Adam. "I can appreciate your wanting to buy the guns here at a bargain, but is it right to mount this armament now, before you get to New York and secure your letters to be a privateer? We signed on as passengers to get to New York, not to participate in naval mayhem at risk of our lives."

"Now, Jamie, you hate what's going on with the country as much as I do. If we have the hardware on board, we might as well mount them while were here in port. We'll be able to take prizes between here and New York. Think of the prize money we can make."

"Adam, *you* think about it! You don't have a large enough crew to fire the guns and manage the ship. You don't have mates to serve as a prize crew or spare room on the ship to put them right now, nor do you have a doctor. People are going to get hurt. You are putting Olivia,

Crispin, and me at risk, a risk we didn't sign on for. The three of us are not trained to fight. Nor do we want to be. Is your crew trained to fight another ship?"

"I can train 'em on the sail to New York. That's easy enough. The crew is eager to get started. We won't take on ships of the line or anything that sports guns. Just tubby merchantmen that'll be sitting ducks." Adam expected resistance to this premature scheme but he was using weak arguments. I think he knew it.

"You and the crew will be much better off if you wait until you get your letters and can train yourselves or, better, get trained by an old timer. If you set up those guns now, you could be captured as a pirate, with the *Raritan* confiscated and you and your crew put in prison, or worse. Think about it, Adam. We'd better get going or we'll be late for dinner. But please, reconsider."

I knew I could enlist the common sense of Olivia and Crispin, perhaps the Governor, to persuade Adam to delay his looked-for adventure. Dinner would be a good testing ground. We went ashore to the governor's mansion..

We were expecting a large room seating many as in a banquet. But the dinner was just between the Governor, Captain Adam, and the three of us, and a small, cozy room had been selected for our pleasant repast. Olivia stole the focal point from the Governor, but he was obviously pleased with her presence and didn't object.

The smaller room did not diminish the graciousness of the occasion. A chandelier boasting two-dozen candles graced the cherry-paneled room with a golden light. Mahogany sideboards against the far wall were neatly arranged with gleaming sterling flatware, china dishes and cups, presumably to be employed for dessert or additional courses. Silver candelabras flanked bouquets of exotic flowers on either side of a large bowl of oranges, the centerpiece, and five place settings glistening on the mahogany table.

Curiously, the fragrance of the flowers mingled with the fumes of the bayberry candles to saturate the room with a heady atmosphere that must have been designed to increase one's appetite. We were ravenous and ready for a feast.

Two liveried servants, trained to respond to the merest wish and answer every question regarding the choices on the printed menu attended us.

Of course, we were offered fine French white wine; the governor said it was a Riesling from the Moselle valley. The governor noted that it had been chilled by a chunk of iceberg that a considerate ship captain friend had fetched drifting south in the North Atlantic. It was of excellent taste and gently inspired conversation.

Heyliger intrigued us by performing an elaborate ceremony that seemed almost religious, though amusing to us uninitiated. After the server poured a dram of wine in his long-stemmed glass, the Governor swirled it around before first sniffing, and then sipping a taste. He tilted his head as he savored the offering, then gave his nod, whereupon the server poured again, this time decanting an exact amount to the requisite level below the rim of the glass.

The ceremony was so intricate, I was afraid the ritual might call for rejection of the first offering. But Heyliger told me later that was unlikely as he had selected all the wine for the wine cellar for as long a he could remember. Not until this ritual had been repeated by each of us around the table did the Governor resume the conversation or partake of his wine..

In turn, presentation and appearance of each entré, garnished with fresh-picked parsley or other herb, always placed alone and at the exact center of a large plate, was as important as the quality and taste of the food, in this case lamb chops. This was the first fresh meat we had had since the first day at sea.

Such service put the four of us on notice to act as dignified and graceful as possible so as not to embarrass ourselves in front of the Governor. From all aspects, it was as different as could be from the fare we had endured in the crowded cabin for the last four weeks.

After the servants had served the first course and retired to their sedate stations by the sideboards, the Governor renewed the conversation. "Please be at ease and not let these trappings stifle our conversation. So, captain, you've met with Hoogs for more arms for your patriot friends back home and struck a good bargain?"

"Yes sir, and he's agreed to bring all to dockside by noon. We should be victualed and have fresh water on board so that tomorrow evening, we can sneak out of port under cover of the new moon. I'm looking forward to seeing those brass carronades gleaming from freshly-cut gun ports the following morning. They'll give any British cutter a different view of things," affirmed Adam for our benefit as well as answering Heyliger.

Olivia was astounded. "You're not going to arm your ship and announce to all comers that you're game for war, are you?"

"Well yes. Everybody else is doing it. Why shouldn't I ?"

"Because Jamie, Crispin, and I are not prepared to be part of your fighting force. That's why. I'm surprised, Captain Adam. I thought you showed a great deal of judgement and consideration for your passengers for the last month, and now this!"

"We don't have to fight every one we see. Only those that are unarmed. It will be a cinch I'll share some of the prize money with you"

I chimed in. "No thanks. If you sport guns on your bulwarks, you won't have a choice as to whom you're going to trade shots with. I expect you to take us to New York in one piece, as you agreed to do at Bristol. We'll hold you to it. Besides, you haven't trained the men. You don't even know how the guns will fire or how well the ship will trim when the guns are installed. You'll have to determine the best location for the guns by trial and error, I should think that would be a time consuming task, and important to get right.

"Adam, you will be making a mistake to mount the guns before you get to New York or someplace where you can train the men and get the range of the guns. The *Raritan* will be so heavily overburdened that if we meet anything but a floating log raft, you won't be able to outrun her. Many will be better armed, remember." With this I had shot my wad at Captain Adam.

The Governor sided with us. "It would be folly to try to get in the game hampered with an overloaded ship, Adam. You would be at great risk at the very start. Give your self a better chance. Get used to the ship's performance with the guns in place when you're not burdened with all the cargo you're taking to New York. Use that space in the hold for a larger crew which you'll need to fire the guns and to bring a prize into port.

"Hold off until your next cruise. I know you will be a successful privateer, but not under the conditions you're thinking of putting yourself in between here and New York."

Adam remained silent.

Crispin piped up, "Besides, you're three passengers would just be in the way, Captain Adam. And we do want to get to New York rather than endure the glories of naval warfare."

Olivia changed the subject in the hopes that the question of Adam's premature military adventurism had been put to rest. "Has the navy been stopping and examining non-British ships for their cargo, Governor?"

"Yes, the British navy have even been coming into the harbor to board non-belligerents to examine their bills of lading, as if Statia was theirs. Search and seizure of non belligerents, they call it. British officialdom has a way of being arrogant and doing such things, you know. They have also made as much diplomatic fuss as possible. But so far, our diplomats have been able to fend off their demands.

"I hope the Americans can take them down a peg or two. All other European countries do, too. Our position, that is, both Holland and that of the Dutch West India Company, has been to help the Americans bring over as much contraband as they can bargain for.

"It's been good business for us and we see no reason why the merchants on this island should give up a lucrative policy which also serves our political stance. We hope that you safely run the British gauntlet when you leave. After you clear these infested waters, I suppose there will be little problem until you reach the coast near New York. They probably are blockading every city on the American seaboard. But I've heard of little so far."

Adam told him, "They seem more interested in foraging for food and bombarding small coastal towns so that the residents are burned out. Washington has created a small fleet of ships that lay in wait for supply ships coming in to Boston. They've been fairly successful and annoyed the British army since it's boxed itself into the confines of Boston and relies mostly on the supply ships for food. It's pleasant to think that they may have to eat hardtack occasionally. And Washington needs every bit of supply he can get his hands on, I'm sure."

Subsequent courses were served in the same stylish manner following removal of the formal serving plate. Thankfully, the conversation drifted away from mundane matters to the social scene. The Governor told us the latest news he had read from Europe. He was excited about taking his next leave in London and attending the Drury Lane Theater.

"The new playwright, Richard Sheridan, has a play, *The Rivals,* being presented there. He has wittily characterized high society and its pretenses and foibles to the delight of audiences, even the reviewer. What's more, the ingenue, Sara Siddons, also new on the scene, has dazzled a London jaded with taxes, a slow economy and the increasingly dismal news from the colonies."

Olivia became interested about the theater. "Does Philadelphia have an active theater season, Governor?"

"They used to, but certain Quakers and Presbyterians have long wanted to have plays banned. The Continental Congress last year, that is in seventy-four, in an effort for frugality and what they called other virtues, called for a discontinuance of such activities as horse races, cockfighting, gaming of any kind, and especially the theater.

"I'm reasonably sure that bias against the theater goes back at least to the mid- twenties when the staid and proper churchmen tried to quash a performance put on by an itinerant showman. They were unsuccessful but the theater, as a profession, was uncertain for some time.

"In the late fifties, David Douglass was authorized to build a playhouse south of the city on so-called Society Hill. But for some reason, he had to sell the theater a year later.

"Douglas supported budding American playwrights, one of whom was a young Philadelphian, Thomas Forrest, who wrote a comic opera, *The Disappointment; or the Force of Credulity,* in 1767. The play lampooned so many local leaders that it was forced to close before it could be performed for the public. Too bad that Judge Allen retired to England last year. When the Quakers asked him to close the playhouses twenty years ago, he was forthright. "Ridiculous, I get more moral virtue from the plays than from the sermons," the judge had replied.

"So I'm sorry to say that, at present, I don't think there is any theater in Philadelphia—a pity," the Governor sighed.

"That's a disappointment. We'll be in Philadelphia to see John Bartram if we can. I was looking forward to the theater, too. New York must have playhouses." said Olivia.

"I'm sure they must, but I'm not up on them. I know about the theater in Philadelphia partially because I read an article about it in *Gentleman's Magazine* last year. And I've never been to New York. Now, if you were going to London, I could steer you straight," said Heyliger.

Captain Adam had been quiet for some time. "I think we had better get back to the ship. Tomorrow will be a long day."

We said our goodbyes and thank you's. We would likely never again see the Governor. As we left the mansion, Olivia said too bad he had to live in the cavernous place virtually alone.

# chapter 21

THE NEXT DAY, Adam and the entire crew had been up and about at first light. It was flat calm with no sign of impending storm so they launched the gig and towed the *Raritan* the two hundred yards to the dock for loading. The crew did this before breakfast. We kept a sharp eye on the lighthouse for signals of any weather change. If the wind should suddenly come to life, we could set sufficient sail and cast off. We didn't want to be caught in an awkward position.

With docking done, all hands vigorously satiated their appetites. In deference to the crew, Olivia, Crispin, and I waited till the captain's cabin was clear before we ate. Cookie had made good use of his time on shore the previous afternoon. We all had bacon and eggs for breakfast.

By noon, Hoogs had kept his promise and all the provisions had been stowed including several butts of fresh water. Olivia had made sure there was adequate set aside for the rhododendron. Much depended upon their survival.

Captain Adam had reconciled himself to not cutting gun ports and installing the carronades, so all his purchases from Hoogs were stowed in the hold, including some molasses, several barrels of muscovado sugar, and a stack of ribbon-grained mahogany, all of which would fetch a good price in New York.

We could have sailed by mid-afternoon, but Adam elected not to depart until darkness would obscure our sailing. There being a slight breeze, we set the mizzen and jib sails only and sailed the ship the short stretch back to our former anchorage to await departure.

Presently, a ketch flying the British flag entered the harbor. Adam scanned it with his glass and was satisfied the ship was not part of His Majesty's navy, and that it had no gun ports. He kept the glass riveted on the ship and said, "Jamie, didn't you tell me of a bald-headed man with an ivory-tipped cane? There's one like that at the stern of that ship. Here, take a look."

I grabbed the glass from Adam and quickly verified that it was, indeed, Mochter. I had enjoyed a pleasant several months without having to think of him, and now, here he was. I didn't think he could be following us despite his presence in Statia. After all, many ships now had reason to sail to the port. We had safely eluded him when we left the Wye valley and again when sailing from Bristol, I had thought. If he is tracking me, why? He can't still be thinking of gold ingots. Since this is a well-traveled route, perhaps it's just coincidence that his ship is here.

Captain Adam saw my distress. "If he represents a problem to you, Jamie, we can try to shake him off our trail. We'll hoist all sail two hours before sunset. If he follows us, we'll have some idea of his speed. If he doesn't follow right away, we'll have a fair lead over him. I'll have Ross in the tops with a glass to see what those blokes are doin'. At first, we'll head northwest toward the Bahamas Channel, a common course taken from here to the colony's seaboard.

"But the channel is tricky and can be dangerous, particularly if you get a blow. So, I prefer to set my course north past the Bahamas, then head a tad northwest and sail blue water until I intercept the stream off the Virginia Capes. So, we'll go north, it's safer that way."

I thought about Adam's strategy. "Mochter was still on dry land when we left Bristol so he must have left soon after we did to arrive here so fast, but we didn't see any ships in our wake. If he left the next day and got here a day after we did, he made as good a run as we did. His ship can, at least, pace us. He must have been running low on victuals and water, as we were, so it would only be prudent for him to refresh their provisions. If he doesn't have to do that, he must have done it at the Madieras, which means he may have a faster ship than we do. Where does that leave us. Adam?" I asked.

"We'll have to make sail as fast as the *Raritan* will let us. That's all, Jamie."

Well, even if he's behind us, I don't want to have anything to do with him I thought. That Mochter was here in Statia rankled me. What foul business does he have in mind? I went to the cabin to discuss the probabilities with Olivia

"Mochter's here, in Statia? He must be dogging us!" she exclaimed. I assured her that Mochter was in a ship at this same harbor, and that he had just arrived. "We must find out what he's up to," I told her.

Even so, she could hardly believe that he would be so persistent after what I had revealed to her. "There must be some other reason that this aggressive man would cross the Atlantic at the same time, to the same place, as we have done," she said.

I continued, "It is possible that his crossing at the same time is pure coincidence. After all, there is a war on its way, and people in the know are trying to position themselves to take advantage of it."

"Pure coincidence, my eye," said Olivia.

"Tell me again about the people he is privy to—from whom he passed on commercial secrets. You remember, the people you mentioned at the Guy Fawkes dance."

"Oh yes, I well remember that evening, Jamie. He mentioned Lord Germaine, Lord Dartmouth, and Lord Sandwich. Also, Lord Grafton and Rockingham and the Earl of Chatham. I thought at the time that he was just boasting of the big names in his circle of contacts—those who might be prospects for landscaping services. But after all, anyone could pick those names out of the paper." Olivia was warming up her memory. I urged her some more.

"I can't think of anyone whom Mochter really seemed to know well, as a friend, I mean. Let me set my mind on it. But the captain is trying to evade Mochter. Wouldn't it be better if we find out where *he*'s going?" Olivia suggested. "Best if we follow him without his knowing. Maybe we will find not only where he's going, but why."

I told her I'd ask Adam to follow instead of lead. "But nudge your memory to tell us anything that might give us a clew about Mochter. That man is trouble."

Our change of plan made sense to me. We could simply turn the ship aside near the harbor entrance and wait for Mochter to sail, then follow at a discrete distance. We should then always have someone at the topmast to keep a vigil on Mochter's ship and any prowling British cutters that could cause mischief.

I went back to Adam and suggested we follow Mochter rather than try to shake him. He agreed that we ought to bide our time until Mochter's ship moved out.

Adam sent a man to invite the Governor to have dinner on board with us. Within an hour, Heyliger was rowed out in the Governor's handsome launch, pleased that his sumptuous dinner was being reciprocated. He had a guest with him.

"Thanks for the dinner offer. I brought along several magnums of that Riesling you liked so much—some for the crew, as well," he said as he stepped up to our deck. His oarsman handed him a sack. "Oh. And some oranges, too. I'll not have you fellows leave my island with a case of scurvy. I took the liberty to bring my good friend, Abe Van Bibber, an agent from Maryland. I thought you might like to compare notes with him.

Captain Adam was more than pleased to welcome Van Bibber. Indeed, we were all interested in meeting another official American. Perhaps he had news from the colonies.

With fresh provisions on board, and a governor and Van Bibber as our guests, Cookie resolved to prepare as fine a banquet as his limited but recently augmented, resources would permit. We had not told him of the ritual wine tasting and the precise presentation of the many courses for fear that he would feel ill-prepared to meet the challenge.

But we found later that Cookie had learned his business in the kitchen of the Governor's Palace at Williamsburg and was familiar with diplomatic protocol. He knew that his offering would be carefully scrutinized. Being the butt of jokes would be his lot for the rest of the voyage if he didn't measure up.

Unannounced to the captain, Cookie had gone ashore yesterday. He thought the cow and it's calf deserved fresh forage after a month on board. On his return to the ship, Cookie loaded them both with bales of silage. He also wangled a dozen freshly plucked chickens and several large sacks of potatoes. The remainder of the ship's spuds had long since sprouted and withered. How he had managed to prepare fried chicken and mashed potatoes for the fifteen of us from the dog house he used as a galley was a marvel we would never comprehend.

The *Raritan's* deck house roofs provided the seating arrangement and the cerulean sky the illustrious ceiling and walls of Cookie's dining hall. Masts, fife rails and marlin spikes held lines fast, and a heavy boom festooned with the brailled main sail and rigging were our other decoration. The wine was served, with no ceremony, in our usual earthenware mugs. The platters of southern-fried chicken were emptied by eager hands and a mountain of mashed potatoes was presented by Cookie, and served in large dollops using his ever-present large hand-carved wooden spoon. Gravy and toasted potato skins were available to the particular.

"Cookie's Revenge" was a masterpiece to salute and satiate the palate of our disparate fraternity. His Excellency graciously honored Cookie with the "order of the gratuitous galley" and awarded him with a bottle of Carioca rum. Sorry to say, for some, it did not mix well with the wine. No matter, it was a day to remember.

Just as the sun set and coffee was served in the former wine mugs, Captain Adam nodded his head toward Mochter's ship. Everyone followed his gaze. The square sails and the mainsail were being broken out to the sound of the rattling anchor chain in the hawse pipe. Adam ordered softly, "Finish your coffee, boys. We have plenty of time."

Adam, the Governor, Olivia, Van Bibber, and I sat by the wheel enjoying our coffee and listening to the crew sing ancient sea ditties. Adam mentioned Mochter's name. Van Bibber opened up, "That name rings a bell somewhere. I think it came up not long ago and had something to do with British intelligence."

"Oh, he's a smart man alright," I said.

"I don't mean in that sense. I mean he's somehow connected to British Intelligence—spies, informants, under cover stuff. Watch out for him, he's trouble." Van Bibber threw in.

Despite others being present, I opened up on Mochter and his strange following us closely, or so it appeared. I mentioned his enclosure of the common and buying and selling the greenwood so beloved by Crispin and me.

Van Bibber added, "Some think Mochter is a genius, some think him barmy. But he's supposed to have made a fortune in land speculation. He's also a close friend of Lord Dartmouth. Or is it Lord Germain? Well, it's someone high up in the ministry." That bit of information, though fuzzy, confirmed our reason to fear Mochter and encouraged more questions of Van Biber.. But he could not answer further question. Either he didn't know or could not divulge it to any but those with an official right to know. We wanted more definite information but would have to find out about Mochter's plans ourselves.

The British ketch had by now moved northwest several miles on a broad reach with the help of the northeast trades. Captain Adam suggested to the Governor and Van Bibber that it was time for them to go ashore as we would be hoisting the anchor soon.

Thanks for the governor's hospitality yesterday and to both of them for being our guests were hailed all around before his Excellency, as he was now affectionately called, and Van Bibber clambered into his launch and were rowed to shore.

As soon as Mochter's ketch was no longer even a dot on the horizon, we set sail and sent Mink up the ratlines to the masthead where he could see what we could not..

Just at twilight, Mink hailed to the captain that Mochter's ketch had turned north north-east. I guess they had changed their minds about using the Bahama Channel. Soon, it would be too late to change their minds again—they would be committed. There were too many shoals and uncharted small islands in that path to risk a change of course, Captain Adam said. But within a few moments, Mink called down again to say that our quarry had a lantern lit and that it had turned to the northwest.

The mate Estrich, who had the helm, asked the captain if he should change course. Adam scooted up the ratlines with his glass and told him to hold his bearing until he came back down. He squinted into the glass held tight to the mast to steady his gaze.

"Just as I thought," Adam triumphed. "Two can play that game," and he quickly shinnied down, his feet hitting the deck with a thump. He called to Estrich to hold course and to "launch the gig complete with sailing gear, extra line, and a lantern. Snap to!" he roared.

After his orders had been followed, he explained to all the hands, "Our friends have sent out a shallop to the northwest with a lantern at the masthead to confuse us. But I'll bet the ketch continues on a straight course north northeast, as they should, if they don't want to swim with sharks. The lantern swings wildly at the top of the shallop's mast, unlike it would higher up on the mast of larger, more stable ketch. They ought to know that anyone familiar with these waters wouldn't take a deep-draft ship into those coral reefs. Their bottom could be ripped out."

Adam told Estrich and Ross to sail the gig to the northwest with the lantern atop the mast. "That way, they might think we bought their ruse and are following them. When you can no longer see their light, douse the lantern and lower it, and sail back to the *Raritan*. We'll slack our sail and have a stern light out for you so you can catch up." Estrich and Ross were away in five minutes. The Delaware, Mink, stayed 'upstairs' to keep watch.

The captain was so pleased to think that he may have thwarted the British strategy that he offered the crew a taste of Calvados that I had given him. I never saw the captain happier.

Adam was eager to be at the topmast at first light. We shared his pleasure when he confirmed his hunch by identifying the dot ahead as the ketch where he had predicted it would be. At the same time we kept an eye to the southwest hoping to see Estrich and Ross hove into view.

Our pleasure eroded each hour as Mink, still at the topmast, reported nothing in sight.

With Estrich and Ross still not visible by midmorning, the captain reversed course in order to find our missing mates. Four hours later, Mink shouted from the topmast that he had sighted them two points off the starboard bow. He said he could just make out the pair of them and the gig on a small cluster of rocks, a mile off, surrounded by shoal water. We sailed as close as we dared in these crystal blue and green waters—beautiful but treacherous.

Even from this distance, we could see that the gig, our only small boat, had a large hole in its bottom. Mink was called down from the top to make a small vessel to float us there. He proved the veracity of the compliments Adam gave him and was up to the task in minutes.

Mink took a three-by-three piece of straight-grained spruce from our lumber supply and chiseled a rabbet on each side as two other crewmen selected ten long boards as he directed.

He planed a gradual bevel on an edge of the last foot-and-a-half of some of the boards and directed his helpers to do the same on the rest. Mink screwed the beveled board-ends into the rabbets on the stem piece so that they overlapped an inch, the width of the bevel, and soon the assembly began to look like the bow and sides of a boat.

He joined several wide boards and cut the piece six feet long at the top and five feet at the bottom to form a boat cross section. With help, he wedged this between the sides about seven feet back from the stem to serve as a fulcrum, and wrapped the far ends of the planks with a loop of line. Mink then took a turn of the loop around a belaying pin and, as he wound the loops to take in line, the aft end of the opposing planks were drawn together so that a transom could be fitted to the drawn-in planks and temporarily screwed in place. Mink called it a Spanish windlass. His crew then rapidly riveted the planks together every six inches from bow to stern and reset the screws holding the transom in place. All this was done in less than an hour by knowing hands and sharp tools. What a gleeful and cacophonic chorus but a masterful production.

The whole assembly was turned over, boards were cut and nailed firmly together to form the bottom with cotton string forced between timbers for water tightness. Caulking the bottom planks with oakum, a stringy bark-like rope, the boat was finished. Although it looked like it had been built by an errant child, at least it was finished enough so that it could meet the emergency.

The boat was put over the side to soak and swell while Mink gathered a piece of old sail, a full canteen, a more than generous slice of cheese from the galley, some extra line, and several other boards and tools. I was flattered that he selected me to go with him.

We hoisted and emptied the makeshift boat of water. When it again rested on the sea, very little water trickled in. Our gear was thrown aboard and, at the last minute, an extra pair of oars was thoughtfully put aboard. All this time, Estrich and Ross were shouting, whether as a sign of joy or foreboding, we knew not.

As Mink and I approached the damaged boat, Mink told me to jump out so that I would be standing between the freshly-made boat and the surging waves against the rocky shore. We dare not allow damage to the new craft, he said. He threw the canteen and cheese to our mates who howled with joy as they swigged and bit off chaws of cheese. Then all four of us lifted the damaged boat so that the threatening reef edge would not cause any more grief. Mink quickly slipped the length of sail under the boat bottom and over the gash, and tied the ends to the gunwales on each side. He then screwed a piece of board tight over the canvas covering the hole.

"Jump in. Let's go. This patch will work only so long," Mink cautioned. Estrich and Ross stepped in gingerly, afraid they might jostle the temporary patch out of place.

"What took you so long to find us?" Estrich said as he crouched in the gig..

Mink always liked to rattle Estrich's dignity. "We first had to decide if we were going to rescue you. And then we had to draw lots to pick the lucky ones who didn't have to do it." said Mink, with a straight face. Ross and I laughed to Estrich's discomfort.

Mink tied the line of the rescue boat to the gig's stern and we towed it back to the *Raritan.* The diminished craft was only a temporary expedient to save our mates. Mink was proud of his quick work. "Only an hour and a quarter," he muttered. He was already looking forward to repairing the gig to its original condition and embellishing the jury-rigged boat.

The crew yelled and applauded as we brought Estrich and Ross and the gig and little boat back aboard the *Raritan.* Cookie was the most appreciated since our rescued pair hadn't eaten since yesterday noon. But they had no bruises; hunger and lack of rest was all the pair could complain of. Adam headed the ship north, carefully picking his way to deeper water.

Within the hour, I heard some distant commotion sounding like a pack of excited dogs, or gulls, but different. I borrowed the captains glass to scan the larboard bow and there in the far distance was another small shipwreck with two sailors waving a rag tied to an oar. We surmised it must be the crew of the ketch's shallop that had tried to mislead us the night before.

Again, Adam told Mink and me that he wanted us to go pick them up. And if at all possible, bring their shallop back. He dropped the anchor in five fathoms of water a hundred yards from the wreck. Mink and I went on a mission of mercy, this time with our temporarily repaired gig and an aching curiosity, to seize our first prize without firing a shot.

The water was roiled by mako sharks darting aside as we proceeded cautiously above a garden of varied-color coral and aquatic life. If it were not for the nature of our mission, I would have dawdled to examine such strange but beautiful growths; some arms of white filigree, stark and immobile, others wafting purple strands in the current. The forlorn crewmen urged us on, grateful that their prayers had been answered.

It was as if our first life-saving venture had been a rehearsal for this one. The crewmen suffered no more than Estrich and Ross had, and their shallop appeared to have been holed by a sharp ridge of coral that had pierced and then worried a larger opening. The sail patch would work, but Mink screwed a plank tight over the hole just to be certain that we could return with such a beautiful craft. We knew Captain Adam would be more than pleased with his first prize.

As we were about to bring the ketch crewmen on board the *Raritan*, I whispered to Adam that they could be a trove of information if we handled it right. We should question them but in a casual manner so that we wouldn't show the nature of our intent. We shouldn't grill them about Mochter or as if they are prisoners or we won't learn what we're after. We have plenty of time to determine their designs before we land at New York, I cautioned.

Captain Adam agreed that we should show that we were glad to be able to save them, as we truly were, and to ask where they're from and other innocuous questions to avoid putting them on their guard. Who knows, maybe they resent Mochter and would like to avenge bad treatment. I told the mates to be friendly and to not let them know that we've been following their ship.

We transferred the first of the sailors out of the shallop and on to the deck of the *Raritan*. But the second tar was nauseous and limp. He threw up over the side and then passed out so that he became a dead weight to deal with. Suddenly, he slipped out of our grip and into the water.

"Quick, get him out of there. The puke attracts sharks," shouted Mink. We grabbed for him but he bobbed just out of reach. Mink picked up a boat hook to pull him alongside but had to use it instead to fend off a shark that had quickly materialized. The huge fish was diverted but he was close enough so that his skin scratched the tar's face. It quickly reversed its course and was preparing to make another pass at the horrified crewman now floundering in his own vomit.

Mink again diverted the shark and in one seamless motion he hooked the spar on the crewman's belt and yanked him into the gig, screaming and flailing his arms. For fear the sailor would mismanage himself overboard again, Mink tapped him hard on the skull with the business end of the hook which made him less difficult to hand up to Cookie and the captain. Other sharks began to congregate so we hooked a lifting line on the gig to lay it on deck while Mink secured the shallop to a towline. We would at least find where Mochter was going; maybe why.

Adam bent on all sail and had Mink at the topmast conning the northern horizon for the ketch. A few of us hovered over the ketch survivors to ask how they came to be in a small boat in this remote part of the sea. The small one, Paul, said they had asked the captain if they could lower a boat and go fishing for red snappers. Just as they were casting out lines, their shallop was holed by the reef. That was all there was to Paul's story; we supposed that he hadn't enough time to make up more than that. Now that they were saved, Paul's fears shifted. He feared his captain's wrath at damaging his specially made shallop, so he said.

Paul's brief story was devious, but we pretended to swallow it whole. We told him and Cyrus, the other survivor, they need not worry about the captain of the ketch. He was probably far away by now. The shallop would be repaired to better than original condition by one of the best. The captain of the ketch would probably never know, or see, the shallop or them again. It was salvaged property and belonged to our captain now, and they were a part of our crew. Cookie produced some 'extract of shark liver', he called it, to salve the abrasion on Cyrus' face. It was supposed to cure bites and alleviate pain from shark wounds.

Paul and Cyrus began to realize that their ordeal had a bright side—they were no longer subject to the harsh discipline of a British navy ship. They would have to pitch in like the rest of our crew, but they were not prisoners. Captain Adam included them in the daily luncheon schedule. They accepted and within a short time, were welcomed as part of the ship's company.

I suggested to Adam that we not have both at the same lunch but separately on successive days so we could compare their stories. I thought each of them might be more open with us if away from the scrutiny of the other. To induce openness, we had Mink retell his story, which we delighted hearing again, this time embellished with death-defying adventures in the mountains of western Pennsylvania during Pontiac's Conspiracy. Paul was then encouraged in his turn to tell of his background and how he came to sea. We hoped he would be more candid, this time.

"I was born in Hazelrigg Mill not far from the Tweed River, the boundary between Scotland and England. My mother died when I was six and my father decided to move back to his home in Somerset. For many generations his family had raised teasels, the kind that have hooked spines on the burrs and are used to tease the nap on woolen cloth. Somerset people have been doing this ever since the Romans, they say.

"I was the oldest of the four of us. My father prospered in Illchester, our new location, and saw to it that we children were well educated according to our abilities and ambition. I was so well educated that I thought to raise myself in life to a better level than that of raising and selling teasel burrs. The other scholars at Tisley Wells Academy were from wealthy homes and on substantial allowances, judging by how they had such disdain for the management of money.

Paul looked around the table, surprised that he was the center of attention. He downed a large gulp of coffee and continued. "An important part of my education was to learn how to be a gentleman. Tisley Wells did not provide suitable conditions for my aspirations. Accordingly, I made the rounds of the taverns with my new-found mannered mentors and met all stripes of men.

"One of them convinced me that I could learn to play cards and win every time. He demonstrated how to win so well that just before he left on an extended trip, he won my last few guineas as well as my note on the balance of the severely depleted account I had with the local squire. My teacher must have considered that I had completed the course for he never reappeared to continue the lessons." We all laughed despite being sorry he had been so taken in.

Cookie came in to clear the dishes and to ask if we wanted a dessert. We shooed him off.

Paul resumed, his story. "I was the source of my friends' merriment until the press gang snagged a few of us at one of the Avonsmouth watering places.

"How long have you been in the Navy?" I asked.

"A little over two years now. They taught me to disavow every genteel manner with slavish tasks and the help of grog on ship and whatever I could afford in port." Paul said.

I thought that his life was reenacting Hogarth's *Rakes Progress* and that we wouldn't learn anything of value from him.

But then, he volunteered, "I wanted to escape the Navy and jump ship but never had the nerve to carry it off. A gentleman on this last run, apparently high up in government, took a shine to me when he happened to see my handwriting—I was good at calligraphy at school—and said he might be able to use me as his secretary if I could scribble his memos and letters well and fast enough to suit. I found that if I applied myself, my handwriting returned almost to its former speed and clarity. He was going to take me with him when he debarks at New York. But then, Cyrus and I were ship wrecked on that small island. You know the rest."

"How did you and Cyrus happen to be on a shallop this far out on the ocean?" Adam decided this was the time to ask this central question.

"The gentleman I mentioned thought that another ship was purposely following us and he wanted to throw them off course and into the Bahama reefs."

"That sounds like a very ungentlemanly thing to do. How was that to be accomplished?"

"We were instructed to hoist a lantern high on the mast after dusk, to appear to the ship aft of us as the ketch, and to gradually turn to the northwest to lure them on. Then we hit the reef."

"Did your scheme work?" I asked, innocently.

"I don't know, sir. It got so dark we could no longer see the ship behind us. Then we got hung up. The next day, you came by."

"What was the name of the man who was going to hire you as secretary? The man who was going to New York?" Adam asked. The question was so pointed, Paul became cautious and claimed that he couldn't remember. Adam acted as if it didn't matter. "I thought it was possible I might know him," he said, and changed the subject.

The next day, it was Cyrus' turn to have lunch in the Captain's cabin. We had asked Estrich to retell his story to get Cyrus into the spirit of the conversation. Estrich's story was the same as he had revealed before, of course, and not dissimilar to what we were to hear from Cyrus. It was perfect to put the man at ease.

He was shy by nature, but I think he was still in shock from the trauma of the close-call with the shark. We showed concern for his horrible experience and for the shark wound on his face which was looking better after Cookie's administrations.

Cyrus had enlisted in the Navy, applied himself, and had advanced in rank. He had never tasted the lash and had indifferent affection for the officers of the ship. But he had a warm respect for his king. He was grateful to us for saving him from being stranded and the shark but, since we were Americans, he showed disdain for us. We doubted that he would reveal any thing useful before we reached port. It was for this reason that we revealed some of Paul's story.

I was saying, "Paul said he was happy to have been saved, not just from shipwreck but from the British Navy, as well. Although he said that he thought he was going to be relieved of regular Navy service to be a special assistant writing messages and memos for one of the gentlemen on board."

Cyrus erupted. "That damned Mochter told me I was going to get that job! When we got to New York, I was to go with him to a place in the Jersey mountains where he needed someone with a fine hand to write notes for him."

I soothed Cyrus by telling him he would be much better off away from British officialdom. "Of course, when we reach port, you're free to go where you wish. If you wish to rejoin the British Navy, you can, but you don't have to." I changed the subject. Paul's story would bear considerable query.

# chapter 22

TREVOR WAS SHAKEN as was Arthur. Nothing like this had ever happened at the Queen's Head to their knowledge. Both wished to leave the scene of this disagreeable experience and forget that there were such people as Cunningham. Trevor walked Arthur to the Cortlandt Street ferry to await the next crossing.

"Have you ever encountered that man before?" asked Arthur.

"No. But it seems like the city has sprouted such men like mushrooms in the past six months. And many of the Old Guard have left. Even though some were notorious Tories, like DeLancey and Roger Morris, I miss them. The city has lost some of its smart men and with them, part of its charm," returned Trevor.

Arthur was very concerned with what Trevor had told him at lunch. "I should think the British are anxious to get out of such a disadvantageous position as they occupy in Boston. When they do, its only natural that they will come here in force and take over New York. It would be a key step to quashing the rebellion. It should be easy for them to bring their navy here and bombard everything of strategic value from every side. Then they can go up the North River into the heartland and separate New England from the rest of us.

"It's only a matter of time, Trevor. We don't have the trained army or the huge navy that King George can wield like toys on a table game." Arthur said in despair. "Both of us would be out of business. You because your buildings and merchandise would be ruined along with other merchants. And I would then lose my main customers. Very likely, my farm would be ravished by whatever army arrives first."

"They have the men and the ships, Arthur, but not the grit. For them, fighting Americans is not the same as Americans fighting off the British. We are defending our families and our home territory. For us, it's fight and win, or lose all.

"From what I can tell, the British people are not in favor of another war. Certainly not against us, or in having to raise taxes. They haven't been successful recruiting men. Hiring mercenaries from German princes reveals this. I understand the Howe brothers are lukewarm about fighting Americans. So is Cornwallis. And Montgomery, Gates, and Lee have chosen our side. You can flip a coin about the outcome, but it's not as bad as you may think."

"I wouldn't want to have to bet on the outcome. But I do think the British will be in New York, soon." was Arthur's parting statement as he prepared to board the ferry. "I'll have the cider and Calvados sent to you in the next few days, Trevor. Thanks for the lunch."

Arthur used to stay out on the open deck and marvel at the reach of the mile-wide Hudson River as the ferry tacked across. But on this cold November day he remained in the ferry's cabin basking in the warmth of the large wood stove with the few other passengers. The buffalo-robe coat was a good choice for the day. At least, the strong wind would help get the ferry to Paulus Hook in time to spur his horse home to his farm before dusk.

When he disembarked, he bought a peck of oats to feed his horse after he was saddled up by Reuben, the stable hand. As much as he enjoyed seeing friends in the city and the excitement of the city, he was glad to be going home and, most likely, to not have to return until late spring.

Trevor was probably right that the British populace were not eager for war but they weren't running things and it would take a while for the leaders to find their place at the head of public sentiment, Arthur ruminated.

In the meantime, the war machine would make its own momentum. Who ever won, the king or the patriots, our countryside would suffer the mere presence of an army. Battles would make it much worse. Aside from the carnage on the field, financial establishments, business relationships, and businesses would crumble to the detriment of everyone; owners, suppliers, and customers. The scheme of daily life would be radically changed. Essex County, so close to New York, would be a no-man's land. How could he arrange to survive this? he pondered.

Arthur had twelve miles to go. At first he must surmount the low ridge behind Paulus Hook and then trudge the causeway across the Jersey meadows, more swamp than meadow, unrelieved by a change in terrain except for the oddity of Snake Hill starkly rising from the flat. The causeway had been built in corduroy fashion ten years before and had finally settled. The ground was unevenly frozen with some stretches that mired wheeled vehicles so that he would have to dismount Blaze and give a shoulder to help clear wagons and carriages on the narrow carriageway. The meadows were windswept and the sooner he made the crossing the better. By late May, the road will have dried but the mosquitoes would drive everyone crazy and give impetus to move traffic at a much more determined pace.

By comparison, it was a pleasure crossing the Hackensack river bridge and shortly after, the bridge over the Passaic. Would that all stretches of road were free of ruts, potholes, and wallows. He would stop briefly at the Royal Arms in Newark to warm up with a draft before the final stretch along Seven Bridges Road. Always good to have the immediate goal in mind, he murmured as he massaged Blaze's withers.

Arthur reflected on how much better to ride this trip rather than trudge the distance as he had to do on the first trip twenty years ago. As Newark grew in size and sophistication, he no longer had to go to New York for his banking. Good to see Trevor, though, and to have a pleasant lunch at Fraunces' Queen's Head Tavern. Too bad that there are constant reminders of the looming ugliness such as Cunningham's challenge.

Having reached the Royal Arms vicinity, he realized he was not cold, tired, or hungry after all and decided to keep moving. Perhaps he would arrive in time to see the sun set over the Watchungs and to reach his dooryard while there is still daylight.

As Blaze took him up the long hill out of Newark, Arthur saw the flag created by Benjamin Franklin during the French War flying from the post office staff. "Join or Die" said the caption on the depiction of a snake cut into thirteen segments, each representing a colony. 'What an inventive mind!' he thought. 'Though twenty years old, Franklin's flag is still appropriate. People in the different colonies may yet learn to join together and make us one country so we're strong enough to withstand the British. I'll bet Franklin could figure how to save my farm.

'Maybe I should throw those crow's feet all around it. No, even if we could plant enough in time, which we couldn't, either Arabella or I would be sure to step on one. Forget that. The place must be made to get a reputation for being dreadful or hazardous to keep marauders away. Small pox would do it. And both Arabella and I were inoculated five years ago; we came through the epidemic in '73. No, that's no good either. I wouldn't wish my neighbors to be subject to such a horror. I'll have to calm down and think of something else.'

He passed the turnoff for Connecticut Farms. 'Only two miles to go and a good forty-five minutes of light left, he might get home before dark. I think it's warming up—the wind has shifted to the south! Maybe I can fix the fence by the brook tomorrow, after all. I wonder if Trevor ever did get to Rivington's. What a tragedy. We won't see a newspaper that good for some time. And Arabella will miss its recipes.

'Ah, Arcularius house and Tuscan Road. Just top that rise, Blaze, and then we're practically home. Look at that stunning sunset. I got here just in time.'

He led Blaze into the barn, unsaddled him, and curried him for a few minutes finding it pleasing to follow the grain of Blaze's close-grown hair. He then gave him the rest of the oats. His wife Arabella had heard the commotion and opened the kitchen door as he trod up the steps.

"How is Trevor? Has he met an attractive girl yet? I'm glad you're home. The almanac says there's supposed to be a hard rain tonight turning into a blizzard tomorrow," The warm aroma testified that his sturdy blond mate had been baking loaves in the Dutch oven.

"Well, I was hoping to rebuild that section of fence near the brook tomorrow. But the almanac isn't always right. Trevor didn't say anything about a girl and I didn't think to ask him. He seems fine." Then Arthur began to tell her of the talk before lunch, going to Fraunces

Tavern, the increasing tension between the rebels and the redcoats, and, finally, the startling attack and challenge by Cunningham.

Arthur poured himself a shot of home-made whiskey into a stoneware mug, mixed in some fresh-cold well water, and sat down to relax after a long day. He shared the thoughts he had on the way home and posed the question of saving their farm from being ravaged or destroyed if it finds itself in the path of a mindless army.

Arabella agreed. "I've been thinking about that, too. I haven't come up with any good ideas yet. Maybe we should sell the farm and move to Sussex County. How would you like to live on Flatbrook near Walpack Center?"

"Well, that would be a last resort, dear. But I do think we're close enough to New York that we could be in the way of the British army, or ours, or both, and all that would likely entail."

Arabella put her hand against her forehead in despair. "Your nephew might arrive just when the British army does. Or maybe he's decided not to come. I wonder if he received our letter yet?"

"It would be lucky if he's gotten it. We mailed it only ten weeks ago. We might not even know if he's coming for another few months, Arabella. If he is coming, a letter saying so might arrive the same time he does..

"What a dilemma! I would love to see him. I haven't set eyes on him since he was two years old. But I don't want him to put himself in danger, so I hope he doesn't come. Well, it's up to him. We'll probably know by mid February."

"Yes. I feel the same way," she said. After a minute, "What would we do with the money if we did sell the farm? How would we invest it? I wouldn't want to take back a mortgage. That could be as risky as keeping the place."

What to do with the money? Arthur thought there were as many places to invest the money as leaves on the trees. He casually mentioned, "Well, we could invest in Silas Menton's venture. Ever since Congress decided to issue letters of marque, some venturesome ship captains have decided to refit and become privateers. They have been asking for backers by offering shares. I saw the notices on the board at the King's Arms. I heard Silas is eager to set up for it but needs money to refit. Risky though." Arthur knew Arabella would not take him seriously.

"Arthur! Don't be silly! I wouldn't want to profit from the war. And I'd want the money in something safe so we could ride it out. Then get back in farming when the war is over. What could we put it in to do that?"

"We could invest in British industrial shares or The Bank of England. Or, to play it safer, invest in British government bonds. Even if they lose, the British government isn't going to go bust."

"I don't really want to sell this place. It took us a long time to make it as nice and productive as it is. We had to battle the East Jersey proprietors so we could get good title. We have a good list of customers, Arthur. We are well located and have a good reputation all around. The farm would fetch a good price. But I want to keep it. Keep it out of harm's way, too, if possible."

"I agree, Arabella. We'll try to figure how to keep the farm and ourselves safe."

The next two months were busy for them. They slaughtered one of the hogs and the black-spotted cow, and smoked the meat. Arthur repaired the fence by the brook as well as replacing old boards in the loft of the barn. When the ice in the brook was as thick as it was likely to get, he harvested as much as room in the icehouse and sawdust afforded. He made some more bookcases for his study, as well as rearranging his desk to better catch the afternoon light.

He sharpened all the saws, scythes, and knives as well as oiling the harness and other tack. He repaired several watches and clocks that had been left with him, as well as a clock he had in the barn, and made notes of parts he should obtain from Walsbruch's in Newark. He put in order everything in sight to minimize down-time during the pruning season and when Jamie was supposed to be here. He almost forgot to arrange for sending the hogshead of Calvados to Trevor.

Arthur missed reading *Rivington's Gazetteer* published by Jeremy Rivington.. He usually reported both sides of an issue, though the factions disliked him presenting the views of the other side. That's exactly why Arthur and Arabella chose to read his paper—an even-handed report on all sides of an issue was more likely to let them arrive at an honest opinion of the situation.

It had been a little more than two months ago when Rivington's press was raided and the special type was confiscated by Isaac Sears and his thugs. Arthur was a patriot but disliked people of his own faction degrading their position by rough tactics.

In late January, Arthur read a pamphlet by an Englishman who had been in the colonies only two years. Already Thomas Paine, editor of the *Pennsylvania Magazine*, had a better grasp of the disagreement with Great Britain than many Americans.

The main thrust of his piece was what a great opportunity it was to break with the mother country and create a system of government in which the people themselves governed rather than being dictated to by a hereditary and unqualified leader and his cronies on a small island three thousand miles away. "Common Sense", already in its second printing, satisfied a growing interest in its articulate commentary.

He also read that Alexander Hamilton, a West Indian student at King's College, had formed the first artillery unit for the New York militia. A few days later, patriots read with pleasure the notice that British officers attending a play in Boston written by General Burgoyne called "The Blockade of Boston" were rudely interrupted by being called to arms. Under Captain Thomas Knowlton, a regiment of Massachusetts militia carried off a raid on Charlestown, destroying several fine houses and injuring a few Tory residents besides disrupting the play's audience. 'Good for them" thought Arthur.

And Colonel Henry Knox had arrived back in Cambridge with forty-three cannon and sixteen mortars hauled through the snow over the Berkshires from Fort Ticonderoga. The British will be out of Boston soon. 'As I thought, events will move quickly now,' Arthur murmured.

Best of all, they had today received a letter from Arthur's brother, George, in Herefordshire saying that their son, Jamie, had left Bristol for New York with his bride two days after the wedding by way of St. Eustatius. Captain Adam Glass of the ship, *Raritan,* had said they would arrive sometime between mid-January and mid-February. He wrote that they also had eight balled-and-burlapped red-flowered rhododendron for Arabella.

Arabella was thrilled at the prospect of seeing Jamie and his bride and decided that she would do her spring cleaning early this year by starting the next morning. And Arthur could help her set up the double bed in the guest bedroom. She could move her loom and spinning wheel someplace else. The ground might even be workable to prepare a plot for the rhododendron, too. Arabella reveled in this energy arising from Jamie's forthcoming visit, with a bride, no less. The sun had finally begun to rise earlier and it set almost an hour later than in early December. The days were now getting noticeably longer and a few were slightly warmer. That snows melted faster was especially welcome since this was the season for the coastal northeasters when Jersey received the most snow of the winter. Daylillies were already just breaking above ground on the south side next to the house. Red-winged blackbirds would soon be arriving. Maybe a few geese would be accommodating enough to land on Pierson's mill pond. All were welcome and heartening signs.

With many of his seasonal chores completed and Arabella's resolve to do major housework, Arthur decided to go to the King's Arms, only a quarter mile away. He wanted to read the notices and hear what his friends were saying about the news. Since Christmas, he and Arabella had been in virtual isolation by reason of severe weather. It was time he renew acquaintances. He also needed to stretch his legs which had no more of a workout than walking back and forth to the barn. Even the short walk to the King's Arms would get the blood moving again, Arthur enthused.

He was surprised to see that the ornate sign composed of gilt passant, rampant, and gardant lions, with unicorns and the harp of Ireland on a scarlet field had been removed. It had been replaced by a comparatively drab sign showing a roosting bald eagle against a blue sky. . Nothing else had been changed. The large clapboard two-and-a-half story house with a wide sitting porch facing south to view the road, and three large chimneys looked its usual, immaculate self.

The yard across the pike was crowded with rigs of all kinds and the paddock was full.. Was there a meeting of some kind that he had forgotten, he wondered. Arthur clumped up the steps, held the door for someone coming out, and walked in. Ralph Twidden, the owner, had just said his goodbye's to a leaving patron and greeted Arthur with the same warm smile.

"Nice to see you Arthur. Haven't seen you since Christmas. What brings you out today?"

"The need to have some of your good coffee, Ralph. And to partake at the old boy's table of wisdom. Have you sold the tavern? I see a new signboard. I assume the new owner is going to call it the Eagle Tavern."

"That's a good guess, Arthur. I *am* going to call it the Eagle Tavern, but I haven't sold it, just changed the name in view of the community sentiment. It pays to keep in step, you know."

"It's good to see a fresh sign, but it will take some getting used to." Arthur summed up this brief greeting and went straight to the table where he usually sought information and opinions. He was pleased to see that Squire Lamsden was presiding and, after signaling the barkeep for a mug of coffee, he sat down in the remaining chair.

"It's the most concise and intelligent presentation of the case for independence I've read so far. Judging from its many editions, I gather many others think so, too." the Squire was saying.

Arthur assumed he was commenting on the Thomas Paine pamphlet but refrained from interrupting. He wanted to sample the positions taken by the unevenly sage group who "held court" here every morning.

"That means war against the world's best trained army and navy. It's like announcing that you're going to commit suicide." said Malcolm Van der Veer, always cautious on any subject.

"It's obvious that we're at war with the King already, like it or not, Malcolm. We might as well set our sights on separation. No sense in risking all for any thing less." said the Squire amidst nods and complements.

"You said it, John. We don't need Britain anymore. They set the colonies up for legal exploitation over a hundred years ago. This is a heavy drag on all of us. As long as we're going to war, let's make the most of it." I was surprised to hear what Doctor Gottschalk had to say.

"Well, Arthur, what have you to say about the goings on these days" asked the Squire.

Arthur hesitated , as if reticent to give his opinion. "It seems that the war is getting closer to us all the time, John. Do we know it? I see that Lord Stirling and Elias Drayton and some volunteers have taken a British transport loaded with provisions near Sandy Hook just the other day. That will stir the redcoats up a bit. And give His Majesty's navy something to do besides provide room and board to ousted royal governors. So far, Governors Tryon, Dunmore of Virginia, and Martin of North Carolina are refugees aboard warships just offshore and Governors Hutchinson and Gage were given free passage to England. Governor Franklin may be waiting for a berth." The table chuckled but looked to the Squire.

"You all may laugh but this could be the beginning of a different way of life for all of us. Look what the British did to the Irish and to the Highlanders. In each case they were vicious, cruel and greedy. What they can't get with legislation they take by making war. They would like to do the same here. We must resist this bullying, stop it for all time."

"I don't see how we have a chance of standing up to them," said Rufus Simpson, looking for an answer rather than making a declaration.

"They have to come three thousand miles with all their provisions for many thousands of troops, Rufus. That's an expensive operation that the English people won't want to pay for for long. If our generals avoid head-to-head battles and make raids that whittle away at their numbers, resources, resolve, and time, we may have a chance.

"And England doesn't have many friends in Europe. We can probably get some help from the French or the Dutch just for the harassment value of it," said the Squire. "If we can pull this off, we'll have made a change in how the whole world looks upon governance."

Conversation at the table began to dwindle to personal plans for planting in the spring and someone else's problems with his horse. One who seemed new in the valley said he was going to plant a crop that didn't have to be tended till harvest time when the war would be over and the speaker would have served out his enlistment. We never did hear what this remarkable crop was but of course such a wondrous item would be kept secret. The few remaining laughed and left the table. The squire and Arthur found themselves able to have a private conversation.

"What are you planning to do, Squire?"

"I'm committed, Arthur, to being a captain in General Maxwell's regiment. I'm supposed to recruit and train as many men as I can induce to back their verbal patriotism with three months of service, including combat, if it comes to that. How about you?"

"I'll probably join your regiment. That's part of the main reason I came here this morning. Arabella and I think that the British will come to realize that they're wasting time blocked up in Boston and will make a strike at New York. That way they can go up the Hudson and isolate the main source of disaffection. But, it also means they will raise hell in New Jersey and maybe strike towards Philadelphia. Maybe come right through here.

"We are worried about our farm being in the war zone. The best thing to do would be to sell it rather than watch the farm trashed. We want to know what to invest the proceeds in that would be safe and provide income at the same time. Do you have some ideas along these lines?"

The squire scratched his chin, drummed his fingers on the table, and finally decided what he wanted to say. "I know artisans and other businessmen in the area who could use some money and would be willing to pay a fair interest rate. This includes some iron mine operators and local foundries who are gearing up to make armaments. They may even be interested in issuing shares. That would be one way for you to invest.

"Or you could buy shares of some reputable British companies on the London Stock exchange, companies like Lloyds of London, or you could invest in bonds issued by the Bank of England. No, I change my mind about Lloyds of London. They insure ships on the high seas, mostly, and the war could cause them severe losses. Candidly, I don't even know if their stock is available to the public. Even if it is, I'd stay away from it. Besides, it would take the better part of three months for you or your manager to receive information as to how your investment fares. It is no longer a stable world where you can trust that business will continue as in the past.

"But I really can't tell you what would be the safest investment. I know Robert Morris. He is a partner of Willing and Morris in Philadelphia and a delegate to the second Continental Congress. He has many contacts, local and foreign, and would be conversant with English as well as American companies better than I. I suspect he would want a commission to put a transaction through for you.

"If you don't mind going to Philadelphia, Arthur, I think it would be worth your while. Write to him and tell him what's on your mind. Use my name. I'll give you his address. That's what I would do. If you decide to sell your home, perhaps I can help you with that. People often ask me for help when they want to buy a farm or home for themselves or for a son.

At that moment, Arthur felt the presence of someone behind him who had just approached the table. He turned to see a tall well-made young man who looked familiar but he couldn't place him.

The young man looked straight at Arthur and asked, "Can you tell me where I can find Mr. Arthur Claveraque's farm?"

Arthur's jaw dropped. "So that's who you are! You look just like your father when he was young. Jamie, I am your uncle Arthur."

# chapter 23

THERE WAS BARELY room in our rental wagon for Arthur, what with normal baggage and the rhododendron bushes, so he walked the distance, insisting that he loved the walk. The road was worse than ours at home. Arthur said it had been nothing more than an Indian trail until about fifty years ago when it had accommodated pack trains only for Indian traders. Then settlers had begun coming with all the encumbrances of civilization.

Wagons were required to bring in larger loads, forcing the trails to be widened. A semblance of roads was built but with many stumps still remaining in the newer ones. Now, Valley Road has evolved with the labor of several generations to be part of the main road from Morristown to Newark. It suffers a lot of traffic, especially the large Conestoga wagons. And looks it, Arthur said.

We rode through the remnants of virgin forest with stands of oak, maple, chestnut, hickory, dogwood and wild cherry, many of the former with girths of thirteen or fourteen feet. The trees were so tall they blocked sunlight and allowed little under-story. A cleared field appeared on the left and on the right, an orchard of apple trees on a slope which was cut by a winding ravine and brook. After crossing the stone bridge over the stream we turned right up the hill alongside the crest of the ravine for a quarter of a mile. As we turned into his yard, Arthur halloed Arabella over the sound of a series of cascades.

A figure quickly appeared at an upstairs window and disappeared for a brief interval before she rushed out the front door with arms wide in greeting. "I knew you'd arrive today. I just knew it!" Arabella exulted. Later, Arabella told me this was the day she had elected to ready the house for our arrival. I loved her the more for her supposition that doing her spring cleaning early could bring on our arrival—and for admitting it.

Greetings and hugs ensued before we remembered to show Arabella her rhododendron which had well endured the more than three-thousand mile odyssey. The day's warmth had unfurled the dark green shiny leaves to appear gloriously fresh. Arabella was over-joyed at seeing the shrubs she had sought so long about to be planted in her yard. She said that the soil here was hospitable to plants such as mountain laurel and rhododendron. If the weather held she could plant them that afternoon, she said.

As we entered their charming clapboard house, I wondered how to extract the gold from the roots unobserved. What could I say if they saw me filching gold from their plants?

Arabella served us a delicious sandwiches which she proudly said was named after a cabinet minister. I tested the political waters by replying, " the man benefitted humanity with at least one good idea." Arthur and Arabella agreed vigorously and relaxed as they eased into non-political conversation. Olivia and I felt at home.

"How was your Atlantic crossing, Jamie? You made such good time," Arabella asked. At this, Arthur produced a battered document. "Well, I see we arrived at the same time as their letter," I replied and began to relate highlights of the voyage.

Olivia cut in.."We were trying to find out why Mochter was on board the ketch, however unlikely that these two seamen would know anything about him. The first one, Paul, told a false story and we knew there was some intrigue of which one or the other might know something.

"Mochter was very interested in employing someone with a fine hand, and had led each of these lads to believe he was to be hired as a personal secretary to write notes for him. We think something big is afoot and that Mochter is in on it. But several days of casual questions revealed only that the ketch was making for New York. We had thought all along that was probably the case. We still don't know what's going on."

By this time, we noticed how dark it had gotten and I scrambled outside to appraise the weather. There was some blue sky left overhead but the clouds approaching from the southwest were solid and dark and the air was damper than it had been in the morning. We would have to plant and retrieve the gold soon or to put it off until after the rain. If I postponed it, I might find that Arthur or Arabella would plant the rhododendron while we were otherwise occupied. They might unknowingly bury our gold.

I suggested to them that we do our planting now so as to let the rain settle the shrubs in. There was no getting around it, we would have to tell Arthur and Arabella of our secreted hoard.

"I will have to change my clothes, " I announced, stalling for time.

"Oh! We'll help you with the digging, " Arabella cried.

"Please! No. I wanted to have these in the ground for you so you could enjoy them right off," I offered lamely.

"Jamie, I want to arrange them so that they present themselves in the garden just the right way—with a bit of *insouciance*, you know."

That was a hard argument to parry politely. Besides, I didn't know what *insouciance* meant. I gave in.

Olivia saved the day. "We'll prepare the plants and remove them from the wagon for you Arabella." This was agreement enough for them and they went upstairs to change.

Quickly, Olivia and I searched the burlap covering for the camouflaged swatches. We were infuriated that this took so long, but comforted that a meddler would have had little chance of finding our hoard. We hid the gold in the wagon's feed box for the moment, just in time, for our hosts stepped from the house as we were wiping our hands on the partially removed burlap.

Arthur and Arabella went to work immediately and, aside from Arabella stepping back to view the *insouciance* from time to time, they finished planting just as the first large drops slammed down on the raked soil. I must admit, she had a knack of eking the most charm from the plants by placing them just so, *au naturel.*

The prematurely warm day chilled as rapidly as if we had walked into a cavern, and we hastened our be-splattered selves into the comfort of the house. Uncorking a bottle of Chablis while embraced by the aroma of bread baking in the Dutch oven was fittingly comfortable for our first evening in America.

"And what happened to your friend Crispin? Is he shy?" Arthur began after his toast to our American Tour.

"He is less shy than he was only a few months ago. He was eager to acquire paints and brushes, and decided New York was probably the only place to get them, after he inquired in Perth Amboy. Captain Glass was anxious for him to not disappear but to do portraits in oil of him and his wife, as promised. He had drawn charcoal sketches of everyone aboard and enjoyed such acclaim that he plans to try portraiture as a living. I suspect he'll show up on your doorstep when he completes the portraits for the Glass family."

"We would like to meet him. Anyone who successfully escapes the British army has to have gumption and his wits about him," Arthur opined.

"This might be a good time to have our portraits done, Arthur. And a painting of the farm with the rhododendrons would be a good idea before we sell the place."

Olivia was surprised. "Are you serious about selling the farm? It's too lovely to think of anyone else living here."

"Arabella and I are just thinking about it, Olivia. We're afraid the war will inevitably involve the New York area and that we'll be right in the middle of the fighting or, at least in a ravaged neighborhood. We are patriots and an island in a sea of Loyalists. It might go badly for us as it already has for some partisans of both sides in New York and Westchester County.

"We haven't made up our minds. We don't know how to invest the sale proceeds to carry us through the war and keep our investment safe. We're going to see a financial man in Philadelphia some time soon."

"We are? When are we supposed to do this?" said Arabella.

"Oh, I haven't had time to tell you, what with our guests arriving so abruptly. I happened to meet Squire Lamsden this morning at the King's Arms—no, that's changed, too. It's now the Eagle Tavern. Twidden's changed the name to be in step, he says, because of war fever.

"Anyway, I talked to the Squire about this problem and he mentioned an expert financial man in Philadelphia by the name of Robert Morris. Trevor Shaw mentioned him last November as someone Jamie should know to conduct him around Philadelphia. Trevor said then that he himself expected to see Mr. Morris about some financial concerns."

"What is so notable about this man that we have to leave our home and go all the way to Philadelphia for financial advice from him, Arthur?"

"Aside from being suggested as a competent person by both Squire Lamsden and Trevor Shaw, the man is a member of the very successful trading firm, Morris & Willing, with many business contacts, as well as being a delegate from Pennsylvania to the second Continental Congress. Those sound like excellent credentials to me. If he's going to be attending Congress, maybe we should do all we can to see him before he gets too mired in committees and politics."

"Uncle Arthur, Olivia and I have reason to see someone like Morris, too."

I told them all about the fall day I was fishing and literally stumbled on the gold ingot, and all that followed, including Mochter's suspicions and interventions on land and sea. "Now that we have successfully escaped from England with this treasure, our concern is how to convert it to some safe, income-producing investment. We want to keep our investment as private as possible and especially away from the prying eyes of Wencesles Mochter."

Arthur offered us a refill of wine, poured Arabella's and his own glass, and sat down to reflect.

"A very unusual and interesting story, Jamie. I think we may all need to see the same man. How did you escape customs inspection at Bristol and Perth Amboy. How did you secrete the gold from the authorities?"

I told them of Olivia's suggestion that, as long as we would be taking rhododendron with us, we could bury a slice of the ingot in each root ball where no one was likely to search.

"So, you see, your plants were given attention every day, Arabella. We not only wanted them to be in excellent condition when we presented them to you but we were afraid that if they died, Captain Adam would insist they be thrown overboard with our fortune tucked inside. We would have been embarrassed to reveal our riches and our secret concealment."

"So that's what all that funny business about planting was about. You wanted to have a chance to conceal the gold pieces in private before the shrubs were planted. I assume you did this when we were changing our clothes." We nodded. "Well, I don't blame you. Congratulations on smuggling your contraband over here. You're great grandfather would be proud of you, Jamie."

Arthur then offered a toast. "To the continued success of the Claveraque clan. Your and Olivia's ingenuity, determination, and daring have assured us that this toast will be fulfilled." We clicked glasses and drank to that in silence.

Arthur put down his glass and exclaimed, "We forgot all about the letter your parents sent to Arabella and me. Let's take a few minutes and I'll read it out loud." He reached for his glasses in his waistcoat, fogged and wiped them clean, and, with a clearing of his throat, began.

*Dear Arthur and Arabella,*

*Jamie and his bride, Olivia, were married in our living room Friday of last week (December ninth) amid our friends and family and much gaiety. We are very pleased that, though this courtship, and marriage evolved over a period of less than two months, Jamie could not have chosen a more charming, level-headed, and responsible girl. We love her already. It is clear that they are deeply enamored of each other and respond to each other's interests. It is certainly more than mere infatuation.*

*Olivia is the daughter of the Farrells that have the greenhouses over near Ross. She and her brother, Alan, run the business. Their parents passed on several years past.*

*Olivia had the kindness to say to me following the ceremony that she felt sure that George and I would be the perfect surrogates for her deceased parents. (Her father survived her mother by several years). When Jamie was busy conversing with guests, she also confided in us her gratitude for instilling in him fairness, intellectual curiosity, and the ability to stand up to overbearing authority. This was very pleasing to our ears.*

*Jamie was delighted by your kind offer to provide a Tour of America, as is Olivia. They are fascinated by the colonies; Jamie has been for years. I believe the prospect of actually seeing that part of our country so appealed to both of them that it was a significant factor in their decision to marry. They were doubly excited about traveling together and they left the day after the wedding for Bristol to set sail for New York in the Raritan commanded by Captain Adam Glass.*

*They hope to arrive at Vaux Hall within eight to twelve weeks knowing that the vagaries of weather and the plans of men can change. But look for them sometime in February, probably about the time that this letter reaches you.*

*It is interesting to us that a younger son influenced the oldest by his actions. Yes, Dordy and Sally Bushnell have decided to marry sometime this spring. It's been a long time coming.*

*Denny Mohan is known to have recently sold a large herd of horses to the army and will accompany the herd to the colonies; New York, I think . You probably know by now that the king has announced that he considers the colonies in a state of rebellion and will do everything to crush the insurgents and cause them to return to obedience.. People over here are upset over going to war with the Americans. After all, they are Englishmen, too, and are greatly admired for making a country out of the wilderness. Walpole's policy of leaving them to their own devices for so long has paid off and shows that, when people have the resources and the will, they do best when unhampered by politicians and excess meddling.*

*Enlistments are slow as a result of this disaffection and the administration has even tried to interest Catherine of Russia in the loan of a part of her army. Thank goodness that she rejected the idea. Now we hear that the king is dealing with some of the German princes to buy the services of their regiments to fight his own countrymen in America. What will he think of next to alienate what remnant of American affection remains for the mother country?*

*The administration is intent on following a course of folly that is dividing the country here and in the colonies and may well lose our most important possession just as it is becoming the goose that lays the golden eggs. Too bad William Pitt was persuaded to become the Earl of Chatham. He has lost his influence in the Commons without gaining clout in the House of Lords.*

*Thank Goodness for the comic relief provided by John Wilkes and Isaac Barré as they continue to prick the pompous and the stupidity of the king and his bumbling administration.*

*It appears that C has eluded Brigandi's squad which has been scouring the countryside in their search for him for three weeks now. We know C. is in good hands.*

*Wencesles Mochter has suffered more contempt in the form of someone pouring gravel into the funnel hole of the running stone at his mill. The term,"grind to a halt", never had more appropriate meaning. George heard at the Green Bottle that Mochter is out of the country on a mission for the army. People are determined to get even with him for selling the greenwood to the army and allowing for its despoliation. One can't help but feel that the miscreant (or hero) who vandalized his mill is a compassionate being who would not have done so if there was no other mill to serve the area. Another reason for competition!*

*May Providence direct that Jamie and Olivia do not become embroiled in the politics and the fighting over there so that they can enjoy their discovery of the colonies. What a wonderful offer of the Tour you made to Jamie. They will bless you and remember it the rest of their lives.*

*Our best wishes to you. Please keep us informed of their Tour and of your dear selves.*

*George and Edith*

We were aware of the sentiments that Father and Mother expressed in their letter. After pleasantries regarding their communication, there was silence.

Then, Arthur continued, "Arabella wants to finish preparing dinner. The rain has let up. Come with me and I'll show you both our pride and joy—our farm."

"I should help Arabella," offered Olivia. "You go with Arthur, Jamie."

Arabella, who was stirring the coals of the fire for roasting our dinner, turned and said, "No, you go with them Olivia. I've got things under control here. I'd like you to see our small piece of the kingdom."

We walked with Arthur over to the brook which ran capriciously in the ravine shaded by willows. The current scoured matts of willow roots first before making a wide swing around the house into a natural pool which spilled over to the base of the hill. "This stream flows cold winter and summer and keeps our milk and cider chilled. It also carries a current of cool air which wafts against the house and keeps it comfortable during the summer." Arthur was proud of how the house had been situated.

"The poor fellow who owned the farm before us ranged too far in his hunting forays. He was killed by Shawnees in the Kittatiny Mountains during the French war. His widow moved back to Newark with her folks and sold the place to us. We've loved it and enjoyed adding to it and shaping it to our own needs." Arthur fawned.

"The stream is called Lightning Brook because a Mohican chief, said to be here on a trading venture, lost his favorite colt to a lightning strike over there in the meadow. The chief was so saddened that he said that when he died, he wished to be buried in the meadow near where they buried the colt. He was, so the story goes. Tuscan Road, that we came along earlier, was named after him, Chief Tuscan. It's one of the main links in the road that goes from Newark to Morristown and beyond."

We moved down along the crest of the ravine. "That stand of oak trees has probably been here for many centuries. It does double duty for us; it blocks the north wind from the house and is our source of good firewood. I cull the stand every year and it seems as plentiful as when I started. I just finished cutting all I need for next year. Good red oak with some white mixed in."

"Somebody's going to get a well provided for house when you sell it, Arthur, what with the wood all cut and seasoned by then, and the ice house full to the brim. You should get a handsome price. You are a work horse, like Father," I said.

"Thanks for the compliment. I had the sale in mind when I tidied up the ice house, the wood pile and some other things.. But we hate to sell the place. We get increasingly attached the more we put into it. I suppose if I hold on to it any longer, they'll have to tear it out of my hands." Neither Olivia nor I spoke after this, we merely moseyed on and followed Arthur.

When we arrived at his orchard, he inspected the bark of one of the apple trees, rubbed off an excrescence, and continued like a docent outlining an ancient cathedral. "We use Canfield and Harrison apples to make our cider and our Calvados. Our orchard and mill is not as large as the Crowells, up the road, but we command a premium for our products, so we're content.

"The honeybees your father sent last spring really paid off in a bumper crop, although the weather helped, too. Not as hot nor humid last summer so we had less scab and more fruit for sale. I wish we owned down to the east branch, it would be a perfect place to put a dam. A water-powered mill could probably operate most of the year, too. It would save Blaze from wearing himself out. The mill could grind the apples." Arthur was talking more to himself than to us. He was just thinking audibly, that's all. He seemed a solitary man.

"You'll be pruning soon, I suppose," I said. "I'd like to help you. I need the exercise. I've done little in the way of hard work for three months. Just tell me when you want to begin."

"Thanks, but I think we won't have to start that for at least a few weeks. We'll probably go to Philadelphia first, both you and us. We might even share a coach," he smiled.

Arthur turned and led us back up the hill to a small graveyard overlooking the stream. Off to the side of the few old stone markers was a smaller one:

John Claveraque
1750-1758
God Rest His Soul

Arthur anticipated our question. "Our only child, Jackie, used to play here in the ravine. He would pile rocks across the stream and then rip mats of willow roots to lay across the upstream side so that, after riling the water, mud and debris would clog the pores in the root mats making it fast against leakage. He and his friend would make little boats and watch them race down in the current when they opened up the dam.

"Jackie died of small pox in the same epidemic that claimed Jonathan Edwards, the evangelist and second president of Princeton College. At least, he was in good company."

It was obvious that it pleased Arthur to think of his loss that way. We sympathized and followed his lead to the barn backed up to the hill.

"The doctor said that it would not be a good idea to have any more children. Arabella was not well at the time. So we never did." He opened the large barn door.

"As you see, we store only a little hay and straw. Blaze pulls the sweep that turns our apple grinder and we use the barn for storing apples and cider as well as a wood-working shop. We manure the orchard with barn leavings and pomace from the cider press and the vegetable garden with droppings from the chicken house. Your grandfather taught us to make the farm be as self-sustaining as possible. The old man was right, it's paid off in both time and money."

Arthur's shop had a small forge for repairing tools. I noticed a sleek-looking musket which was about five feet long hanging on pegs in the wall.

"That musket must be an old timer, and very heavy," I said.

"That's a Pennsylvania rifle, made in Lancaster. The barrel is long and spirally grooved inside to give the bullet a spin for better accuracy than a musket. They call it rifling. It belonged to Arabella's brother, who treasured it—he even gave it a name. He said it saved his life several times when he was with General Forbes in the Fort Duquesne campaign. Here, feel the heft and balance of this thing."

He handed the rifle to me. It wasn't as cumbersome as I had thought it might be although I admitted that I had no familiarity with guns. I admired the heft and balance of the piece. "This feel invites one to bring it to your shoulder to sight and fire. We use bows and arrows for hunting at home. You know, it's illegal to own guns in England," I told him.

"That's right, I forgot. The establishment over there is afraid the commoners will start an insurrection. I suppose the aristocrats may have guilty consciences and are paranoid.. Here, every brother's son has a gun, though maybe not as fine as this one. In this generation, they serve mainly to add variety to the table. In previous generations, they were to keep the Indians at bay.

"You should learn to use one of these, Jamie. It's fun to hunt with them, though the need to stalk your game closely is not as pressing because of the longer range. Here, I'll show you."

Arthur took the gun from me and reached for a powder horn and a leather pouch. From the small end of the horn, he poured a tad of powder down the barrel and then rammed a half-inch lead ball followed by a small leather patch down the barrel with a thin rod tucked under the barrel. He jarred the rifle butt on the floor to seat the charge. Finally, he clicked open the lock, as he called the trigger and ignition mechanism, against a hidden spring. "This is called cocking the piece," he said and poured a pinch of powder in the pan. "Priming," he said.

This ritual was time-consuming but he explained. "When I pull the trigger, it takes the lock off the safety position in which no one can shoot it unintentionally. If the gun fires then, it's called 'going off half-cocked'. Pulling the trigger a second time releases a spring forcing the flint against the steel to send sparks into the pan. This ignites the powder in turn igniting, through the touch hole, the main charge in the breech. That fires the gun and propels the ball out the barrel."

"It sounds complicated," I said.

"Yes, but it works surprisingly fast, in a fraction of a second. See that white stone embedded in the bank by the hickory tree, behind the mossy log? Watch!"

Arthur pulled the trigger, and in less time than a tuppence could drop to the floor, a loud bang accompanied by black smoke, shattered the stillness and some dirt near the target. He missed the white stone. But it was only as big as a walnut and close to a hundred yards distant.

"Bravo!" I cried. "You didn't miss it by much! Good shot."

Olivia called out, "You must practice a lot, Arthur."

Arthur blanched, disappointed that he missed, but thanked her. He reloaded the gun and handed it to me. I aimed at the white stone but then, I lowered the barrel. I didn't expect to hit such a small object so far away. But how embarrassing it would be for Arthur if, by remotest chance, I did hit it. I aimed again but announced, "I'll try to hit that fungus on the hickory tree.

Here goes," and I pulled the trigger. Nothing happened. "Oh yes," I said, and I squeezed again.

BANG!! assaulted my ears and punched my shoulder. My head was in a swirling cloud of dark smoke that obscured my target. A light breeze cleared the air and I could see the fungus was still there but hanging by a shred.

Arthur asked Olivia if she would like to try a shot which she politely declined. He then said that I had promise and offered to coach me some day later in the week.

He showed us the small cabin, the original residence on the tract, packed with ice and sawdust, next to his cistern just up from the pool. "We're lucky to have a sawmill nearby. I could never store this much ice without their sawdust. It keeps our meat and cheese fresh. We also like our milk, wine, and cider cold."

Returning to the house, we had some more of Arthur's chilled wine and Olivia helped Arabella with putting dinner on. A polished cherry table with silver candlesticks holding lighted bayberry candles at each end glistened in the firelight. Arthur and Arabella had not spared the fine touches, so that we were reminded of the grandeur of Governor Heyliger's banquet for us at his palace at Statia. Arabella favored us with a roast of lamb to celebrate our successful crossing. We felt as at home.

"The more I think of it, the more I look forward to seeing this Morris fellow. You may want to have his counsel regarding the gold, Jamie," Arthur declared.

Olivia and I were delighted at the prospect of having Arthur and Arabella accompany us to Philadelphia. We told them about John Bartram and his nursery. They had heard of it, but had never been there. The idea of seeing the self-taught botanist who had hiked the wilderness to bring wild plant specimens to the gardens of civilization whetted their enthusiasm for the trip. Departure was set for a week hence.

The next morning I noticed that Arthur's wagon had no springs. The thought of traveling ninety miles to Philadelphia on primitive roads on such a crude contrivance prompted me to ask if Arthur had any old iron or machinery that I could work to makes springs for his wagon.

It was all I could do to pump Arthur's small forge bellows to develop enough heat so that his scrap iron became malleable. Even so, working at his forge was as pleasing as ever I found it, and I felt that serene sense of accomplishment by producing a set of springs by mid-afternoon.

I hitched Blaze in the wagon traces and went for a spin towards Vaux Hall at the south end of the valley to call on the smith there to see if he had any bolts and nuts or could make some. As much as the hardware, I wanted the ride in Arthur's wagon for comparison with what I was sure would be a much more comfortable ride when I had fitted it with springs.

I had gone only a mile when the clang of someone hammering iron reached my ears. A ramshackle elongated hut made of upright logs and wattle-and-daub next to a grove of trees at the river bank assaulted my eyes. Guinea hens and chickens picking over the remnants of last summer's weeds strutted to and fro, clucking indignantly at my intrusion.

Upon hearing my quest, the smith was anxious for conversation. "You sound like a smith, yourself. What do you need the bolts for?"

I told him.

"More power to ye, but don't let the word get out. I get more business hammering axles bent from the beating this road gives them. When you install the springs, come back so I can see how well they work. I may equip my own wagon with springs to demonstrate to my customers." His jaws worked constantly, undulating a pepper-and-salt frost of beard as he talked or chewed.

As he worked, he altered his conversation with deftly hammered blows to the cherry-red end of a strap of flat iron. "You sound like you might be English," he spat.

I introduced myself.

"Are you planning to set up shop here or just visiting?" He reversed the iron to heat the other end, and double-checked his measurement. Despite his sloppy appearance and his crude shop, it was clear that he was an expert seat-of-the-pants metallurgist.

"Oh no. I'm just visiting Arthur and Arabella and touring the country," I hastened to say. He seemed relieved.

"Hardly enough people here to keep two smiths occupied. But in another five years or so, we'll have more custom to keep us busy. More people and more of them getting wagons, carts, and even carriages. That is, if the Tories and Whigs don't get carried away with fighting each other and destroy all that four generations have built here."

The other end was now cherry-red and his style was to deliver a strong whack followed by a tap or two for aiming the next blow.

"Elkanah! Come out here," he called. "I'm just about ready. Bring Jed, too." Two youths Jonathan's age appeared but they were sturdy and heavily muscled, like wrestlers.

"Elk. Hold that end on the horn so I can butt this end to it. Yes, like that. Now, hold it still." Elkanah concentrated on holding the ends tightly together.

"Wham!!" The smith hammered while the ends dimmed to grayish-red as they fused. Satisfied, he quenched the welded part of the piece in a mossy bucket and set it aside as he reached to shake hands. "Glad to meet you, Jamie. I'm Henry Pierson, but call me Hank."

Henry turned to the boy waiting for instructions. "Jed, set that tire on the coals and build up a blast. Elk, bring the wheel."

He relaxed and turned to me, "This is a new technique in applying the tire. Makes better sense than the bother of making up ten curved plates and bolting them in place like we used to do. Saves time, and so far, no tires have come off, unlike the plates. "

He pulled out his pipe and makings, loaded it, and fired up with a wisp of reed he ignited in the coals. He coughed and blew out a cloud of heavy leathery-smelling smoke.

"I think I have enough carriage bolts and nuts on hand. Get 'em for you in a minute," Hank said.

Elkanah produced the wheel and laid it down on a thick wooden platform that had seen extensive service. A void in the center made room for the wheel's hub so the wheel could lie flat. Elkanah and Jedediah then grabbed their tongs and carefully picked up the iron tire and placed it on the bed of coals as Hank began pumping the bellows.

Flames furiously shot up from the aerated coals and engulfed the iron band.

After another draw on his pipe, Hank admonished, "Boys, have your mallets handy as well as full buckets. You know what to do. Be careful now."

The black iron ring now radiated a greyish-red, the signal for Hank and his boys to clasp the band with their tongs and carry it the short distance to the wooden wheel. They carefully placed their burden concentric with the rim before lowering it to embrace the wheel assembly.

"Wham! Wham, Wham." Their mallets drove the iron circle down evenly in place around the wheel quickly so that they could douse it with water before it set fire to the wooden rim. The water cooled and shrank the iron so that it gripped the whole assembly like a wedge, firmly seating the spokes deeper into both the hub and the felloes. Smoke, steam, sweat and yells filled the shop and Hank and his boys collapsed with joy and exhaustion.

"You boys earned your money on that job. Let's all have a mug of cider. How about you, Jamie? Join us in a mug before you take your nuts and bolts along." Hank offered.

I recognized the rare taste of Claveraque cider which satisfied so well after the heat and concentration in Hank's forge. Hank must be a customer of Arthur's. When I set the mug down, he handed me the wrapped package of hardware and shook hands again as did each of his boys.

"Come back, now, Jamie. I want to try out your rectified wagon!" I offered a ten shilling note but he dismissed me with the wave of his hand and disappeared into the dark of the forge.

As I fastened the springs, I thought about our forthcoming trip. It would be far better to delay at least another month till mid-April and see spring unfold as we progressed south, particularly at Bartram's nursery. Leaving next week would be way premature. We might even be caught in a storm. No need to rush into the Grand Tour on either Arthur's or our account.

At dinner, all agreed. Arthur was glad to have the time to show us his neighborhood and friends, and to assure us that we could use his farm from which to range the countryside.

The next day, he hitched Blaze to the "rectified" wagon and we all took our seats to tour the valley. We went down Tuscan Road to the Valley Road, zig-zagged north, then west to ford the narrow river. Red-winged blackbirds had claimed the marsh reeds, a sure sign of spring.

There had not been much snow that winter but there was a good flow of water. Several decades before Arthur had arrived in the valley, grist and saw mills had been erected where dams backed up substantial reservoirs that assured uninterrupted operations. Many orchards blanketed the hillsides to satisfy the voracious market in Newark and New York.

We started to climb the rise at the foot of the mountain up the road that erosion had badly rutted, a perfect place to test my efforts to make a less miserable ride. Arabella noticed it first. "I usually ask Arthur to avoid this road it at all possible. It's such a series of jolts that I can hardly walk for days afterwards. But the springs have made even this endurable. Jamie, you are a genius. Thank you." Arthur and Olivia concurred.

Arthur announced, "If Blaze can hold out, I thought we could go up the mountain to a lookout where the view of the valley and Newark and New York is superb."

The road was a long sloping gash in the mountainside but was too much for old Blaze with all of us in the wagon. All but Arthur got out to lighten the load and occasionally to give Blaze an assist as required at difficult stretches. There being no brakes, I cut a stout pole to shove through the wheel spokes should we need to resist gravity's pull. The sluggish pace of pushing behind the wagon allowed closer observation of the bank cut in the side of the hill where colt's foot had embedded itself to bloom and confirm the almanac's forecast of spring.

Near the top was a clearing where the breeze refreshed our overheated and disheveled selves as we rested, we said, for Blaze's benefit. I gave Blaze a handful of oats and an apple to compensate her for her exertions..

When we mounted the crest and arrived at the overlook, there was a stiff breeze. Arthur asserted, "On a clear day, you can just make out the steeples of St. Paul's and Trinity Church and the heights of Staten Island." He pinpointed the steeples and swept his hand south to the headlands framing New York Bay. As yet, this was my closest view of the city.

# chapter 24

CRISPIN HAD BEEN enthralled to see his first real land since leaving England, part of a continent rather than a small coral island like St. Eustatia. From the ship the Atlantic Highlands had come into view several hours before that province's southern flat lands so that New Jersey first appeared as an island.

As the *Raritan* closed to within five miles of the shore, the ship rounded Sandy Hook and Crispin had his initial view of New York Harbor. The terrain satisfied his artist's eye with the contrast of steep cliffs next to the bay, islands, large and small, two wide rivers emptying into the splendor of an expansive estuary, and a toehold of civilization clutching the southern tip of Manhattan Island in the center. What an awesome sight, it would be rapturous to view the scene in its spring verdure, he thought.

A large British warship bristling with armament and arrogance in the distance confirmed the information they had received a few hours earlier from an outbound sloop. The presence of HMS *Asia* dissuaded Captain Adam from any further thought of docking at New York and the *Raritan* changed course to the starboard tack and began preparations to land at Perth Amboy..

Crispin was anxious to discover and paint scenes of this new land that beckoned with beauty and bounty. But the only paints he could obtain there were for the hulls of ships and shop walls—nothing for artistry despite Perth Amboy's stature as the capital of East Jersey. The ship chandler suggested he try New York. "One can get anything in New York," he said.

Captain Adam loaned him several pounds in advance against payment for the long-anticipated oil portrait of the captain and his wife. Crispin said his thanks and hastened to step aboard a sloop glad to sail with one more passenger.

As he savored the view of the Staten Island hills and the lengthy Long Island shore across Raritan Bay, Crispin felt a nudge at his side. "You new here, son?" Crispin did not turn but only nodded, intent on admiring such an overwhelming scene.

But the man insisted and repeated his query, again accompanied by a nudge. Crispin felt obliged to respond, "Yes, I just arrived at Perth Amboy yesterday," and, without further word, firmly returned to his view of the magnificence of the Narrows just coming into sight.

"You be from England, boy?" This time, Crispin turned and stared at the bulk of the unwelcome interloper who withdrew a step from Crispin's glare. Crispin didn't care for this intrusion nor for being addressed as a boy even by someone perhaps twice his age.. He had followed the lead of the *Raritan's* crew by not shaving for the duration of the Atlantic crossing and sported a man's full beard trimmed with style and finesse by first mate Estrich.

"Yes, I am. But, I want to enjoy this incomparable view without interruption, if you please," Crispin declared and quickly turned his attention back to the intriguing panorama unfolding before him as the sloop swiftly advanced. Indistinct points of interest and headlands came into better focus and the distant traffic of sloops, ketches, snows, ferries and whitehall taxis, and bulky round-hulled merchant ships became larger as they beat up the harbor. His sloop was favored by a flood tide and a northwest wind so that it raced to this appointment with an indelible moment in Crispin's life.

The Staten Island shore was forested with many varieties of trees but mostly a type of evergreen more easily detected from a mile offshore for its pungent pine or cedar-like essence. Now and then an eagle or osprey would hover, searching the surface, before plummeting to its target. A splash, grappling and flapping its wings, the strong bird burst into the air again grasping the wriggling prey to retire to a branch of a sentinel tree on the headland.

Fully fifteen minutes passed before Crispin was annoyed again.

"If you be new to the city, you be needing a place to stay, to whet your whistle, and maybe some female company. I just wanted to say I can take you to any of these places. We try to offer hospitality to strangers." His demeanor hinted of many years of unremitting labor as did his clothes. He may have been forty years old or fifty but without much to show for it.

Crispin wished to spend the entire two hour ferry ride as if it was a solo excursion. To politely gain this privacy, he smiled at the man, "I won't be staying the night. Just tell me where I can buy some artist's supplies, please." This ought to discourage him, Crispin thought.

"Why, that's easy. I'm going to a shop joined to a book store where artists bring their paintings for sale and buy brushes, colors and canvas and easels and such like. It's on Maiden Lane. Just remind me when we dock and I'll take you there. In the meantime, enjoy the sights. I won't interrupt. My name's Jedediah Peters, by the way," and he thrust out his hand.

Crispin had no choice but to accept the man's hospitality. His rearing obligated him to introduce himself. "I appreciate your understanding and courtesy, Mr. Peters," Crispin begrudged and turned back to the ship's rail. Sailing up the Narrows was like passing through a gate to a new world, the same feeling he had when he had fled the hated army camp at the greenwood. He foresaw an exciting future successfully painting portraits and fixing on canvas the magnificent landscape of a new and vigorous country. While he couldn't wait to begin this career, he wanted to savor this moment and be able to recall it many times. He was grateful that Mr. Peters refrained from conversation. The man had some sensibilities, after all.

The ferry veered to starboard to make for the East River flowing between the island's eastern shore and a bluff opposite which he later found was Brooklyn Heights. They passed an island of perhaps forty acres on the right which Jedediah said had been traditionally called Nutten Island for its many nut trees but was now called Governor's Island. As they approached Manhattan Island, Crispin noticed that many buildings were as high as three stories and even with the tops of the highest trees in their winter tracery. Many church steeples rose much higher.

At the island's tip, a battery was being enlarged with more guns. Nearby, Fort George, marked by years of neglect, was now clambered over with workmen on scaffolds. It was the first building they passed. Then a row of ships with bowsprits over-reaching the quay crowded by shore-side taverns and shops spread northeast along the river. As they neared, Crispin noticed that the wind was blanketed by the island, making it easier for the sloop to navigate the difficult approach. This arrangement of piers on the leeward shore explained the concentration of ships docked on the southeastern side of the city.

The sloop bumped the huge knot of hemp protecting the bow from chafing against the dock, and passengers bustled about with their burdens ready to disembark while others on shore waited impatiently to board. Jedediah joined Crispin on the landing and pointed the way from South Street to Broadway. Crispin quietly kept in step with his un-sought guide. He admired the change from taverns, shipyards, rope walks, fish markets, and ship chandlers between Cruger's Wharf and Whitehall Slip to law offices, shops, churches, and fine residences on Broad Street. Soon, they arrived at lower Broadway and an oval of well-kept grass within an iron fence.

"This is the Bowling Green, where gentlemen play at bowls. Now, we turn right and go a few blocks up Broadway," said Jedediah.

"What! A statue to the man who makes war on his own subjects?" Crispin bawled. The sudden view of a gilt King George III, dressed in a Roman toga to simulate a statesman, mounted on a charger all about fifteen feet high and set on a white marble pedestal. It was startling.

Jedediah calmed down Crispin and vowed, "This monstrosity was erected a few years ago when some Tories wanted to grand-stand and curry favor by crediting the king with repeal of the stamp tax. Can you imagine? What a waste of the thousand pounds spent on its erection. Notice that the sculptor omitted stirrups. We take that to mean George has no base to stand on."

With that statement, Crispin's opinion of Jedediah changed forever. 'Just because his clothes are shopworn doesn't mean he's stupid like some who are well dressed,' Crispin thought. As they strode Broadway, Crispin admired the three-story red brick mansions mixed in with the older Dutch step-gabled homes and shops. Troops were laying up barricades on the cross streets and building batteries for gun emplacements at strategic locations. Jedediah said that they were largely militia under the command of newly arrived General Charles Lee, a disgruntled former English officer, now Washington's second in command.

In the absence of adequate barrack space, some troops had desperately broken into fine homes that had been vacated by terrified families and made quarters for themselves. It was estimated that almost a third of the citizenry had fled. The city appeared trashed.

Crispin was awed by the Trinity Church steeple—Jedediah said it was one hundred and seventy-five feet high. Within a short walk, they reached Maiden Lane and turned right. A few steps off Broadway brought them to a narrow storefront wedged between two townhouses. Upon entering the shop, a small bell tinkled and soon a ruddy-faced man with remnants of an Irish brogue stepped from behind a partition to introduce himself.

"I am William Farrell, owner of the shop. How can I help you?" he said.

Crispin's only answer was a nod to avoid appearing impolite. Books lined most of the walls but some shelves displayed paper, stretched canvas, wood panels, pallets and brushes, various styled frames, and most sorts of painter's colors, ready mixed and prepared for use by being put up in bladders.

At eye level were portraits and landscapes by artists unknown to Crispin. He decided that his work must soon be presented in this fashion to gain notice. He introduced himself to Farrell who was delighted to have a new customer. "I need a quarter ream of paper, charcoal stubs, two stretchers of canvass, brushes, and a rainbow of colors," he declared. As soon as Farrell placed the items on the counter, Crispin reached for a sheet of paper and a stub of charcoal and began to sketch. The shop keeper and Jedediah watched in amazement as Crispin's firm strokes quickly captured the essence of Farrell's countenance and character.

Farrell snatched up the picture the second Crispin completed it and walked over to the framed mirror on the wall by the wash stand.

He carefully compared the rendition to his reflection and shook his head in disbelief.

"Where did you learn to do this? To be able to recognize the main features of a face as well as its overall character and render them so faithfully in such a short time is astonishing. I would like to add this portrait to the gallery in front, with your permission," said Farrell.

"I was hoping that you would," Crispin responded.

"Do you do portraits in oil, Mr. Johnson? There are many in the city who would be glad to have you paint them and their families, particularly in view of the uncertainties facing them now. As helpless as they feel, having their likeness recorded for their posterity would give many great comfort, I'm sure." Farrell said.

"I have a commission to do an oil portrait of husband and wife friends of mine. It will be my first___"

The shop bell tinkled with the entrance of a stocky self-assured middle aged gentleman. "Bill!" he greeted. " What's that you have? Someone do a charcoal sketch of you? Is this the man who did it? One of your artists? Introduce me. I want him to show me some of his work."

Bill introduced Crispin to Sedgewick Pettit " Pettit is one of the most perceptive connoisseurs of art in the city. He visits my shop frequently for artwork and fine books. He bought all the books written by, or about, Samuel Johnson. He brings fine conversation wherever he goes."

"This caricature of me is his most recent work," said Farrell, as he handed the sketch to Pettit

Pettit pinned it to the wall and examined it from several angles and degrees of light.

"This is excellent. Do you have any portraits done in oils, young man?"

"I have only one—-of a ship captain and his wife. And that is still in my studio in Perth Amboy undergoing completion of collateral detail." Crispin was sure this would be an honest statement within another week. One must not pin himself down by time, he rationalized.

Pettit would not be put off. "Can you arrange to have me sit for you a week from today at my town house which is nearby?"

Crispin was amused and delighted that he was able to arrange a commission so quickly and from such an influential and highly vocal authority as Mr. Pettit. "I believe I can arrange to be in the city that day and can see you that afternoon, sir."

"Fine. I shall ask Adrienne, Mrs. Pettit, and my daughter to be present. We will probably want you to paint them as well. May I call you Crispin? Please call me Sedgewick."

Crispin readily agreed whereupon Sedgewick reached out his hand, shook Crispin's hand vigorously, and, without further comment, departed.

Farrell sighed and cooed. "You certainly nailed that down in a hurry, Crispin. May I call you by your first name?, Indeed! I think we have a winner here. Don't you, Mr. Peters?"

Crispin spied a thin leather portfolio on display in which to carry these supplies and asked Farrell the price.

"Please, be my guest and accept it as a token of my admiration and friendship. You have made an otherwise bleak morning interesting, pleased an important customer of mine, and started a promising career for yourself here today. So, please take the case. I hope to see much more of you, Crispin. Did Mr. Peters bring you here?"

"He did indeed, sir," said Crispin, smiling. "He nudged me into it, you might say."

As Crispin and Peters turned to leave, Farrell called out, "When you see the Pettits next week, come by to see me. I'll probably have more patrons interested in your work. At any rate, it will be good to see you."

Crispin turned to Jedediah as they stood on the curb. "Well, Jedediah, I'm glad we met and that you introduced me to Bill Farrell. Thank you. It being early afternoon, I think I should head back to Perth Amboy. I hope to see you again, perhaps at Farrell's shop."

"No need to leave so soon, Mr. Crispin. The ferry won't sail until three thirty or when they have enough passengers to make it worth their while. As we're in the neighborhood, let me take you to meet another shop owner who may be as useful to you as Farrell."

Crispin agreed and the pair crossed Broadway to Greenwich Street and walked a few blocks north to Trevor Shaw's emporium.

Jedediah led the way past Marty Mittens, who looked like she might be dreaming of her successful mouse hunt the previous night. A flick of the ear was her only recognition.

"Hello, Jordan. Is Trevor in this afternoon?"

"You're in luck. He's in, Mr. Peters, and will be glad to see you. He's been fussing about what to do with the business. Talk him out of selling it, will you? Go right in."

"Trevor, what's this about selling the store, just when business is bound to improve?"

"Come in, Jedediah. I have a problem and can use your opinion. Who is this?"

Introductions were made, hands shaken and both men quickly took stock of the other.

"We have just come from Bill Farrell's where Mr. Johnson, an artist, sketched Bill, and a few minutes later obtained a commission to paint Sedgewick Pettit and family. I wanted Crispin, ah, Mr Johnson, to meet you since we have some time before boarding the Staten Island ferry. He just recently arrived from England but sketched a remarkable likeness of Farrell on sight."

Trevor called out to Jordan, "No more visitors, Jordan. I want to chat with these gentlemen, and that will be it for the day." He turned to Crispin. "Can you do a sketch of me? Here? Now? May I call you Crispin? Are you from England?"

"The answer is yes to all your questions, Mr. Shaw. Or, may I say Trevor? I will begin right now, if you please." Crispin removed a charcoal spud and paper from the leather case and set up his newly acquired easel a few feet from Trevor's chair..

"Yes! By all means, call me Trevor. But before we begin, Crispin, let me ask you how people over there feel about the protests over here."

Crispin was direct. "Many in the West Country, where I am from, are in sympathy with the Americans. But in England tradition is strong and loyalty to the crown has been ingrained for many generations. There is the heavy expense of the French war still to be paid and the almost certain prospect of war with Americans. So we have the gentry, burdened with a heavy land tax, twenty percent of the property's value, and other groups opposed to the war, regardless of political opinion, because they simply want their taxes lowered and their lives left undisturbed."

Trevor appreciated Crispin's candor. "Thank you, Crispin. Well said. Enough of politics. Where do you want me to sit?"

"Stay where you are and talk or do what you want. I want to capture Trevor Shaw as you are—not some staid and solemn replica of him."

"What did you do in England and why did you decide to come to New York?"

Crispin drew the initial stroke of Trevor's profile before answering.

"My family had a dairy farm and I did the usual chores, mostly milking, shoveling manure, scything hay, and other menial tasks. My father was very dictatorial, insisted I make a life of farming, and never offered a word of encouragement for my interest in art. I was convinced that my life would be nothing more than doing dull farm work. I hated such confinement and was both humiliated and distressed by it.

"In its recruiting program, the army offered a chance to come to America where I had heard that a common man could do well, even be given land. I thought I could never afford the voyage on my own, and so I took the king's shilling and joined the army.

"Trevor, turn your head a bit to the left for more light. That's good." Crispin dashed the charcoal spud across the paper and the caricature now featured Trevor's high cheekbones.

Crispin continued his sketch and commentary. "I was so centered on my misery that I acted too hastily—without realizing what I was getting into.

"At that time, a local businessman man tricked dozens of people, who used the commons for a living, by offering to loan them more than they could pay back. When they defaulted, he foreclosed and dispossessed them. Then he took over the commons by right of enclosure.

"This may seem like a long-winded answer but anything less would not justify my actions. The same man bought a part of an adjacent and ancient forest through which a magnificent trout and salmon stream flowed which many generations have enjoyed. Being well connected, he sold this tract to the government knowing full well that it would be desecrated and made into an army training ground.

"Whole squads of recruits, including me, were ordered to level this beautiful greenwood where my friends and I and generations of our fathers had fished and hunted. England has always admired the beauty and sport of its countryside, especially ancient tracts.

"Yet the present administration insisted on ruining some of the oldest and most glorious woodlands. I just could not have a part in destroying what I so loved. Besides that, most of the officers and non-coms were arrogant and mean-spirited. They made life unbearable, an affliction I had to refute and abandon.

"So I fled into the nearby woods and made for my best friend's little forge and work shop on his family's farm. He put me up for several days and a day before he and his wife were to sail, he sent me to Bristol, disguised as a teamster, with a wagon load of cider,—his family owns an orchard and cider mill—and I made it safely to the ship because of my friend's wit and planning."

"You mean that your friend was leaving the country, too?"

"Yes, but not permanently. He was planning a grand tour of the colonies and it so happened that he had met a wonderful girl whom he began to court. Their wedding coincided with my bolt from the army. When I asked for help, I knew nowhere else to turn. Jamie came through as I knew he would, and gave me safe haven and passage with them on board the schooner they were taking for New York." Crispin refrained from telling about his sketching the captain for his passage. He thought it would lessen the illusion of his professional status.

Crispin's story had a familiar ring. Trevor had heard of a situation similar to it but he could not put his finger on it. He stepped over to see what Crispin had sketched. "That's beginning to look like me, alright," he said and returned to his chair. "Keep going, but take your time, Crispin. I've never been sketched before and not likely to be again."

There came a great rattling of the front door accompanied by barking dogs. Someone was demanding that Trevor open up for business. Trevor was annoyed and told Jordan to ignore them, but the racket persisted.

Crispin spoke up. "Better let him in. Your facial composure is being affected and I won't achieve the normal likeness I want with this agitation. Perhaps it's important."

Jedediah went to slide the bolt and the door was pushed open by a large-nosed, very tall, middle-aged, gangling fellow dressed in a bizarre military uniform and adorned with a cockaded cocked hat. Epaulettes glittered in the fading light but a white lace stock held with an emerald pin between the lapels of a yellow satin jacket stood out like a candle. He strutted with authority and demanded serious attention. He was accompanied by a stiff-backed aide and two pomeranians, Jedediah thought that was the breed, that ran ahead of him and threatened to dislodge brooms and kitchen hardware on display.

The man yelled, "Sit!" and the dogs instantly flopped to the floor. Marty Mittens, greatly affronted by this intrusion, screeched as she got to her feet and raised her hackles, almost doubling her size as she ran to the basement steps. The interruption astounded us and tied our tongues on the instant.

"I am here to examine your wares, sirs. I am particularly looking for darts with which my men can kill the thousands of rats that infest the streets of this foul, promiscuous, and mismanaged city. At the same time, this should entertain the troops away from wasting their energy and health trysting with the denizens of what you call the 'Holy Ground'. I also will require several dozen whetstones to repoint those darts that are flung wide of the mark."

Trevor winced, "Welcome to New York, General Lee—you are General Lee, are you not?—and to your aide de camp. We have about five dozen dart sets and perhaps two dozen whetstones on hand. You may purchase what you want and we can order more of both, if you wish. But, for the moment, I am having my portrait done, as you can see.

"Please make yourself comfortable with some coffee and examine the store and the merchandise. I'll be glad to give you my personal attention when the artist has completed my likeness. It will only be a few moments more."

The general grunted his displeasure that he had met with a will equal to his and turned to browsing the shelves and counters loaded with such widely diverse items.

"Crispin, please continue with the sketch. I am anxious to see the finished portrait," Trevor implored.

Noting wrinkles around Trevor's eyes and forehead that weren't apparent before, Crispin changed the subject to relax Trevor to his former composure. "Do you sell fishing equipment here, Trevor?"

"I have both salt water and fresh water tackle, including fine fly rods made of Tonkin cane by local craftsmen. Crispin, I'll bet you prefer trout fishing to all else. Am I right?"

Crispin deftly shaded Trevor's lapels and his collar on the drawing while he awaited a more desirable facial expression.

"Yes, I grew up with a fly rod in my hand and tied my own flies. I read Izaak Walton's **Compleat Angler** many times and, as well, learned fishing lore and techniques stream side on my own. Because of the crossing I haven't fished in four months and am anxious to get back to it. So I'd like to buy some equipment and would appreciate your consideration if you'll tell me of some secluded riffles and a productive pool. Do you wet a fly now and then, Trevor?"

"I haven't in some time. I'm glad you raised the question. I'd like to get away from the city and its troubles and fly fishing would be just the thing. Do you know that Walton lived to be ninety? The pleasures of fishing may have helped him live so long. I know just the stream near Westchester. When you finish the sketch, I'll show you some light tackle that'll pitch a fly twenty yards but still let you fish those ignored tree-encumbered rills loaded with brook trout."

"That sounds exactly what I want. I can't wait to be wading a rushing stream again.

I'm almost done, but I don't want to be hasty or add any superfluous lines. Don't let me forget to secure a map of the area as well as the tackle."

"The ferry will be leaving soon, Crispin. We mustn't dally if you wish to return to Amboy tonight," Jedediah chimed in.

Crispin stepped back and looked at his work, then at Trevor. With a flourish he approached the easel and made one last stroke with the charcoal spud. "There! It's done. Take a look."

Trevor quickly vacated his chair to see the product of his imposed immobility.

"Ah. That does look like me. But do I look that old? It appears almost as I remember my father," he said.

"I hope you don't feel you have been advanced in age, Trevor. My aim has been to show you as an experienced businessman, a successful entrepreneur as opposed to a young hustler—a man at that time in life when he is enjoying the fruits of his vigor and enterprise." General Lee returned from his round of the store. "Ah. I see we have an accomplished portraitist in New York. The picture looks very much like you, Mister Shaw. Very shrewd. Very handsome," he declared.

Trevor mellowed and agreed that he was very pleased. "I think I want another done in colors," he said.

General Lee ordered shovels and wheelbarrows besides the darts.

"Do you think the city can be defended, General?" asked Trevor.

"Were doing the best we can, Mr. Shaw. But we will see." The general paid for the merchandise with a handful of fresh bills of credit, had his aide load the wheelbarrow with darts and shovels, and as he opened the door, called out, "My aide will call to carry back the rest."

Crispin began to pursue his conversation with Trevor but Jedediah cut him short. "We have to hurry to catch the ferry. I'm sure Trevor would like to spend the afternoon telling you of his fishing exploits and you would like to listen and buy tackle, but it will have to wait."

As they retraced their steps to the ferry slip, Crispin gloried in his good luck. "This has been a very successful day. I owe much of that success to you, Jedediah, for which I'm grateful. When I am able, I will repay you several times over."

Jedediah smiled and put his hand on Crispin's shoulder. "Crispin, you made good use of your day in New York so I'll see you off now. I have some business in the city, but I'll be back in Perth Amboy in a few days, " he said.

The ferry must have been delayed for it was just pulling into the slip. There were about fifteen passengers, all in a hurry to disembark as soon as the crew made the lines fast. Especially anxious was a tall baldheaded man wielding an ivory headed blackthorn cane.

Crispin was shaking Jedediah's hand as they were about to part but pulled Jedediah closer to him. "Don't look now but the tall bald man with the fancy cane bears watching. He is the man I told you of who foreclosed the common. If you can, please keep an eye on him, where he goes and whom he meets. Keep him in sight but avoid his seeing you, if at all possible. My friend, Jamie, and I think he is on a mission of more trouble."

Jedediah smiled, for this was the very man he was looking for.

Trevor had been looking forward to an interesting afternoon but it had suddenly changed from one of convivial conversation to being alone in his office with the store closed for the balance of the day. He was sorry that his friends, including the artist from England had commitments elsewhere.

The unexpected opportunity to have his portrait sketched was welcome but precluded getting Jedediah's opinion on business prospects for the foreseeable future. Jedediah had been a successful merchant up to five years ago and had had to make a similar decision. And he had opted out, though for different reasons. I'll take him to lunch the next time I see him. I'm sure he'll have a considered opinion on my situation, Trevor decided.

Trevor had read several weeks before of Colonel Knox's crew of soldiers who had struggled to bring desperately needed cannon and mortars from Fort Ticonderoga across the snow and ice of the Berkshires to Washington in Cambridge. He knew that the stalemate in Boston would soon be over. This artillery could be set up to bear on the besieged redcoats in the city and the British fleet in Boston harbor. The trick was for Washington's troops to get all this armament in place before the redcoats could stop them.

Anyone could see that the British would soon be in a disagreeable position from which they would have to fight or disengage and leave the area. He did not claim to be knowledgeable in military matters but suspected they would choose the latter. Otherwise, it would be like Bunker Hill all over again.

Other news a few days later revealed the king's determination to suppress what he now referred to as a rebellion and a state of war existed. Trevor was certain that New York would be the focus of the British fleet and army. A bull-headed king and ministry would now use massive force to put down a persistently annoying throng.

His store business had suffered since June when the last of the British regulars had been shipped off to Boston. And, as the tension due to a brief naval bombardment on the city and patriot raids increased, many Loyalists fled to the outskirts. Trevor was reasonably sure that the British would return to New York, but in far larger numbers and with blood in their eyes. They could easily take the city from Washington's troops who were far from being trained to the same high degree of proficiency as the British regulars. He felt sure that a naval barrage and many battalions of His Majesty's army could quickly subdue the area.

Washington's troop strength would be far from reliable since enlistments for the state militia as well as the Continental Army were for short periods. As they did in the French war, many troops would return home when the fighting became fierce or the crops needed harvesting. And there were only a few men of officer material by reason of their French War experience who could command the respect of and direct troops under fire.

Trevor wanted to help the rebel cause but he doubted that he would be a good soldier. He had no qualifications as a fighter except in street brawls when in his teens. The thought of firing a gun to kill someone, with whom in other circumstance he might have coffee, was a repulsive distraction which precluded his joining the Continental Army. He could better help the patriot cause by making use of his contacts, he mused. He would appear neutral but silently join with the patriots and provide them with valuable information.

So he would keep his store and newly acquired apartments and become an informant—not a spy—an ugly word. He would be in a unique position to overhear unguarded conversations of British officers in taverns and coffee houses, and his store after they took over the city.

There was a knocking on the door and a polite call, "Mr. Shaw, I am Captain Rawls, General Lee's aide. I've come back to pick up the rest of the general's order. Please let me in."

Trevor opened the door wide and directed him to the pickup items. "It's better to secure the wheels and nest the barrow shells, and to tie the shovels together, like spoons, Captain. Then, use one shovel handle like a wagon tongue for a manageable package," Trevor told him. He showed the captain what he meant and sent him on his way with his unwieldy burden in tow.

When Trevor closed the door, he sighed and turned back to his office. He was surprised to find a young women in the store with a half-dozen candles in her hand.

"How did you get in, miss?" Trevor asked.

"The door was unlatched. That soldier left it so when he entered your place. Why, shouldn't I be allowed in the store?"

"I'm sorry, I didn't realize that the door was open. What can I help you with?"

"I need these candles and hope that you have some stationery on hand. Maybe I could use a quarter wheel of cheese and a loaf of bread, too." She spoke in a pleasant tone.

Trevor called her to come nearer. The lass was perhaps in her early twenties and wore a linsey-woolsey slip which was becoming to her figure. In better light he could see that she was a person of sensibilities, she spoke well, her auburn hair was modestly coiffured, and she had used a subtle perfume.. She must live close by to come out coatless in this cold.

I don't think I've ever seen her before, Trevor thought. I would certainly remember such a good looking woman. She looks like the lovely girl you see for a fleeting instant walking the opposite way or looking out a carriage window—one who instantly catches your eye but whom you know you will never see again. But here she is right here, now.

"Are you new in the area?" Trevor asked.

"My husband went north to Montreal with Montgomery's army last summer. I couldn't manage the farm alone or find any qualified person to run it, so I rented it to a neighbor and moved into the city. You have a nicely provisioned store, Mr. Shaw."

"Thank you. Is this your first visit miss, excuse me, missus, what's your name?"

"Annie McLauren, sir. I've been here only a few days. Neighbors told me I could get almost anything I wanted at your store, and that you would help me. So, yes, it's my first visit."

Trevor realized he had other reasons to remain in the city after all.

# chapter 25

OLIVIA AND I grew impatient waiting for better weather to travel to Philadelphia. February had been bitter cold and Arthur said that there had been no January thaw that year. To while the time, Arthur and Annabella took us to various friends who seemed interested in meeting travelers from the mother country. They were interested in our opinion of the king, Parliament, Lord Sandwich, Lord Germain, John Wilkes, Samuel Johnson, Isaac Barré, General Howe, George Washington, ad infinitum. Others thought that we must be wealthy because, to them, our manner of speaking hinted of a classical education, although no one intimated that we were "uppity."

One woman noted that, unlike another English visitor who was evidently a social sport, we did not use such inanities such as *split me; Madam; by Gad; and damn me*. She fancied that we were from London or Bath. She did not recall where the sport was from.

Hearing that Americans were largely levelers, I was surprised that Henry Pierson was not included as one of their friends although he was engaging and occasionally did smithy work for Arthur. Their circle was composed of shop keepers, lawyers, doctors, a tavern owner; and all were Anglicans. None were farmers, house wrights, blacksmiths, cabinet makers, tailors, shoemakers, or leather apron artisans who worked with their hands.

I had no brief against this, but they were all of one mind with little diversity of opinion. They professed to being Loyalists. Perhaps, because we were so recently from England, they assumed that we would be, too. Arthur and Arabella seemed to be firmly on the patriot side when conversing alone with us. But when called upon by their friends to confirm a political opinion they acquiesced in favor of the crown—I think only to avoid controversy.

One morning a neighbor came to borrow some sugar which I learned was her usual pretext for gossip over a dish of tea. After she knocked on the door, much to the dismay of Arabella who had plans for the morning, Mehitabel Blith barged her way in, bowl in hand.

"Arabella, I'm so sorry but I was planning a mince pie for Denny and found I was out of sugar. May I borrow some?" Her question was so practiced that no one could refuse her the time. But Arabella did not offer a dish of tea nor did she sit down, which would have allowed *Mettie* to anchor herself for most of the morning. Arabella readily proffered the sugar, though.

"Oh, thank you. I don't mean to bother you but Denny will be celebrating his fiftieth birthday and I must prepare favors, you know."

Arabella graciously replied, "You're welcome, Mettie. It's nice to—-"

"Denny so loves mince pie, I think it was when you served pie at your dinner last—- no, it was at Mary Lou's dinner party just before All Saint's Day. I remember because we had just heard about the Second Continental Congress adjourning and Denny wanted me to get her recipe, Mary Lou's, that is. Mary Lou is a good cook and pie maker but I don't know where she gets her funny ideas about the colonies separating from the mother country. Maybe that pamphlet I saw on her kitchen table, Mr. Paine's *Common Sense*. Well, where was I…Oh yes, Denny is thinking about serving in a new regiment, the King's Own, I think it is. Denny says…"

Not wishing to appear to be eavesdropping, I entered the kitchen. I also wanted to help Arabella disengage from this prattle.

Arabella quickly introduced me. "Mehitabel, this is Arthur's nephew, Jamie Claveraque, from near Bristol, England. He and his bride are touring the colonies."

"Well, we live twenty-five miles north of Bristol in the Wye Valley. I'm glad to meet you miss Mehitabel—"

"You're newly weds? How cute! Denny and I were married—I can't believe it—twenty-three years ago last month. Father paid for our European tour and we traveled for seven months until I became with child and had to return home. Father is a distant cousin of William Livingston, you know."

"I remember when you moved here, Mettie. You celebrated your anniversary the next day. Dear girl, I'm sorry to take so much of your time. I'm glad to loan you the sugar, but I must not delay you any longer. I hope the pie turns out well." Arabella moved toward the door. Mettie dallied, "To think that those rebels had the audacity to set up their own congress. Don't they know that King George rules the freest, the richest, the happiest country in the world? The nerve to think that they can tell him and Parliament how to run things. Denny says—-"

"Excuse me a moment miss Mehitabel. Arabella, can you finish mending my shirt? I really must arrive in Newark on time." I urged. I was hopeful that Arabella would recognize this ploy. She saw my meaning and clutched on to it as a drowning person would for a thrown line. I inched towards the door and Mettie.

"Oh yes, I'll get right back to it, Jamie. You must really come over and have coffee, Mettie. Someday next week. Be sure to come now, dear. Bye!" Arabella was firm but not unkind.

As the door closed and Mehitabel trudged home, Arabella sighed, "I was afraid she was going into her usual diatribe on the patriots. Thanks for enabling me to save the morning."

Arthur came in at that time. "I'm glad to see that miss Mettie didn't stay long. I couldn't wait out in the barn all day. You must have threatened to beat her with the rolling pin to send her on her way so quickly."

Arabella and I laughed. "It was something like that," she admitted.

Olivia had been weaving a throw on Arabella's large loom upstairs. When she heard the outburst, she came down to find what it was all about.

Over coffee, Arthur said his mind. "I know you're both anxious to get to Philadelphia for financial advice, Jamie. A jeweler I know in Newark might give you some ideas which, if nothing else, would help you ask the right questions and understand the jargon these fellows use. You can get there in about an hour and I'd be pleased to introduce him to you, if you wish."

"How could a jeweler help? I don't want to buy jewelry."

"But they deal in silver and gold and are most careful of the safety of their investments and husbanding their income. Besides, everyday you let that gold just sit, you are losing money—interest or capital—profit you could be earning if it is invested in something that pays dividends or grows in value, or both. So it behooves you to seek advice soon. What say you?"

Olivia stood up. "You two go to Newark. I want to do some more work on this throw. I think I can finish it if I devote the next few days to staying on the loom. Tell me all about it when you get back." Arabella followed suit.

As the rain seemed to be coming to an end with a dry northwest wind, Arthur and I went the next day in his chaise to his jewelers in Newark.

Arthur introduced me to Mr. Bunkrot, who smiled behind a glass counter loaded with watches, eye glasses, brooches, bracelets, rings and silver service. He shook hands warmly with the prospect of a sale. When told that we wanted to see Mr. Walsbruch, his smile faded, slightly, and he led us to the back room where Walsbruch sat at a large desk surrounded by trade books, newspapers, and his pewter whale oil lamp. I noticed the papers were from Paris, London, Frankfurt, Boston, and other cities before I turned my gaze back to Walsbruch.

He pushed his chair back and stood to greet Arthur as an old friend. "More watches for us to fix today, Arthur?" he inquired. "How did that last batch work out?"

His deep-set eyes behind thick eyeglasses, high cheekbones, and a high, wrinkled forehead on a thin face suggested a constant mental intensity.

"Only two watches this time, Alan. Everyone was pleased, as they usually are, to get their timepieces back again. And they were most happy with the reasonable repair fee. I don't see how you can afford to charge so little. But I'm here for another purpose today, Alan. Please meet my nephew, Jamie Claveraque, recently arrived from near

Bristol, England. He and I are here to ask your advice on financial matters. Can you spare some time, perhaps be our guest at lunch?"

Arthur, who knew that Walsbruch favored Braunschweiger, pepperoni, and strong pale beer, steered us to the Golden Ox where we occupied a corner table away from most of the noise.

It was easy to see that Alan relished this treat to relieve his usual frugality although Arthur was sure Alan had accumulated a comfortable estate during the fifteen years he had built up a substantial clientele.

Arthur didn't waste time getting to the main subject. He explained his dilemma of risking the farm should Essex County find itself in the path of terror and destruction, versus selling it and investing the proceeds. What reinvestment options did he have, he wanted to know. He then allowed me to tell my story to Walsbruch.

I did not reveal the details of how I had enriched myself and Walsbruch did not raise an eyebrow at this sudden acquisition of a gold ingot. I was sure he had heard many similar revelations and was pleased that people sought him out and confided in him. He seemed particularly self-assured and that his years of study and experience had enabled him to amass a comfortable living and that he was in a position to tailor advice to suit each client's situation.

"Arthur invited my wife and me to tour the colonies for an extended period but I feel that it is unseemly for me to accept his generosity much longer in view of my extraordinary circumstance. How can I best convert the gold to an income producing property and keep it safe?"

Alan Walsbruch hesitated briefly before he spoke, "Your questions are somewhat similar but let me deal with Arthur's first. I assume that your farm is the main, if not sole, source of your income and that you do not want to buy another farm even if it is located where, in all likelihood, it will not be endangered. Is that correct, Arthur?"

"Not until the threat has passed," Arthur nodded.

"Is this a long term investment or just for a year or less?"

"It will be an investment for at least as long as the war lasts—or only three months if we have no war. Or for eight years if the war goes on that long. God hope it does not. Who knows, maybe there will be little to invest in if the ministry pushes its vengeance to the limit. I want the investment to be as flexible and safe as it can be and, if possible, to earn at least as much income as I earn now. You can appreciate that we want to maintain our style of living, Alan."

"Of course," Alan agreed. "You could buy stocks or bonds of companies in England on the London Stock Exchange that has been there for almost a hundred years. For example, you could own such companies as The East India Company of recent infamy or The Adventurers of Hudson Bay, The Bank of England, Lloyds of London, or some of the recently formed midland canal companies which have dug canals for increasing trade in the heartland of England.

"How much do they pay and how safe are they? What would you suggest, Alan?" Arthur was anxious to learn as much as possible during lunch.

"I wouldn't, at this moment, buy any of them. The East India Company was seriously mismanaged and had millions of pounds of tea accumulating in warehouses as a result. This is why the government tried to bail them out and, at the same time make it unprofitable to smuggle the stuff. As well, the big shots limited the sale to certain well-connected agents thus creating a monopoly. They should have known that it would ruin the market and upset colonial merchants.

"With war likely, I'd be wary of investing in companies in which King George's government has a hand or would be affected by the conflict. Manipulation for reasons only known to insiders can damage the small investor and you wouldn't know to sell out until it is too late. Best to stick to local, that is New Jersey, New York, or Pennsylvania companies so that you can keep current with their operation. I only mention these mother country investments to familiarize you with the dimensions of the investment world."

"What does that leave to invest in?" said Arthur.

"I can think of several prosperous businesses owned by solid, substantial families. The Wistar family and their glass works downstate, Joseph Galloway and the Durham Iron Works near Easton, Robert Morris and his commodities trading and banking company, and some boatbuilders who should do well in the war building and fitting out privateers and warships.

"But these are family owned businesses that would probably only be interested in borrowing funds to beef up their operations for the war. They wouldn't likely let an outsider in as a part owner. You would have to approach them and see."

"You could invest the sale proceeds with a private individual or bank firm that makes loans to those companies. This would be safer than a direct loan to just one company because you would be spreading the risk, though there would be a lesser return because of bank fees. Of course you would not have an ownership interest—you would be a creditor only." Alan declared.

"How do I know I can trust them?

"It's implicit in any type of investing that the management of the investment must be trustworthy. Of course, there are shady operators. That's why reputation is so important—and how long they have managed to stay in business. Does a succeeding generation have the interest and the brains to do as well as their father or uncle? Their customers and colleagues wouldn't countenance incompetence or trickery for one minute. So stick with venerable firms with good reputations." Alan said.

"What would you suggest if you were in our situation, Alan?" I cut in.

"Frankly, I wouldn't invest in any of the options I have mentioned so far. The times are menacingly unstable. This may sound self-serving on my part, but I would put my money into gold certificates. You turn over your money or your gold to a jeweler, like me, and receive back a fancy printed piece of paper which says it is redeemable in gold at the issuing jewelers.

"The certificates will fluctuate in value, depending upon the market for gold, but usually not very much. Gold, or its equivalent, generally holds its value, or even increases in value when investors think they see hard times ahead. It's considered a financial haven when the value of all else is endangered such as now. It's reasonable to believe they will be more stable than the new issue of Continental currency."

These certificates seemed promising. "Suppose I'm in Boston, or Philadelphia, and I want to cash some of the certificates?"

"Jewelers there will recognize their value since gold is internationally recognized as a safe medium of exchange, subject to market conditions. They will take them in and give you the market equivalent of their denomination. A ten pound note will fetch ten pounds assuming the value of gold is the same as it was when you obtained the certificates. You may even receive more than you paid if gold increases in value. Gold is a haven for money in bad times" Alan waited for questions.

Alan asked Arthur, "Did you say most of your income comes from operating the farm?"

"Oh yes. Both Arabella and I work in the orchard, although I do most of the physical work like pruning and harvesting. Arabella does the bookkeeping and some of the marketing. We have very little income from other pursuits. She sells bed covers, table cloths and other items that she weaves on her loom occasionally, and I handle the watch repairing."

"So your main income earning asset is you and your wife and your experience in managing the farm."

"Yes, that's right."

"I would suggest, that if you're really worried about the farm being ruined and beyond the possibility of rebuilding, that you sell it and put the proceeds into gold certificates. That will give you safety but not income. Many farmer's are enlisting in the militia or the Continental Army and are worried about their family being able to get a crop in. You could hire yourself out to provide labor and management to farms that have lost the owner or manager to the army. But likely you will earn less than you do now.

"Arthur, I must warn you that I suspect that the value of farms in this area has already dropped in anticipation of the possibility of a British attack. But, I don't involve myself in real estate transactions and can't advise you as to how much value they have."

"Arabella and I have been thinking about selling the farm ever since Bunker Hill and the threat of war became imminent. I suppose we waited too long to put the place on the market."

"Are you enlisted in the militia? Could your wife manage the farm without you."

"The work is too demanding. I wouldn't want to lay that responsibility on her alone. We do have two men who help out during the pruning season and at the harvest but they are both talking of joining the militia. I have made somewhat of a commitment to General Maxwell's regiment through John Lamsden who is a captain in the militia."

"So maybe the die is cast?, Arthur? You may be in the army before you know it and your labor force may be, too. But someone has to stay at home and raise the food for the populace and for the army. The country can't afford to have your farm or those of other farmers gone into service left unproductive. Some one has to work and manage them. I think you should talk to Squire Lamsden about managing those farms that will have need of your management skills. There may be some provision to exempt farm labor from military service. That may well determine what you are going to do."

Alan turned to me. "Tell me more about your plans and finances, Jamie."

"We want to enjoy a safe income while here, and return home with the balance."

"Very straightforward, Jamie. That's good," said Alan. "I would suggest that you visit Jason Witherspoon, here in Newark, only a few blocks down the street, and inquire about depositing the gold with his firm where it will be safe as can be anywhere. He is a banker who helps finance firms in northern New Jersey.

"His firm is loaning money at all times, usually on a short term basis. He has two kinds of customers; those to whom he loans funds, and those from whom he takes in funds so that they can earn interest until they have some other need to use the funds for. And some deposit funds with him and still borrow for business or personal reasons. With war looking us in the face, many firms are gearing up to make supplies and provisions for the army. And Jason will need funds to loan to them. He's only a few blocks down Market Street. I would go see him."

"How much interest would I earn?

"You'll have to ask him that. It's a fluid situation, particularly now. Probably around two or three percent over a years time. Do you need any gold certificates for spending money?"

"Yes, I do. I'm low on money. I have only a pocket full of Spanish milled dollars plus some Portugese Johannes I have left from Saint Eustatia. I brought along one of the gold slices in case we could do some business now," I told him.

"This is the place to get 'em," said Alan, as he pushed back on his chair, stood up, and thanked Arthur for lunch.. "When we get back to my office, see George Bunkrot, the fellow you saw in the front of the store. He'll take care of you."

We returned to Alan's store where he said goodbye and disappeared to his sanctum after introducing us to his clerk. Bunkrot was pleased to do business but, again we disappointed him. I requested of him that my gold slice be halved to buy the gold certificates. I stowed the paper in my money belt, and reserved the other half for possible business with Jason Witherspoon.

Fifty-four Market street was only a few doors away and Tracy, Brown and Witherspoon was handsomely gold-leafed on the window of a grey stone building, all suggesting financial solidity. Soon after the clerk invited us to be seated, Witherspoon appeared and invited us into his office. Arthur let me do the talking since he was now doubtful of doing any business on this trip.

"I assume Alan Walsbruch told you of our banking business. Did he mentioned that we have recently become stock brokers—that is, we buy and sell securities of publicly-owned companies for our customers?" This seemed fortuitous since I was encouraged by a surging war economy despite the possibility of battles in our back yard. If we had to suffer because of the conflict, maybe we could profit by it as well.

"I want to get as much as I can in terms of growth and income as safely as possible.".

"Mr. Claveraque, it would be wonderful to obtain high income, growth of capital, safety and flexibility all in one investment, but it doesn't work that way any more than your orchard produces both cider and steak.

" If you crave maximum safety, you will get little growth and a reasonable income, but usually, at a fixed rate of income. If you're looking for rapid growth, you have little assurance of safety. You may get growth, but you will likely get little income—what with earnings being reinvested to enhance growth, and may have rapid losses also. I would advise that you not speculate but go a medium route. Moderate growth and moderate income based on a reasonable income and expense statement and a conservative balance sheet. Hold on to shares of a company that gives you that. You'll make money and be able to sleep nights."

"What firms do you deal with?" I asked.

"We will be dealing with all the firms in the New York, Newark, and Philadelphia business community that are publicly traded. There are some twenty firms that we presently handle and they have interesting histories to tell. From what you say, I will tell you of the most conservative, though I must say, I think the outlook is very bright. There are other firms, but so far, we deal only with these."

"Well, I'm listening."

"I have in mind the Brown Belt Transmission Company. "

Arthur cut in, "I never heard of it!"

"No, most people haven't. Their product is not something you would be familiar with unless you had a mill or machinery you needed turned. They make all manner of leather belting for taking power off a water-powered wheel and transmitting it in a way to drive machines for milling, sawing, lathe turning, drilling, planing, spinning wool or flax, or otherwise.

"Their product is not limited to just one industry but many, and more uses are being discovered and invented every day. Of course, the belts can be used in grist mills for turning a run of stone or in a saw mill for operating saws for cutting dimension lumber. The belts are as long as fifty feet and as small as three feet depending upon their application in the mill."

"Don't gears do all that?"

"Yes, of course they do and the company makes gears, too. But the future seems to be in the leather belting. The company has been in business for twenty years and began selling shares to the public fifteen years ago. Their earnings have increased nicely every year what with industries beginning to defy the mother country by competing with English manufacturers. "

"Aren't they in danger of being attacked by the British?"

"I wish I could say that nothing in the country is vulnerable, but war is war. You've read about Falmouth and Salem and that town in Connecticut on Long Island Sound bombarded and set fire to by the redcoats. Some mills have been damaged. But they've been repaired and the use of leather belting has speeded up the rebuilding and is being used as never before.

"Where is the company located? Here in Newark?"

"They have but one factory now but are planning others. Safety in numbers, you know. The factories are necessarily near stock yards since they buy hides. The factory is in the largest city on the seaboard, Philadelphia."

"Do they share the profits? Pay interest or make some kind of an annual payout?" I asked.

"They pay interest on their outstanding bonds to their creditors but I'm talking about the stock shares which would make you a part owner. They pay an annual dividend which they have increased as their earnings have climbed each year. The last dividend was thirty-five pence."

Arthur was getting interested. "How much does a share sell for?"

"The last shares we sold—about two weeks ago—went for ten dollars. That would give you a yield of three and a half percent. If they keep increasing the payout each year your yield will become quite handsome. I should mention to you that some manufacturers are considering using Mr. Watts steam engine rather than having to locate their factories on a strong current and trusting to the weather. This could add immensely to the proliferation of factories and the need for belts and gears. Most of all, breaking away from Great Britain and their restrictive laws against American manufacturing is the best outlook for all investors.

"We have no shares in this company available for sale because no one wants to sell a comfortable investment like this at the moment. But someone may have a need to raise cash by selling his shares. I will get word to you when that happens."

I wanted to believe what this earnest and articulate gentleman had to tell us.

"Mr. Witherspoon, I'm impressed with your expanse of knowledge and would like to do business with you—and probably will do business with you. But I have no funds readily available at the moment. You can see that I'm not conversant with the investment world and that is part of the reason we asked Walsbruch to direct us to you. Thank you for your time and patience. We will meet again, I assure you."

We left in mid afternoon. The winds had shifted to the southwest and the air became balmy. Perhaps spring was about to embrace us. Arthur felt so encouraged by this that he suggested that we return by a round-about way through the Oranges. At a corner a kiosk with newspapers caught my eye and I quickly jumped down from the chaise to buy a copy of the New York Gazette. News of any significance had been scarce recently.

Amidst the local gossip, horse sales, and ads for runaways appeared a story that counterfeiters had been caught in north Jersey with many thousands of pounds of continental currency which the paper said had been circulating recently. It was alleged that authorities were alert to several other sources and would soon have them closed down. I turned the page and was delighted to see an ad placed by a Boston carriage manufacturer, Adino Paddock, selling luxury coaches for *ƒ*200 and used coaches for bargain prices.

Just below the ad, in smaller type was an article headed, **British evacuate Boston on St. Patrick's Day. Washington's Army occupies town**. The general's strategy was paying of off.

# chapter 26

ON THE WAY home from Newark, we saw large flights of red-winged blackbirds wheeling over marshy-ground crowded by reeds. Their appearance and vibrant song, like a jews harp gone wild, were harbingers of spring though Arthur said they were almost a month late in arriving this year. Arthur, Arabella, and Olivia and I were anxious to finish the meticulous task of pruning the orchard before we could think of leaving for Philadelphia.

Just as we were finishing clearing the orchard of cut branches, a nor'easter came raging up the coast to drop fifteen inches of wet snow which justified our delay. We were glad we hadn't left on our long-planned trip south only to mire on the road in the cold.

Arthur said this was actually a good sign since the snow would melt quickly under the spring sun and that we could be assured that it was the last snow until next November. I was not dismayed by this. Another week in the gully practicing target shooting with his rifle might help me to attain the marksmanship I was aiming for. And the increased melt would speed a wood chip along the creek and help me become more nimble with moving targets.

Storms of pigeons blackened the skies as if another blizzard was in the offing. I started to shoot them for the pot but Arthur said this was a waste of powder—they could easily be clubbed off the branches when they settled down to roost. Indeed, we could see eager neighbors out in their wood lots with the entire family, young children included, swatting and bagging large numbers of the dumb, trusting birds.

We followed suit and Olivia and Arabella were kept busy plucking and cleaning them. They fried some and roasted the rest in anticipation of our soon-to-be-realized trek. They also cut and dried in the spring sun several pecks of apples. The day after the storm when dainty spring beauties poked through the snow and began blooming, was to be our day of departure.

Arthur had gotten a copy of the map made by the cartographer and surveyor, Lewis Evans, from Squire Lumsden. He proudly held it up. A General Map of the Middle British Colonies, published in 1755 in Philadelphia, it said.

"This is the same map that was supposed to have been used by General Braddock in his ill-fated campaign to take Fort Duquesne at the Forks of the Ohio. People migrating west over the mountains are using it all the time. Let us hope they have more success than the general did.

"Even though Evans' map is much larger than what we need because it shows the whole of the mid-Atlantic provinces it will be useful because it is so detailed," Arthur said. He propped the large chart on the table, covered it with a sheet of pattern paper, and laboriously traced out two copies of the map. One he limited to south-eastern New York and most of New Jersey and eastern Pennsylvania for our trip to Philadelphia. After writing in the names of towns, mountains, watercourses, and other particulars, he folded and creased it several times for compactness.

Olivia pressed her hand to her forehead. "I have been trying to think of where I heard that name, Lewis Evans, before. Now, I remember. He's the one who accompanied Bartram and Conrad Weiser on their trip to Onondaga in '43. Some of the surveying he made on that trip probably went into the making of this map. Imagine the territory he had to cover on other excursions to be able to put it all together to have a map like this. I assume it's accurate."

"It has had twenty years of other's explorations to prove it wrong and I've heard no contradictions," said Arthur.

The other map was full size copy of Evans' original. Arthur liked to study maps and the four of us became entranced with the expanse of the country. We spent several evenings examining points of interest and the distance to them. My imagination of what these far-flung places in the wilderness looked like ran amuck and when we retired for the evening, I could hardly get to sleep in the excitement.

The next afternoon, just before our scheduled departure, a knock on the door just after dinner gave us pause. We were expecting no one, but the animus between Patriots and Loyalists had grown alarmingly and we were on edge. I guardedly opened the door and was delighted to see Crispin dressed in the bright satins of a gentleman, a genuine macaroni, and sporting an expertly trimmed beard. He was the epitome of wealth and fashion.

"Come in! Come in! You look wonderful after two months of not seeing you or hearing a word. Come in and meet my father's brother and his wife. Tell us what you have been doing!

Introductions were made all around. Crispin quickly formed a liking for Arthur and Arabella, probably helped by the lay of their patch of land and other signs of their tidy husbandry.

"You won't believe what I've been doing" Crispin said as he smiled and shook hands with Arthur and Arabella and kissed Olivia on the cheek. Arabella offered him snacks and coffee and we all sat down at the dinner table to hear of his adventures.

"I met the most interesting man on the ferry to New York. He was well-spoken but in shabby clothes so I thought he was just a sophisticated beggar trying to talk himself into my confidence. He surprised me by leading me to an unlikely friend of his, the owner of a well stocked bookstore which also had artists supplies. Remember I had to get colors in oils to paint Captain Adam and his wife's portrait."

Olivia asked, "Did you finally get to do those paintings? Adam was very eager to have them done before he outfitted for profiteering."

"You mean privateering, Olivia," I corrected.

Crispin continued." Yes, I did. But let me tell about it as I get to it. Right after meeting Bill Farrell, the bookstore owner, I did his portrait in charcoal, just like I did those of the crew on the *Raritan*. I thought it would be a good way to bring my work to people's attention. Farrell was pleased and impressed by the likeness and pinned it on the wall next to works of other artists."

Olivia needed to know right away before she forgot her question, "Did he pay you for doing his portrait? How much?"

"He didn't pay hard money but did let me have some supplies for nothing. I didn't even have to use any of the money that Adam loaned me, except for the ferry.

"Right after that, when Farrell pinned his likeness on the wall, one of his wealthiest and most influential customers, a noted connoisseur of art in New York, came in the door, as if on cue. After seeing the Farrell portrait, he wanted one done of himself and each member of his family. We set an appointment for a week later at his town house. That same afternoon, Jedediah, the one I thought was a con man, took me to another friend of his who had a store nearby that sold general supplies—from seeds to tomahawks to defend against Indians or to trade with them.

"Jedediah starts telling the owner, Trevor Shaw, a friendly guy, about what happened at Farrell's and Mister Shaw decided, then and there, that he wanted to be sketched, too. So, I sketched him which took about twenty minutes during which General Lee came into the store with his aid and his dogs and tries to order Trevor around to get him some stuff right away, while Trevor's in the midst of sitting for his portrait.

"Arthur chimed in. "That sounds like Trevor. He's an old friend and customer of mine."

"I'll tell you, Shaw wasn't about to be ordered around like that, business or no business, and, politely, tells the general to—no, he invites the general to stroll through and inspect his store saying he'll be with him in a minute. I was disappointed that the general wasn't curious about the sketch I was doing but he was set on getting some more tools for digging up and barricading the streets and building redoubts for defending New York against the redcoats."

I broke in, "All this took place on the first day after we landed?"

"Yes. No, the next day. Excuse me, Jamie. So much happened, I've been running on at the mouth telling about my own adventures. What have you and Olivia been doing?"

"We'll tell you later. Keep going with your story."

"Well, alright. Jedediah reminded me that I had to get back to Amboy, so we walked to the ferry slip and arrived just in time. And here's what I didn't want to forget to tell you. One of the people getting off the ferry, I swear, was Mochter, with his bald pate and his fancy ivory-headed blackthorn cane. He didn't recognize me with my two-months growth of beard.

"I pointed him out to Jedediah whom I asked to keep an eye on him, since Jedediah was going to stay the night on York Island. Jedediah surprised me. He said they were looking for him, too. I didn't know who "they" are, and I hadn't time to find out. The ferry was casting off."

Olivia was anxious. "What did you find out about him?"

"Well, later Jedediah told me a few things. Mochter has been planning something with Governor Franklin at Proprietary House. He was at the governor's mansion overnight last week and returned from Perth Amboy a few days ago. He also had some dealings with other people near Morristown. They don't yet have details but they know that Mochter has contacted the Tories and is up to some kind of mischief.

"I'm sorry, I have much more to tell you. But what's the map for—are you planning a trip?

"We've been planning to go to Philadelphia for some time. One of the reasons, you may remember, was to visit John Bartram at his famous nursery. We have purposely delayed because we want to see his nursery when it's growing and in bloom. We were planning to leave tomorrow. Would you like to join us?

"Are you going all that way just to visit a nursery?"

"We also want to visit with Robert Morris, if he isn't too busy with congress, and to inspect several mills and manufactories on our way there and back."

"I can only spare tomorrow. Perhaps I'll accompany you for the first day. There may be some prime landscapes I'll want to paint, or a trout stream to wet a fly in on the way. But, I have some important people I'm scheduled to do in oils when I return to New York. One of them may be Wenceslaus Mochter if we can wangle it. He doesn't know that I'm the artist and I don't think he'll recognize me in these duds and with this beard.

"Nor do I think he will remember my name, if he ever knew it. We didn't travel in the same circles, you know. Anyway, I've got to think of questions I'll put to him during his sitting—questions phrased so that he has no inkling I'm trying to find out his plans. Our group thinks this may be a good way to go about it.

"In early May, I'm going with Trevor Shaw to Fort Stanwix on the New York frontier. He's attending a meeting with some Indian tribes, and I'm hoping to paint some chiefs in their native surroundings. I bought my new fishing tackle from Trevor and we're going to try some of the streams that feed the Mohawk River." Crispin was in his long-sought heaven.

Arthur was surprised. "This fellow, Jedediah, is the one who led you to his store?"

"Yes."

"A middle-aged man who shuffles a little and is not too careful in his dressing habits?"

"That's him. He literally bumped into me on the ferry to New York. He knows everyone in the city and introduced me to Bill Farrell where I bought my artists supplies."

"I think I have met the man on occasion," Arthur's confusion was cleared up.

"It's been some time since we saw you. What else have you been doing?" I became a little envious of Crispin's prosperous adventures.

"Well, I returned to Amboy and painted the captain and his wife in oils. They were both pleased with the result- especially her. He's fitting his ship as a privateer and soon expects his letters of marque. She's afraid that he may not survive despite the chance at making a fortune.

"Adam's looking forward to humiliating the British and becoming rich at the same time. He thinks the supply line to the British army in Boston is poorly guarded and that there's no way that they will have enough ships to convoy the provision ships across the Atlantic when they try to take New York. This is a golden opportunity that come's but once in a lifetime, he says. He's willing to take the main chance.

"Adam and I went hunting in Barnegat Bay for ducks and geese—downed enough to feed the crew for a week. It's a lot easier with a shotgun than with a bow, you should try it, Jamie. The crew are all going to ship on with Adam when they've finished refitting the *Raritan* to his satisfaction, sometime in the next month, he hopes. "

"Estrich, Mink, Ross, Cookie, and the rest? How are they?"

"They're fine, but I saw only the four of them busy with the refitting. The others had gone off to Tom's River to get some supplies. They asked about you and Olivia—wanted to know how far you've gotten on the tour. Then, I went back to New York and painted a merchant and his family and he referred me to others. This kept me so busy painting and making money that I didn't leave York Island till just now.

"By the way, I saw from a distance Ancie and Downey Cohan. They were all decked out in fancy clothes talking to some businessmen. His horse trading must be paying off. While there are no redcoats in New York anymore, none in uniform, anyway, there are a lot of Tories, and I thought it best to stay clear of him since he must be over here to do business with them. They didn't recognize me for which I'm glad. It's providential that I grew the beard. I can see a lot from behind the leaves on this tree." Crispen tapped his cheek.

I hadn't thought about Ancie since the Guy Fawkes Day dance in November. But I did marvel at how much had happened in five months. How lucky I was to be able to slip away from Ancie and meet Olivia at the same affair . And Ancie had made it to America, thanks to Downey.

That evening, we heard the murmer of peepers, reassuring us that spring was anchored in place. We all talked on and on. It became so late before we retired that we almost decided to delay our start one more day. Fortunately, the weather held. We wanted to be on the move.

That morning, conditions were so much like the day Olivia and I left for Bristol, that I thought it forecast good fortune. We took the valley road that skirts the Watchungs. By the time we rounded the western end of the mountains, people we met in the small settlements along the way were in shirt sleeves, glad to get out, take the air, and enjoy the noon-day sunshine. The soil was dusty red—the same color as at home on the Wye..

Crispin had his easel and colors at the ready and was adept at setting up beside the roadway with blank canvass and dashing off a painting of someone's house or grange. It took him no more than ten minutes to create a likeness usually of the grandest house in the settlement. Crispin could spot the most likely buyers. And he made a theatrical production of his artistry. He would pause and pose before making each additional brush stroke, as if performing magic. Then he made a ceremony of packing up as if to catch up with us. The proud householder, thinking this potential personal treasure would be lost to him, invariably asked Crispin if he minded parting with the picture and would offer to pay well for this rendering of the ancestral home.

Occasionally, when the villager seemed more than pleased with his purchase and began showing the painting off to his neighbors, Crispin let it be known that he was celebrated for his likenesses drawn of New York personalities. How he managed to appear modest by this not so subtle announcement is beyond my comprehension. But he derived several quick commissions before he caught up to us with his saddle bags jingling with Spanish milled dollars.

Many times since I have been pleased to look at sketches Crispin made of the journey, made not for the purpose of making money alone , but to capture the sheer pleasure of being on the road. Many families were fleeing from New York and the threat that General Lee's fortress building foretold. With heirlooms and household furniture stuffed in fine carriages to farm wagons, and even hand carts, families were migrating west because of cheap land in Pennsylvania, Virginia, or the Carolinas or to escape the wrath of the king's army.

The Pennsylvania Dutch over in the Conestoga Valley had fashioned a commodious wagon with the wide-rimmed wheels and running gear painted a dark crimson which contrasted sharply with the sky blue of the wagon box. I admired the outward slope of the sides and ends which, with the concave floor, kept the cargo anchored in place. The whole was neatly covered from the weather with white linen canvas supported every yard or so by steamed hickory bows raked to overhang the wagon box front and back.

Conestoga wagons were large enough to accommodate even two families under the stress of flight, always with some of the party walking at the easy gait of two teams of oxen. They settled for the night by making space among the boxes and barrels. Others were satisfied with what shelter they could manage under the wagon or in the lee of the large wheels.

A cold spring was welcome when we arrived at a glade near Somerville. The milestone had a large twenty-three carved on its face. For many, this represented a half-days travel from Newark. Those coming north from McConkey's Ferry were gratified to see that they had made thirty miles of their day's trek and could escape the wind in the lee of a row of cedars. For both, the meadow and spring warranted a stop to break out lunch. A wise soul had tied a swing on a sturdy horizontal branch for the diversion of children and the long-awaited relief of their parents.

We stopped to rest, taste the spring, and graze our horses. Our goal was to make forty-five miles the first day; we were on schedule and could afford the rest time. Several wagons had stopped as much for conversation with strangers as any other reason, judging by the alacrity of their greetings.

Olivia had been admiring the first of the spring signs. Willows had drawn on their spring gold. Robins were chortling and yanking worms from the occasional greensward. Swallows had appeared from nowhere to show off their daring dexterity of flight. Some of the gardens of the finer homes displayed magnificent forsythia radiating golden jewel-like strands of flowers higher than first-floor windows.

Lilac buds were swollen but needed another day or two to bloom. Olivia knelt down to investigate more closely wild flowers she had seen from horseback. "I'll sketch these so I can ask Mr. Bartram what they are. We don't have these at home."

A middle-aged man, called Tim by his wife, walked over, wiping his brow, "Afternoon! Nice day, ain't it? Wife and kids and I are goin' to the Susquehanna. Nice country here but we bought a quarter section on bottom land. Gettin' away from Connecticut fields of stone. Where are you headed, stranger?" he smiled as he offered his hand.

"It surely is a nice day," I agreed. "We're just on our way for an outing to Philadelphia. We're taking our time so long as the weather holds," I volunteered.

"I take it you're from around here?"

I nodded.

"We bought some supplies back in Springfield and the clerk give me change in Jersey bills, but they look funny to me. Care to look at them?"

I looked at the bills but saw nothing unusual and handed them to Arthur. He squinted and put on his glasses. "They look alright except they look brand new—unused, I'd say."

Olivia smiled at Tim and asked if he minded that she look at them.

"There was a notice in the paper a week ago warning that a flood of bogus bills had been passing around the county—usually given to people passing through. First thing to look for, it said, was; did the bills look too perfect? Second, was the counter signature." It was in black ink, same as the rest of the bill. "It should be black to be authentic, the notice said. Look for yourself," Olivia observed, and passed the bills back to him.

The poor fellow scrutinized his money and shook it, as if to throw off the wrong colored- ink. "Dam! That clerk got the best of me. I've a notion to go back and raise hell."

"It's only a half-pound note," I said. "You'd waste a day going back to straighten things out. Cost you more in time than it's worth."

"I can't let that happen. I got the time, but I ain't got much money. Mary, get the kids, we got to be on the way." He stepped up to his board perch, looked to make sure all were aboard, and cracked the whip over the heads of his patient oxen. The Conestoga, chocked full of tools, kids, and supplies, trundled back to the dust of the road going east.

"It's good that you're so sharp-eyed, Olivia. I didn't see that."

"I've seen about three notices like that. Arabella pointed them out to me."

Arabella confirmed, "The notices started about two weeks after you and Olivia arrived. I'm surprised they escaped your attention," she said. "The Gazette says the British are passing these to depress the value of our currency so everything costs more." I began to worry. I had obtained a fist full of pound notes from Alan Walsbruch. I'm sure he's honest—he has to be. I'll look at the bills tonight, just the same, I thought.

We rode on west into higher hills, fewer fields, less prosperous looking farms, and more timber. Fortunately, light clouds began to obscure the sun which, as it moved lower and westward was beginning to shine into our eyes. Eventually, we arrived at the Clinton House, whose thirty-year reputation for fine food and accommodations we later found was more than justified. A small committee was selling lottery tickets in the tap room to raise funds to build a steeple for the local Dutch Reformed Church so we had to wait to get a place at table. Since they were mostly local, we had no difficulty obtaining a room.

When Crispin viewed the stream over which the main road in Clinton crossed, he said he was certain it must have magnificent trout in it. The wait to be seated was unbearable to him, so sure that this stream, only a hundred feet distant, was chock-full of trout nourished and strengthened by the mountains and lush meadows upstream. Though only ten or so miles from the great Delaware river, this was the South Branch of the Raritan which debouches so tamely fifty or more miles downstream into the Atlantic Ocean at Perth Amboy

Crispin told us to order anything that would give him a half hour, as he dug his tackle from his saddlebags and scurried to the pool below the bridge. He was desperate to renew his acquaintance with the sight and sound of the slurp and burble of fast water against mossy rocks and the tug of sleek beauty from the depths. Just as our waitress delivered his chops he beamed as he sat down and presented the house with a fifteen-inch speckled trout. A fair trade he thought. Crispin arose at first light to take his morning walk and to look for scenes of interest to sketch. He chose a low, round stone building. A granary in former years, it had been designated for a more topical purpose. He set up his easel with fresh canvass and began to anoint his palette.

This attracted a casual onlooker even so early in the day. He was dressed in a black vest and buckskin breeches, covered by a black wide-brimmed hat and shod in black shoes with square pewter buckles. He looked even more severe with his long blond hair clubbed in back.

He observed Crispin's first strokes with interest. "Thee chose a handsome building to paint, young fellow," said the gentleman in an authoritarian and pleasant voice..

"I have a weakness for round buildings, especially if they are built of stone," said Crispin, with fixed gaze on his work.

The gentleman noted in Crispin's voice a residual tang of London's East End where his parents originated. "We have perhaps forty buildings of one kind or another in Clinton and thee chose this particular one. Why?" asked the man.

"I told you, sir. I like round buildings and I also like buildings made of stone with the shady side carpeted in moss. They make interesting pictures."

"Art thee from England, young man?"

"Yes, and glad to be."

"What brings thee to West Jersey? Are thee with the Royal government?"

Crispin turned and assessed the questioner. "God, no. What kind of a question is that?"

"Our village has never had an Englishman paint pictures of its buildings. Now, with a war on, thee, an Englishman, have come to paint its buildings, maybe its citizens, too. Eh?"

"Yesterday I painted half a dozen houses and several residents on the Somerville Road. They all seemed happy about it."

"Art thee an artist?"

"I would like to think that someone watching me with brush and palette in hand might draw that conclusion. These people paid hard money for a picture of their house or person. They didn't seem to mind that I'm from England." Though annoyed, Crispin continued, now carefully shading-in the mossy growth on the stones.

"Well, we're at war with England!"

"Yes, of course. But that doesn't mean we shall discharge Gates and Charles Lee. And General Montgomery died in Quebec for our cause. They're all English, you know."

"Thee say "our cause". Does that mean thee are on our side?"

"I was born in England and came over here just this February. I had a quarrel with the King's army and decided I couldn't win if I stayed there. Besides, I have admired that Americans have made a better living out of a wilderness in a relatively short time against massive odds. Now they are resisting the bullies in the ministry and the regulars to protect what they have gained. So my friends and I crossed the Atlantic. Now, please to stop badgering me and let me finish this so I can go back to the inn and have breakfast."

The local gentleman didn't know what to say. Indeed, he wished he had said nothing. But he felt this interchange required an ending. "That's a nice painting of our old granary. But it's where we store a more useful grain than wheat now." Then he walked away.

The Clinton House made bacon and eggs so well that Crispin and I had a second order. Languishing longer than intended, our group finally got underway. Shortly we passed the turnoff to Easton when Crispin left the road for personal reasons. A minute later, he called out in fright. "Stay here." I commanded and ran into the bush. Crispin had heedlessly stalked into a nest of rattlesnakes basking on the sun-warmed rocks of a south-facing knob. His encounter left him pale and in a sweat, grasping his lower leg. I pulled him away from the rattler's nest into the shade and pulled off his boot. Already his calf had swollen around two red dots a half-inch apart. Arthur entered the glade, gasped, and immediately knelt down with his knife.

"Crispin, this will hurt some, but I have to make two small cuts to suck the venom out. Try to stay still as I do this. We don't want the poison to get to the rest of your body." He handed a short stick to Crispin. "Here, bite down hard on this. I won't take long. Jamie, hold him snug."

I was impressed by Arthur's management. He sharpened his knife on a handy shard of limestone before making the incisions. Abruptly, he scrunched down to suck out the venom, spitting out the poison several times. He offered water to Crispin whose fortitude was commended by all of us hovering round. Arthur took a drink himself but was careful not to swallow but to swish it around and sluice any residual venom in an elaborate spit to the side. He poured water on the wound to wash it. We heard a cracking—Crispin had bitten through the stick.

.Arthur cut a length of the horse's rein and tied it in a loose loop just below Crispin's knee. He grabbed an end of Crispin's biting stick and stuck it under the loop before twisting it into a tourniquet. "If you can, hold this, Crispin." Crispin held it tightly.

"Grab his legs, Jamie and we'll carry him to his horse so we can get him back to the Clinton House. It' not too far. How are you doing, Crispin?"

"I'm a little woozy and my leg hurts, but I'm alright. Somebody better make sure I don't fall off the horse." He wavered precariously even as I held the horse's halter and Arthur carefully boosted him into the saddle.

Olivia and I led the horse over to a stump and she stepped up to mount the horse just behind our wounded comrade. The gravity of Crispin's predicament laid a glum determination on all of us. We would make sure Crispin recovered and regained his strength.

Arthur led the way. "A slow gait should get him to town and a doctor soon enough," he pronounced.

Within ten minutes we were back in Clinton and a villager spotted our need for special attention to Crispin. "Do you need a doctor?" He asked, and pointed a finger at the round stone building. "Doctor Bolster's dispensary is in that old granary," he said.

Crispin was not too faint to recognize his morning antagonist. Despite his despair, he smiled. He almost passed out as we lowered him from the horse and into the doctor's office.

"Well, I declare, the artist from England. What have thee done?" said the doctor.

When he saw my friend's swelled and purple calf, he motioned for Crispin to be lowered on the cot and bent over to examine the wound and Crispin's grip on the tourniquet.

"Someone knows what they're doing." He put his hand on Crispin's brow. "Did thee have a fever? Probably did and it's gone down. How long ago did the rattler strike thee?"

Crispin still looked spent and confused so I answered. "Half an hour ago, no more. It happened off the road about a mile past the fork to Easton."

"I think I know the spot, a few bushes and many rocks piled on each other, south side of the road. We've had snake roundups there for years but never seem to get them all. My name's Fenwick Bolster. I met Crispin, without benefit of introduction, earlier this morning when he was sketching my building. I think thy quick action saved him a lot of pain, even his life."

I introduced Arthur, "It is Arthur's care that saved him."

The doctor opened one of the many small drawers in a large wooden case against the wall and withdrew a small jar of white powder. He poured alcohol on the snake bite and rubbed an alcohol-saturated rag over the area before mixing the powder to a paste with only drops of water and gently applied the poultice on Crispin's wound. He also raised Crispin's upper body and positioned cushions to support his back and head. "It's important to keep thy wound below thy chest," he whispered to Crispin as he handed him a cup. "Here, drink this."

Turning to us, Bolster said, "He needs quiet and rest. I gave him a sedative. He'll be alright resting here for a while. The poultice is a powdered root given to me years ago by a Lenape healer. It's for drawing poison out of the wound and works very well. In a few hours we'll give your friend some sassafras tea. I don't think thee need worry about him. He'll be alright and out of pain. Where are thee from?"

Arthur made a modest reply to the doctor's complement about his quick attention to Crispin's snake bite. He introduced us, including the now slumbering Crispin. He explained our trip to Philadelphia to visit John Bartram and his botanical nursery and to admire the city where the Continental Congress was sitting.

Bolster explained his early morning's acquaintance with Crispin. He added, "I suppose thee know that thou art taking a roundabout way of getting there. Thee could have stayed on the McConkey's Ferry road or gone by way of Princeton and Trenton and spared thy horses and thy selves."

I wanted to talk to this interesting individual. "We know. But we wanted the pleasure of passing through the uplands of West Jersey at this time of the year, visiting the Durham Furnace, and traveling by the river as far as the falls at Trenton. We were on our way to Easton when Crispin was struck while answering nature's call."

The doctor picked up on our interest in the natural beauty. "The forks of the Delaware are exciting this time of the year with the spring runoff, and if thee has a reason for visiting Easton, then the road thee embarked on was correct. But if thee are only interested in getting to the Furnace, I will tell thee of a short cut."

He began scribbling on a small paper. "Instead of the fork you took to Easton, take the left fork down to the river through Pitts Corners and Everittstown. Then go up the river to Milford and give this paper to my man on this side, Moses Brinton, and he'll take thee across on my scow. It should be able to accommodate thee and thy horses. Durham Furnace is only about five miles from there up the west bank."

"That's very kind of you. Will you accept some pigeons we roasted the other day."

"Thank ye, but no necessity of that, Mr. Claveraque. I need some supplies from the other side so I was going to send Moses anyway. But thee will have to allow Crispin a few days rest so he can recover easily. I will instruct Moses to introduce you to Thearon de Laye, our manager of the furnace."

"I don't think Crispin is coming with us. When we left Vaux Hall the other day, he said he would accompany us the first day but that he had some important portraits to do back in New York. He's a very determined fellow. I doubt he will let even a snake bite deter him for more than a day. We will stay in Clinton until he can return on his own before we cross the river. We'll, move him to the inn later this afternoon—that is if it's agreeable with you, doctor," I said.

"That would be best. No one is here in my clinic overnight. I have a litter thy can use to take him back to the inn. Rest is the best cure for such a trauma. I think Arthur sucked much of the venom out. I'm surprised he doesn't complain of pain in his mouth. He must have sound gums. In the meantime, we'll let Crispin sleep. When he wakes, we will see how he fares." Olivia had been paying close attention. "What medicine should he take with him to New York? In case one of us gets a snake bite, shouldn't we have that powder to make a poultice?"

"All Crispin needs is rest. I will give you a small quantity of the powder but it is unlikely thy will need it. Rattle snakes usually give warning of their presence by rattling their rattles and then slither out of sight when they hear some one coming. I guess Crispin tread too lightly to be sensed, was impatient to do his business, and heedless of the rattle's warning."

Curiosity got the better of my manners. "Did I understand that you are one of the owners of Durham Furnace, Doctor?"

"I'm pleased to say that I am. That's right, you did say that you wished to see the furnace. May I ask if thy has a special reason."

I told him of Arthur's and my interest in investment possibilities.

"I'm not active in the management of the furnace. Nor am I familiar with their present capital requirements. But talk to Thearon De Laye who runs the operation. He knows the business in and out."

The name De Laye struck a cord in my memory but I could not readily bring it to mind. I put it aside, confident that the answer would surface.

Crispin slept all afternoon. He awakened at sundown with much better color and spirit.

"The doctor recommended some sassafras tea, Crispin. They talk about it much in the colonies-and not just to avoid the East India Company variety. Will you have some with me?"

After taking the tea, which he quickly favored, as did I, Crispin promptly fell into a second deep sleep. I reported this to Doctor Bolster who agreed it was the best thing for him.

The next morning Crispin woke with his vigor restored as if by magic. It is natural phenomena like this spontaneous healing that forms my spiritual foundation rather than a pompous cleric reciting timeworn and tinkered-with dogma from the pulpit.

In the same motion of putting his feet to the floor, Crispin declared, "As long as I'm so close to the Delaware River and must delay my start back to New York, I might as well try fishing the river. It is probably as unspoiled as a river has a right to be."

He hopped out of bed, dressed more rapidly than I have ever seen him do anything, and cheered the serving maids in the dining room as he ordered bacon and eggs, toasted cinnamon rolls and a pot of coffee to be left at table.

Crispin insisted that he was well enough to fish, I could not dissuade him. We decided to continue our journey with him in tow and to by-pass Easton as per Doctor Bolster's suggestion.

Several Conestoga wagons were preparing to leave which spurred our departure. On the narrow trail to the river, jokingly called a road, there is no chance to pass a laggard and no opportunity to stop for reasons of nature without complaint from those behind. Our haste served us well; as we found the short-cut river road had virtually no one on its twelve-mile length.

From a meadow just beginning to turn green the road entered deep woods where clusters of hepatica thrust their purple blooms through matts of leaves. Sunlight filtered through rose-tinted branches of red maple about to bloom. We descended a steep hill along a rushing torrent which shared the ravine with virgin hemlock, all numbed in cold. It was clear that the stream overflowed the trail at times as the roadbed showed signs of severe erosion. Drifts of snow that never saw sunshine would have to be cleared for wagons but caused only minor concern to us and our horses. Trees lining the road had been shorn of bark at axle height. The road builders begrudged making the road wider and stopped short by only pushing the axed trees aside. They left the trimming of stumps to teamsters whose wagons would not clear. We were happy to be on horseback

The ravine flattened to a small meadow edged by skunk cabbage where the stream washed into the Delaware. The river made its own noisome wind by the force of the rapid current there we had to shout to each other to be understood. It was deep enough with no visible boulders to bother navigation but there were standing waves which resembled haystacks. In sunlight again, we still shivered from the cold river wind. Within a half mile we arrived at a clearing with a small crude cottage and an outbuilding sided with hemlock bark.

In the shed, Moses Brinton, a trim and muscular young artisan, was shaping the blade of a fresh pair of oars with a drawknife. He was an agreeable fellow, happy to have an excuse to delay this tedium and cross the river. He alluded to his girl friend who worked for the furnace. It seemed strange for women to be employed at an iron foundry. She was one of the cooks.

Crispin found no place where he could cast a fly unhampered by trees. Wading in the shallows risked being carried away by the current in his still-weakened state. He decided to fish from the scow as we were being ferried across and began to set up his equipment.

He had prospered painting New York society so well he had not spared expense buying his new tackle. The first of the three oiled three-foot sections was tiger-grained maple sporting a reel holding fifty feet of line. The other sections were hickory fitted with wire guides and brass ferrules. He proudly flexed the rod. "If you'd had something like this, you wouldn't have lost that big one at Wedlich's pool." He still was not aware of my more significant catch that fateful day.

Moses was quick to get us under way and said that if we left for Philadelphia during the spring runoff, we could get there before sundown provided we left at dawn. Olivia's mare balked and whinnied in fear at stepping into the scow until Moses put a blind over her eyes and with soothing words led her on board. The other horses followed easily. He and his crew poled us upstream where an eddy's back current assisted. At a point jutting into the river he waved his men to drop their poles and grab their oars to push into the main current. They rowed vigorously so that the scow careened across the black water at a crabbed angle to the strong current.

Crispen disjointed his rod as he realized he would hinder the crew if he attempted a cast. It would have been heedless for him to idly cast for fish while the crew strained to reach our landing. As well, he was showing signs of fatigue from the day's travail.

I asked Moses, "Why are there so many Conestoga wagons on the Easton Road?"

"Probably because the Yankees from Connecticut are determined to stake their claims in Wyoming and Forty Fort. They've been battling Pennsylvanians over their claim to the valley for a dozen years now. With the weather improved they want to overpower the opposition. That's my guess," he yelled over the wind and roiling of the river.

"Why would Connecticut think they have any claim on Pennsylvania. They're way over on the Eastern seaboard," I shouted back.

I had been watching a large double-ended black bateau coming down the river. Several of these boats had come along since we arrived on the stream. Moses had not heard my question about Connecticut, so I asked, "What are these large boats continually coming down stream?"

"Most of 'em are carrying pig iron from the furnace on their way to Philadelphia. They carry so much and draw so little water that they have been copied up and down the river to carry all kinds of cargo. You asked me another question?"

I repeated my question about the territorial dispute.

"Connecticut claims that their land grant under the charter from England out dates William Penn's and that it runs due west to the South Seas, including Pennsylvania. They got their grant from King Charles in 1662. About twenty years later, Charles granted Penn some of the same land west of the Delaware to settle a large debt owed to Billy's father, the admiral. I guess that neither the king or his advisors paid much attention to earlier grants."

"What started all the fuss?" Olivia wanted to know.

"The Susquehanna Company in Connecticut bought land from the Six Nations in 1754, just when the French war broke out. No settlements started until '63 when some Yankees began building cabins at Mill Creek in the Wyoming Valley. Five years later, the Penns persuaded the Six Nations to renege on the purchase and sent troops to take the Mill Creek blockhouse.

"The latest face-down was last December, Christmas day in fact, at Rampart Rocks. The Pennsylvanians think they won, but, with all those Yankees on the move, it isn't over yet.

"Don't the Indians have any local land anymore?"

"The Lenni-Lenape, that is the Delawares, and the Shawnees were cheated out of it almost forty years ago now. They were affronted, and sought redress at Onondaga, but the Iroquois held for the treaty. Some think the Penns pressured them. But the Lenape and Shawnees had to vacate the land after all. They moved, of all places, to the Wyoming Valley."

"What happened?"

"Were coming to shore and I can't talk now. Remind me to tell you later."

Moses directed the rowers so that the scow came to shore just downstream from a congregation of log rafts. The lumbermen who ran this armada were jocularly occupied in the tavern on this point known as Upper Black Eddy and making enough ruckus to drown out the roil of the rapids. Moses tied up to a downstream raft, swung our bow ramp on shore, and rolled his eyes. "Sounds like they won't be leaving soon," he said.

As we rode north along the river bank, I renewed my question "You were going to tell me how the Lenni-Lenape were cheated out of their land."

Moses turned his horse close by to be heard. "Unlike their father, William Penn's sons had few scruples in their dealing with the Indians. They wanted to add another tract to the ones their father had bought along the Delaware years before. The original purchases were for as much land as a man could walk around in a fixed time.

"They had walked, stopped for lunch or to smoke a pipe and they ate, drank, and made merry when the sun went down. They resumed after breakfast and at mid-day concluded the walk and celebrated the rest of the day. It was a fair, pleasant way of doing business. Indian and white were pleased with the outcome; there was peace here and in the Ohio Valley.

"Why did this affect the Ohio Valley?" I asked.

"Indians want to know what the whites are doing whether it's here, in the Ohio Valley or the Carolinas. They aligned themselves with the French or the English depending upon the quality and prices of goods, fairness in treaties, and our military strength. Word travels fast. Talk about the grapevine! They know what's going on before Franklin's post can get the word out."

"In 1737, the local agent for the sons who had remained in London said that they had found an old treaty between their father and the Indians but that the day-and-a-half walk, for some reason, had never taken place. The agent rounded up three trained runners. They had no intention of dawdling, you understand. They had a trail cleared and streams bridged so that no delays occurred and a rapid stride could be held for hours at a time. There was to be nothing leisurely about this event."

"What time of the year was this? Where did it take place?" I asked.

"I'm told it was a cool, sunny day in September, just right for a long run. The race—for it was more an endurance test than a treaty—started at Newtown, about five miles west of Trenton, and went northwest, parallel to the Delaware. Right at the start, the Indians knew something was amiss. The runners outpaced the surveyors and judges who were there to verify the proceedings, ignoring the fair-mindedness Brother Onus had always practiced. Onus is what the Indians called Penn and successor governors because it's the Lenape word for quill, as in ink pen.

"No idle stroll, no break for a friendly smoke, no need to clear the path of downed trees, it soon became apparent that this was a race to see who could last, who could endure and run the longest on this prepared trail to stretch the boundary as far as possible.

"First one runner dropped of exhaustion. Then the second could drive himself no longer despite the promise of choice land as the winning runner's prize. The most enduring ran sixty-five miles—all the way to Mauch Chunk.

"The Penn's agent then said the boundary went northeast back to the Delaware which took the line all the way to near Minisink Ford and contained not just thousands of acres, but hundreds of thousands. The braves had thought that a casual walk, like Onas had done years before, would take the parties to a point where the next leg would intercept the river only a few miles distant as would any reasonable person. Instead, the run took that crucial point far past a major bend in the river so that the leg back to the Delaware was sixty miles long. The Walking Purchase was nothing but a gigantic swindle that defrauded the Delawares and Shawnees of many more thousands of acres of hunting ground.

"They complained to the Iroquois, to whom they had to defer in such matters, in the hopes of a just settlement. The Iroquois denied them redress for reasons of their own. The Delawares and Shawnees thought that Sir William Johnson had something to do with this unfair decision. They allied with the French from then on as did many tribes in the Ohio Valley when they heard of the land grab.

"When the French War broke out, the Indians took their long-repressed revenge out on the settlers and especially the runners who had made them squatters on their own land. Several treaties have tried to make amends in fear of just such raids. And we are mindful of what could happen if the Indians now take the British side."

So tricky wilderness dealings may have some bearing on which side the Indians fight. A chance for someone to do some finagling, I thought, but I refrained from comment.

We arrived at the furnace after riding two-and a half hours up the west bank. We were surprised to be confronted by a large clearing for a manufactory, including a blacksmith shop, a boat-building shop, a barracks with a large kitchen, a store, tavern, grist and saw mill, stables, a paddock, and a barn seated in the middle of fresh-tilled fields and an orchard.

The most commanding were the long sheds for keeping large stacks of charred wood from the weather. The mine was nearby by the center of six thousand acres of hardwood timber. Many workers were dedicated solely to felling trees to make charcoal for the operation. An acre of chestnut, hickory, and oak was necessary for each day's production, Moses said.

He strode to an elegant building and introduced us to Thearon De Laye as he passed Doctor Bolster's note to him. De Laye read it and smiled as he offered his hand. "Nice to meet you folks. But we just received a fresh infusion of capital. Thanks for your interest, anyway.

"Perhaps you'd like to look at our plantation. I can take a few minutes to show you how we make and market our iron." Before we could utter our thanks and hide our disappointment, he bid us to follow him in the yard.

The main feature of Durham Iron Works was the furnace, a twenty-foot stone tower that was served by an equally high ridge. The tower and the ridge were joined by a bridge over which men brought handcarts of ore, limestone, and charcoal to dump into the maw of the furnace and to feed the fire. A water-powered bellows charged the charcoal fire in the "bosh" with large gasps of air to generate the heat necessary to melt the iron from the ore.

De Laye explained, "The limestone is thrown in the mix to serve as a flux. The stone actually melts and the liquid limestone acts as a sealant to keep the molten iron from corroding, which would weaken it. The molten mass runs down to accumulate in the crucible, and the iron workers, using those long poles, continually skim the surface of impurities, known as slag.

"Iron smelting has to be a continuous process to be efficient. We keep the fire going full- blast day and night and avoid banking the fire and start ups which waste time and materials. Every twelve hours a clay plug is removed from the hearth to drain enough molten iron to fill the sand molds which you can see on the ground at the sides. Does anyone have a question so far?"

He checked his watch and signaled to a worker and the clay plug was quickly flipped away. A river of exactly measured molten iron was released and rapidly flowed into the plump channels carved in the sand where the ground steamed as the metal congealed.

"Notice the similarity of the configuration of the molds to a sow and its nursing piglets. That's why we call it pig iron. Years ago we would ship the pig iron to forges that would hammer the pigs into a more useable product for the making of flat metal stock and rods to be further worked into nails, kettles, stoves, fry pans, and raw metal for blacksmiths and farriers to use.

"Now, we have our own water-powered trip hammer to produce a stronger and more marketable product in less time. As you can see, we are busy making shot and cannon balls for Washington's troops. Soon we'll be manufacturing cannon."

De Laye walked us over to the nearby docks on the creek. "We have our own fleet of boats, named after Bob Durham, who designed them about twenty-five years ago. You may not believe this, but they are based on the way the Indians make their log dugouts. But our fifty-foot boats which can carry up to fifteen tons of iron, can be rowed, poled, or sailed if the wind is just right. With all that weighty a cargo, they still draw only about two feet of water.

"We're proud to say that they have been copied and used on this and other rivers for carrying just about anything imaginable. Would you like to see anything else?" He said this in such an intimidating manner that no one spoke. He was dismissing us. I decided not to mention great grandfather's meeting in Marseille with Captain De Laye.

I thanked him. After all, he had performed on such short notice. I also asked if they had room at the tavern for overnight guests and if they took passengers on their boats to Philadelphia. The answer to both questions was a cordial "yes".

# chapter 27

THE NEXT MORNING, Crispin said he felt sick, likening it to influenza. His brow was cold and sweaty and he looked miserable. This could be so serious that I told the others that I felt obligated to take him back to the doctor They said they would go back with me. But I insisted that there was no reason they should cut their trip short. They could be in Philadelphia by evening if they left early on the Durham boat.

Olivia protested that she would accompany me but I suggested that she had better have her visit with Bartram, if she's ever going to, considering our limited schedule.

"What about you? I know you want to see him and his nursery, too," she said.

"Crispin has been my friend as long as I can remember. I can't leave him here, in limbo, I don't think he could make it to Clinton alone and I wouldn't want him to have to get to New York in his condition. I'll just have to visit Philadelphia some other time."

A boat was leaving in a half hour giving us just enough time to eat a quick break-fast and get aboard. Crispin wrapped himself in a blanket and sat on the middle of the fore deck, out of the way of the pole men. With the pig iron aboard and the five of us with horses, I was the last to board and would be the first to disembark across the river from Upper Black Eddy.

It had taken us more than two hours to reach Durham Furnace up the west bank by horseback; an hour was all it took racing with the current to get back. We passed islands we hadn't noticed earlier and the flow of the Musconetcong River hastened our rounding the bulking shoulder of Musconetcong Mountain.

On shore we had been too closed-over by trees to be able to notice the sandstone palisade reaching far above the west bank. But coming down the river we were awed by the five-hundred foot high soft-red crags and their brilliance in the early morning sun..

Moses said that some fancied the profile of an Indian head in the rocks but I think they either had another vantage point or were influenced by their corn whiskey to think that.

As we approached the east bank, the boatswain threw several loops of line over a sturdy stump onshore and payed it out to bring us gradually to a halt so the horses would not be thrown off balance. Olivia reminded me of our schedule and lodging in Philadelphia just in case I could rejoin them, depending upon Crispin's recovery.

Circumstances allowed such a brief moment to kiss goodby and get ourselves ashore. Our good byes lingered so briefly in the damp air as the boat regained speed in the current and was soon a dim specter floating off in the dawn mist.

Crispin turned to me. "You're good to do this, Jamie. I'll be able to travel better if you let me warm up a bit at Moses' shed. The river air is heavy with cold—it's soaked me to the bone."

A workman had a fire going in the fireplace of the shed. I believe that first sniffing, then seeing the thin column of smoke rising from the chimney warmed Crispin by the mere thought of the fire's warmth minutes before he seated himself by the hearth. The brief halt invigorated both of us so that in half an hour we were impatient to crown the hill on the way back to Clinton.

As I helped Crispin on his horse, he remarked, "Did you notice how long and straight the logs of those rafts at Upper Black Eddy were? Like they are going to be used as ship's masts?"

"No, what about it?"

"I was just thinking about how this stretch of river reminds me of the greenwood. And then, I thought of Wenceslas Mochter who ruined the greenwood, and how he might do other diabolical things to make an obscene profit and to further ingratiate himself with the ministry. Those handsome timber specimens would be mighty welcome by the Royal Navy about to lose a source of beams and spars they have relied on for over a hundred years."

"What makes you think they're for the Royal Navy? They could be going to the shipyards in Philadelphia to be used for American ships."

"But I think I saw the king's broad arrow on a few of the logs. Confiscating hard-to-get items would be the kind of thing Mochter would do if he had a chance. And being over here, and unknown, he has a chance."

"It's possible. But just because you saw premium logs in a large raft doesn't mean Mochter's here on the river, or if he is, we could do anything about it. It's too remote a suspicion, Crispin." Crispin didn't respond and I thought this would be the end of such wild conjecture.

Crispin sat his horse with no signs of weakness or threat of falling off. I insisted that we go slowly and stop often. Happily, our return to Clinton was uneventful. The inn's groom took the reigns of our horses after I gave each nag an apple. We refreshed ourselves with sassafras tea at the Clinton House and then Crispin went to bed. To this he gave no argument.

It was late afternoon when I walked across the street to Doctor Bolster's infirmary.

"Aren't thee going to Philadelphia?" he said with surprise. I told him of Crispin's relapse, our visit with De Laye at the furnace and his disinterest in additional capital.

"I'm sorry for your disappointment but De Laye gave you an interesting lecture, I'm sure. He came from an old ship building family in France, you know."

I gagged. "He must have been a direct descendant of great grandfather's benefactor in Marseille." I told Bolster the story of grandfather's encounter with the authorities in the 1690s.

"You should have mentioned it to him. De Laye is very proud of his ancestors and his own success in the colonies. He would have enjoyed hearing of your great grandfather's adventures and his success in England."

I did not respond, so upset was I with my failure to connect with De Laye.

Doctor Bolster continued, "Getting back to Crispin. It's always best for a snakebite victim to rest for three or four days. I'll look at him if you wish, but I think you're doing the right thing by putting him to bed. Crispin was lucky to survive at all. Arthur's quick work and the poultice must have drawn out most of the venom. That's why I think he will be alright after a few days convalescence. But there is no way to pound common sense into young men. Medicine will have come a long way when it learns of a method.

"Will thee join me in a drink, Jamie? I have a hideaway on the stream behind the granary."

We walked down a few steps behind the old building, out of the wind but within sound of the rapids, to chairs set out on a level paved with flagstones. Bolster poured rum into a pair of stoneware mugs and handed one to me. "Some like it straight, others prefer it mixed. This water came right from our well," he said, and passed me a small pitcher beaded with moisture .

"I'm sorry that Crispin did not get a chance to fish the Delaware, it's good fishing for trout and black bass. But the best sport of all is soon to start. The shad begin to run up the river from the ocean to spawn. In another week, and for the next two months, they will crowd the river as the wild pigeons cloud the air. When hooked, they leap out of the water several times. Or they may sound and turn their bodies flat to the current for better purchase. They fight with diabolical fury so that the fisherman may be the first to become exhausted. Shad are also delicious, a delight for the epicure. When the shadbush bloom, you know the shad are running."

"That sounds like great sport. Crispin and I would delight in it. I hope that shad run up the Hudson, too. But what do shadbush look like? I've never heard of them."

"Be assured that shad run up all the coastal rivers. The shadbush is really a tree no higher than forty feet and, in profile resembles a slim lance point. The oyster-white blooms cover it like a cloud and you can't miss them. But when the petals fall, the shadbush fades into the greenery."

"I think I've seen some already. Your Moses is a library of information about the area. He told me of the plight of the Lenni-Lenape," I said as I poured the cold well water into my mug.

Bolster nodded, "They're a remarkable people and some of the whites have been barbaric to them. The Delawares have had honorable leaders like Tamanend and Teedyuscung and we've had the likes of William Penn and the Friends, and Christian Frederick Post and the Moravians. Otherwise the Delaware Valley would still be a dark and bloody ground. Moses is part Indian. He can recite their history back ten generations. His uncle is the one who told me of the snake root I used for Crispin's poultice.

"Thee know, Indians aren't dumb as many like to think they are. Whites just use that and their paganism as a pretext for taking their land. Well, what are thee going to do now, Jamie?"

"I've got to convince Crispin to rest for a day longer than he thinks is necessary and then, either accompany him to New York, if need be, or go to Philadelphia."

"I understand thee are going to visit John Bartram. He's traveled the back country more than most except for some Indian traders such as George Croghan and Conrad Weiser. He used to be a Quaker years ago before the Darby Meeting read him out for his departing from doctrine. He is an intimate friend of Doctor Franklin. But the doctor has been in England so much in the last twenty or so years that his recent return must seem to Bartram like greeting a stranger."

"My wife and her brother run a nursery and have bought seeds and specimens from Bartram for years. Now that we're on this tour, she wants even more to meet him. So do I."

"He is highly regarded by Linnaeus, the Swedish botanist. Not an inconsiderable distinction since Bartram is self-taught. But thee will have to hurry. He's in his late seventies and frail." "It would be a shame to miss him because of my dawdling. I pray Crispin recovers soon."

"If thee are going straight to Philadelphia, take the Flemington road to Coryell's Ferry. It's thirty-five miles to the river, sixty more to the city—a long way to go in a day."

"Alone, I can make it in a day. I like to travel, and Crispin, my wife, and I are English—-"

"Ah yes," the doctor laughed. "Crispin made sure I knew that on our first meeting." "—- so your countryside is a new adventure for us. People seem more prosperous here than at home, and we are from the West Country where our orchards and grain fields keep us better off than most. I wonder the reason for your colonies' wealth."

"I think it's probably because most of our farmers own their own land. The same is true for many of our artisans; they work in their own shops. So they have the incentive to work hard and expertly, knowing the effort will accrue to their own benefit instead of someone else. Apprentices are encouraged by the fortune they observe of their masters rather than being soured with no prospects. They see all around them men who have started with little but grit and determination. I understand that, on average, Americans make four times the wages of English work-men. It also helps that there is more than a thousand miles of cheap, available land to our westward."

The conversation lagged briefly. We both knew that most of the land would be wrested from the Indians or purchased from them at very cheap prices. Bolster sighed and continued.

"We are favored by many, such as Doctor Franklin, who came to Philadelphia with nothing and not only prospered but has shown much ingenuity and energy for the betterment of the city, indeed, for mankind. But thee probably know all about him."

"I know he's given the ministry something to think about and they seem to have it in for him. I'm not familiar with what he's accomplished in the colonies."

"Let's see, there are so many things, it's hard to know where to start. Of course, he published the *Pennsylvania Gazette* and was notable for *Poor Richards Almanac* through which he dispensed common sense, humor, and barbs at pompous political personages. Papers in the main seaboard cities are owned by him and managed by operating partners, and these companies publish books and pamphlets, sell stationery and print state documents, even state currencies.

"He's known here and abroad for his experiments that prove lightning is electricity. He wasn't just dealing in theories or gimcrack toys, he devised the lightning rod to protect our barns and houses. That's why he's called doctor, for the honor awarded him by Oxford

University, the Royal Society medal, and honorary degrees from Harvard and Yale.

"As with electricity, Franklin's a practical man and has devised a heating stove which is so much more efficient than a fireplace that half as much wood is needed to keep a body warm. Didn't try to monopolize it either. He established a circulating library system in the city, and organized a volunteer fire company and a hospital for the poor as well as an academy. You must realize all this energy and invention has developed a considerable economy here and elsewhere."

Bolster paused as if to rest from this recitation. He took a draft of his rum, changed position on his chair, scratched his nose, and continued.

"Oh yes, he became Deputy Post Master General for all the colonies which, to be sure, helps him sell newspapers. But he speeded delivery of the mail considerably up and down the seaboard. That is until the ministry fired him because of the Hutchinson letters. He's acted as agent in England for Pennsylvania and several other colonies for the better part of twenty years. .

"What about the Hutchinson letters?" I asked.

"It's a long, complicated story. Essentially, Franklin came into possession of letters written by Governor Hutchinson which advised the ministry to limit liberties in the colonies. Massachusetts published the letters. Publishing of the governor's letters gave the crown the long-sought opportunity to embarrass and publicly humiliate Franklin. The event did discredit the doctor in the eyes of many colleagues and friends and from then on, Franklin stopped trying to negotiate conciliation with what he considered a corrupt government.

"As a doctor, I should have headed the list of his important accomplishments with his making a silver catheter. If this was the only thing he ever invented, his name would be gratefully remembered by many of my patients forever. I could go on, but tallying up the list becomes almost tedious. It is an honor to know him."

"You know Benjamin Franklin?"

"Well, I met him once about ten years ago. He and his son had just come back from England. We talked for maybe fifteen minutes about medicine and philosophy in general."

"You also know his son, the Governor of New Jersey?"

"Yes. For a while I was a member of New Jersey's assembly. A smart, reasonable man, just like his father—a chip off the old block. But politically, they differ as night and day."

"I would love to meet them. So would Olivia. But, I'm sure the Franklins are both far too busy to spend time talking with everyday people."

"Thee would be surprised. I used to think it was impossible to see important men, but it's not, really. I girded myself for the ordeal but had no trouble. It's the smaller-minded men who have no time for visitors. Successful people are busy and prosper partly because they do see a lot of people. But when one gets in their office he shouldn't lollygag and waste their time. He should state his business, stick to the point, and leave when the business is concluded. When thee go to Philadelphia, try seeing Doctor Franklin. I'll wager he'll see thee. And he'll put thee at ease."

I savored the thought of conversing with the Franklins or even one of them. I was afraid I would stammer or remain speechless in their presence. The thought prompted my next question.

"Crispin and I noticed large rafts of lumber being maneuvered down the river. One tied up at Upper Black Edy had remarkably long and straight logs. Crispin thought they were probably going to be employed as masts and spars for the Royal Navy because some were blazed with the Royal Arrow. Could that be true?"

"Until very recently, England commanded much of the timber since she denuded herself of serviceable timber by much shipbuilding for commerce and her many wars. As well, industrial charcoal for centuries has consumed much of the natural forests. The Royal Navy lays claim to the finest boles and the easiest to take out by marking those specimens with the king's broad arrow mark. The blaze is a warning that these are reserved by royal privilege. Crispin's conjecture could well be correct, Jamie."

"I understand that the King has proclaimed that all ships of the American colonies are considered contraband and subject to confiscation. If that's so, we are in a state of war and should confiscate these prime logs so they won't be used against us. How would we find out the purchaser of these logs? Any ideas?"

"When thee get to Philadelphia—I would assume the rafts in question may arrive about the same time thee do—go to the customs office or the pilot's association and they should know. Or see where the rafts are being loaded onto vessels for transport overseas.

"Then visit nearby taverns. Surely some denizen of these places will know. Proceed carefully else someone will wonder why thee ask and may cause trouble. But thee may not have to ask. Just have a drink, remain private, and keep thy ears alert to gossip. But be prepared."

He offered another draft of rum. But rum does not agree with me that well, and I stood to go. "Thanks, but no. I must check on Crispin, get dinner, and go to bed. It's been a long day."

Crispin was still sleeping soundly so I prepared for a dinner long delayed.

The next morning, Crispin was up and about. "I think I'll be alright now. Let's have breakfast soon so I can leave. New York's a long way off," he declared.

"That's what you said a few days ago and look what happened. I'm glad you feel better. But you better be sure this time because if you go to New York, I will be going to Philadelphia. Take it easy for one more day. I'll stay here with you to make sure you're able to manage.

"I saw a billiard table in the Long Room of this place. I've always wanted to try the game. Have you played in New York?"

"Trevor Shaw taught me the rudiments and it was fun. But I haven't won a game from him yet. Billiards is a skill like archery; it takes a lot of practice."

After breakfast, I had Crispin show me what he had learned on the New York playing tables. Grabbing several cues, he rolled them on the green baize to see which were straight and which wobbled. He selected the straightest and gave me my choice. Then he became thoroughly intent sizing up a shot, aiming and following through with a smooth glide of the cue stick. He stabbed the ivory cue ball so that it collided just so with the solid yellow ball next to the side rail. It ran smartly along the edge of the table and dropped into the corner pocket.

With him the cue ball always seemed to be aligned for the next shot. He showed me that gaining position was second only to scoring. I managed to drop a few balls in the pockets, but the effort of putting "English" on the cue ball to be in position for the next shot nixed my aim. As I missed easy shots he made difficult ones. With fewer balls remaining on the table, my chances to even the score diminished. Each shot was important, each miss critical.

Shooting billiards proved to be an important part of Crispin's therapy although I had not planned it that way. After the two hours it took us to play one game we stopped for tea. He showed no sign of fatigue, only exuberance for the day's offerings and a further chance of winning pool games. Good, maybe he could return to New York the next day and I could leave for Philadelphia. God, how I missed Olivia.

At dinner, I repeated Bolster's comment on the approaching shad run. He was interested but said he had heard about the sport on the Hudson from Trevor Shaw. He and Trevor and Trevor's new friend, a young widow who had recently lost her husband in the Quebec campaign, were planning a trip to the Esopus around the first of May.

"Tell me about the young widow. Is she much younger than Trevor?"

"Trevor's thirty-five and she's probably about twenty. I think she had been married for only six months when she received word that her soldier husband had died of small pox."

"How is it that an old man has endeared himself to a woman so young? Is she attractive?"

"She's beautiful and charming. She moved to the city when her husband's regiment marched off to Quebec. She was referred to Trevor and his store and he wanted to help her. Three months later she heard of her husband's death. We've both been trying to console her. I did her portrait in charcoal just before I left. I think—I know—I have it with me."

He rummaged in his duffle bag and pulled out the sketch, unrolled it and weighted the edges flat on the table. "See for yourself. Her name is Annie McLauren. Trevor doesn't know it yet, nor does she, but I am going to marry her."

She was beautiful with a pleasing, sensitive face. I congratulated him on his choice of mate and wished his courtship successful. Though I was pleased that Crispin was doing so well in New York, it seemed ominous that our friendship might drift apart; our paths had diverged from the moment we landed in the colonies last February.

Doctor Bolster dropped by the next morning to check over Crispin and have breakfast with us. He pronounced the patient well and able to resume his life. We had a cordial and memorable meal, so memorable that I feared that the event could never be replicated. In the social mire about to take place, we might not see each other again. I rode the short mile east with Crispin to the crossroads. A stylish sign pointed east to New York. At right angles to it, another said sixty-five miles to Philadelphia.

The road to Flemington was cluttered with Conestoga wagons carrying freight and people south and west, away from seaboard congestion and likely military strife. Others were hurriedly pushing hand carts overloaded in their haste to flee New York.

The highway going south had more and better-styled homes than the road to Easton and the many fields were being plowed now that the ground had thawed and dried out. The lay of the land was less hilly than only ten or so miles to the northwest and sloped gradually to flatter land as the road left the Raritan Valley. The farther south I traveled, grass was greener, buds bursting, and a pale green suffused the woods along the way. The shad run must also be beginning—shad bushes were outstanding white clouds in the woods, islands in a landscape on the verge of spring.

# chapter 28

Coryell's Ferry was larger than Clinton as I expected. Sluiceways channeled river water to power grist and saw mills. Taverns lined both sides of the road and ware-houses commanded both shores of the river. Wharves were piled high with stacks of lumber, barrels of grain, and barrel staves. Several craft, mostly Durham boats, were loading local products at the same time others discharged cargos. Of the fifty homes or so those on low ground by the river were ramshackle compared to the few mansions gracing flood-free bluffs.

Just as the ferry was about to shove off for the opposite shore, the ferryman let me and my horse step aboard. My stomach was grinding on nothing but I put off having lunch rather than be delayed. Close scrutiny revealed no rafts of logs, only a few random logs of ordinary dimension drifting in the eddies and backwaters. There were none blazed with the royal broad arrow.

My poor horse had scant but an apple since morning so my first stop in Pennsylvania was at a livery stable for a quarter bale of hay and a bag of oats to relieve her hunger, with plenty left over to tie behind the saddle. The sun had moved an hour past noon; the almanac said sunset was about seven o'clock. I had a little more than six hours of daylight in which to reach Philadelphia.

Despite all the taverns, I had little choice for a decent meal and relaxation. The Old Ferry Tavern had several carts and many horses drawn up at the rail—the best endorsement. I gathered that they served good food or something interesting must be going on inside. A tall well-formed, mustached gentleman in a cocked hat and bright blue long coat appeared through the smokey haze. Through the smokey haze he was gesturing and holding a small bottle to an amused crowd. His long black hair was clubbed and exaggerated the staccato bob of his head as he emphasized each statement. I pressed forward to the edge of the attentive throng.

"I myself hazarded the wrath of the Six Nations to procure this small portion of elixir, said by the Seneca to cure or even ward off mankind's worst malignancies. How many of you have had the misery to witness loved-ones die of small pox, cancer, plague, measles, snake bite, cholera, consumption, diphtheria, myosotis, and the ravages of peristalsis?" He waited for favorable response or argument to his recitation.

The crowd mumbled only 'amens'.

"My condolences. I only wish I had been there to serve you in you're hour of need. How many times have you or a loved one suffered food poisoning, horse kicks, scalds, and abrasions, and wished you had an ointment to salve or forestall further agonies?"

Some poor souls raised their hands while others laughed. The scoffers abruptly restrained their skepticism to avoid missing more gems of medical knowledge from the speaker's dissertation. After all, it didn't cost anything to listen.

"I can commiserate with you, my friends. But condolences and commiseration are not enough. This pint bottle of Doctor Honeoye's Seneca oil will, after two swallows, cure what ails you in only a matter of hours.

"Why, I have personally witnessed a brave Seneca warrior fight a black bear, suffer many bites and gashes and the loss of his left hand in the process. Despite these injuries, he brought the bear to heel. Then he drank half a bottle of my Seneca oil and was cured of his wounds in only a few days. For a measly two shillings, you will thank the day you stand here dithering whether to reach deep into your pocket in exchange for this elixir, guaranteed to allay the severest pain and mend the worst wounds."

He repeatedly said Seneca so fast it sounded more like *snake*. But whoever heard of snake oil? It's a dry meat. He must mean Seneca, I thought.

"I, myself was scalped in an unhappy misunderstanding with a chief of the Cayugas. A squaw friend of mine forced half a bottle of this elixir down my throat. You can see with your own eyes that my scalp has grown back to its former luxuriant condition—the envy of men five and ten years younger than me.

"Think of it! I have only fifteen bottles left. I dare not visit the Seneca lands to replenish my supply as long as war threatens. My friend Red Jacket may not be as kind if the Iroquois join the British. Who will be the first to take advantage of this unique medical opportunity?"

As the crowd surged to accept his offer, I bought four crusty rolls and a chunk of cheese for the road. This was to be my dinner so that I could stifle my hunger en route. The bar man insisted that my New Jersey currency was worth fifteen per cent less this side of the Delaware. As I left, the "doctor" pleased the crowd by being able to "find" a few more bottles in his commodious portmanteau.

The Old York Road passed through towns like Lahaska, Furlong, and Hatboro. My haste deprived me of learning the derivation of these memorable names except for the hatters' signs..

The deeper I traveled into Pennsylvania, the more mansions there were, most were built of fieldstone. This was in sharp contrast to the mostly raw, unpainted wooden buildings at Coryell's Ferry. The finest had quoins of lighter stone interlocked at the corners similar to dovetails in fine furniture. Veils of ivy clambering the walls added to their charm. Most were surrounded by a magnificent and expansive greensward kept trimmed by flocks of sheep.

Many outbuildings, shops, and barns testified to the plantations' being self supporting. Fields, commonly bordered by stone walls laid dry, had already been fitted and rows of Indian corn, wheat, flax, hemp, burley and oats would soon make their appearance above ground.. I was told that tobacco seedlings would be planted in a few weeks. Winter wheat, six inches high and deep green, promised a bountiful harvest in a few months.

Cattle and other stock appeared sleek and well fed. Especially fine were those spirited fleet-footed steeds drawing sulkies whose proud owners insisted on challenging a race with countrymen in similar equipage. I was envious of such grace and speed. Orchards had been well pruned and a pink blush hinted an early bloom. Prosperity was the rule wherever I went.

An hour before sundown, I came to the small settlement of Jenkintown.. Gunsmiths, drapers, silversmiths, book sellers, general stores, liveries, blacksmiths, tack shops, and taverns sported their distinctive signs over the walk. Even local cabinet makers could compete against those in Philadelphia. No human need was neglected. Their tidy presence testified that the residents made a comfortable living and presented a prosperous market. In contrast with the plantations, most of the town homes were red brick, regimented side by side for several blocks with scrupulously scrubbed white marble stoops abutting the sidewalk close to the street.

The road bent sharply to the right, luring me to the edge of Germantown, a thrifty area indeed. It was as if I had crossed into a different country; no one could understand my questions as they spoke only German. The road progressed to Wissahickon Creek, a gorge deep in hemlocks where the sparkling-silver stream capriciously made its way to the Schuylkill River, the last few miles of which defined the western boundary of Philadelphia.

The west bank of the river had been reserved for fine mansions such as Stenton, Lemon Hill, Cliveden , and Walnut Grove, lying just outside the city limits. The leaders of the business and political world had surely prospered from the Delaware Valley and its seaport..

Philadelphia claimed the plain between the Schuylkill and the Delaware Rivers, known as the Neck. The citizenry were concentrated in a plat of a dozen east-west streets and seven blocks spreading west from the Delaware with ample space north, south and westward to the Schuylkill for fifty times as many residents. The city boasted that is was third largest to London and Bristol in the English Empire: thirty-five thousand people by last count. It looked like a large small town basking in the shade of its many trees. Reverence for natural beauty was expressed by streets named Locust, Chestnut, Walnut, Spruce, and Pine, with Vine and Lombard thrown in. Cross streets were numbered first, second, etc.

William Penn designed this grid which made it easier locating people and places. I found the newly built and extravagant Smith's City

Tavern on Walnut Street, which Olivia had written for reservations. Except that we hadn't realized that its newness and location near the state house merited Congress' complete possession of it.

The clerk was sorry that he hadn't been able to honor our reservation.

"Your wife and party arrived a few days ago Mister Claveraque. I referred her to a nearby reputable boarding house, one of the best in the city, run by Mrs. Bunting. Many of our overflow customers have enjoyed a stay at her establishment since Congress went into session," he reported in a remorseless monotone as he continued sorting papers. I was weary and hoped for no more usurping congressmen.

Twilight was delightfully descending on the city as lamp-lighters went about with tapers and ladders to kindle the street lights—another convenience championed by Doctor Franklin.

Most of the houses in the city were built of red brick and were fronted by white stone stoops as they were in Jenkintown. Fifth Street was no exception.

Thanks to the street lamp close by, I could just barely read the large letters graven on the brass plate on the front door, ***Bunting's Boarding for Ladies and Gentlemen.***

Loosely tying "Nellie" to the hitching post, I approached her stoop. The front door was flung open.

"I have been expecting you! You are Jamie Claveraque, aren't you?"

I nodded.

She held out her hand and smiled. "Welcome, Jamie. I'm Gertrude Bunting, but please call me Bunny."

As I crossed her threshold her chandelier cast a bright light on a buxom woman of fifty, with her blonde hair in a bun, who obviously enjoyed hosting travelers.

"Let me take that bag, Jamie. Linus, see about Mr. Jamie's horse. I have some hot coffee and scones. Sit down and take a load off your feet."

I was able to utter, "Thank you, Mrs. Bunting," before she added, "Olivia, Arabella, and Arthur have gone to a local carriage house to see a Shakespeare play performed by a local amateur troupe. It's the final performance and they didn't want to miss it, especially since I told them that plays, along with other entertainments, have been proscribed by prim and proper Quakers. Oh, please call me *Bunny*. Everyone does."

Linus, a ten-year old black boy appeared, ready to see to Nellie. I stopped him, drew out two apples from my pack and gave both to him. "One's for you, Linus. The other is for my horse, Nellie." I added a pence, "Please give her a good rubdown." It had been a long day. I thanked Bunny while gulping the coffee and devouring the scones, made my apologies and asked directions to our rooms.

"Top of the stairs, first door to your right. But first, I think you'll be interested in our refreshment room. Follow me."

At this I hoped that she was not one who insisted on delaying urgent business with endless and blithering conversation. She led me through the kitchen to a recent addition to her lodgings and opened the door to a chamber floored with flagstones laid in sand and equipped with a pump and wooden pipes to a keg overhead.

"This shower will do more for you than a bathtub. Use it all you want, but pump the keg full for the next bather. It has had no use today so the water should be warm enough. Enjoy!"

When I left home, I thought never to see this luxury again. I haven't, except Captain Bob's simple device on the *Raritan*. But that was seawater—refreshing but at the cost of itching from the salt until one could rinse off with fresh water.

"Bless you, Bunny. You make me feel at home and one of the family."

An adjacent room had a two-holer with a quaint direction carefully printed by Bunny:

> "It is well to put in a dipper of ashes after each use. After each major use, please add a spoonful of chloride of lime. Keep cover on lime."

The next morning I was pleased to waken and see that Olivia was by my side and just beginning to stir.

"I can't believe that I was so numbed by sleep that I didn't feel you slipping into bed. You must have been especially careful," were my first words to her in what seemed like weeks.

"My dear, I knew you had to be very tired for such a journey and I didn't want to wake you. Besides, we would have exchanged greetings and carried on at length, as you're trying to do now, and neither of us would be able to sleep." She half-heartedly fended me off and laughed.

I caressed her back, seemingly her most sensitive part and starting point for our amours.

"Oh, that feels so good and I haven't had such treatment since you stayed with Crispin. I missed you dreadfully. Scratch my left shoulder, will you?—-a little higher. Don't stop."

But then she realized it was to be a busy day. "You had better stop after all or we'll be in bed all day. We have an appointment with Robert Morris this morning. But, I'm so glad you are here. We were worried about you and Crispin. How is he?"

I told her briefly about Crispin's recovery and his parting for New York as we both washed and dressed. "When do we have to see Morris?" I asked. We heard stirring in the adjacent room. Arthur and Arabella were up.

"Are they joining us in the interview with Morris?"

"We're all going. The appointment is for eleven-thirty. He's giving us fifteen minutes."

Mrs. Bunting had heard our commotion getting dressed and had timed breakfast perfectly.

"Everything smells so inviting. I'm glad you're a good cook, Mrs. Bunting."

"Thank you, Mr Claveraque, but remember, I want you to call me Bunny."

"In that case, Bunny, call me Jamie," I insisted.

Olivia explained, "Jamie, we arranged such informalities when we arrived the other day."

I changed the subject. "How was the play? What have you been doing in Philadelphia?"

They all started to talk at once. Olivia triumphed, "Hamlet was well performed considering the players were amateurs. But they ignored Hamlet's own advise to his players "to speak slowly with words trippingly off the tongue." Arthur and Arabella nodded but looked guilty since they had violated the law with ten others by attending the banned performance at the make-do carriage house theater.

Arabella joyfully revealed that they had walked around much of Billy Penn's city, especially noting the better shops, Carpenter's Hall, the State House where the Second Congress was sitting, the many parks with daffodils, forsythia, flowering crab and redbud trees in bloom, the ships at Front Street, and a long-delayed spring.

I related my conversation with Doctor Bolster, the raft of masts with the king's broad arrow, Crispin's interest in Annie McLauren and what I wanted to accomplish in Philadelphia.

"Who is she?" Olivia asked. I told her the details as Crispin had related them to me.

"What does a raft of masts floating down the Delaware River have to do with us?"

"We could have the satisfaction of slowing down British ship building if we could confiscate the masts, maybe capture the party trying to sneak them out of the country. Who ever is doing this most likely is doing us other damage. Catching them is worthwhile,"

"Why is it you wish to meet with Robert Morris? Who is he?" I explained again. "I would like to leave a little early to visit the river front. I understand there are about a hundred ships in port at any given time."

Olivia had other ideas. "Why not visit the ships after we meet with Mr. Morris? Then you and Arthur can inquire about rafts of logs and ships as much as you please and Arabella and I can do some serious shopping." Arthur said he wanted to walk inside the State House, maybe talk to some congressmen. Conveniently, I would be alone in my inquiries.

We arrived at the modest appearing offices of Willing and Morris at exactly eleven thirty.

Mr. Morris did not keep us waiting. Tall, well proportioned, and robust for his age, about forty, I'd say. Morris' high forehead, large nose, and thick lips commanded attention. His bass voice and manner of speech was authoritative and convincing. I gave our reason for seeking him out.

"I can understand your desire for investment," he began, 'and now is a good time to do so. American industry has been held back for well over a hundred years because of England's so-called Navigation Acts favoring industry in the mother country. Now we can ignore that law.

"We are desperately in need of war supplies, not only muskets, cannon and gunpowder, but blankets, shoes, farming tools, medicine, soap, uniforms, paper for cartridges, flour and meat, money to pay the troops, down to canteens, fodder and horseshoes. And wagons. God, how we need wagons. The army can't move without horses and wagons, you know.

"We have little money to pay for these things and no authority to tax the public or to secure tax money from the states. The problem is that much of our protest to Britain is about taxes. This makes it difficult to assess a tax on the public determined to shuffle off one government, partially because of taxes, in favor of another which, right away, wants to tax them.

What brief time we were allotted was running out and I wanted Morris' advice. But he was so obsessed with the complexities of his concerns that I dared not interrupt.

"With only the trace of government affecting most people, they see little reason to pay for it, especially to people they don't deal with every day. Politicians enter the average man's life only to take something from him—so they say.

He paused. The mahogany clock ticked in time with its pendulum. He kept our attention.

"But no one can provide these things for nothing. So we have to get the funds in the easiest, most unobtrusive manner—where the taxpayer is not confronted with the tax collector. Can you guess the solution?"

He waited but briefly for answer. "Customs! That is import duties on items like spices, sugar, tea, coffee, wine, salt, high fashion, dueling pistols—any thing from overseas. The tax is simply added to the price as the cost of the heat of the oven is added to the cost of a loaf of bread.

"Taxes also call for specie—gold or silver in any form—not payment in kind. Few of our country men have it. So we issue paper money largely to assist in the payment of taxes and to expedite trade. Well, that's our problem. How can I help you?"

"Can you advise us on investments? I have some gold and would like to put it to work."

"We have a stock exchange in Philadelphia but I hesitate to make specific recommend-ations. I'm too busy trying to find money to pay for the war as I have mentioned. I also find that people seeking investment advice, in their innocence, expect infallible results and tend to tag after the advisor for further renderings. If years later the investment falls on hard times, the adviser is held personally responsible for not being able to see ten years in advance.

"The best investment you can make is in your own government, young man. One where you can have a say in what goes on, and prosper."

"But, I'm a visitor from England!"

"Then move here and invest your gold in this country. No, you don't have to move here to invest in our country. But you can't make a better investment. I was a visitor from Liverpool and here I am thirty years later."

I was finally able to pose another question . "How much interest or dividend will the government pay? It doesn't sound like it's in a position to pay anything and I need income now."

"Well, I'll give it some thought. You seem like a bright young man. We can use men like you." He glanced at his watch, courteously suggesting that the appointment was over.

As we arose from our chairs, I thanked him for his time and asked, "Where will I find out who is exporting lumber to England from the port of Philadelphia?"

"We used to send a lot of lumber to England. They needed it desperately and we have plenty. But, of course, we don't export any to them anymore. Why do you ask?"

I told him of our seeing logs blazed with the king's broad arrow on the upper Delaware.

"Those logs were blazed years ago to show the lumber men what to cut. Non-exportation agreements ended supplying the king's stock. There shouldn't be any of them left. They've long since been sold or confiscated by authorities up river. But you're right. Some one may be trying to steal leftovers out from under our noses to send them to England. Years ago, anyone stealing logs with the broad arrow would be hanged, no doubt about it. The Brits can get plenty in Canada, but their rivers are still frozen and they probably need them as soon as they can get them.

"How do we find out before they leave our shores?"

"Pennsylvania started a navy of its own only last summer. We have more than a dozen mid-sized, ship-rigged row galleys patrolling the river and Delaware Bay. If you saw the rafts five days ago, they might be this far down river by now. Probably in some out-of-the-way cove waiting to be picked up on the sly by a redcoat Indiaman. We can have our local patrol keep an eye out for them. Where are you staying and for how long? I'll get word to you."

"We're at Mrs. Bunting's boarding house. We'll be there another week..."

"You're at Bunny's? I've known her for years. She accommodates extra visitors for me when my house and the inns are overflowing. She also buys ice from me at my ice house. "Perhaps I can scrape up an investment for you but remember, the new governments can use that gold. I'm sure we can work out a fair return for you. If you wish, you can set up an account at our personal bank. Then you can designate investments to be purchased merely with a check on your account." He scribbled the captain's name for me.

As we were leaving, Morris called me back. "The man to see for opening an account is William Bingham." He smiled, bowed slightly, and turned away. He kept his word. He had given us fifteen minutes.

Outside, we talked briefly in the balmy noon sunshine. Arabella and Olivia were anxious to begin shopping. They had spent enough time on the interview part of the trip, they said.

Arthur tarried a moment, then excused himself and went into the nearby coffee house. In five minutes he returned and meekly whispered, "Bunny's coffee goes through me like a sieve." He stayed with me only long enough to ask if he could borrow ten shillings which I handed over to him. I watched him as he departed for the State House.

He had only gone about a hundred feet when a cluster of urchins, no more than twelve years old, who had been playing innocuously on the walk, swarmed about him, yelling, "Daddy, Daddy!" for no apparent reason. Understandably, he threw out his arms in an attempt to avoid being hemmed in. They took advantage of this posture and confusion, all searching his clothing for whatever it would yield, and then ran off in all directions. I hastened over to see if he was all right as he straightened his clothing. We declined with thanks offers of help from onlookers.

"What's that all about?" he wailed. Then he realized that he had been thoroughly frisked. He dug into his pants pockets, front and back, then his shirt and sighed with relief when all seemed in place. Then he checked his coat breast pocket where he usually put his wallet with the bank notes I had given him. All were gone! They had seen him put the money there and quickly relieved him of it by encasing him in confusion. The devils had gotten his watch and fob, too.

"I feel so humiliated! Those little heathens. My father, your grandfather, gave me that watch twenty-five years ago, just before I left England to come here. I'll never see that again."

I tried to calm him. "Let's go over to that bench and sit for a spell. You've had a frightful shock that would upset anybody. When I can do it with out anyone noticing, I'll pass you ten more shillings."

Arthur finally relaxed when I asked him simple questions and told him of my plan to call next on the navy captain Morris had mentioned. He was still determined to visit the State House. The urchins did not return. No doubt they had a lookout for when all seemed clear. Arthur had stopped shaking and regained his color and composure. I suggested we leave this area and come back when the little thieves had time to set themselves in readiness for their next diversion. Arthur shook his head and declined any further confrontation. "What would we do with them if we caught them? They have probably passed off the watch and shillings to a confederate. We would accomplish little even if we could find a constable."

I suggested that we go back a block to the coffee house he had used before being assaulted. He hesitated but then agreed that a dish of coffee might calm him back to normalcy.

After savoring the coffee, Arthur insisted that he was recovered enough to see the State House and observe Congress deliberate their resolve to outwit the ministry.

In the dim light of the coffee house no one was paying any attention to us so I passed him another ten-shilling note. "I hope this will be enough."

He patted my arm as we rose to leave. "Thanks, but no matter," he said and we parted.

I referred to Bunny's map of the city and noted that it was a short distance to the river and the naval wharf. On the way, I entered a men's establishment and purchased a handsome brass-headed cane. The clerk kindly called it a walking stick. I knew I was a little young to be using a cane for support or even for the formality of it, but I wanted to be prepared with some kind of sturdy cudgel should threat of an assault occur again. City of brotherly love, Indeed!.

The clerk pointed out that the wood was the finest hickory, varnished with a badger fur brush, and that the end of the walking stick had a pinned brass ferrule to protect the wood from being scuffed or split. It was thick brass so that "it could be sharpened if you wanted." He also brought my attention to the spur on the brass handle. "Gives you a firmer grip," he said.

As I left the shop I twirled the piece and slashed once or twice, rapier-like, before tapping the flagstones in cadence. The walking stick in hand enlivened me and my step.

The Pennsylvania Navy wharf jutted far enough into the water to accommodate several ships but only a small sailing vessel such as one would hire for an afternoon sail with his sweetheart was at the dock. The wharf looked more like a rookery for seagulls than a necessary facility for an official navy. I enquired for Captain Kells Oakley but was told he was on river patrol and wouldn't be back until the day after tomorrow.

The Delaware was about a mile across here with the waterfront boasting at least fifty wharves, crammed with ships, and these were sheltered by a sandbar called Windmill Island. Hydraulic conditions had deposited many similar islands in this part of the river. I could see shipyards beyond the myriad masts up and down for two or three miles, but no sign of log rafts.

A tavern was at hand and doing a good noon-time business judging from the cacophony coming from the open door. I went in, sat at the bar, and ordered a mug of beer. Of all the bottles lining the back bar, my eyes fixed on the brown pint bottle of Doctor Honeoye's Seneca Oil Elixir. I asked the bartender if the bottle was his or if he ever tried the stuff.

"It's not mine, but I have tried it and it does allow you to feel better when you have a painful gut. We sell it for the doctor and it's the last bottle of this month's consignment. He's due any time to renew our supply and harangue the customers. Like them, I always enjoy his show." The bartender, Dick, left to tend a customer at the far end of the bar. He returned in a moment.

"Do you know the doctor?" .

"No. I watched him make his pitch to a crowd at a tavern in Coryell's Ferry. He drummed up a lively business. I admired his performance and handling of the crowd."

Dick started to polish a tray of glasses. "Are you a traveling man, too?"

"No, I'm just making a social visit. But this is my first trip to Philadelphia."

When I ordered lunch and he quickly placed two baskets of strange food within easy reach, one filled with what he called peanuts and the other with many pieces of dough that had been rolled to finger thickness and tied in a three-inch knot and baked and salted to a pleasing crispiness. He called them pretzels. They were made by the Pennsylvania Dutch near Lancaster.

The peanuts were easily shelled by crushing the brittle covering and extracting the one or two nuts. Both peanuts and pretzels were enticing: to eat one was to quickly require another.

Bunny's map showed many coves, islands, and channels through a swamp at the mouth of the Schuylkill on the Pennsylvania side. Just the place for avoiding observation away from the main stream of traffic. I'll just have to wait until the day after tomorrow to talk to Captain Oakley. Or better, go on patrol with him.

Dick asked if he could remove the plate and the bowls of peanuts and pretzels. "I'll clear a space so you can look at your map," he said. "Looking for anything special?"

I hesitated but realized that my answer need not reveal my true quest. "I'm trying to see where lumber floated down the river might be corralled and picked up for shipment overseas."

"That would probably be upstream of the city so the logs don't float free and disrupt shipping. They used to have awful problems with strays staving in the hulls of smaller boats. Hey, Tom, come here a minute," he called.

Then he turned back to me, "Tom would know. He used to work for a shipping company that specialized in exporting naval stores and spars to England. Non-exportation agreements slowed business and he lost his job."

"What can I do for ye?" said Tom, mug in hand. He had come to the bar for another one.

"Is that lumber exporting company you used to work for still in business? This gentleman wants to know where they do their loading of logs from up river?"

"They don't export from here anymore what with the rebels saying you can't ship stuff to Britain now. I think the Brits can only get naval stores from Nova Scotia where they get the really large mast stock anyway. There and from Maine. Any logs now coming down the Delaware would be picked up higher upriver and used locally for construction, ship building, papermaking, fuel, or suchlike. A few may be shipped to Holland and France."

"Since they can't be exported to Britain, why would there be logs blazed with the king's arrow?" I asked. "Those days are gone." I took another swallow of my beer.

Tom thought for a bit. "There are a lot of people in Philadelphia who don't think so. Maybe the logs are being marked for when the British resume their authority."

We conversed a while longer and then I slapped a tuppence on the counter. "Thanks for your information. Here, have a beer on me," I said and left the place.

There was now a fifty-foot ship at the dock, possibly part of the fleet for the Pennsylvania Navy. I enquired. The captain was on the town but the mate on watch said they patrolled the river up to the falls at Trenton.

"Have you seen any rafts of lumber floating down the river?" I asked.

"No rafts, sir. Just the occasional tree undermined by an upriver flood or a log or two that escaped the loading at Bristol. Nothing like a bundled lot of them at once. Not like it used to be ten years ago." he said. There might be something to that, I thought, and thanked him.

As I walked away, someone called my name. Strange, since I knew virtually no one here.

He called again and I could see this young man beckoning to me as he walked in my direction.

"Mr Claveraque! Don't you recognize me? I'm Cyrus. Remember, you saved me from the shark."

Cyrus was an agreeable lad. I never expected to see him again but was pleased to.

"Cyrus. Yes, I remember you. It seems like years ago that we finally pulled you from the water and the jaws of that shark. How nice to see you again, Cyrus. What are you doing in Philadelphia. I thought you were going to New York to rejoin your regiment."

"I did that, sir! They, that is Mister Mochter and his men thought they had lost Paul and me. They had no way of knowing that you saved us. I had to explain all this to avoid being treated as a deserter.

"And you did persuade them, I see. Are you on assignment here in Philadelphia?"

"If you don't mind, let us go into that tavern. I'm expecting to meet someone there and if Mr. Mochter saw me with you he'd have at me with the cat, he would."

When we had found a corner booth and we could talk in private, I replied, "Who is Mochter? Why would he react in such an extreme manner?" I asked innocently, hoping to draw from Cyrus something of Mochter's mission in the colonies.

"Don't you remember? He's the man I work for on special assignment. If it weren't for working for him, I surely would have been flogged within an inch of my life. I was accepted back in the army with no punishment because he said I was innocent of the charge of desertion and that I did my best to return to his direction. Besides, he needs me. He—-."

A striking, fully endowed blonde arrived out of breath and seated herself next to Cyrus with a heave of her hip. She was beautiful. That is until she opened her mouth. She spoke in a screechy whine. "Cyrus, this place is so dark, I couldn't find you and thought you were late again. Introduce me to this gentleman," she demanded as she made herself more comfortable.

Cyrus obediently performed introductions and was about to continue when—

"This is the man who saved you from the shark? I expected that it was some burly sailor to have done that. What do you do, Mister Claveraque?"

Betty Ann Button had a surfeit of feminine pulchritude, too much for her best interest, I suspect. And little of the cultured coquetry and nuances that should go with it. She presented herself as if for immediate consumption. But Cyrus seemed proud to show her off as his. At least he had her for the afternoon.

"I'm just visiting the city, Miss Button. We saved Cyrus as any decent person would do."

I did not care to lead the conversation but rather hoped Cyrus would be allowed to continue revealing what he and Mochter were up to in the city of brotherly love. But the conversation flagged as Cyrus and I surveyed Betty Ann.

I urged him on. "As I remember, you were taken from the ranks for special work because you have such excellent handwriting, Cyrus. Wasn't Paul chosen because of his calligraphy, too? What do you write? Royal commissions? Advertisements? Letters to the editor?"

"Paul got the job but began putting on airs. But his undoing was being insolent to Mr. Mochter several times. So Mochter sacked him and gave me the job. Paul was ordered back to his regiment in Halifax. He was simmering with rage. Since we returned to New York, I've stayed clear of Paul. And Mochter has treated me well. Says I might be granted some land in one of the colonies if I continue to do good work."

"Good for you, Cyrus. It must be important work to be valued so highly."

"Thank you, sir. I like doing it and I especially would like to own land in the hills of New York or New Jersey. I hear Philadelphia is very hot and sultry in the summer. Mister Mochter says we will be going back to New York in two weeks. He's looking forward to having a famous New York painter do his portrait in oils. What brings you to Philadelphia, Mister Claveraque?"

I wanted to veer the conversation back to finding out what Cyrus and Mochter were up to but answered his question. "Misses Claveraque and I were invited by my uncle in New Jersey to tour the colonies. We're looking forward to seeing Bartram's Gardens tomorrow, then perhaps a cruise on the Delaware before we go north to visit New York province."

"Better see New York soon. Mr. Mochter says the regulars are going to land in large numbers and take New York this summer.

Betty Ann's impatience intruded. "You said you would buy me a rum flip this afternoon, Cyrus. Get the waiter's attention. I'm getting thirsty."

"Alright, Betty Ann, but just one. We have to be going soon."

Cyrus ordered the drink and the waiter set it down for her within the minute. I offered to buy it, but Cyrus pulled out his wallet, thick with bills, and put several crisp-looking two shilling notes on the table. He said he needed some small change.

My eyes had adjusted sufficiently to the dim light to make out the right hand signatures on the notes. They were in green ink. Could Cyrus be counterfeiting with Mochter?

This chance meeting was soon over and prospects of gaining further information were doomed, thanks to Betty Ann. It was as if she was intentionally hindering me from obtaining useful information. She was very possessive of Cyrus implying he had some special value other than as a supplier of rum flips. I also thought that she was pretending to possess a weak intellect. She was pretty good at it, but something was fishy. This supposition later proved to be the case but in a surprising manner. I also wondered if Crispin was the "famous New York painter" that Mochter was looking forward to sitting for. The answer to this would take a little longer.

# chapter 29

Olivia could hardly sleep that night she was so excited about the next day and the long-awaited visit to John Bartram and his nursery. I was excited, too, but walking around the city in the balmy spring weather set me so that I could hardly keep my eyes open despite Bunny's fine supper of prime ribs and potato pancakes.

Olivia and Arabella told of their bargain hunting in the fashion salons of the city happy in the thought that their purchases were only slightly behind London's stylish modes. Arthur was thrilled that he saw Benjamin Franklin from a distance. I divulged little of my sleuthing but tried to keep up my part of the conversation. It was no use. I went to bed early and slept like a log.

At breakfast, Bunny hummed happily. She said that for this week, anyway, we were "her family". She put a platter full of a strange looking food on the table and began serving.

"My Henry was a good shot. He usually had half a dozen deer carcasses hanging in the carriage house to last us for the winter. He always saved the last for when we had our best friends for dinner in the spring. Then he would prepare this venison scrapple as a mark of his appreciation for their friendship. Henry's been gone these five years and so have some of the friends. But I wanted to show my appreciation even tho' he and they ain't here anymore. For the moment, you're my friends. Please dig in."

I have always been hesitant to try new food, and the appearance of this stuff left me even less adventurous. The other three wielded their spoons with vigor so, with reluctance, I nibbled a small fork full of sausage made of ground corn and diced venison. It was delicious. We showed Bunny our appreciation by devouring her entire production. She said that scrapple was introduced by the Pennsylvania Dutch and is peculiar to this region.

Bunny glowed with gratification that her Henry's recipe was so acceptable to outsiders, even me. We also pronounced that we were happy to be in the city of Brotherly Love and that we admired the Quakers for their civic mindedness.

Bunny quickly replied, "The Quakers have done a lot for the city and have an unequaled social consciousness, but they have gained a lot of enmity when they blindly refused to put up money to defend the province against the French and Indians, and now many are hesitant in their stance against the British. They are too tight with money when it comes to business.

"Around here we have a saying about the Quakers, 'On First Day they pray for us, the rest of the week they prey on us.'" With that, she sat down and 'dug in' herself.

Knowing our day's destination, Bunny searched the pigeon holes of her ancient desk and produced an old map which she marked with the location of Bartram's. It was not technically in Philadelphia, but in Chinsessing, on the west bank of the Schuylkill in farming country. At the most, the nursery was less than three miles from the Delaware River and nearer the tidal swamp I spotted on Bunny's map yesterday.

After breakfast, Linus had our horses curried and ready at the carriage house adjoining Bunny's establishment. This day promised to be even warmer. Many plants at the nursery should be up and blooming: some would at least break dormancy. The over-sweet fragrance of honey locust trees filled the air. Alas, the pungent smell of horse apples tainted the effect.

Land west of Seventh Street was part of the city, but shops and homes left off and flat meadows, enormously tall virgin woods and a few tilled fields began. Bunny had said that her Henry shot much of his game between Seventh Street and the Schuylkill. Judging by the city's rate of growth over the last two decades, the verge would be fed into the market at the most favorable pace—a study in assured prosperity for the owners.

We made straight for Gray's Ferry and crossed the Schuylkill with no delay. I reflected that many of the great had followed this same path to Bartram's humble font of botanical knowledge and had left to happily furnish their gardens with seed or specimens.

Bartram had made available to English and American estates many unique plant, shrub, and tree specimens brought back from the American wilderness. Mountain laurel, rhododendron, moccasin flower, bloodroot, several varieties of ferns and much more graced their gardens.

The man was now almost seventy-seven years old and had long since stopped tramping the backwoods looking for botanical material. We hoped he was up to giving us a tour of his plantation or at least a morning's conversation about it and his travels.

The entrance road to his place was inconspicuous and his drive had several curves which created the same pleasing sensation as when suddenly encountering beauty on a twisting forest trail. First we came upon a table-top sized plat of low-growing bloodroot at the peak of its waxen daisy-like bloom. They were surrounded by a sea of purple violets.

This was followed by a succession of pinxter rhododendron sporting delicately recurved pink blossoms on dainty branches just showing leaves in the mouse-eared stage. They resembled intricacies of the jewelers art.. A day earlier or later and we may have not seen these dainty beauties. An April downpour would have quickly demolished them.

Under cover of the pinxters were trailing arbutus just breaking their buds. Olivia was delighted and slowed her mount to explain what we were seeing. Islands of Daffodils covered feet of honey locust trees. Fecund fragrance flooded the tract.

At the end of the drive the greenhouse and potting shed promised a kaleidoscope of color inside. A hitching post inviting us to dismount. Mr. Bartram appeared, slightly bent over but gracious and eager to share his plants. He was enthusiastic about the display brought on by the sudden warmth of the past few days. It was plain that he had enjoyed a robust physique in former years. His stout voice compensated for the ravages of wilderness travel and belied his age.

He greeted Olivia, honoring her by remembering his correspondence with her parents initiated by their long-time mutual friend, Peter Collinson, a successful London draper. Even though Olivia had written Bartram only a few months ago, I don't think he expected so many of us. But he accepted our party in stride.

We approached the three-story gray stone house which Bartram had built himself in 1731. It had since been enlarged by stone sheds built at both ends he explained.

The house was attractive in the local style with one important difference. In the middle of the side facing the river, there were three two-story stone columns about ten feet apart and carved as if they were from an ancient middle-eastern pantheon. Space between the columns left a cavernous porch from which he could enjoy the view of his garden and the river.

Three dormers pierced the roof on the river side. Several large American chestnut trees had leafed out early and shaded the grounds. They had been carefully situated in line on the slope down to the river to not shade the gardens or block the view.

Within a few minutes his wife, Ann, a small, keen and soft-eyed lady, appeared and offered sassafras tea on the porch. His son, John, who ran the nursery now, interrupted his supervision to join in for a moment. We all sat down.

Olivia began. "Mr. Bartram, which of your many achievements do you consider your most significant?"

Bartram cocked his silver-locked head slightly and clenched his jaws several times before answering. "I guess I would have to say that getting away from farming, that is, escaping from the formidable pressure of the agricultural market, dependence upon weather that can be resolute and contrary, and the ravages of pests that eat your crop or otherwise destroy it, and the incessant hard labor entailed. Those forces are difficult to contend with. Farming is a dogged, day-after-day discipline that requires constant dedication in the face of disappointment.

"Yes, you describe the management of a farm or nursery very well. My brother and I are familiar with those problems," Olivia nodded.

"Becoming a hunter of and collector of new and different species of plants, trees, rocks, animals, insects, and marine life by traveling our great rivers and mountains is much more interesting and diverting. Luckily, I was able to drum up interest with the right people like Peter Collinson, God rest his soul, Doctor Franklin, Peter Kalm, and Carl Linnaeus. There are many more, such as my friends in the Philosophical Society here in Philadelphia and the Royal Society in London although I never traveled to England."

"Is there a section of the country that you enjoyed more than the rest, sir?" Olivia posed.

He seemed embarrassed by this respectful curiosity regarding his life. "Oh, just call me John. Everyone else does. I'm glad you could come visit." He put his hand to his mouth and coughed several times and pulled a handkerchief to dab his face.

"We have so many grand and charming sights and some are hard work getting to. One of my favorite spots is only fifteen miles from here where a small stream enters the Schuylkill. The water is so clear, and the bottom of the pool is scoured to coarse sand and pebbles. Forget-me-nots and daisies bloom in the clearing in season. Moss covers the rocks and the stream bank to gladden bare feet. It's an out of the way private place. On a warm day, like this one, you can't wait to strip and dive in.

I could not help but think of choice scenes similar to that in the greenwood. I wondered if this old man had had dalliances in his youth which enhanced the pleasure of his memory.

"But that's not what you asked. I think I like the mountains surrounding the Susquehanna Valley from Pennsylvania through the Endless Mountains into New York through which Weiser, Shickellamy, Evans and I traveled to Onondaga and Oswego in '43. The Hudson Valley and the Catskills are beautiful, too. The climate in those hills agrees with me more than any other place."

Arabella joined in. "We live in the first valley of the Watchungs, five miles west of Newark. What do you think of New Jersey?"

"If you don't mind me saying so, Arabella, I think of it as an extension of the Hudson Valley; the Watchungs are practically part of the Hudson Highlands. There is something about the area that provides a wide variety of fauna and flora. Perhaps it's the climate made more moderate by the Atlantic Ocean close by. You only have to go a day's travel west of York Island to escape the excessive heat of summer. In the winter, the short distance enables one to skate in Morristown even when you can't in New York.

"And North Jersey is so different from South Jersey. North Jersey shares trees and plants with New York and southern New England while some of the plant life at Cape May closely resembles that in the Carolinas. Residents of Cape May say that their growing season is as long as that in Georgia because Delaware Bay and the Atlantic nearby moderate the local climate.

I chipped in. "When's the last time you made one of your excursions?"

"I think it was the year after I returned from my Florida expedition. That would make it in '65 when I went to the Pine Barrens in New Jersey. You know, there's an industry mining white cedar from the swamps in the barrens—trees that died centuries ago, and sank into the mud where they defied decay. Atlantic white cedar is very durable—it's light and used for boat planking. It's also used for roof shingles. They're known to last seventy-five years or more. Several generations have made a comfortable living recovering the logs and splitting them into shingles. Thousand of tons of cedar are shipped from Philadelphia each year."

Olivia continued, "What are your sentiments about the political situation?"

"I'm afraid of the destruction that will occur. Unlike the French wars battles which took place largely far from seaboard cities, this will threaten New York, Philadelphia, and Charleston. Boston was lucky; the damage there was, as we're reading now, much less than it could have been. I dread what could happen here if the British have designs on the capital city. I don't like it.

"I must admit to some partiality. The Englishmen I've known, primarily through correspondence, I've liked and admired, and largely been benefitted by them.They have flattered me and even honored me by reading my botanical reports and findings to the Royal Society.

His wife Ann spoke up. "George the third made John his official botanist and he receives an annual pension for this."

"Oh yes, Collinson arranged that just before I went to the Floridas. How I miss that man. We never met but had the most interesting conversations by post for thirty-five years. Though distant, he was a true and enjoyable friend." Bartram coughed several times but caught his breath.

Ann interceded. "Are you feeling a little tired, John? He hasn't been feeling well lately." She turned to her son, "John, do you have a few minutes? Can you show our guests around?"

Olivia was quick to respond. "Oh! I'm sorry. We should have been more considerate and not encroached on so much of your time. We have appreciated your interesting answers to our questions, Mr. Bartram. Oh. Excuse me—- . Thank you, John."

"Not at all. Your questions have renewed warm memories and I appreciate your coming by. Young John will be glad to show you the grounds. He knows more about them than I do."

John junior was a younger version of his father. "Let's walk down to the river," he said, as he rose from his chair, "you'll get a better idea of the scheme of things."

He pointed to the garden down the slope where tulips in red, pink, yellow, orange, and even bronze, sparkled with dew still dappling the petals. "The tulips just opened. Several varieties from Holland will come into bloom next week, and others will continue well into May.

"Then the perennials will take over for the rest of May and into June. Daylillies, fox glove, delphinium, snapdragon, swamp candles, lupin, and coreopsis, in succession—ah, I see our columbine has opened this morning. And we have annuals in the greenhouse to fill in when the spring flowers finish and danger of frost is over—in another ten days or two weeks. "

With a start, John said, "You know—this is the first anniversary of the battle of Lexington and Concord. I am right, aren't I? Isn't this April nineteenth?" I assured him that it was and remembered that I was in Hereford a year ago worrying about my brother Dordy. in America. John excused himself and said, "be back in a moment", and ran back to the house.

Arthur had listened carefully, admiring what he had seen. Now, with John gone, he criticized, "It's distressing, but even such an exalted garden as this has a full complement of plantain, dandelions, and veronica infesting the lawn. I feel better that my place is no more susceptible to weeds than the estates even of experts. Like the Bartrams, I like the Quaker ladies in the lawn and low blue spires of ajuga and clumps of ferns in out-of-the-way places."

We all agreed. "If they worried about weeds, they would never have time to prune shrubs, propagate plants, and run their business. Thank goodness they don't." I pointed out.

We stopped and bent down to inspect some low growing plants in bloom. Little spires of dainty blue cups Olivia called grape hyacinth and low-growing blue-petalled chionodoxa showed their brightness in otherwise dormant gardens still strewn with leaves. Bronze-red shoots of peony appeared amidst them to promise dominance and fragrant bloom for the middle of May.

A long bed that flanked the larger rectangular gardens in the center of the yard had a profusion of low-growing shiny green leaves with single blue-petaled flowers. Olivia said it was vinca minor but that it was easier to call myrtle. Lilies of the valley were encroaching on the myrtle and about to challenge the tulip fragrance. A large bed of trillium was back under some oak trees. Olivia said she recognized it from a drawing in one of her herbals but she preferred to call it wake robin. At fifteen inches, it was as tall as it would get and ready to bloom she said.

During John's absence we just roamed at will, and with no one asking questions, we could hear a plethora of song birds few of which I recognized. The Bartrams had many nests hanging from trees, secured under eaves, and some bird apartments mounted on special poles. One bird was especially notable. It was black and orange with a little white on its wings. It called from different high-up vantage points and tended a hanging nest that, from the ground, looked like a small sack. I believe the bird could throw its voice, like a ventriloquist, for it wasn't easy to locate him despite his bright colors. Later, we realized that the colors are those of Lord Baltimore, Maryland's founder. Of course, the bird was a Baltimore oriole.

Arabella heard a cardinal and located the red bird on its perch. Higher up, flitting in the branches, were others of many colors, too small to identify with the naked eye. Large echelons of geese streamed north high above the river, chortling their way back to their breeding grounds.

Something like an old-time merchantman appeared on the Schuylkill. It was hoisting something out of the water and loading it through the bow but it was too far to see clearly. I didn't mention it, not caring to interrupt the conversation with this extraneous observation.

John returned. "That's better. We couldn't be caught not observing this day." He pointed to the house now proudly flying a flag with a rattlesnake coiled on a yellow field with the caption DON'T TREAD ON ME. "A friend in the Continental navy gave that to me," he said proudly. Some dusky workers doffed their wide-brimmed straw hats as we passed. "Good mornin' John," said one. "We just finished unclogging the ditch. Can we plant the sorghum tomorrow?"

He turned to us, "Years ago my brother William and I helped father reclaim the riverbank. It was a dry summer and the water level was low. We put in a bulkhead of logs which extended our property and protected it from flooding. It retains some of the best soil so we planted sorghum to supplement our colony of honey bees. Many of our neighbors think it's corn but they buy sugar and molasses made from it locally now for a lot less than that from the West Indies."

We walked by a tree no higher than the lilacs nearby. John pointed to it, "My father brought seeds of that tree back from the deep south. At first he thought it was related to the gordonia. He described it as flowering with snow-white blossoms and very fragrant while at the same time it bears ripe fruit about the size of a white oak acorn..

"The large flowers resemble magnolias with prominent gold stamens in the center. It makes a handsome ornamental with flowers at every twig end. The fruit is a round, dry woody apple We named *it Franklinia alatamaha*, to honor the doctor which pleased him mightily. We call it the Franklin tree but we're not sure how well it will do."

"My brother, William who is down south now, wrote that he found some but only in a small sandy section. It's truly rare and may be close to extinction. Perhaps we can save it."

"Since it is so rare, don't you give it special protection?" Olivia asked.

"We started the seed in the greenhouse but only a few germinated. We sent seeds to England and we understand a few survived. That's why William is looking for them down there now. But a small area along the Alatamaha River in Georgia, is the only place father and William ever found them. If they don't do well down there, we doubt if they will in more northern conditions. We hope it survives but we don't protect it It's mostly an experiment at this time."

We inspected some white low-growing flowers by the path and others, also white, but with evergreen foliage. John bent to our curiosity. "The larger, mounded ones are candytuft and the smaller ones are arabis which, as you see, spreads in profusion. We sell a lot of them."

Iris and blue flags were up, clustered along a drainage ditch but there was no sign of flower stems yet. John said it would be another three weeks.

Olivia was impressed by the layout, the variety, and the whole scene by the river.

"Do Peter Collinson, Carl Linnaeus, Doctor Fothergill, and others send specimens from Europe and exchange information with you?"

"Oh yes. Father asked for seeds and roots and often they, particularly Mr. Collinson, volunteered plants that he thought may be unknown in America. He sent some potted roots of English oak, I remember," said John pointing to a specimen leafing out down by the river.

We approached a swath of evergreen shrubs on a small ridge and under light shade. Arabella was especially attracted to them. "Oh, what is that shrub? It looks like it may be related to rhododendron. The leaves look so neat and green, almost as if they had been varnished. What does the flower look like and when does it bloom?"

John was pleased. "It's mountain laurel and we find a lot of it growing here. It's named after Peter Kalm, an associate of Linnaeus, you know, one of father's house guests over twenty-five years ago—*kalmia latifolia*. It blooms in early June, Arabella. I hope you plan to be here that long. The bloom is a lemon-sized umbel of pinkish-white flowers. The flower buds are dark pink and just as fetching as the open flowers which gradually turn white during its week of bloom."

"I can't wait to see that. Arthur, we should buy some mountain laurel from John and take it back with us. If Jamie and Olivia can bring rhododendron three thousand miles across the Atlantic Ocean, certainly we can bring laurel ninety miles across New Jersey!"

Arthur was obviously troubled about something. "John, why do the scientists insist on complicated latin names for plants and trees? Why not just call it the Franklin tree rather than something or other *alatamaha* or mountain laurel instead of *kalmia latifolia*?"

"I probably get that question more than any other, so it's a good question. It helps us, scientists and lay people alike, to identify plants more accurately. For example, Many plants are called mayflower. The binomial system was devised to avoid confusion.

"There had to be some system of classification better than the Doctrine of Signatures which is outmoded. The ancients believed God designed some plants so that mankind would know that they could be used to cure certain diseases. Hepatica is based on a Greek word meaning liver. So the liver-shaped leaves suggest the plant could cure diseases of this organ.

"In the binomial system, the first word tells us the genus; the second gives the species and often gives the main characteristic that sets it off form other species in the genus. Maple trees are the genus, *acer*, but there are many kinds of maples such as red maple, *acer rubrum*; sugar maple, *acer saccharum* and so on. Same thing with oak or *quercus: quercus alba* is white oak, *quercus palustris* is pin oak. You may not care what kind of oak it is but the man buying trees or lumber and the scientist wants to know exactly what he's dealing with."

"But the names selected are puzzling," pursued Arthur.

"Yes, that's true. But the old system involved as many as ten words to describe the plant which was unwieldy. Linnaeus simplified it to two names such as *acer rubrum* for red maple. Are you familiar with the Black-eyed Susan, a yellow daisy-like flower that lines the roadsides in July? Its botanical name is *rudbeckia hirta*.

"Carl Linnaeus, a Swede, established the system for not only naming and classifying plants, but insects and animals. It was his pleasure to confer the name *rudbeckia* on the genus that includes the Black-eyed Susan and give immortality to his friend and mentor, Olaf Rudbeck, the Younger.

"Many plants are named after eminent men but some plant names defy understanding. Take *taraxacum officinale* which is the plain Dandelion we use for salad greens. The leaves are sharply indented on their edges giving the French reason to call it "Dent-de-Lion" or "lion's tooth." Even botanists prefer *dandelion*," John said.

John led us along the waterfront past an "old cider press". Here I had a better view of the ship hoisting large logs from the water into its hull through ports on either side of the bow.

I asked John, "How long has that ship been there putting logs aboard?"

John had to squint to see clearly. "I haven't seen it before. It must have just started this morning—look at how she floats high in the water. She's very close to shallow water and the tide's going out. Maybe she's stuck and unloading logs." As one of his workers was passing by, John called to him, "Billy, take a minute and run to the house and bring me my spyglass, will you?" Billy wasted no time and returned, scope in hand.

John took the glass and held it firmly. "Yes, that's exactly what they are doing—they're loading. They don't have too much time, it will be dark in a few hours and it's a slow process with many logs still in the water. Looks like they're short-handed."

John scanned left and right for any other activity. "I haven't seen anyone loading large logs in a long time, and it was not done here but up the Delaware just below Trenton Falls. There's something fishy about it. But they'll be there tomorrow, the tide won't change until dark and they'll need both a flood tide and daylight to get free of the mud bank and finish loading."

As the ladies and Arthur moveed on, I dallied to ask John where I could get hold of a boat. He pointed to a dock where a wherry was bottom up on the shore.

"She's got a pair of oars and a sail if you get a wind in the right direction. Help yourself."

"I would like to come some time, perhaps tomorrow, and use your boat to investigate."

"You're more than welcome, Jamie. Perhaps I'll join you," John said with relish.

# chapter 31

WHEN WE RETURNED to Bunny's for supper, Olivia asked about my talk with John. I told her of the logs being loaded aboard ship in a cove of the Schuylkill where they are probably ignored by everyone. "Some shenanigans are probably going on," I told her.

I did not want to worry her and so treated the event casually despite my intention to inquire into it. Arthur and Arabella loved the Bartrams and their nursery, which included most of the plants, known and unknown of Europe and America. Olivia was delighted by the extensive gardens along the river. The conversation shifted back to the garden, the advance of spring and to laughing at the ridiculous binomial Latin names which they applied to friends. Arthur was the first to be abused by this sport and was bemused at being called claverakis arthuria.

Suddenly, I realized that I had been talking against the British as if I wasn't from the merry old island myself. In only a few months, I had become of such sympathetic mind as to become an American, and a rebel at that. I decided to hold my tongue until I was more certain of my contrary attitude. On further reflection, it became clear to me that American thinking was being crystalized by the pamphlet written by an Englishman arrived in this colony only two years ago. Thomas Paine's *Common Sense*, and its many editions had been available to the public only about three months but had focused American thinking on seeking independence.

"Jamie, Mrs. Bartram invited us to come back tomorrow to see the rest of the nursery. She said that many plants would likely come into bloom in the next few days. Let's take advantage of her hospitality." Olivia was thrilled by our tour of the gardens which to her was the high point of our American tour so far.

"I have been invited to go on patrol down the Delaware on a ship of the Pennsylvania Navy tomorrow. If Mrs. Bartram's invitation extends to Wednesday, I'll go with you then." I hadn't been asked by the navy but was planning to foist myself on them to be part of the crew on one of the patrol boats. Phrasing this adventure, as if by invitation, was an acceptable answer to Olivia. She was disappointed for the conflict of events, but we parted in good spirits.

Arthur decided to avoid adventure and went shopping with Olivia and Arabella, possibly to protect the family pocketbook from persuasive store clerks it not from aggressive adolescent pick pockets.

I grabbed my cane and sauntered along Front Street, admiring the bowsprits, carved figureheads, intricate rigging, and ships on my way to the navy wharf. As I passed the tavern where Cyrus, Betty Ann, and I had chatted briefly, I was hailed by Cyrus again. He had Betty Ann in tow (or did she have him). He asked me to join them for breakfast. This presented another chance to find out what mischief Mochter was up to, and so I agreed and held the door for Betty Ann. She accepted this courtesy with the grace and decorum of a maid making her social debut at the squire's ball, a little out of character with the Betty Ann portrayed a few days ago.

This time we sat by a window and the morning sun streamed in. Good, thought I, the light would enable me to view any currency Cyrus might offer. I hoped he would get the check again. Since he had been so fond of spending his fake bills there was no reason to think he wouldn't spend them a second time. After all, they cost him nothing.

Betty Ann was cordial. "Have you seen the gardens you planned to visit?"

"Yes, and they are beautiful with the flowers opening in this early spring weather. Mr. Bartram is a very pleasant and interesting gentleman. You must visit there.

"I would like to take in the garden some afternoon soon. Cyrus, why don't you take me there next Saturday. Where is it Mr. Claveraque."

"It's on the Schuylkill, perhaps three miles southwest of here as the crow flies,"

"Is there anything else near by to visit?" Betty Ann seemed sincere in wanting to know.

"Only a few small farms, nothing else. But, you can see ships on both rivers from there.. I saw one loading logs from the water in an eddy of the Schuylkill. It looked very mysterious, like one of those old merchantmen that pirates used to board and pillage the passengers. You can get to the gardens by crossing at Gray's ferry and then taking the river road south."

Cyrus was attentive. "What day were you there, Mr. Claveraque?" He was concerned.

"It was Monday. That ship had just started salvaging logs. I think for the shipyard."

Betty Ann had just dug into her scrambled eggs and was listening closely. But Cyrus revealed nothing of importance.

I ventured, "Loading those logs into the ship like that must be a ticklish job—like trying to eat a leg of fried chicken suspended by a string from your outstretched arm." I paused for Cyrus to respond. But he was oblivious to what I said. Betty Ann changed the subject. About to leave, I remembered to check Cyrus's currency. Could he really be passing out phony bills?

After another ten minutes of banter, Cyrus swallowed a final fork full of pancakes, shoved back in his chair with a screech on the floor, and grandiloquently fished from his pocket some coins to put on the table for a generous tip (**T**o **I**nsure **P**romptness, the sign on the wall urged). At the counter, it was awkward straining to see the color of his money.

Fortuitously, there was a bowl of peanuts on the cashier's counter. I stepped forward and grabbed a generous handful just as Cyrus laid down a five-pound note. I offered some peanuts to Betty Ann and, at the same time, could see that the ink of the right hand signature was definitely green not black, as on legitimate bills.

We parted and I walked to the navy wharf, with my cane counting cadence, and with more confidence than I had had this whole trip. I entered the Navy office but saw no sign of authority as no one was in uniform. I thought that the day might end up being wasted.

"May I help you, sir?" said the man at the desk.

"I am looking for Captain Kells Oakley. I'd like to accompany him on patrol and will earn my way as a member of the crew or in any way he may think best," I said.

"I'm Captain Oakley. I'm taking out a patrol this morning but we don't take passengers unless they are naval personnel or connected with the navy."

"That makes sense. They would only get in the way and ask too many questions," I said.

This was the proper response. Oakley bent closer to hear what else I might offer.

"I have reason to think that a British agent is stealing logs coming down river—such as can be used for masts and spars. If this is so, the logs should be confiscated," I declared.

He laughed. "Now that we are in a state of war with Britain, the king no longer has his choice of trees. God hope he does not regain it. The White Pine Tree act went into effect fifty years ago. But it only applied to New England, not to Pennsylvania or even New York. Surprising, since we have just as stout boles as do they. No matter, Britain has to get its mast stock from Canada or the Baltic. But why do you think someone is stealing these timbers?"

I told the captain what Crispin and I had seen on the upper Delaware. "They were marked with the king's broad arrow like this.." I began to draw the mark when he stopped me. "I know the mark your talking about. I used to live in Falmouth until the British bombarded the town and left us all to freeze. So you think someone is trying to salvage these timbers for the British?" "Well, yes. Something had to happen to those rafts of logs. And they did have the king's mark on them. I saw them with my own eyes!"

He asked my name. "Well Mr. Claveraque, those logs were probably shipped down river to some of the shipyards at Trenton, Bristol, or Frankford.. As for the marks, I can only guess. Could be that some woodsman slashed the best trees he could find so that anyone else might think that the law applied along the Delaware, and leave them alone. That way, he could claim them for himself. Maybe he died or, for some reason, couldn't carry through on his plan. Or there may have been some of these trees still standing and someone cut them and rafted them downstream. There are many possible explanations."

"But the marks looked like they were branded, they were so uniform," I insisted.

"Those marks were made by hand by expert axemen. I've seen them mark logs in a few seconds. They looked as if each letter was painstakingly carved with a sharp chisel," he retorted.

"Well, the other day I saw a large ship on the lower Schuylkill hoisting logs out of the water. The ship was designed to take logs through special ports on either side of the bow. I remember Captain Adam Glass telling me about ships like that."

"You know Adam Glass? Skipper of the *Raritan?"* he said. I had touched pay dirt.

"Yes my wife and I came over on the *Raritan* from Bristol in January. We took our meals in Adam's cabin every day and had the opportunity to know him well."

"How is Adam? I haven't seen him for several years."

"I haven't seen him either since we landed.. Adam was well and excited about fitting out his ship to be a privateer. He and his crew were eager to sail. They must be at sea by now."

"What a coincidence!" Oakley said. "What is it you wish to go on patrol for? You sound English to me. How do I know you're not spying out the defenses of Delaware Bay?"

I thought to say that he could suspect everyone on the river, but thought better of it. "Half the people I've talked to since I arrived sound like they're from England, too. I just want to get a better look at that ship as I enjoy the scenery, Captain. Besides, a fortress, or whatever is being constructed, is there for all to see."

"Come aboard then. We leave at ebbtide—about nine-thirty. The ship is being rowed over from the shipyard a mile upriver.—it just came off the stocks a few days ago; this is to be it's trial run. Do you have any gear? The men will be here to stretch their legs before the tide change and we begin the patrol. You might as well come with us. Help yourself to some coffee."

I saw the fifty-foot, double-ended ship threading traffic down the blue Delaware. I could not determine the color of the hull but the oars on either side flexed and glimmered in the sun in an unrelenting cadence.

It was a galley just like the ones I had read about in great-grandfather's journal.

The sail could not be set but the ship came on with remarkable speed considering it was battling strong head winds. When it came close, the bosun barked, and the starboard bank of oars back-watered so that the ship made the turn neatly to it's berth. The bosun barked again and the oarsmen (twelve a side) set their oars to stand straight up. Lines were secured at the bollards and with the bosun's final bark, "dismissed", the men shipped their sweeps and scrambled ashore.

I stayed clear except for the introduction by Oakley to the ship's executive officer, Lieutenant Gushea, who had commanded the brief cruise from the shipyard. The crew were all young men selected for their brawn and eagerness for sea duty. Within a half hour the tide would ebb when the order would be given for all to go aboard and stand to their stations.

I hopped on with Oakley who maintained the helm while Lieutenant Gushea stood in the bow to con the ship down the channel. The order to cast off was given, the ship drifted free of the wharf, the cadence began and the ship came alive. The port oars only, back-watered with the starboard oars dead in the water. The ship turned smartly as it backed into the channel. At the bosun's bark, both banks of oars dug in and the ship clawed forward to course down the Delaware. Gulls cruised above the waters in their relentless search for morsels dumped over the side by fishermen cleaning their catch.

Within a mile, the ship cut to starboard as the river narrowed and turned west. The south wind offered its steady power; and the men unfurled the large lateen sail which snapped and billowed as it caught the surge of the wind. Small fishing boats were returning from the bay with their day's catch. As oyster trawlers fought their way upstream and dried their nets in the wind, duck hunters along the shore spread armadas of decoys. The last stragglers of geese squawked their way north.

Oakley broke the silence. "That's League Island to starboard, one of many islands in this part of the river. They aren't a problem like the sandbars. The narrowing of the river at the bend speeds up the current and scours the bottom. Where the river widens, the current slows and deposits the sand resulting in islands and sandbars." Other ships kept their distance since the navy pennant was flying from the taffrail and a twelve-pounder in the bow announced authority.

Below League Island the Schuylkill added its vast volume to that of the Delaware.

As we passed the tributary's mouth, I could see the merchantman hoisting logs.

"There's the ship I told you about, Captain. You can see that she's been busy."

He nodded, "We'll check it out on the way back." He went forward and talked with Gushea briefly and returned. "Gushea says the gun is charged and ready for action."

Below the mouth of the Schuylkill, two islands appeared. The captain explained, "The colony built some batteries there to stop French privateers in the forties. Then the British started building a fort a few years ago on Mud Island but never finished it. We're going to complete it and also build some redoubts on the Jersey shore. The channel is quite narrow here. A ship coming up river has to proceed cautiously which will make it an easy target. Don't be concerned. We don't draw enough water to worry about it." He then directed the helmsman to change course a little to the southwest so our passage would run parallel to the Pennsylvania shore.

Oakley pointed to the next and final island. "That's Billing's Island where the merchant ships are waiting at moorings for their turn to make it down the channel. Usually, there are more than that lined up. Commerce must be easing. The British blockade is responsible."

The Jersey shore was flat for as far as I could see. The Pennsylvania side was, too, but low hills appeared a few miles distant. The wind had increased and we were moving at a good clip with waves pounding the hull. "How fast do you think were going, captain?" I ventured.

"I think we're making about thirteen or fourteen knots. We left at nine-thirty. It's now about ten o'clock and we're a little more than halfway to Chester. So that's about right—fifteen miles an hour or thirteen and a half knots. She seems like a good ship." Oakley ordered a pair of oarsmen in the bow to trim the ship by taking position in the stern. As the ship continued, he said he could notice an improvement.

Thunder rumbled and a dark patch of sky to the south enlarged ominously and eclipsed the already gauzy sun. Gusts strengthened and became more prolonged and nudged us faster as larger waves slapped and splashed the hull. The oarsmen kept the pace—nothing fazed them.

As we coasted Chester, Oakley pulled out his watch. "Ten twenty-five! We must be doing fourteen knots! We'll keep going for a quarter hour, and then I'll let the first watch take a five-minute rest. We'll be off Wilmington before noon, even with both watches taking a break."

Lightning was striking over the Jersey countryside, briefly brightening the landscape, with claps of thunder soon after each strike. The air began to cool and we could see rain coming down in straight falls not far down the river. We were going to get soaked.

The captain turned to me, "The men will appreciate the rain. They've worked up a real sweat and if we get caught in a rainstorm it'll refresh them and give 'em a second wind."

Just as he spoke, lightning struck the ship. It splintered the mast and the fractured top fell overboard with the sail blanketing a dozen rowers. Several sailors amidships were thrown to the deck amidst screaming. We suffered a sudden loss of speed. The smell of charred wood permeated the air. Three sailors recovered but were badly shaken. A fourth had been severely burned and was still unconscious. Oakley ordered men from both watches to haul in salvageable rigging and the sail and to cut away the rest. As the mess was cleared, the sail was brailed and stored below. Lieutenant Gushea ordered the men to continue rowing to maintain headway. He then attended the burned sailor with a tincture of tea leaves but the prognosis was not hopeful.

Captain Oakley said that he was satisfied with the ship's trial run and more than happy with how the men handled the emergency. There was no sense continuing the cruise especially with a man in dire need of medical attention, he added. The helmsman was ordered to reverse course and we turned and headed back to Philadelphia.

I'm glad to say that due to that decision of Oakley's, the injured sailor's luck enabled him to recover under the care of Doctor Benjamin Rush. The sailor was especially fortunate since the doctor was a delegate to Congress, but was not in attendance at the State House that day.

As for the royal logs, I did not see anything which would help solve the problem. Under the circumstances, we had no time to spend time investigating the 'timber' ship. When the galley pulled into it's home berth back at Philadelphia, less than half the afternoon remained for investigating the goings on at the hulk in the Schuyllkill.

I hastened to Bartram's and as I dismounted, Mrs. Bartram came out from the greenhouse.

"Mr. Claveraque, how nice it was to have such a charming and knowledgeable guest as your wife and, of course, your aunt and uncle. They left right after lunch, about an hour ago."

I thanked her and decided to call it quits and go 'home' to Bunny's.

At Bunny's, all of them were in the parlor in a state of excitement. On the way home from Bartram's, they had stopped briefly at the stalls on Market Street. Arthur had been idling as Olivia and Arabella shopped for groceries.

Olivia related the story. "Just as I was paying the grocer, a runaway carriage suddenly came roaring down the street scattering shoppers out of the way. A boy, in the act of pilfering some potatoes, was about to be trampled by a team of horses run amok, when Arthur ran over and scooped him out of harm's way. It had been a close call and the boy suffered only minor abrasions on his arms and back from grazing the hitching post as Arthur swept him aside."

"You should have seen the potatoes fly out of the boy's pockets!" laughed Arthur.

Olivia continued, "A small crowd gathered as Arthur inspected the wound and brought the boy round to consciousness. Soon, an older lad, presumably the boy's brother, arrived. The brother removed his scarf, ran to a nearby pump where he soaked the scarf and ran back to soothe his charge with the wetted cloth. "He could have been killed.

I saw the whole thing." ventured an older gentleman standing by. The crowd murmured in agreement.

"Can you stand, Billy?" said the lad. Billy stiffly got to his feet and said nothing more than, "Yeah." The crowd cheered and then dwindled. Billy began to limp off with his brother. Billy's brother then stopped and turned. "Thanks, Mister" he waved to a still-shaken Arthur.

Olivia added, "The boy looked as if he knew you, Arthur."

"Arthur, this must have been a scare for you, too. Were you hurt?" I asked.

"I was so busy grabbing that boy from the street that I didn't have time to notice. But, no, I didn't have a scratch, Jamie, just a scare. But, you know, there was something familiar about the older boy. He might have—-" Then Arthur stopped short. He hadn't mentioned the urchin's assault on his person and the loss of his personal effects to the ladies the other day and he didn't want to now. "Never mind. It isn't important." he said.

The next morning we could hear Bunny downstairs singing as she prepared a breakfast that would probably be something new to us, but toothsome. A popping sound filled the house simultaneously with the pleasant smell of food cooking. The popping increased for a few minutes and then stopped. Then Bunny called that breakfast was ready if we were.

We romped downstairs to see a bowls of clusters of white acorn-sized solidified bubbles. They resembled candies carved from wax. But that couldn't be—not for breakfast.

"Haven't you ever had pop corn? The local Delaware Indians showed grandfather how to prepare it. In the evening we eat it dry or mixed with melted butter. But for breakfast we pour on milk and perhaps some honey. Try it." Bunny said and poured the milk into each bowl. "Then we add some of the syrup you bought yesterday, Olivia. That's what inspired me to make popcorn."

Olivia was game for anything and pronounced it light and refreshing. She was right and we all had a second portion, as much to finish Bunny's offering as to enjoy more of the unique taste. This made Bunny's face beam. "What are you folks going to do today?" she asked.

"I'm planning to find the answer to that merchantman down at the mouth of the Schuylkill. Something fishy is going on there. John Bartram, the son, said he would loan me his boat, might even go with me. If the rest of you are going to inspect some more of his father's nursery; this is the time to observe the flowers from the wild. Isn't that right?" I asked Olivia.

"Yes, that's what I'm most curious about. And I want to know what to order for our nursery at home. We can go to Bartram's together."

I hadn't thought about the Wye Valley since my parent's letter had arrived in February. Strangely, a few moments after breakfast a lad from City Tavern arrived to notify us that a letter had arrived for us. It had only been two months since the last one and we hoped this was not bad news. I put on my coat to go pick it up.

"Since you'll be going by Biddle's, pick up several pounds of butter, will you? Bunny asked. "I'll give you the money. Oh, wait a minute. I don't have to, I have a credit there."

Arthur stood up. "I'll join you. I'll get my coat."

As we went out the door, Olivia called, "Don't get into a long conversation with anyone. We want to leave by nine."

After a few blocks, Arthur whispered. "Don't look know, but someone's following us."

It was all I could do not to turn around. "Let's cross the street," I suggested. As we crossed, we looked behind us with the usual precaution. Sure enough, a young lad was walking fast and catching up with us. "I think it's the brother of the kid I saved yesterday. Billy was his name. Let's slow down and see what he wants." Arthur said.

"Thank you, mister." he said as he approached. "I was afraid I wouldn't catch you in time." He turned to Arthur. "Mister, you saved my brother yesterday. He could have been badly injured, even killed. I just wanted to thank you and to give you this." From his pocket he pulled some pound notes and handed them to Arthur. "There's more." He dug into his trousers pocket and produced a gold watch. "I think this is yours, too." and handed it to a dumb-founded Arthur.

Arthur hesitated at first; he couldn't believe that this uneducated and dirty Godless waif was actually performing a friendly and contrite act. He took the watch in hand and looked closely at it to verify its identity as his valued keepsake and slowly wagged his head. "I didn't think I would ever see this again," he said, more to himself than to Billy's brother or me.

"I'm sorry, mister. I can see you're a good man and I didn't mean to hurt ye. Keep the money, too." Then Billy's brother turned and fled.

"Thank you, lad." Arthur called. "I'll be damned," he repeated several times.

The whole affair, the theft, the close call with the spooked horses, saving Billy's brother, and the return of the lost watch and money seemed providential. As it happened, it was the beginning of a streak of good luck.

We went to the desk at the City Tavern, picked up the letter and paid the clerk the postage.

I was expecting it might be from England. But it was from Crispin in New York. Just as I looked for a table in the coffee shop two gentlemen paid their bill and rose. We overheard one say,…"I heard Doctor Franklin isn't feeling well and may be delayed returning from Montreal." This disappointed Arthur. He thought he had seen the doctor the other day coming out of the State House.

We ordered coffee and I read Crispin's letter out loud for Arthur's benefit.

Dear Jamie,

*People are concerned here that no one in New York has seen Mochter in the coffee houses or taverns for several weeks. It's not because they miss him, but because, if a snake is loose, it's best to know where he is. How well I know that! Ha, Ha. I just thought to warn you to be on the lookout down there. As for me, I have an appointment to do Mochter's portrait in oils, which means big bucks. I hope he returns in time.*

*It may have nothing to do with Mochter's disappearance but Annie Mclaren, who has been working as clerk for Trevor Shaw, hasn't been around for a few weeks either. Trevor was very attracted to Annie and I realize I had better find some beautiful ingenue more his age to introduce him to if I want to be able to court Annie. I have in mind the mistress of a wealthy loyalist who has been abusing her—-stupid man—-a good woman is hard to find.*

*That's why I'm writing to tell you that I'm coming to Philadelphia to find Annie. I have reason to think she is down there. She lost her husband in that miserable siege of Quebec last winter and I suspect that she is still a little unstrung by it.*

*I'll be looking for her, but, as long as I'm there, we might as well try the Delaware for the shad fishing. So get out your fishing gear and we'll have a day of it.*

*your friend,*
*Crispin*

# chapter 30

AT BARTRAM'S I thanked my stars when I found that the wherry, despite the shoddy paint, was in good shape. The boat was manageable and the oars were light and well-balanced promising me the prospect of shortly arriving at the merchantman. It shipped not a drop and felt gratifying to body and soul to again be pulling a well-crafted boat.

As I approached the old ship through an armada of timber, a large log had been hoisted twenty feet off the water and was ready to be maneuvered into the ship. Cyrus appeared on deck in a collarless white shirt with horizontal red stripes and black trousers, the working uniform of a British tar. He wouldn't have passed inspection, he looked so unkempt, as if he had continually wiped his hands on the shirt and pants. He was the only visible member of the crew, presumably now a skeleton workforce. Instead of a friendly greeting, he snarled, "We were expecting you, Mr. Claveraque. Mr. Mochter is on the other side of the ship."

I was so engrossed looking over my shoulder while rowing my way through the clutter of logs that I did not realize that the suspended log was following me and that I was almost directly underneath it. When I looked up at the hulk's quarterdeck, there was Mochter in a British army officer's uniform, including a sword. He grimaced, "Ah, Claveraque, we meet again."

He slashed the air with his sword, signaling someone, and the log dropped. Thanks to the lapse between his signal and the log's release by the hoist operator, I was able to quickly scuffle the wherry so that the log missed. But the large splash and wave almost swamped the craft which would have left me at a disadvantage indeed. I blessed the little boat's buoyancy.

Mochter then had run out to stand on a small raft of logs and was chagrined that, despite all of his preparation, the log had missed its target.

"I see your hospitality is in your usual style, Wencesles. What is your next presentation?"

He jumped from the raft and charged across the logjam like an enraged bull. He managed to get within an oar's length of me without slipping. In his rage he slashed again. I parried with an oar and his sword clattered to the close-packed logs, bridging two of them.

He scrambled to reach the sword but slipped as the log rolled and spilled him into the water. He splashed about, cursing, "Dam thief, stealing my gold, dogging my every move, son of a bitch. Think you're an American now, huh?"

Cyrus was nowhere to be seen. As friendly as he had been the last few days, the prospect of obtaining land and promotion under Mochter's sponsorship would guide his actions and I could expect no help from him. He soon appeared alone rowing a large unwieldy whaleboat. I had lost track of the hoist operator—hopefully he had fled with the rest of the crew.

Mochter continued his incoherent clamor. "Claveraque, you thief. You took my gold. You stole Olivia from me, too. You hound my every action, here as well as at home. God, this water is cold. Cyrus, get me out of here." He ranted on, not waiting for answer, oblivious of my presence.

Cyrus was rowing full tilt to ram me. But he was obedient to Mochter's command and changed course. "I'm coming, Mr. Mochter," he answered.

Mochter quieted some and swam to his sword laying precariously on the logs. He was shaking with cold and so water-logged that he had trouble reaching the weapon. I grasped my oar and slid the flat of it neatly under the sword blade and lifted it so that it clattered safely into the stern of my wherry and out of his reach.

"Goddamn you, Claveraque. I'll get you, damned if I won't. Cyrus! come over here and help me out of the river," he cried.

Cyrus had maneuvered close to my wherry, grabbed the bow, lifted it up and twisted it, throwing me into the water. With my cane I whacked Cyrus who had lost his balance. He fell in yelling that he couldn't swim. I neglected him and turned to Mochter.

Mochter could swim, but with great difficulty in his wet uniform which must have been heavy. He was now within arms reach of the log between us. With my cane, I stabbed under the log at him with great effect. But the confusion of logs soon pressed hard against me, clasping my head as in a vise. It was all I could do to duck underwater to escape its grasp and the pain. This was a mistake. The logs closed over me so that I was prevented from surfacing for air. I jammed the cane between the two logs and tried to pry them apart. They stayed fast together. Underwater, I could see Mochter's coat clinging to him as if glued on and I struck out again. This time a vicious jab to his lower abdomen relaxed his hold.

I saw a open water several logs behind me and swam under them to calmer, less crowded waters, though greatly hampered by my clothes.. My lungs craved relief and I was fearful that other logs would block my way to the surface. I needed air desperately!

Finally, I broke the surface and breathed deeply to relieve my pained lungs. Suddenly, neither Mochter or Cyrus was in sight. As if nothing had happened, the wherry was still upright but low in the water, almost awash. It was boxed in a cove full of logs which conveniently provided a platform to assisted my climb out of the frigid water back into the boat.

The air was cooling off making me even colder. I had been drenched starting with the log's fall and Cyrus' flipping me into the river. Now the sun had gone lower and behind a cloud. Alas, the breeze freshened, compounding my chill.

Denizens of the river had stopped to witness these theatrics but, with Mochter's bully blustering, no one had offered him help. They dispersed as Cyrus magically appeared and hefted Mochter, still incoherently blubbering, into the whaleboat. Daylight diminished much too fast for this time of year. I turned the wherry around and started rowing back to Bartram's.

I had rowed only a few rods when someone lit a fire on the near shore. A moment later, a sonorous voice called, "You must be very cold and wet. Yes, I saw the whole thing. Come over and dry out by the fire." I recognized the voice but could not place him. This invitation I could not ignore. Weak and shaking with cold, I welcomed this timely gesture. Who was my savior?

As the bow of the wherry touched the river bank, this Samaritan reached out a hand to steady my step to shore. This done, he pulled the boat up, but emptied it slowly to relieve the strain on keel and planks, and then turned it over against the impending rain.

The fire, now in full glow; marvelously revived my strength. He draped a buffalo robe on my shoulders. "When you've recovered enough, strip off your clothes and I'll dry them by the fire. The robe will keep you warm until you can put them on again."

As he spoke, I caught his face in the firelight. "You're Doctor Honeoye. I saw you pitch the crowd at Coryell's Ferry. You were doing quite well. You must have run out of bottles!"

"Yes, I did well that day, and did run out of bottles. But I keep a cache of reserve supplies at Coryell's. Since the boys were buying, I quickly got extra rations to satisfy them. So you were in the crowd?" He extended his hand, "I'm Daniel Reittenhaus, also known as Doctor Honeoye."

I introduced myself and told him how much I appreciated his hospitality.

"I witnessed that man's assault on you for no discernable reason," he said.

"He attacked so violently. Never have I had to defend my life. I must have looked a ninny when he rushed me with his sword. If the oars hadn't been handy, I would now be sliced meat."

"You handled yourself and the situation very well, I thought. The oars were there and you made use of them and saved yourself. Wit is the essence of self preservation whether in physical or oral combat. Would you like some coffee or soup?—I can make either. Here, sit down and rest on these pine needles. They're more comfortable than the thwart of a boat."

I thanked him, elected soup, and relaxed as he searched his pack for the makings of my succor. I fell asleep briefly until he offered me a mug brimming with steaming peas and ham..

The first gulp sent a surge of strength through my body. I was overcome with gratitude. "Thanks, again, Dan. You've returned me to one of the living." The fire crackled and the embers glowed from a whisper of wind.. He had draped my wet clothes on two cross sticks by the fire. The buffalo robe was cozy especially as a thunderstorm was coming.

"Have you really come from the Indian country? It sounds like a long way," I said.

"It is, but I came down the Chemung, the Susquehanna, and the Delaware. The river does all the work except for a short carry at Oquaga. The Indians helped me make the portage."

"How long were you up there?"

"I went up last spring and stayed the whole year. I have a lot of friends there and it's pleasant if you have enough firewood and your own cabin. Besides, I have to get the magic medicine oil, but that doesn't take long to do."

"I've heard they have long, cold winters and unimaginable snow in the northern region. You must be glad when spring comes."

"Yes, but I like the Indians, especially the Onondagas. They're more friendly and aren't as eager to go to war as some of them, like the Senecas. But, it's nice to return to civilization. The southeast shore of Lake Ontario gets an unbelievable amount of snow and for a long season. Around Crooked Lake and Ochenang they don't get so much. You have to enjoy it. There are redeeming activities like hunting, trapping, and making maple syrup."

"Where do you get the snake oil, do the Indians catch them?"

"Oh no. It's not made from snakes. It's a natural oil that comes from a spring in Seneca country. *Snake* is what Seneca sounds like when said fast and repeatedly. Seneca oil surges from a spring and floats on the surface of the small pond. The Indians take it up with blankets and then squeeze the oil out into pans from which they funnel it into bladders."

"Do they treat it to enhance it's properties? Like filter it? Or add anything to it?"

"No. That's the way it is when I buy it. The oil carries well in the animal bladders except when the donkey wants to scratch her side on dead spruce stubs. When I get it to the city I bottle it, put fancy labels with instructions for use on the bottles and sell it.

"I forget what you said it cures when you sold it at the Ferry. Does it really work?"

"If you have a stomach ache or you're constipated, take a couple of ounces of the stuff and it will clear you out fast. And then you feel better. Since it improves your well-being, I think it relieves the distress of other diseases the customer might have. It does as good a job as other potions prescribed by so-called physicians. It's certainly better than the hammer cure."

"What's that?"

"You hit yourself on the head with a hammer because, when you stop, it feels better."

We both laughed and I felt at home with this surprising and congenial man.

"It's also a good lubricant for wheel bearings, polishing gunstocks, clockworks, machinery, softening leathers, sharpening knives, waterproofing boots, fighting off black flies, a lot of things. It also works well in a lantern, a little smokey, but it makes a good light."

"Aren't you afraid to be among the savages? I've heard some horrible tales of how they torture captives, force them to run the gauntlet and then burn them at the stake."

"The tribes have lost many people since the whites came on the scene; some due to war but far more to sickness, smallpox especially. They want to increase their numbers in self defense. So they adopt if they don't see the captive as a liability. I was captured when the French and some Onondagas made a raid on my parent's clearing near Unadilla about twenty years ago when I was five. A family that had lost a son adopted me and I was accepted into the tribe.

"My new family's lodge was on the banks of West Canada Creek, a wide and beautiful stream, which feeds into the Mohawk. They treated me with patience and affection and I came to consider them my family as they considered me their son and brother. I can hardly remember my white mother and father who were killed during the raid. To answer your question, yes, they make war and sometimes treat captives badly, but so do the whites who are often worse. And we *whites* are supposed to be Christian."

"Does that mean that you are a full-fledged Indian? An Onondaga, did you say?"

"That's a good word to describe it. I was fledged or grew into my manhood with the help of this family and the tribe. They themselves had been lured north from near Onondaga, an important Iroquois town, by Abbe Piquet, when they were in their teens. Piquet was a tyrannical Romish priest who had nothing good to say about Englishmen and distorted his religion and political realities to suit his politics and his fur trading. He was *bizarrerie*, as the French say.

"But most of the priests I met were moderate and tolerant. Above all, they were kind. Are you warm enough? Do you want a bit more soup?"

Dan got up, put more wood on the fire, pushed two pieces of a burned-through branch over the embers, and tested my clothing. "They're almost dry," he said and returned to his log.

I was digesting my host's story when he said, "For several days I've noticed people coming and going to that ship. When they go ashore, their pockets are bulging. You'd think they'd be loaded with supplies coming back. But they don't return with much. Also, it's peculiar that they have been lifting logs into the ship and then they unload the same logs, accomplishing nothing. That water is too shallow to be loading and the tide's going out. When you came along, I was about to paddle out to give you a hand. But you handled the situation very nicely."

I explained about Mochter and his shenanigans. "In my opinion, he's half British, half mad, and whole son-of-a-bitch. Now he's come to America on some mischief that you can be sure is profitable for him but troublesome for everyone else."

Honeoye interjected. "I doubt if he'll last long. Or if he'll get back to England in that ship. It's an un-seaworthy hulk—it'll break in half when it feels the ocean swell. But who cares?"

I could hear a slight pattering of rain and felt a few drops. I grabbed my clothes from in front of the fire. "I had better be on my way. My wife will wonder what happened to me."

"You'd better stay here. This is going to be a heavy rain and it's cooling off. You'd get soaked, your boat will fill and slow you up, and you could get a bad cold. Your wife will feel better if you get home, alive and well, even if it isn't until tomorrow," said Dan with authority. "Let's get under the open camp, out of the rain. There's more soup, if you want."

We moved a few feet into his hut with an overhanging roof and a pine-needled floor to enjoy the fascinating flames and the sound of fusillades of rain pounding the bark roof.

After a few moments, I asked, "What side are the Indians on in this obstinate war?"

"The Iroquois haven't decide yet. The Mohawks, because of their admiration and long friendship for Sir William Johnson will most likely side with the Crown. Americans have told the tribes to stay out of it, that the war doesn't concern them. Of course, that's nonsense. The tribes' major concern is the massive western emigration that's taking over their hunting grounds.

"Like the tide, it's unstoppable. It's what prompted the Iroquois to sell the British the western part of Virginia and Kentucky, to divert the path of migration away from Iroquoia. And Pontiac saw Indian lands being engulfed by whites. He was also miffed being denied supplies and ammunition by General Amherst but went to war to stop whites from invading Indian land."

"I've heard of Johnson. Tell me about him."

"He's an Irishman who came over forty years ago to manage the Mohawk River trading post of his uncle—then a captain in the British Navy. He attracted settlers and sold supplies and rum to the Indians and tenants alike. He befriended all, especially the Indians whom he treated fairly, learned their language, even hunted and danced with 'em. He was an unusual white man in their eyes, since he didn't cheat them or show contempt for them like most traders . He also bedded many of the squaws, a not unusual practice with traders. But Johnson married Molly Brant. She and her brother, Joseph Brant, are heirs of a powerful Mohawk family.

"Johnson did very well. So well that he decided to acquire land and set up his own trading post across the river on the north side. In the meantime the Mohawks adopted him into the tribe with the name "Warraghiyagey", meaning "man who undertakes great things." They don't bestow honors like this on just anybody. Tiyanoga, a gruff but long-respected Mohawk chief was who Sir William went to for advice.

"Johnson set up trading posts at Oswego on Lake Ontario, and at Oquaga, on the Susquehanna as well as at Johnson Hall and attracted farmers, mostly Germans from the Palatinate and England. His reputation with the Indians and his tenants grew so that he was appointed commissioner of Indian affairs by Governor Clinton. Just the same, he was rebuffed by the old-line Dutch in Albany who were affronted by his earthy friendship with the Indians and his tenants. Besides, his trade was eating into their profits."

I was awed by this emigrant to the wilderness who bucked the entrenched crowd in Albany and was so successful at it.. "What's Johnson advising the Indians to do?"

"Johnson collapsed and died suddenly as he was addressing a large Indian conference at Johnson Hall two years ago. But his son and son-in-law continue to sway the nations to the side of the Crown. As I said, they can probably persuade the Mohawks since they and Sir William have been chummy with them for years. The other tribes?—- it's anybodies guess."

"You called him Sir William. Has he been knighted?"

"He was made a baronet after he sort of won the battle of Lake George in '55. I say 'sort of' because his campaign didn't accomplished all that was desired. But, the battle took place only a month or so after the disastrous rout of General Braddock's campaign to take Fort Duquesne, and the Crown wanted to put a good face on the progress of the war.

"But, I'm running on too long. Why are you still concerned with this nasty guy on the old timber ship—if you don't mind my asking?"

"When my wife and I left England, we saw Mochter embark on a British ship. We thought this was only co-incidental and didn't think much of it. At sea, we saw his ship in the distance several times and, believe it tried to lure us into dangerous waters near the Bahama Strait. We rescued two of that ship's sailors wrecked on a small shoal. They both worked for Mochter. He was in New York and now he's here in Philadelphia. We think he's dogging us."

"I suppose that could be coincidental." uttered Dan, urging me on.

"Yes, but there's more than that. There's been a flood of phony paper money. It's easy to associate Mochter with this sham. By coincidence, or design, I have been hailed by one of his ship-wrecked sailors here on the street in Philadelphia. Not once, but twice, he and his girlfriend have invited me for breakfast. He even paid the check, both times with counterfeit bills."

"Well, that's not surprising. One can be generous using cheap money to pay the bill rather than gold or silver. We use wampum belts for recording treaties and other important deals. Many tribes also use it in trade since it is so much more convenient than bartering. So the Dutch began making wampum in quantity, cheapening its value. So it was counterfeit money but they thought it acceptable since they had little in the early years after they arrived in America."

I was surprised to get such a learned answer from one who has spent most of his time in the wild. He must have been tutored by someone. I felt somewhat challenged.

He added, "What I mean is that he must be a source of the stuff, he has so much of it. Maybe that's what I saw in the bulging pockets of his men going ashore from this old hulk."

"That would make sense. I'll bet that's what their doing. They are unloading it on the public and they print it on the ship. Hoisting logs is just a cover to satisfy the curious. I was barking up the right tree but for the wrong reason. It's is just a subterfuge for printing their phony money." Finally, I realized what was going on. I felt like a fool chasing around for log robbers. I sat there in self humiliation. This man from the wild who sells a laxative elixir to persons desperate to relieve their suffering had really thought it out. Where did he learn so much growing up in an Indian village. He speaks with authority, as if he went to Princeton or Harvard. I'll have to find out.

That was the last I remember of that exhausting day.

# chapter 31

THE NEXT MORNING, I woke to a calm, dense fog on the river. It was cooler and everything had been thoroughly drenched. The fog lifted as I washed with wet from rain-soaked ferns. Deep blue sky and strong sunshine bathed the valley to proclaim the new day. Swamp marigolds had been nudged into bloom to radiate their cheer on the scene. A crane stalked carefully among the shallows. Mergansers swimming nearby were the sole disturbance of the waters. Protesting squawks of unseen geese high overhead suggested the wild, not the city, not Philadelphia. No human activity disturbed the scene even on the sinister ship.

Dan squatted in front of a small fire frying eggs and a rasher of bacon. He looked smaller than he had in the rustic costume he wore to sell his elixirs. "Have some coffee," he offered.

"Your friends are either not up yet or they have fled. You put up such a good defense yesterday that they may have decided to close up shop," Dan added.

"I'd be surprised if Mochter did that. He's a tenacious character. He's proven that once he determines to do something, he'll see it through. He may lay low for a while but he won't quit."

Dan handed me a trencher of bacon and eggs. "What are your plans now?"

"Well, I don't want to lose track of Mochter but I can't stay in Philadelphia much longer. I'm sure my uncle wants to get home to his farm. It looks to me that Mochter is a counterfeiter and I think I should inform Robert Morris or some authority. I don't think they'll act unless

I can produce phony bills or something tangible. I want to pin him with evidence of some villainy."

"I'll be here for another few weeks, most likely, Jamie. If something turns up, I can get in touch with you. Where are you staying?"

"Bunny's boarding house—owned by Gertrude Bunting—on fifth Street."

"Oh, I know her. When I want a good meal and a shower, I visit Bunny. I'm due soon."

"That's a coincidence. Another curious incident is that Cyrus, the young man who works for Mochter, now has a girlfriend here in town. There's something about her that doesn't ring true. The first time I met her, she acted like a blowsy bar maid who relies on her feminine charms to get what she wants. Yesterday she acted like a debutant. I think she may be trying to pump something from Cyrus, maybe about Mochter. I don't know exactly what. I have a hunch that I'll be seeing more of both of them.."

"I see no distinction in that regard, Jamie. In my experience both the bar maid and the debutante use their charms to get their way. Perhaps you mean, Cyrus' girlfriend was brazen about it but now she has become more sophisticated."

"Exactly.

"I had better get back to Bunny's. Olivia, my wife, will be upset as it is. And I've got to return this wherry to Bartram. Besides, I feel grimy and need a shower, too. Thanks for your hospitality. I hope to see you again. What do you plan to do? Are you going back north soon?"

"No. The Indians are being stirred up by John Butler and his son Walter, large landowners up north who are a loyalists and close friends of the Johnson's. Joseph Brant, a protégé of Sir William's and his widow's brother, is in England along with Sir William's son-in-law, Guy Johnson. When they get back, chances are that disagreements with the patriots will get ugly. So I'll wait it out 'til the dust settles. I'll be here in Philly for a while, or near here.

"By the way, John Bartram is a friend of mine, too. If that's his wherry, let me row you back to his place. I'll be going that way this morning, anyway. A friend has my canoe and I suspect he'll be a while coming back. Just say when you want to leave."

Dan rowed the wherry at an even and powerful pace so that it made a respectable complement of waves. Bartram's place on the river became distinct in a short time.

"I've been scanning the hulk for activity with every pull on the oars," he said, "and now, I see some movement. But I can't make out just who it is. At least, we know they haven't left. They must have kept an eye on us and haven't stirred until they thought we were out of sight."

In another few minutes, we landed at Bartram's dock. We paid our respects to Mrs. Bartram and John, I thanked them for their hospitality and the use of the wherry, refused their offer of lunch, and we parted.

Olivia must have been watching out Bunny's window, since she greeted me by opening the door just as I approached the steps. "Are you all right? We worried about you all night. Arthur was all for searching the shore of the Schuylkill with torches but I thought that would be overdoing it. Come in and sit down. Have you eaten? Come tell us what happened."

Relating my encounter with Mochter and my fortunate meeting with Doctor Honeoye, alias Dan Rittenhaus, elicited great concern from the three of them. And it helped me sort out what I should do next. I should bow out and get the authorities to take over, I decided. After all, I am not an adventurer skilled in combat. (Although, my bout with Mochter ended favorably.)

Olivia sighed with relief. "I'm glad you're back here, safe and sound and that you were out of the weather with that Indian over night. Crispin was here, but only long enough to leave his pack and to say that he was sorry he missed you. But he said that he'll be back this evening."

I had almost forgotten about Crispin. "He arrived almost as fast as his letter. I'll be glad to see him. Perhaps you and I should have our portraits done in oils, Olivia. He's probably gotten even better in the last month."

"There was another person here to see you, Jamie. A Miss Betty Ann Button. She said she had to see you in private." Olivia said this with severity. "Is this how you have been entertaining yourself when you went looking for what you called 'specimens'? Tell me about it."

Betty Ann was of no personal importance and it didn't even occur to me to mention her when I told Olivia of my unexpected encounters with Cyrus.

This was a mistake. It was alright with Olivia for me to meet other women occasionally in the course of social or business events, but I had better explain the circumstances of the Button situation to avoid misunderstandings. I was upset that the relationship, for lack of a better word, had to be explained. I explained it now.

"Betty Ann is Cyrus' girl friend and she was accompanying him on both occasions when he saw me. After brief conversation, he offered to buy breakfast on both occasions.

"Betty Ann acted differently the second meeting in that she seemed refined compared to the first time when she appeared to be just a floozy he picked up. At the second breakfast, she seemed out of character. Maybe I'll find out now."

Olivia was adamant. "I want to be in on that conversation."

"That's all right with me. But it sounds like you think I had an affaire and hold me in contempt which I don't deserve. I resent it," I said in self defense.

"No, I do trust you. It's simply that a woman can see through another woman, and a man usually can't. Cyrus is a case in point. It sounds to me that Betty Ann is trying to find out something from him and he is resisting or is, more likely, too obtuse to notice."

Olivia had not even met them yet she was describing their character! I marveled. I went to my room, shucked off my grungy clothes, put on a robe and returned downstairs to take a long-delayed shower.

Before I had a chance to shower, someone knocked on the front door. The uninvited guest, of all people, was Betty Ann Button. Olivia welcomed her into the house. Introductions were not necessary and there was an awkward moment which was easily overcome by Betty Ann.

"Mr. Claveraque, I am sorry to trouble you and Mrs. Claveraque but the situation with Cyrus and his boss has come to a point. I hope I can discuss this with you alone, sir."

"Anything you tell me, you can tell my wife. Why don't we move to the kitchen. I think we can have some privacy there." Surprisingly, Bunny was not cooking something at her stove.

"This is official business, Mr. Claveraque. I am pledged by our new government to secrecy. If my boss, whom I can't divulge, ever finds out that your wife has been made privy to this conversation, I can be sent to Simsbury Mines. I insist that I talk to you alone. Mrs. Claveraque, this is strictly government business. Please be good enough to let us have the sole use of this room." This serious statement convinced Olivia and me that Betty Ann was bona fide.

Olivia did not protest this challenge but left the room as would a disciplined errant child.

"All right," Betty Ann began, now that we were alone. "For some time, I have pretended to have an interest in Cyrus because I know he works for Wenceslas Mochter whom my superior thinks is affiliated with the British Army. When they came to Philadelphia from New York, I followed. When we had breakfast with you the first time, I realized that you are a recent arrival from England but that you either sympathize with the American point of view or are neutral.

"We think that Mochter is, among other things, involved in printing large denomination notes in quantities large enough to weaken the value of our currency and our ability to finance the coming war. You may have concluded that, too. I watched you and listened closely during those meals, and I thought that you were on to something and were trying to verify whatever it was.

"Your encounter with Mochter and Cyrus yesterday was serious in that it not only endangered yourself, but you are interfering with our plans in apprehending Mochter. You are spooking him and he may go into hiding so that we can't pin him with the necessary evidence to satisfy a court. We also think that he may lead us to other counterfeiters so we do not want to arrest him before any additional information has a chance to emerge.

"Even though it is not a royal court anymore, we have set up the tentative organization of the new province of New York with its own court jurisdiction. It will adhere to most of the English principals of law.

"So, we want you to stay away from Mochter. We appreciate your good motives and we know something of your past experience with him in England. This operation requires professional people who are competent, authorized and able to handle the risk. If you have questions, I will answer them to the best of my ability and within the limits of security in the case."

This was startling. But Betty Ann justified my suspicions about her. She was pretty and could act saucy enough to attract a lout like Cyrus and charming and clever enough to keep his attention without revealing anything hazardous to herself.

I quickly assured her that I would not be a problem. "I reached the decision to stay out of the Mochter affair after yesterday's scary adventure. I was surprised Mochter became so belligerent. He has been unpleasant in the past, but never dangerous. He must feel hard pressed."

"Yes, that's where we have tried to steer him, and then you came along and forced the issue, and ruined our careful planning. If he goes underground, we may have to start all over again. Promise us that you will have nothing to do with Mochter from now on, Mr. Claveraque."

I assured her. "I promise to stay out of it."

Betty Ann looked keenly at me. "We know that you have known Mochter from the Wye Valley for a long time and the tragedy he brought about there to the people and the countryside what with the army base despoiling the local park.

"But he also did something worthwhile when he arrived here—-probably not intentionally, to help the patriot cause. He sold Washington a ship load of gunpowder just as the General moved to New York. Chances are he intended to sell it to General Howe but the British evacuated Boston for Halifax before Mochter could make a landfall. That left him no one but Washington to sell to. And Washington was desperate for powder. So we know that Mochter can be induced to support either side.."

"I think that's a fair estimation of his character. Whatever works best for Mochter has always been his guide. Go on, Betty Ann."

"We want to intercept Mochter and bring him to court with hard-bound evidence so that he knows his fate is certain to be a resident of Newgate Prison at Simsbury. I'm referring to the dreaded Simsbury Mines."

"It would be desirable to get him off the street and out of circulation. Mochter is cunning and he can cause no end of trouble. But what is so terrible about Newgate Prison?"

"That's the point. We want Mochter to know just how terrible Newgate is. It's a hundred year-old copper mine that has played out. Prisoners, mostly notable Tories now, are held in subterranean cells deep in the mine. It is continually dark, cold, and damp so that prisoners have been known to loose their mind, certain that they'll die before they ever get out. Even if a prisoner is not claustrophobic when sentenced, being confined at Simsbury soon makes him so. We want Mochter to know that this is what awaits him if he doesn't come over to our side."

"Come over to our side? To do what?"

"Well, of course we want to put a stop to his operation. But we want to use him to find out British plans, supplies, Crown stamina, which of our operations bother them most, their secret agents—things like that. He has the contacts with the upper echelon. As my indelicate boss says, he's a son-of-a-bitch, but we want him as our son-of-a-bitch. Pardon my coarse speech."

"How can you trust him? He is only concerned about his own welfare. Even if it causes disaster to the other guy."

"Exactly. That is the kind of agent we want. And Mochter fills the bill. We will let him make as much money as he can. Just so long as it isn't at our expense, or if it is, it proves to be worth it." Betty Ann had stated her case and conducted herself well.

I sat back in my chair. "I see what you mean. My chasing after him could have screwed your elaborate plans. What do you want me to do?"

"Just stay away. We'll take over. Just so long as it isn't too late. When we're ready, we'll stop his printing of pound notes. But, after all, we are printing our own currency to finance the war, so he is saving us the expense of paying Doctor Franklin too much for fancy paper and the use of his printing presses."

Besides staying away from Mochter and Cyrus, is there anything I can do to help?"

"I can't think of any way you can. I know that Mochter seems to carry a grudge against you and that he is guilty of following you as much as you may be interfering with him. Cyrus told me how he was set to have that log drop on you and when that missed, he came after you with a sword. A good thing you had a cane with you."

"A walking stick, not a cane," I insisted. "It was an oar that I used to ward off the sword."

She ignored my correction. "If he bothers you again, try to avoid a confrontation. Most of all, don't hint at, or in any way, let him know that I or the authorities are on to him."

I nodded assent.

"If we are agreed, Mr. Claveraque, let us join the others," she said.

# chapter 32

WE LEFT THE kitchen in a state of elation so much that Bunny said,"You all look so relieved, why don't we celebrate what ever it is with a bottle of Madeira I have been saving for the right occasion?" Not waiting for an answer, she opened a cabinet next to her desk and pulled out from a cache of special liquors a full crystal decanter, and said, "Don't worry. I haven't been eavesdropping ." She also brought forth six crystal glasses.

At that very moment, we heard another knock on the door. "Good gracious! I hope it's an abstainer. I only have six glasses," said Bonnie.

Olivia opened the door and Crispin appeared, in fine fettle, fine clothes, bearded, and bottle of wine in hand, to greet us. We were all standing as if to celebrate something, which indeed we were, "I see that I'm just in time," he said and Crispin re-entered our lives.

As his vision adjusted to the candlelight, Crispin's eyes bulged with delight. "Annie McLauren. What are you doing here!"

We all turned to look at Betty Ann. Or was it Annie McLauren. We turned back to face Crispin. "Well, she was Annie McLauren when I last saw her. I wrote about her in my letter. Or hasn't it arrived yet?"

"I can explain," said the besieged girl. "I am both of those person's and for good reason. Crispin is right, I am known as Annie McLauren. But my maiden name is Elizabeth Ann Button and my friends called me Betty Ann. My husband, George McLauren, preferred to call me Annie, and so that is how I am known as Annie McLauren in New York. But then my husband died last winter with the army in Quebec. We had been married for only four months.

"I have come to Philadelphia in the interest of settling my husband's estate. He was from a family who lived near here, whom I had never met, and I wished to share condolences with them. A merchant in New York, by whom I am employed, thought I should have protection during my journey here and assigned another in his employ to accompany me to Philadelphia.

"But..." Crispin stammered.

"Wait. Let me finish. I am almost finished wrapping up my husband's estate and, aside from visiting some friends, I plan to return to New York soon. Because of my employer's kindness, I hope to do all this as quietly and as soon as possible." She smiled and moved in Crispin's direction. "I am so glad to see you here, Crispin. What a coincidence," she said.

"Annie, if you had only told me I would have been delighted to be your escort."

"I considered it, Crispin, but you were so engaged in painting the grandees of New York, I didn't have the heart to ask, much less accept, for such a sacrifice on your part. Besides, Mr. Shaw provided an escort." Crispin considered this revelation and was devastated. He had expected a better response from Annie. I secretly commiserated with him.

Annie relaxed when she saw this explanation served to allay suspicions.

Crispin gasped. "I don't know what to say. But I'm delighted to see you Annie and Jamie, my friends, here in the same house in a strange city. Let's not waste this, Jamie," he said, brandishing the bottle and loosening the cork. "Introduce me to this lady with the tray of glasses."

Introductions were made, the glasses were filled. Bunny and Crispin took to each other immediately. A toast was offered, and Crispin shared his charm, especially with Betty Ann and Bunny. I was bursting with curiosity as to what was happening in New York.

When Bunny, Betty Ann, Olivia, and Arabella were running out of questions to ask Crispin, I was able to wedge in and the four of them began talking among themselves which conveniently excluded Crispin and me. We moved to a corner of the room.

"Well, General Washington and some of his Continental Army have arrived and are digging entrenchments on Brooklyn Heights and putting in more redoubts, making a mess of city streets. Word is that Washington's sure that Howe is in Halifax, regrouping, and will be joined by more troops from England to make an attack on New York this summer."

"Sounds scary. What are you planning to do?"

"I don't know, Jamie. I have a lot of clients to paint yet and many of them are Loyalists. I don't agree with them or their arrogant manner, or let them know my sympathies. But in the meantime, I'm making more money than I've ever dreamed of. Having a portrait appeals to every one's vanity. Also, they want a picture of themselves and their wives to hang on the wall for posterity, or to show that they are prominent in the war. Many tell me that they are afraid they may not be around a year from now. You know what they say?—- strike while the iron's hot."

"Aren't you concerned? Are you going to join the militia? Or, at least, learn how to handle weapons in combat?"

"You know I can handle a bow. Handling a musket can't be much harder.. Afer all those years we've gone hunting together?"

"That's not the same, Crispin. You have to know how to fire and reload quickly, and to follow commands so you're not the last one to move forward or to leave the field. It helps to be part of a group that knows what it's doing because it has been drilled in doing it many times together. You will have to know how to defend yourself in hand-to-hand combat these days."

"I agree with the patriots, but somehow I don't think this is *my* fight. I don't know, I haven't thought about it that much." Crispin wavered.

"Crispin, I don't know what I'm going to do either. But, at least, I'm going to get some training. This is likely to be a long, bloody war and we will probably be caught up in it. I don't want *to happen* to be caught up in it. I want to join it on my own, not because I can't avoid it.

"I'm reminded of that speech of Henry the Fifth just before the battle of Agincourt. Shakespeare said it so well. I can even remember it from school—well, part of it. 'We few, we happy few, we band of brothers; For he today that sheds his blood with me shall be my brother; be he ne'er so vile, this day shall gentle his condition: And gentlemen in England now a-bed shall think themselves accursed they were not here, and hold their manhoods cheap whiles any speaks that fought with us upon Saint Crispin's day!'

"I think Henry's challenge is apropos to this situation. If we are here in the path of two armies, and agreeable to the cause of one of them, and seek to avoid the fight, we will always be haunted for not doing our conscientious duty."

"So that speech was made on St. Crispin's day, my day, in a manner of speaking?"

"Yes. And with this speech he made to embolden his troops, King Henry won the battle of Agincourt. His archers decimated the French lords and grandees by unseating them from their horses. They fell to the ground and the weight of their armor and the confused congestion on the battleground prevented them from rising up to continue the battle. Historians say that it was all over in less than an hour.

"Many French nobles were captured. The ransoms obtained by the English became the foundation of many of the great family fortunes to this day."

Crispin considered this for a few moments. "Was it on October the twenty-fifth? That was the day of the battle?"

I nodded.

"That's my birthday! That's probably why I was named Crispin!" He was overjoyed.

"Unless you have an uncle or a grandfather whose name is Crispin."

"No. I must have been named for the day." He was happy to be associated with the battle so famous in English history and so eloquently commemorated by Shakespeare.

"Well, what else is new?" Anyone coming recently from New York would know what is going on, I thought. At that, Arthur came from the kitchen and offered us a refill. He made the rounds to the ladies and returned.

"This was over a week ago Jamie, but North Carolina has told its delegates to Congress to vote for independence. They are disgusted with sending petitions to the king only to have them come back denied or ignored completely. They think Paine's *Common Sense* outlines the situation very clearly: no sense in people on a small island telling people on a rich continent three thousand miles away how to live."

"That's right. But we know by now that the English aren't going to let us go our own way without a fight. I'm going to get some military training.. I've hunted but I don't know how to shoot a gun. I don't know how to use a bayonet. I don't even know how to use my fists. And I don't know where to go to learn these things without signing up in the army or the militia. But I was on my way to take a shower. Have you ever done that, Crispin?"

"Done what?

"Taken a shower, I'll show you when I'm done. Are you staying here, at Bunny's?"

"I am. I have never taken a shower but I've heard you mention it. So I'll try it. Don't use up all the hot water."

With Crispin expecting to shower after me, I had to be thrifty with what was left of the warm water. The ladies must have used the shower for a prolonged period. This meant that I had to get myself wet, then shut it off and soap myself thoroughly and rinse. I went through the necessary motions—all in the space of two minutes. The water was getting chill.

So I suggested that Crispin wait a half hour to let the sun heat a fresh supply. He couldn't wait and so ignored my suggestion by pulling the on-off cord. The whole house could hear his howls of shock and pleasure.

Crispin appeared in a few moment refreshed, scrubbed, and in his new suit of clothes. A bright scarlet coat, not quite hiding a fluffy white stock, and finely-worked white soft leather knee-trousers complemented by embroidered green stockings and black patent-leather shoes mounted with silver buckles.

"You look like the eminent New York City portrait painter we hear so much about," I shouted, followed by "hear, hear" from the others. Bunny suggested a toast, "May you derive much coin from your Loyalist friends. To Crispin and his own Revolutionary movement!"

Bunny was so taken with Crispin that she announced, "Everyone have another glass of wine. I have a special dish I'm preparing for dinner. It'll be ready by the time you finish your drinks. At least by the time I finish mine." and she tromped into the kitchen, glass in hand.

Crispin turned to me. "I'm happy to find Annie so easily. This means we'll soon be able to go fishing for shad in the Delaware. Trevor Shaw, the merchant in New York—Annie works for him—took me fishing to a delightful stream in Northern Jersey called Flatbrook.

"It's between two mountains and is full of speckled trout. I swear, Jamie, you'd think you were back in the greenwood. It's beautiful and no British army around to mess it up. Hardly anybody else either. And this will be the best time to fish it—the trout will be feeding again after a long winter. What say?"

"If it looks like the greenwood, I'm game. We'll never see the greenwood again. So, if Flatbrook is it, I'm anxious to see it. We're leaving the city in a few days anyway. Olivia and my aunt and uncle are anxious to return home and we can accompany them and then head north."

I expected sandwiches or cold cuts for dinner if Bunny was able to prepare it in only a few minutes. And, in a way, it was sandwiches. She served toasted slices of bread covered with a special cheese sauce.

Bunny explained. "My husband taught me this recipe which was a favorite of his family's who came to Billy Penn's city from Ireland at the turn of the century. They called it Welsh rabbit- reflecting their opinion of Welsh marksmanship." We all laughed, even Crispin, whose Welsh uncle had taught him how to hunt.

Bunny quickly added, "Some call it Welsh rarebit to soften the slur on Welsh honor."

Toward the end of dinner, my nose began to run, annoying me and the others for my attention to it, and I developed chills. I shook so that I could hardly convey a glass of water to my mouth. I had to go to our room to get a second handkerchief and when I returned to table, everyone said I looked faint. At that, I admitted that I felt faint and went to bed.

Even the bed sheets annoyed my flushed and burning skin. Olivia came up to see how I was, but I had developed a fever which along with my unceasing runny nose and head ache made me poor company. I mumbled thanks. She kindly patted the covers, assured me I would feel better in the morning, and left for the conversation downstairs. I dozed off to a dead sleep.

I awoke in the early afternoon with Olivia next to the bed with a glass of orange juice and a dish of rhubarb sauce, my share of the concoction Bunny made to save us all from the "vapors". The deep sleep had cured my headache and my skin no longer burned. But I felt a malaise which all but kept me from being able to down the sweet, refreshing juice and the tart sauce. Olivia felt my forehead for fever and declared it had gone down.

Just hearing her voice made me feel better. "Your ordeal with Mochter and being soaking wet in the cold must have done this to you. It's just a matter of time now. All you need is rest. If you need any refreshment, just call. Do you want to talk to Crispin or Arthur?'

I shook my head. I didn't think I could carry on a conversation. Nor did I care to. I thanked Olivia and she left the room. This must be God's way of teaching us to how it feels to die. Death even seemed the better choice. But I was feeling sorry for myself. If one had any vices, this would be the time to begin giving them up. This depression mercifully melded into a sweet sleep.

I slept into the next day. Olivia was there with more orange juice and toast. I was free of the malaise but felt weak. "You have eaten very little in the past few days. I'll bring you some more toast. Then you can have dinner with us tonight, if you feel up to it," she said. I looked out the window to see a beautiful day with the poplar trees coming to life again, the leaves half unfurled and shimmering in a light breeze. What a waste it is to be sick in May, I thought.

I began to recount this trip to Philadelphia. We had accomplished something, with all this travel. We had enjoyed the beauty of Bartram's Gardens and seen the Delaware River up close. We have met many people about investing. But our gold slices are still buried in Arabella's garden and uncommitted. Perhaps Squire Calloway's idea to make springs was the best idea.

We have seen at first hand the workings of representative government and heard convincing arguments against the harsh policies of parliament and King George. And now, gossip says that Congress is considering separation from England. It must be a sizzling debate going on there and in City Tavern. Some want to stay linked with the British Empire while others think that the colonies should form a confederation, that a new country will prosper much more without the restraints that have been enforced on a bustling economy.

I could hear the unmistakable tread of Crispin' footsteps coming up the stairs. "Bunny thought you might like a cup of soup. If you don't drink it, I will. I've already had a taste of it," Crispin smiled. "How are you feeling? You look much better than yesterday."

I mumbled, "Yes, I'm better—but it's miserable being sick during this beautiful weather.

He handed the soup to me and sat down. "Here. This will make you feel better. I rode up along the Schuylkill to near Matson's Ford yesterday and hooked into seven heavy shad just below the falls. You're right. Shad fishing is exciting and vigorous. I pleased myself and Bunny was pleased, too. We're having shad tonight."

"Did Annie accompany you? I hope she likes fishing as much as you do."

"She said she likes it, and that she would like going with me. But she had some business she had to attend to. Here I am trying to woo her away from Trevor Shaw and she comes down here to be with some one else. At least, she said she was genuinely sorry she couldn't join me."

"I can't tell you the details, Crispin, but she's on government work. Something having to do with the Continental Army. And it has to do with Mochter. That's why she came to Philadelphia. She swore me to secrecy; if word leaks out about her activity, she might be in danger and would have a severe penalty to pay. Just trust her through this. It shouldn't last long."

"I was hoping that Annie would join me in returning to New York. Now, it looks like that's out the window. Jamie, how soon are you going to return to your uncle's place?"

"We were going to leave right away. But then I came down with this damn illness. I still don't know what it is. Olivia was afraid it might have been smallpox in it's earliest stage, but if it is, I would be in very bad shape by now. As soon as I get over this, we plan to return. It'll probably be only a few days before I'm fit for the road."

"I've spent so much time checking out what Mochter's doing, that Olivia may resent my spending more time away from her. I'll ask her to come with us."

"What do you mean, 'checking out Mochter'?"

I explained what had happened in Philadelphia.

"Why not turn him over to the authorities?"

"I did tell the authorities about what I think Mochter is doing and they said they were aware of it but wanted to get more evidence so they could nail him for sure. Now you know as much about it as I do." I hoped that this would end all further discussion of Mochter. Of course, I didn't tell Crispin that the 'authority' was Annie McLauren.

I changed the subject. "Olivia probably won't fish but she'll enjoy the scenery. Might even do some cooking for us. How's that sound? Fresh-caught trout cooked right on the stream bank?"

The next day was sunny and warm and I was feeling much better possibly because of the prospect of looking forward to the thrill of fishing a clear, virgin stream combined with spring in full bloom. Bunny suggested that I sit out on the porch to absorb the warmth of the sun. Arthur brought out chairs to join me. The front of Bunny's house was shielded from a light breeze and enjoyed a double portion of sunshine from the direct rays and the reflection from the brick wall.

After basking in this coziness for a while Arthur broke the meditative silence. "So, we'll be going back home in a few days. Do you think you will be up to it by Friday?"

"My cough no longer has the depth of my lungs. My nose can no longer float a fleet of ships, nor require an acre of handkerchiefs. I feel good enough that I could probably leave tomorrow. We've had a pleasant time here but I'm looking forward to getting back to your farm and feeling at home again. I imagine you and Arabella want to enjoy your garden after the long winter and doing any fixing necessary."

"We are anxious to get back. But we don't want to rush you. We can wait another day. And think you should." Arthur replied, and then lapsed into silence. The pleasant warmth on the porch and the settling of my lunch made my eyelids heavy. I began to nod into sleep, when a nearby voice shouted, "Mister, Mister! We've been looking all over for you."

Arthur and I shrugged out of our reverie to see Billy and Billy's brother approaching. They were trailed by beautiful golden dog that came over to me and slavishly licked my hand and eagerly moved from side to side as if looking for something. She wanted to nuzzle and her large brown eyes seemed to plead 'give me something to eat or pet me.'

Billy's brother got right to the point. "This dog has been following us for a few days and we thought she would make a perfect gift for you." He directed this announcement to Arthur.

Billy added, "She's a good dog, but she hangs around all the time. We can't play the games we like to because of her, so we thought you might like to have her as a guard dog or something."

"Yeah." said Billy's brother. "Besides, you were real nice to us."

Bunny, ever inquisitive, opened the door. "What's all the fuss about?" Then she saw the dog. "She's beautiful. What's her name? She looks hungry." Without waiting for an answer, Bunny receded into the house and soon returned with a bone. "I was going to use this to make soup, but she looks like she needs it more than we do." and she offered the bone to polite, but eager jaws.

Arthur realized that he was the intended recipient of the dog. "Thanks boys. But I don't know what I would do with her. And we'll be leaving the city in a few days."

"Nobody is likely to bother you if you have a dog." said Billy's brother. "We thought you would be the perfect one to unload it on. I mean to make a gift to."

I piped in. "I'll take her, if you don't mind, Arthur. Bunny, I'll take charge of the dog if you have a place we can keep her for a few days."

"I was going to take her if you two didn't. Sure, I can find a place. Giving her a good meal will probably keep her here. What's the dog's name?"

"We don't know." said Billy's brother. "She just saw us and began following us. All we had was candy, so we gave her some licorice. We didn't have to call her. She just came with us."

"Well, I think she is a nice gift, boys. Thank you. We will take good care of her. And you can play your games unmolested. We'll think of a name," I said and Billy and his brother disappeared from our lives.

We thought of names such as 'Candy', 'Goldie', and Polly, but decided that, even though she was cute and feminine, a one syllable name would be more direct and unmistakable for commands or when calling from a distance. The rest of the 'family', including Crispin, joined in.

All the one-syllable names like 'Bob', 'Sam', and 'Dick' seemed to be male gender. Olivia settled it. "She won't know it's a masculine name, let's call her 'Sam'. And 'Sam' it became with approval from 'Sam' herself shown by her tail wagging even more.

Having Sam around to pet, throw sticks for, and teach tricks was fun, pleasantly rewarding, and took my mind off getting my strength back. While looking for lost-dog ads, we saw an advertisement in the Pennsylvania Gazette about a turkey shoot to be held the following day in Newtown. I suggested that talking to marksmen at the shoot might be instructive in the use of the Pennsylvania long rifle, famous for its accuracy and developed in Lancaster only fifty miles away.

Newtown would be a good place to stop the first day as not too ambitious for one just recovering from the vapors, or whatever it was, and so we decided to leave on the morrow.

Bunny knew our stay would end soon. When she heard we would leave so abruptly, she behaved as if 'her family' was abandoning her. We would miss her, too. So we all decided to treat Bunny to a dinner at The City Tavern.

To Bunny, this was cause for a brand-new wardrobe. She could consider the cost part of her advertising budget, she said. I was surprised that Arabella and Olivia were not so inspired, despite having satiated their shopping appetites, if that accomplishment were possible. But they offered to accompany Bunny to advise her of the bargains of their previous day's shopping..

When they came back all excited at helping Bunny, Arthur, Crispin and I gathered to see what they had in their shopping baskets.

"No, No. Not until were ready to go are you to see Bunny's new dinner gown, nor ours," Olivia said. The sun had been beating down relentlessly all day so there was plenty of hot water stored in Bunny's shower, and the ladies drew down the water supply as Arthur and I pumped a new charge of water into the system. Unfortunately, there was not any warm water left for us. Good thing that we were not in desperate need.

After this effort, we dressed for dinner and waited for the ladies. Arabella appeared first. She was quite proud of her two-piece suit. The top was a bold green velvet with a white puritan collar. Her skirt was a finely worked gray doeskin, soft as suede, with sequins and beads sewn into an attractive Indian pattern in the material.

Olivia came down stairs, as if on cue, sporting a bright crimson blouse with large gold buttons spaced down to her dark-brown belt. She also had the gold earrings I made for her (and for emergency money) before we sailed from England. Wasn't there another gold item, I wondered. Her skirt was black with many pleats all around. She was very beautiful and reminded me of our first meeting only six months ago. Touring had not depleted her radiance. I was proud of her.

Perhaps to enhance her entrance even more, Bunny delayed her appearance five minutes. We were excited by her exuberance when she finally presented herself. She wore a plain dress of blue taffeta overlaid by a fine white lace jacket. She had a gold brooch securing the wings of the vest in the middle. Alas, that was the gold jewelry that was missing as part of Olivia's ensemble. I wondered if this was a gift made by Olivia or was it Olivia's way of paying our room and board? But this was not the time to find out.

Arthur, Crispin, and I applauded their finery. We made much ado over their loveliness.

We proceeded to the City Tavern where Bunny was greeted by name by many of the patrons. We were honored by the manager himself, a Mister Smith, who seated our party at a table commanding the fireside. If we had arrived any later in the day, and without a reservation, we would have been out of luck. Later I found that Congress had not adjourned for the day though several congressmen were absorbed in heated conversation at a nearby table. I also found that Bunny, sly one that she is, was one of the stockholders of the company that owned the place.

Our order was taken and brought to table promptly. The mutton was perfectly broiled, sliced and presented. We couldn't have been better served or sated. As we were about to consider dessert, I glanced to my left and was surprised to see Dan Reittenhaus, known to many as Doctor Honeoye, dressed in high-society attire, seated with gentlemen, or so I assumed by their attire. He returned my nod with a wink and a smile. Within a few minutes, he gestured in our direction to his companions, rose from his chair and came over to our table.

"How good to see you so soon, Jamie. You don't look any worse for wear," he said in his most agreeable manner. Introductions were made, small talk followed, and then he said in an aside to me, "I saw your friends on the merchantman this morning. One of them happened to come over for some sugar and I gave him a drink of rum to loosen his tongue. Seems they are going to vacate the area and go north past the Water Gap to inspect some old forts used in the French War in the Kittatinny Mountains. Thought you might be interested."

I was aghast. It was as if Mochter could read my mind! Flatbrook, where we plan to fish, is in that same area. Dan understood my surprise. "Let me know if I can be of any help," he said as he sweetly smiled to my dinner party, especially Bunny, and went back to his companions.

Bunny had been concentrating and finally said, "I think I know that man. Henry used to go hunting with him. Henry even admitted that when he missed a shot, Reittenhaus unfailingly nailed the quarry. I probably owe many a venison dinner to him. What's he doing now?"

I retold the table my experience with Mochter, and how Reittenhaus, or Doctor Honeoye, was kind enough to befriend me that unforgetable evening.

"No wonder he was such a good shot!" said Bunny. "Growing up an Indian would make anybody an excellent hunter."

As the men at Dan's table disbanded, Dan returned and spoke to me alone. "You mentioned that you want to learn to use a rifle, Jamie. I'm attending a turkey shoot tomorrow afternoon at Newtown.

Perhaps you all would like to join me. I'll guarantee you'll see some fine shooting."

"I saw the notice in the paper, too, and we already decided to see the shoot on our way north. We want to leave the city as soon as possible before the yellow fever season starts. We would like to have you join us."

"That's settled, then. We are leaving at eight in the morning, sharp. Or close to it. Join us when we start or on the road, at your convenience, Dan."

# chapter 33

WE ALL HUGGED Bunny goodbye, especially Crispin. The instantaneous bond between them was as if he was a long-lost son. She handed me a small packet. "Scraps for the dog," she said. Linus brought our horses from the stable. He had groomed them well, for which I was grateful. He was wide-eyed when I slipped him a crown for his good service. To the saddle I fixed a pannier to hold the mountain laurel and some other plants Olivia had fancied.

During these final minutes before departing, Bunny, Olivia and Arabella conversed as if they were prepared to chat for the afternoon. The discussion was so intense and likely to digress in several directions that it was difficult to politely terminate it. Indeed, at the last moment when I thought we could leave, a new subject was introduced. At that, I gave Bunny a parting hug, mounted, and nudged my heals into Nelly's flanks and moved off. This was rude but necessary to nip endless conversation so we could depart. Sam trotted behind.

Dan caught up with us on the road to Langhorne just when we stopped for lunch where there was a spring in a pleasantly fragrant grove of honey locust trees.

He was dressed the part of a frontiersman in a soft doeskin shirt covered by a dark brown hunting smock down to his hips. It was secured by a wide belt leaving no loose clothing to limit his actions. Finely worked buckskin moccasins were surmounted by heavier buckskin leggings to his knees to protect against snake bites, brambles, nettles, and such. Soft leather fringes, the length of your index finger, adorned the hem and seams of shirt and pants. He had a mean-looking tomahawk tucked in his belt. With his Pennsylvania rifle and engraved powder horn, he gave fair warning to anyone contemplating mischief.. I was glad to have him as an accomplis.

Dan must have remembered what a good cook Bunny was. She had given us the shank end of a ham and a bowl of potato salad. His timing was perfect. He joined us at a table set out for travelers by a canny farmer who had a vegetable stand nearby. In this season it was stocked only with last season's left-over apples, honey, jams and jellies, and fresh-made maple syrup.

Dan continued the conversation where we had left off the evening before by producing his pride and joy, a magnificent rifle which he lay on the table.

It was more than four feet long mostly due to the length of the barrel and the lock mechanism. I admired the polished black walnut stock and how finely it was fitted to the barrel and lock-- a fine piece of marquetry. A brass plate hinged to the stock covered a cavity for patches. Similar to Arthur's rifle but it had been kept in prime condition through usage. Arthur agreed.

Dan appreciated my admiration for the piece. "I bought it from a trader who said he had bought it at a gun shop in Lancaster where it was made. I, too, thought it was a Kentucky rifle but the trader brought me up short and said the gunsmith insisted that it was a Pennsylvania rifle. He admitted that many Pennsylvanians had used pieces like it a few years ago fighting the Shawnee and Delaware at Point Pleasant.

"Arms like this will give you confidence and respect from those you meet on the trail."

"I agree. But I don't know how to shoot one of these things, and they weigh quite a bit to hold steady on a target," I said.

"Well, the first thing you should know, that many shooters don't, is which eye you're aiming with. This makes all the difference. You might be right-handed but left-eyed. So, you probably would shoot with the rifle butt against your right shoulder. But you will miss your target most of the time if you aim with your left eye because you aren't aligning the rifle properly with the target. So, if you naturally aim with your left eye, you should hold the rifle against your left shoulder, even if you are right-handed. Your aim will be much better that way."

I was pleased to hear this. "As simple as that, huh?"

"Well, you have to practice a lot, as in anything. But, failing this essential knowledge, you're doomed at the start. Maybe doomed literally."

Olivia hesitated to interrupt. "Slice off some ham and make yourselves a sandwich. We have to eat and get going if you want to make that turkey shoot in time." She shoved the bowl of potato salad down the table.

Dan insisted. "This will only take a minute to show him, Olivia." He sliced the ham as he explained. "Look over to that martin house on the pole—the one by the barn. Now, put your hand over your right eye. Does it seem to move?

I did as he said. "Yes, it jumps a little to one side."

"That means you naturally look at things with your right eye. Of course, you're looking at it with both eyes but your right eye dominates. If the target didn't move, that would mean you look at things with your left eye rather than your right because blocking your right eye wouldn't interfere with your sight. See?"

Olivia was intrigued, "Let me try it!" She looked at the martin house and put her hand over her right eye."The martin house didn't move." Then she covered her left eye. "Now it moves, just as happened to Jamie. What does that mean?"

"It means your left eye does the main seeing. It's your dominant eye which means you should put the rifle on your left shoulder so the rifle can align with the left eye. Even if you're right-handed. You'll shoot better."

"I've never shot a gun." she said.

"Then you'll have the advantage of not having to unlearn bad habits, Olivia."

I looked at Crispin. "Did you know that, Crispin? You might have to handle a bow differently, too, if you're not aiming the right way. Is that right, Dan?"

"I'll show you when we get to the shoot. We had better eat as Olivia says."

Crispin was busy eating potato salad. Only now did he show any interest. "Let's eat so we can get to the shoot before it starts. If we have enough time, I would like to put what Dan says to the test. I hope I'm aiming the best way. It would be so awkward to shoot as if I'm left-handed."

"You'd be surprised, Crispin. It *is* awkward making the change, but only for a week or so. After that, it becomes second nature and you begin to see your marksmanship improve way above where it had been. Believe me, I've been down that road, myself."

Newtown was crowded. Every mother's son wanted to show his competence with a gun. And everyone in Bucks, Philadelphia, and Chester counties was curious as to how good were these Pennsylvania rifles that they'd heard such fabulous stories about. The organizers of the shoot had arranged for it to follow the weekly militia muster to boost attendance.

Dour Quakers in their sober garb to Indians in buckskin leggings topped by ruffled shirts and businessmen in fancy silk waistcoats and satin knee breeches were present to watch and bet..

Not encumbered by a wagon or cart, we elbowed our way to the front row of observers. White targets with a black bull's eye and several concentric rings were nailed to sturdy posts at one hundred yards for smoothbore muskets and two hundred yards for long rifles.

The shoot was sponsored by the Anchor Inn which reaped a harvest of customers and offered generous and attractive prizes. Dan wanted to see these first as did we all.

Knots of spectators gathered around to inspect the prizes. A fine Pennsylvania rifle was first prize. Such a gun would command a premium price if traded later. Dan said that it was most likely contributed by the gun shop to promote business. The shop had a good reputation, he said.

Second prize was a pair of pistols seated in a red velvet-lined carrying case. Third prize was a fine three-section nine-foot fishing rod made of Tonkin cane with an English reel wound with braided horsehair line, including a hard-leather rod case and a willow creel. "We should see fine shooting," opined Dan.

A horn blast announced the beginning of the shoot. Musket shooters were to go first to show deference for the local militia, Dan explained. The main event was second, testing the elite long rifle marksmen. With a war imminent, this was likely the last local shoot for some time.

Everyone moved to the one hundred yard mark for the first event. The smoothbore had little accuracy, even in the hands of a good shot, at longer distances. The range master announced the contestants as each was about to fire. Friends, family and girlfriends held their breath as their champion took his chance at station. Then, Bang! The shoot began.

As the bluish white smoke drifted away after each shot, the official by the target called out the reults to a cacophony of cheers and catcalls. Of the ten contestants, only five hit the target within the outermost ring, disqualifying the other five. The crowd of spectators backed away so that the top five shooters could move twenty-five yards farther out for the next round.

The names of the survivors were called and then the first of them took his place. The crowd quieted. A dog barked; a child's cry was stifled. The entrant hefted his piece, squinted, and squeezed off a shot. Bang! The score was called out and the surviving sharpshooters sighed their thanks for their good luck when their rival missed the target. They knew that a gust of wind, a distraction, or a nervous muscle twitch could account for a win or loss. It was practice, the endurance of nerves, strength to hold steady, and trigger savvy that told in the end.

Only one put a shot in the small black circle. With a smoothbore; that was good shooting. He would be looked up to in his militia company, maybe be voted an officer.

For the devoted shooter, as opposed to the farmers and artisans who largely comprised the militia, the main event was about to commence. It attracted marksmen mostly from southeastern Pennsylvania, Jersey, Delaware, and Maryland. And the game was now played with rifles which had pin-point accuracy and range that could change the course of a war.

Now the range began at two-hundred yards. Fewer contended with the long rifle and they were a different breed of men. Several wore fur caps, buckskin leggings and soft doeskin shirts with frills along their sleeves and pants. Slung over their shoulders were inscribed powder horns resembling scrimshaw. While the long rifle set off this elite group, a second badge, of sorts, was the scent of stale wood smoke, fried bacon, and the malodorous smell of old sweat.

Many were from Virginia under the command of Daniel Morgan, one of the heros of the miscarried Quebec Campaign. Dorcas Murray, reputed to be born near the Water Gap, was known to be a crack shot and when the word got around, money was put on him.

Because of such formidable competition, our Dan had hesitated to participate in the match. But Crispin and I encouraged him, even bet some shillings on him, so he signed up.

The first two contestants, local men, put their shots in the edge of the targets from two hundred yards; good shooting in any man's language.

Dan was next; he put his shots just outside the center disc and the crowd oohed and awed. As good shooting as this was, it left room for someone to better it.

Dorcas Murray approached the firing line with aplomb He stretched and stared at the target. As he brought his rifle up and sighted, he let go the trigger to swat a black fly on his left forearm. The swat should have dismayed the fly long enough for Dorcas to get a shot, but it did not.

"Damn," Dorcas seethed. He brought the piece to his shoulder again and, again the fly settled on his arm. He concentrated his aim, trying to ignore the fly long enough to fire. Too long, the fly pierced Dorcas's arm just as he squeezed the trigger. The shot went wild, hitting only the outer edge of the target. Dorcas's mumble partially obscured his curse..

Dorcas unstopped a small vial and dabbed himself with an oil that made his arms and face glisten and stink. He waited to test its efficacy. The crowd empathized with his aggravation. Satisfied that the fly was kept at bay, he brought his rifle to sight his second shot. He held the piece as firm as a rock. Everyone held their breath as Dorcas's trigger finger tightened.Bang. Several spyglasses fixed on the target. The crowd uttered a collective sigh, "He missed. Dorcas missed!"

Dorcas said nothing. He marched to the target followed by his admirers. "Here it is, right in the black, the center of the target," he said. The three judges agreed and Dorcas was the winner of that round. The distance for the second round had been set at two hundred and fifty yards.

The first contender missed both of his shots and was eliminated from the shoot. The second missed with his first shot but he corrected on the next attempt and placed in the second ring.

Dan was determined to show better this round. There was calm in the lee of blooming lilacs at the firing station, but a strong left-to-right wind blasted the target. He slathered his arms and face with fly dope and flexed his arms before lifting his rifle to firing position to help compose himself. He was very deliberate There was no need to fire in haste; he took his time.

The last shoot he was in had these same wind conditions and he had not taken them into account—-not enough anyway. He should allow a little more elevation and aim to the left edge of the target, he told himself. He adjusted and held at that for a second and then squeezed off the shot. Bang! A bulls-eye! The crowd roared its appreciation. Despite the high regard for Morgan's riflemen, Dan was considered local and favored.

Dan was ready for the second shot. He was more confident after scoring the bulls-eye especially since he had remembered to sight his rifle ahead of time. The wind by the target had dropped. He went through his aiming routine again to calm his nerves. Aim as high but not much to the left this time he whispered to himself. Bang! The black center had a slight bulge on the left this time! He had a fair chance of winning the fine rifle. Not that he needed it. But he did want to win to prove to himself he could do it and to please us.

The wind gusted again. Every one had been so absorbed by such fine shooting that they had been oblivious to the dark thunder heads amassing and gathering height in the west. A few heavy drops fell, but that was all. If the remaining contenders hurried, the shoot could be completed before the storm. They could celebrate the winner and settle bets in the large stone barn.

Dorcas, Dan, and the remaining contender were escorted by the judges back to the three hundred-yard station. The crowd kept in step and the betting intensified. The third marksman shot first. Both of his shots missed. He was eliminated and promptly disappeared in the crowd.

Dorcas was next, exciting his followers. He took even longer than last time preparing for the shot. Whether he was a born exhibitionist or it was really necessary for him to perform these elaborate exertions we did not know. The crowd appreciated the exercise but Dan and we were concerned lest the delay and the weather would prohibit Dan from getting his shots in.

As a few spectators cried "get on with it", Dorcas finally performed as expected. Both shots pierced the target, one in the bull's-eye, the other within the second ring. His backers roared their applause and banged noisily on whatever they had at hand.

Dan leaned my way and said, "Dorcas has a reputation for starting a fight with anyone who beats him. Not just fists, but eye gouging, groin kneeing, shattering fingers, anything brutal he can think of. I know I can out-shoot him, but I wonder if it's worth it."

I was dumbfounded; afraid he'd back out at the last minute. But that was not to happen.

As the clamor abated, Dan took his stance, flexed his arms overhead several times, splashed fly dope on his arms, threw a pinch of dust to test the wind, and finally brought the polished piece to his shoulder. A boor yelled "put it in the hole". With studied aplomb, Dan waggled the rifle barrel as if to find the perfect focus for the shot. He held firmly a second and then squeezed the trigger. Bang! At that distance few could even see the target, much less the bull's-eye and rings. A judge signaled that he had hit the bull's-eye.

Even Dan's detractors shouted their approval. Dan had to wait for the crowd to quiet under the judge's orders. He now went through an even more elaborate routine, perhaps to outdo Dorcas's performance. You could hear an acorn fall. Not even the boor dared interrupt his focus. Dan breathed deeply and held stonily still. He tightened his trigger finger and bang, the gun fired.

The target judge shouted something but no one could make it out over the noisome confusion. The judge approached fifty paces and called again, "bull's-eye". Dan had won!

Then the crowd went berserk, lightning flashed, followed instantly by a crack of thunder, and large raindrops began to fall, drenching all. Most of the crowd skedaddled into the barn where the noise and the malodorous humidity of the crowd soon dampened the merriment.

Confusion was restored in the barn as the judges announced the winners and awarded the prizes. Dan stepped up and received his Pennsylvania rifle with pride and modesty.

"What are you going to do with your old rifle?" I asked. "I'm going to continue using it. After all, I know how well it shoots. I'll trade the new one for a good horse."

Most of the crowd had moved into the barn. In deference to the ladies and to our own sensibilities, we quitted the barn and festivities for our lodgings nearby which Bunny had recommended.. We went to bed early to assure an early start the next day.

The rain had cleared the air but had not much muddied the road. There weren't even any standing puddles. The patrons of the lodging house all wanted breakfast at the same time, so to avoid a delay, we decided to defer breakfast in favor of having brunch at Princeton. It was only three hours away. We could stifle our hunger while crossing the river.

The imposing title, ***The College of New Jersey***, implied a spacious campus, a large faculty, and a proportionate and eager student body. But many students and faculty had left to join the army hastily recruiting in anticipation of coming battle.

Doctor Witherspoon, a Presbyterian preacher in Scotland, was invited to serve as president of the college eight years ago. More recently he has become active in New Jersey politics and trading insults and insinuations with Governor Franklin and the Loyalist faction in the New Jersey assembly. The college campus has only a few buildings, most notably Nassau Hall, an impressive stone building that foretells the college's prosperous and grand future.

Just outside town, we passed by one of the finest homes one could view on the Atlantic seaboard. The owner, Richard Stockton, member of the Second Continental Congress, lavished money and tasteful thought building Morven which, even from the outside, was large enough to meet all anyone's needs and idle wishes.

We had a pleasant dinner at the Hudibras, a fine tavern on Nassau Street, the main street in the town. The Sign of the Hudibras burned to the ground in 1773 but its successor was promptly rebuilt by Colonel John Hyer, the congenial and optimistic, proprietor. He made a point of telling us that he had hosted the entire New England delegation to the First Continental Congress.

What we could not eat, because of time constraints, we wrapped in yesterday's paper but not before scanning the news that a British gun ship had attacked a plantation on the Delaware coast south of New Castle. The aggressive ship backed off under fire from a Pennsylvania Navy row galley, a ship probably much like the patrol boat I was on only a week ago.

From Princeton the road paralleled the Millstone River, a small, looping, lazy stream but chock full of ducks and other water fowl. A green heron flew off every time we got to within fifty yards of her. She would fly a hundred yards down the river and then settle in the water only to repeat this game as we moved downstream. Soon afterwards, as we crossed at the confluence with the Raritan, Arthur began to recognize familiar landmarks. His farm was only ten miles east along the road in the shadow made by the first range of the Watchung Mountains.

We felt rushed—sunset being two hours off—that we might not reach his farm before dark. Knowing the local roads and folks was a comfort, he said and we arrived home without incident. We fell into bed as soon as we stabled and fed the horses, and slept to almost noon the next day.

Olivia and I were most concerned about the 'health' of the rhododendron. The only sign of intrusion was a series of holes made by chipmunks which spring had made active. We thrust a thin rod in several places until satisfied that our trove was unmolested.l. At the same time, we helped Arabella plant the mountain laurel which had endured the trip so well that the buds were bright red and swelling. Arabella was delighted when they bloomed within a few days.

Dan, and I went to Cowell's store to obtain supplies for our sojourn to the Kittatinny Mountains. Crispin went to New York to keep his appointment with Mochter, and Arthur and I resumed tidying his orchards and seeding his vegetable garden.

Alas, Crispin came back from New York without painting Mochter who never showed up to sit for his portrait.

# chapter 36

BY THE TIME Crispin returned from New York, our party had expanded to Trevor Shaw, Dan Rittenhaus, besides Olivia, Crispin, me and our dog, Sam. We had more than enough supplies and staples for our trip to last us for two weeks.

"We'll have to bring an extra horse to carry all this stuff," I said. Trevor countered, "We can either come back in ten days or leave some of the load here." Dan argued, "I'll soon have two horses. Why not use them. They can carry the load easily and we can stay as long as we want."

We all agreed that this was the best idea since we had looked forward to getting away to the mountains and away from the constant talk of politics and threats of war. But, it meant that Dan would have to sell his newly-won Pennsylvania rifle and buy a horse that met his qualifications.

Just before leaving I checked to see if any mail had arrived while we had been in Philadelphia. It was providential that I did since what my parents had to say had a definite bearing on our later decision though we did not recognize its importance at the time.

*Dear Jamie,*

*By the time you receive this you will have been gone about six months and have much to tell us about your ramblings in the colonies. We look forward to such a letter.*

*We have just read and had verified by Squire Calloway that Wenc-esles Mochter, who was continually financially embarrassed, and being pressed by creditors on all sides, was forced to sell the mill he had in-*

*herited from his uncle. A group of businessmen formed a committee to arrange for the payment of debts and for the sale of sufficient assets to satisfy his creditors (mostly the committeemen). Squire Calloway made the purchase and has yet to select the man to manage the mill. We believe that Dordy has a good chance at getting the job.*

*This will certainly effect Mochter's standing in government circles as well as his social standing here in the Valley. It has surprised and mollified many local people whom Mochter offended in many ways. They are pleased to see him taken down a peg. Then, too, it will be nice to have Dordy increase his position and living since, though it has not been announced yet, we believe he and Sally are going to be parents in the fall.*

*Imagine! You and Jonathan being uncles! We hope that you and Olivia will make Dordy an uncle soon. Send us a message of your doings, even if it's only a note.*

*Love.*
*Your loving parents*

I found it difficult to believe that Mochter had mismanaged the mill so badly. I'm always sad when someone has misfortune, even Mochter. I was also sorry not to be able to answer their letter. I had no opportunity to compose a reply since we were about to depart for the Walpack in a matter of minutes.

The most direct route to the Kittatinny Mountains was the Minisink Trail which that band of the Delaware Indians had made through the forest centuries ago to make their annual spring trek from the mountains to the Jersey shore for oysters and clams. Huge mounds of shells left at Sandy Hook were concrete evidence of this. Going north, the path skirted the First Watchung Mountain to Springfield, then cut through Hobart Gap and the Short Hills, past the flat lands to Whippany, to Netcong where we decided to stay the first night.

Since the weather was clear, and in Dan's opinion, likely to stay that way, we elected to erect our tents on the meadow by the lake for tavern patron's horses to forage. We all felt a deep sense of embarrassment for Dan when, within an hour, a thunderstorm whipped up, forcing us to quickly repair to the tavern after all.

"You forced me to make a hasty decision," he said as we fled from the tents to the welcome light and warmth of the tavern. We all laughed as we ran for cover.

"Our rooms are filled. You'll have to share the Long Room with another party but we don't close the bar until midnight," said Mr. Hankins, the tavern owner. He nodded in the direction of four people by the fireplace. "They just came in from Stroudsburg. Name is Ellis."

We had our dinner in a leisurely manner and took the opportunity of inspecting Dan's prize rifle. "I knew this was a prize piece when I saw that it was made by Lefevre in Lancaster. Look at that beautiful black walnut stock and the way the barrel and lock fit. It's light, well balanced and feels made to fit my shoulder—I can't wait to try it out."

Raising the gun caught the attention of the other party in the room. The patriarch of the group came over. "Mighty good-looking piece you have there, stranger. Mind if I hold it?" Guardedly, Dan said, "no."

"My name is Robert Ellis, this is my wife and these are my boys, Adolf and Richard. We just came through the Water Gap from Stroudsburg." said Ellis as he accepted the rifle. "How's it shoot?" he said as he carefully studied the lock.

"I haven't fired it yet. Just won it in a shoot a few days ago."

"Which shoot was that?"

"At Newtown."

"Oh, we heard about that. You must be Dan Rittenhaus." He paused."With two rifles, I assume you may want to sell one of them."

"Which one do you want to buy?"

"Why, I'd like to buy the one that won the shoot.

"I can't sell it."

"Why not?"

"Because I don't know how well the new one handles or shoots. What do you want to pay for the old one? We know how well that shoots."

"I'll trade you my best horse. I was just offered fifty pounds sterling for it.

"Why did you turn it down?"

"It's a good horse. I thought it was worth more."

"How many horses do you have?"

"I have three. Let's go outside and I'll show them to you while there's still enough light."

Two of his three horses looked like they had been ridden hard, way past their endurance. The chestnut hadn't been rubbed down but appeared sleek and in good form.

"Which one do you want to trade?" asked Dan. As he suspected, the one that was spavined was the one Ellis tried to pawn off. The chestnut, looked like a worthy trade.

"I might consider this one but I think I'll sleep on it if you don't mind. I also want to check out my recently won rifle as you may want to test my old one. We can do that in the morning."

As we all returned to the Long Room, Ellis was reluctant to break off the conversation since the bar would still be open another few hours. "Where are you folks headed?" he wondered.

"We're on our way to Kittatinny Mountain," pronounced Dan. I wondered why he was so open about our destination. Dan later said since the mountain stretched from the Water Gap to the New York border or about forty miles, he didn't really tell Ellis where we were going. "I wanted to keep him talking. Never know what you might find out." Dan explained.

Ellis opened up. "We met some people this side of the Water Gap who were eagerly buying horses—a tall fellow who didn't seem to know as much about them as you'd expect from someone in that occupation. He also mentioned something about an old copper mine established by the Dutch over a hundred years ago. The mine is supposed to be somewhere on Kittatinny Mountain near the Delaware River."

"There's a number of operating iron mines and forges over near Morristown and Greenwood Lake but I never heard of copper mines up this way."

"Maybe it was an iron mine. I wasn't paying that close attention. He also mentioned an old road used to carry the ore north to Esopus. I thought this unlikely, but that's what he said."

"Maybe the mine isn't so old but it would take a lot of men and machinery and horses to build a road, house and feed the men, fight off Indians, and dig a mine at the same time. There must be a town, or what's left of it, somewhere near." We separated from the Ellis' to a far corner of the Long Room to ponder what he had said and what it implied.

I mentioned these things to the tavern owner who immediately dismissed the idea of an old mine up in the mountain. "I've been here for fifteen years and never heard anything definite. The Van Campen's built a substantial home there in the Walpack Valley around thirty years ago. Old Isaac never said anything about a mine of any kind near by. I think it's just some old legend, like ghost stories people like to tell around a campfire. And hardly likely when you think about it. The Delaware, Shawnees and the Mohawks have been resisting settlement in this area for as long as anyone can remember."

I suggested that we bring in the tents that had finally dried. We brought inside all our equipment which pleased the tavern owner, by reason of increasing business, to offer us a beer on the house. Then we went to bed.

Dan was up early that morning with his new rifle pacing off a distance from a small rise where he had placed a target. The air was clear and calm. Conditions couldn't have been better for sighting the gun. He wasted no time lining up a shot with the rifle firmly braced on the crotch of a small tree about two hundred yards out.

Bang! The sharp crack of his rifle reverberated among the hills. From where he stood he could see that the bullet hit about two inches below the mark but was perfectly aligned. He adjusted the sight, loaded the gun and squeezed off another shot. Bang! This pleased him and he made up his mind; he would trade his old gun for the chestnut mare if Ellis would go along with it. At the first shot, Ellis made haste to witness the second. He was just in time to see Dan do the best shooting he had ever seen outside a turkey shoot. All thought of dickering any longer disappeared. He wanted the rifle—he wanted to be able to shoot that well.

"I'll trade the chestnut for the new rifle," he volunteered.

Dan acted startled. "Oh, I want to keep the new gun. It's the old one is the one I want trade for the chestnut."

"But it was the new gun I wanted. You were going to keep the old one, don't you remember?" argued Ellis.

"Try a shot with the rifle that won the turkey shoot. In any event, I should keep the new gun. I won it and it will be expected of me. My name is even engraved on the lock. People will wonder about your having a rifle with my name on it."

"But..."

The old one is the one you said you wanted It's either that or we have no deal.

Dan took the prize rifle from Ellis' grasp and forcibly placed his old gun in Ellis' hands. "Now, where is the chestnut's saddle?" He spotted it, gave the chestnut an apple, and slung the saddle on the chestnut. The mare accepted Dan's handling and he threw himself on her back with a "chuck". He walked the animal a short distance to get her feel, and then into a trot of a hundred yards, before shifting into a smooth canter. They streaked off to the far end of the field.It was plain that Dan considered the transaction complete. He returned, dismounted and turned to Ellis. "I posted a new target in place. Now take a few shots. You'll be able to win prizes with that rifle."

To show Ellis that he wanted him to be happy with the rifle, Dan tarried to witness Ellis' marksmanship. After watching Ellis get off two shots, he pronounced him a good shot and shook his hand. Then he turned to see that all of our party, including Sam, were ready to go. We waved to the Ellis's and departed for Newton and Kittatinny Ridge on the Minisink Trail.

The Indians had chosen good ground for this path as it wound through country mottled with small ponds but we had no trouble with swampy ground. By noon we arrived at the Sussex County Court House where numerous people chose to eat lunch on the grounds. We thought this a good idea and broke out some food.

Trevor Shaw produced from his voluminous coat pocket a map he had drawn at the instruction of his friend who had the estate on Flat Brook. It portrayed that part of the Minisink Trail from Newton to Minisink Island in the middle of the Delaware River. The map featured Kittatinny Mountain running from the bottom left side of the chart to the upper right and continuing into New York State where it becomes Shawangunk Mountain.

The mountain is breathtakingly prominent and runs parallel to the Delaware River a few miles north. At the Water Gap, the river cuts through the massive barrier and turns southeast. On the Pennsylvania side Kittatinny becomes Blue Mountain.

On Trevor's map, Newton was called Wallpack which was confusing since Walpack Center is only a few miles farther along the trail but they differ in spelling. From here we were close enough to see the mountain clearly on the northwestern horizon. We could also see a small gap just this side of Kittatinny where Culver Lake sits and where we would be passing that afternoon. From there it is only a few miles to Trevor's friend's estate.

Crispin, who had been here once before with Trevor Shaw, edged his horse over next to mine so he could converse. "Not only is the fishing good but they go snipe hunting here using only sticks and a bag. Snipe look like Herring gulls only they taste much better," he said.

"How do you catch them with only sticks? They must be dumb as pigeons. That doesn't sound like much sport to me."

"Oh no! They're very cunning. You have to be patient and crafty to catch them. They hide out during the day so they are active only at night, or as Samuel Johnson's dictionary says, they are nocturnal. If conditions are right, we'll probably go snipe hunting. You'll find that it can be a lot of fun and they are delicious roasted over an outdoor fire."

We had passed through several miles of deep woods and we were about to cross Papakating Creek through which opening of the forest canopy loomed the great Kittatinny range considerably grander than before. Spring had barely left a smudge of green on the top of the ridge but had engorged the valley with dense green, almost cold shade. The under-story would receive little sunlight for the season making less cover for game. I was getting more excited by the yard as we advanced into virgin forest.

When we came upon the shore of Culver Lake and a vast meadow, Dan wished to stop and rest his horses which had been burdened with more than their share of baggage. "This chestnut has earned a rest. Too bad she's so loaded up. I'd love to take her for a fast gallop over level ground, " Dan said. We all could stand a rest, except for

Sam, who sensed that the meadow was loaded with fat mice as did some hawks skimming the grass on the far side.

There were unmistakable signs of many horses corralled here recently. Soon a ranger, whose days-old beard and rouged cheeks testified to his outdoor exposure, appeared. "Can I help you folks? You may need directions since this isn't any place to be. Dingman's Ferry across the Delaware is about five or six miles more. Just turn left and cross the Little Flat Brook at Layton's."

I spoke up. "We're on our way to Van Campen's on Flat Brook. We must be close."

His temples wrinkled and his eyes glittered happily as he explained, "that's even closer. Just take the road that turns left just past a pile of rocks. That'll take you through Tillman's Ravine. Nice and cool in there this time of day," he volunteered. "But I wouldn't want to go that far in these woods at this time of day."

Of course, I asked "why?"

"Because it's virgin woods and very dense shade. It'll be dark in there in another hour or so. Better to camp here and go the rest of the way tomorrow. When you do it, you'll be glad you did. So will your horses.

"That's kind of you, mister," said Dan. "Let's take him up on it. Is that the outlet of the lake?" asked Dan, pointing to the north.

"Yes. That's Culver's Gap, there's an open camp and a fireplace there. I'll round up some firewood for you to get you started. But help yourself."

"Mr. Culver is trying to interest people in settling here. With a hundred acres in meadow you don't have to wait but a season to get a crop. Only thing is the mosquitoes…"

We decided to stay overnight never thinking that mosquitoes should be a consideration. The open camp was large enough to accommodate us comfortably. The ranger, Joe Macomb, had collected more than enough driftwood from the lakeshore for a fire that lasted well into the night. By the time we had set up camp, the mosquitoes had got wind of us and like an armada, gathered for the feast. Every other effort was a slap and our arms became bloody with smashed bugs and sore with itchy bites.

As he piled the final branches of firewood, Joe announced, "Don't use the lake water, it's tainted by the runoff from the pasture. There is a spring just up the hill from the outlet which has proven safe."

Dan threw a few green branches on the fire which then billowed clouds of smoke, "to discourage the mosquitoes," he said

Trevor Shaw broke out bottles of wine, one of the reasons for needing more horses when we left Arthur's farm. We stacked several bottles of Chablis against the rocky wall of the ice-cold spring—I have always thought the cold brought out a depth of flavor in a good wine. Despite the risk of broken glass in transit, Trevor preferred packing regular wine glasses to help capture the gastronomical pleasure. We invited Joe to join us, sensing interesting conversation from him. He did not let us down.

"What brings you up this way?" said Joe as he graciously accepted a glass.

"We came to do some trout fishing at the invitation of Mr. Van Campen, a friend and customer of my store in New York."

"You've come all the way from New York for a few fish? I don't mean to be disrespectful, but surely there's good trout fishing closer to the city than this?"

"I'm sure there is but we have an invitation to come here. Invitations from the Livingstons, the Phillipses, the Van Cortlandts and others closer to the city are not easy to come by."

"You're welcome to all the fish you can catch. A good spot is either up or down stream of Haney's mill. It's not hard to get a line in the water there and, for some reason, the fish seem to congregate in the pool there."

"So, you're a fisherman, too?"

"Yes, I grew up around here."

"You were here during the French and Indian War?"

"Yes, I was a youngster then. We had to get to the stone fort when they fired the alarm gun or remain outside and risk an uneven fight. Those forts saved the folk around here in the mid-fifties but it was hard to get much farming done." Joe savored another sip of his Chablis.

"How many forts were there?" asked Dan.

"There were about ten of them including those on the Pennsylvania side of the Delaware. The first one this side of the river was Fort Reading twelve miles north of Easton. Then Van Campen's Inn is eighteen miles up from that. And our fort, Fort Shappanack is just up a knoll from Van Campens'. There were several more forts, not much more than stockaded homesteads, spaced about five miles apart all the way to Fort Maghaghekmek. That's where the Navesink River joins the Delaware—near the New York line."

"Are these forts still in good condition?" I asked.

"Some of them are. Van Campens, though home to that family, is an inn because the law says certain, selected places, the better ones, have to take in travelers on the road. It's in good shape because Isaac keeps it that way. Fort Shappanack was headquarters but nobody has lived there for a while. It could be fixed up without much trouble, I guess."

"Mr. Van Campen invited me and friends to stay and fish or do whatever we want, but we have more of us than he probably expected so I thought we should look for alternative quarters," suggested Trevor.

"That's of no concern Mr. Shaw. Mr. Van Campen is in Burlington attending the provincial congress. Something big and important is taking place there, maybe a showdown with the governor, Doctor Franklin's son. He'll be gone at least a fortnight. I can have Dick and Pegg stock either place. They are Mr. Van Campen's slaves. And the other people shouldn't be any problem."

Not thinking that we might have to share the place with anyone, I said, "What others?"

"A gentleman from New York is buying as many horses from Sussex County farms as he can and is grazing them and raising forage for the winter."

"He must be the one who owns the horses that pastured in this field."

"I think he's part of a syndicate—there are so many horses—not just the ones that were in this field but several other pastures, as well. It's too much for one man to own and manage."

"Yesterday, we heard about a group who owned a large herd over near the water gap.

What's going on, Joe? Any idea?" I asked.

"It could be a syndicate that wants to corner the market for horses or transportation in north Jersey. Or it may think that there will be a shortage of horses soon or next winter since they're laying up forage. It's got to be more than setting up a stage line with that many horses. Whoever they are, they have a lot of money. They're paying top prices and in specie, too."

I changed the subject." How's the fishing, Joe?"

"I've been too busy to wet a line. But one of the horse buyers who said he just took up the sport said he's caught so many he could feed his crew for a week. 'course, he's just using worms. He said he grew up in London and just recently took up the sport."

This statement reminded me of a similar recitation made by somebody in the last six months, but, for the life of me, I could not think who it was.

Olivia came into the conversation. "You have a wide diversity of trees and wild flowers. John Bartram—we visited his nursery in Philadelphia recently—said this section of the country was one of his favorites. I can see why."

"He visited Mr. Van Campen years ago, if I'm not mistaken. He's the one who travels the country for new specimens of plants and trees for his patron's gardens, isn't that so?"

"Yes, but he's an old man now—in his late seventies."

"He was no spring chicken when he was here. I remember showing him some of the mine holes. He made a close inspection and said that no experienced mining engineer would bother trying to extract copper from those sites. And to my knowledge, no one has."

"But someone had reason to dig those holes in the first place?" said Olivia.

"Yes, but they were probably natural caves when first discovered, someplace to get out of the weather when overtaken by a storm, say," Joe agreed.

"We've heard that the early Dutch may have heard from the Indians about signs of copper and came down this way from Kingston. Even before the English took over, they're supposed to have dug a mine that was promising enough to build a road through the wilderness all the way from the Hudson so they could ship the ore back to Holland for refining. Where is the road?"

"Maybe I can show it to you tomorrow. It goes right by the river and Van Campen's place to Pahaquarry, a few miles south. It begins there, where the mine is. Or where the mine is supposed to be. In places you can't make out a road unless you have a vivid imagination. It also helps that it closely follows the river. That's the Old Mine Road."

"But you said the road goes all the way to Kingston?

"Yes. The Dutch called it Esopus after the Indian tribe there. The road goes north along the Delaware to the point where the river swings southwest and the Neversink joins it. Then it runs up the Neversink Valley, crosses the height of land near Napanock, and follows Roundout Creek to the Hudson. All in all, from Esopus to Pahaquarry, it's over a hundred miles long."

Olivia was appalled. "And the Dutch were supposed to build a road like that to transport heavy ore through a wilderness infested with hostile Indians for over a hundred miles? And the mine didn't even pay? Nonsense!"

"Nevertheless," Joe insisted. "There is a road there."

For a few moments there was just the crackle of the flames consuming the driftwood.

"Well,"" said Crispin finally. "We came up here to fish. If in our wanderings, we come across the old road, and the mine, that's fine. But if we don't there's no harm done. No offense to Joe here, but even he admits that in some places it strains the imagination to verify that such a road has existed here for that long a time."

I was more concerned about the wealth and power that was busy amassing horses. It sounded ominous to me. Such a power could only be a nation state and it certainly was not being funded by the treasury of the new United States. Great Britain was going to bing the war here and it will need horses in large numbers to move men and supplies.

"Have you met any of the men who are managing the collection of this large herd?"

"There's the fellow who catches so many trout with worms, but I told you about him. There's another who raises horses in England but saw a better opportunity doing it over here. There's at least a third one, maybe more, but I haven't met them yet. They've only been here about a month. They been buying horses or acquiring them somehow and hiring wranglers."

Dan poked the fire and asked, "Is this where the infamous Tom Quick hung out?"

"You've heard of him, have ye? Yes, Tom made a name for himself. But there were two of 'em. You're probably referring to the son, the one who vowed to kill a hundred Indians."

"Yes, that's him. Why did he become so obsessed with killing Indians? He sounds crazy."

"Well, I think he became so. His father was one of the first to build a cabin in these mountains. Naturally, he had to get along with the Indians. So he had been nice to them. All the Quick boys were. They learned the Indian's ways and language. They helped the Indians and the Indians helped them, as if they was friends. But after the Walking Purchase when the local Indians were swindled out of their hunting grounds, they suddenly turned on him, the father that is, being as he was the first white man to invade their country.

"They killed the father, took his scalp and some silver buckles that caught their fancy and left his body in the field. Tom junior and his brother could see this going on but they were on the Jersey side of the river and powerless to get there in time to save their father. Tom decided then and there to get revenge on these people he had considered as friends. He swore to kill as many of the local tribe as he could, even a hundred if possible."

Dan was reminded, "I was brought up by the Onondagas from when I was very young. Even as far away as the Mohawk Valley, the story of Tom Quick was known I never did hear how many victims he claimed, nor do I know if he's still alive. I should think that one of them would have gotten him by now."

"I don't know for sure. Old Tom was pretty crafty. It's said that he claimed ninety-nine victims."

Dan hushed us all. "Did I just hear something out there? I think it was something on the left. Let's be quiet."

Sam growled, but softly as if she understood Dan's warning.

Crispin whispered, “Let me go out there. I think I know where the sound came from.”

“Even if you do, chances of catching him are unlikely. Best to not have any extra footprints messing up the landscape. We’ll be able to know more in the morning. Let’s resume our conversation, let the fire die down, and then retire for the evening, as if nothing happened. I don’t know about you folks, but I’m tired and want to get up early tomorrow. How about it?”

In the next few days answers came in quick succession.

# chapter 34

THE NEXT MORNING cold air had slid down the side of the mountain and engulfed our camp. We all threw off our blankets and got into warm clothes quickly. The sun had not risen enough to challenge the chill. Joe broke the quiet.

"I'll go over to Van Campen's with you. I'd like to find out what's going on," he said.

"Don't anyone move away from the camp yet. I want to examine any foot prints or tell-tale signs of our visitor last night," Dan directed.

We spread out to look for sign among the grass and weeds. I saw nothing except myriads of wild strawberries with which I soon filled a cup for breakfast. "Anyone for strawberries?" I called. Crispin came over, accepted some, and went off picking for himself.

"You're supposed to be looking for sign," said Dan. "Spread out farther and look for broken stems or bruised leaves. Notice prints of moccasins, shoes, or boots or anything which could give us a clue of who were looking for. You can pick strawberries later."

Crispen called us over to his piece of ground. "Be careful, don't mess up the footprints. Looks like regular boot soles, to me." Dan bent down to inspect the dew-laden soil closely. "Looks like new boots, there's so little wear. Can you read it, Olivia? Of course its backward."

"It must be *London* where these came from. I can just make out, *nodnoL*. Doesn't tell us much," said Olivia.

"No, but the indentation suggests someone literally well-healed and from the city. It's not likely a country boy. Joe, have you seen prints like this before?" Joe shook his head. "They might be made by shoes owned by that fellow who said he grew up in London," he added.

Before making the short trek to Walpack Center, Dan wanted to find out if the chestnut mare had the speed and stamina suggested by her sleakness. He gave her an apple before throwing a saddle on her. As soon as he mounted her, it was clear they were meant for each other, she was obedient and he was lenient. Dan spurred her into a trot before signaling he wished to go all out.

They quickly disappeared across the meadow. Dan whooped with joy and satisfaction with her speed and gait. He returned with glee. "She's fast and responsive. I might even win some races with her. Thanks for sparing me the time to find this out. We can load up and move out now."

We retrieved our wine bottles, filled and corked the empties with spring water, and packed up for our final arrival at Van Campen's. We moved through the gap in the eastern side of Kittatinny Mountain marveling at the immense height and diameter of specimens of oak, ash, chestnut, elm and maple growing from the shady ferns. Massive hemlocks grew in the deeper confines of the ravine.

Joe was right—the shade made by the impenetrable canopy gave the impression that the sun had not risen though, in fact, it was midday under the dark hemlocks. It was as quiet and serene as a church yard except for the trickle of the rivulet.. Occasionally, when we neared the brook, a field of winter wheat opened the sky to us. Mostly it was dark until we arrived at the fields of Van Campen's plantation. Crispen said that it reminded him of the greenwood. Indeed, it would have been impossible for the scene not to remind him of our former sylvan utopia..

Joe offered us the house to stay, especially as we had "a lady" with us. Even though this was a camping adventure and we wanted to sleep under the stars, we took advantage of his hospitality and stayed in this substantial frontier home.. The stone house had a conventional center hall with two large rooms upstairs and down as any prosperous Dutch burgher would have enjoyed in a settled community such as Bergen or even New York

The crude cabin known as Fort Shappannack was only a few hundred yards down the road. It had been built twenty years ago during the French war. Though it was called headquarters, it was just a frontier outpost built in blockhouse fashion with the second story overhanging the first. The log walls were cut with loopholes to give the defendants a field of fire.

A shallow moat had been dug less than a hundred feet surrounding the place, and all trees and shrubs had been cut providing an open field with no possible cover for attackers. The vegetation had grown back but in no sense did we rate the run-down cabin as a place of defense.

We surmised from pack baskets by the door that this was where the others Joe mentioned were lodging. The stone house was where we parked our stuff and after we fed the horses, we ate a simple meal. Then Crispin, Olivia, and I went upstream to Haney's mill to try long-awaited casting in the large pool backed up by the mill dam.

Snow melt and recent rains glutted the brook and the pool was roiling, but clear. Just so, a hatch of may flies was lifting from the lucid ripples. Crispin and I cast from opposite sides of the pool just below the overshot wheel which was not in operation. Olivia ensconced on a mossy bank to study our techniques which entertained her more than providing exemplary instruction.

Trevor and Dan went downstream. We could see them casting and, at first, they looked professional. But closer inspection revealed dexterity only in recovering from hang-ups and snags but not in bringing in trout.

Despite our piscatorial ineptnesss, I enjoyed the natural setting, so much did it resemble our beloved greenwood. Honey locust trees were in bloom, pulsing their lustful perfume. They were a full ten days behind those blooming in Philadelphia though we were only a hundred miles north of the city. The dew of the previous evening had enlivened the lichens from grey to efflorescent green on the numerous boulders strewn randomly on the wild landscape. Meadow rue and lupine, jack-in-the-pulpit and bunchberry were competing with each other and myriad ferns on the verge of the faint trace of a path. Close attention rewarded one with a handful of wild strawberries.

God hope that this bower is not endangered by greed, war, or legions of humanity come to overrun and stamp it out.

I finally realized that I was standing too close to the stream and scaring the fish as were my clumsy casts. Brush along the stream was scarce here so there was plenty of room to step back and make my offerings unhampered by errant backcasts. Crispin reinforced my decision; he began to play a trout ten feet back from his side of the pool. He took his time deftly managing the unseen but definite force at the end of the line. It was a pleasure watching him exercise his skill in anticipating the trout's thrusts.

"My first trout from Flatbrook!" Crispin called across to me. "I'm going to let him go, he put up such a game fight."

Over the rush of the stream Trevor and Dan heard Crispin's triumphant call and looked up in time to see him return the fish to its transparent element. They became more determined

The water surging in the pool was so clear and mostly free of sun glare that it was easy to see trout rising to the hatch and turning for submerged food even back from the stream's edge. I tried a cast upstream and set the fly gently on the surface amidst emrging mayflies. Swiftly this brought about a strike so firm, that I almost lost the rod.

That would never do. The last fish I hooked had been the otter-like creature that had got away and led me to the gold ingot on the stream bottom fixed in the roots of the old sycamore. Now, I recovered from the strong surprise and kept a taut line, but not so taut as to tear the hook out of the trout's delicate mouth. I gentled him in by letting him go where he wished, but played it to it's exhaustion. I called Crispin triumphantly as I released the catch back into the cool waters.

Every cast after that elicited a strike. By tacit agreement neither of us kept any fish. They were so plentiful and trusting of our lures that we assumed the conceit that we need not lay away a supply for dinner; we could catch trout on demand. Of course, that proved to be faulty and unrealistic. Within minutes the show ceased—as inexplicably as it began.

We continued to search the stream for hungry trout, but they were satiated and it was hopeless to raise their interest. After rounding up Olivia who had become interested in the wild plants springing up among the ferns, we returned to Shappanack. Our ranger friend Joe was there with the Van Campen help, Dick and Pegg, who were adolescent Indians.

They had been trimming the gnarled roots of a small plant they called shang. They said it helped restore strength and good health to the tired and sick. It was most sought after for it was also thought to reinvigorate old men to that state enjoyed when they were romantic youths.

They offered us a tea made of the fine root shavings. The more they talked, the more Olivia thought she had heard of it—it's full name was ginseng, she said.

The boys were digging it for the market in New York City which they said returned as much as six months work in the fields from less than a week of searching for and extracting the plant from the shaded and usually rocky soil. The peak harvest did not come until the white ash trees began to shed their leaves. They worked continuously, especially since someone had filched their basket yesterday. They thought it was one of the horse buyers.

I spat out the first sip, the tea was unpleasantly bitter, but they assured us that the refreshment was worth the astringent taste. Secrecy of their find was important otherwise its presence would draw large numbers from miles around and ruin the market for them. If their find became known, all they could do to protect it was to mention the large number of rattlesnakes and copperheads in the locality. But the plant was hard to find, especially in the spring when it became indistinguishable from other new growth.

The next morning Olivia said that she wanted to go searching for plants, not just ginseng. I felt so refreshed by either the good sleep or the shang and I wanted to encourage her to accompany me on similar expeditions that I agreed. The others went fishing as I expected.

Pegg showed us how to identify the frail stems and how to dig them so as to not mangle the roots which would destroy much of their value. The shang stems were elusive and it was easy to confuse them with other plants until Pegg set us straight. Those with the most fronds were the most valuable. Once the first plant was located, careful examination often revealed other shang close by

We didn't see any copperheads or rattlesnakes, just a few harmless garter snakes. But a careful probe with a spade was supposed to scare the poisonous varieties away. I'm sorry that this was not true of poison ivy which infested the area. Before she left to join Dick, Pegg showed us some impatiens plants, the juice of which when rubbed on inflamed skin, soothed the itch.

All afternoon Sam gleefully ran through the under-story so as to bruise every poison ivy vine. We didn't realize this until it was too late for we had complimented Sam and petted her after her every sortie.. We spent much of our time rubbing our hands with impatiens and still hadn't completely stemmed the ivy's curse. We ignored Sam for the rest of the day.

Later the wind shifted, and we could now hear the sound of splashing water which turned out to be a waterfall. It was a three-foot wide rivulet splashing from boulders to fall free from a twenty-foot precipice into a trumpet-shaped splash pool. Immediately brought to mind were the small falls sheltered in the Wye River Valley where no more than eight months ago Ancie and I cavorted and came dangerously near to spoiling a future.

Olivia and I rested by this charming glen. I listened politely but half-heartedly to her comments on the surrounding flora and shuddered to think of what misery could have come to pass had Ancie and I not exercised at least a little restraint during those trystings.

Olivia sensed my distraction but, of course, I could not reveal what had passed through my mind. As darkness settled on the woods, we went back to Van Campen's to prepare for dinner.

Joe came to the campfire waving a paper in his hand. "I can't wait to read this to you folks—it's from Mr. Van Campen in Burlington," he said and sat down so as to get the last rays of the sun to illuminate the letter. He began to read:

"Dear Joe and our house guests,

> Congress has finally gotten around to a discussion, which has turned into an argument, about separation from the mother country! We are not supposed to reveal our deliberations to

the outside world but by the time this gets to you, every one will know about it anyway. I think every table at the City Tavern has been discussing the wisdom of independence since Mr. Paine's Common Sense came out last winter. More recently, to show its independence, the colony of Rhode Island announced that it had become the "State of Rhode Island and Providence Plantations" by act of their General Assembly.

A few cases of yellow fever have broken out already. The natives say it is early this year because of the hot weather. Farmers are worried that the British may attack Philadelphia. Their fears were reinforced when two British warships were sighted at the mouth of Christiana Creek, near Wilmington. They, the Brits, were ganged up on by thirteen Pennsylvania war galleys and were forced to withdraw down the river

The farmers have been moving their livestock farther from the Chesapeake and the Delaware just in case. I trust that our cattle and horses are safely out of reach. Please ask Pegg and Dick to roundup..."

"The rest is just some business around here that he wants me to tend to. It looks like we'll be fighting soon."

We had something like fifteen pounds of shang roots which would have been an incumbrance. We turned the lot over to Pegg and Dick who had come by just as the sun was setting. They were grateful and rendered us a service later which saved us from serious trouble.

"The ginseng looks a lot like poison ivy to the uninitiated. Do you ever make any mistakes? I guess you'd pay heavily for it if you do," I said.

"We been digging it for years. Never make a mistake. Sometimes make a mistake on purpose. To pay somebody back. They never do it again." With that obscure statement, they thanked us again and receded into the darkness.

Ranger Joe Also had a creel full of speckled trout which provided dinner with wild onions and radishes. We kept throwing sticks into the brook for Sam to fetch in hopes that the poison ivy poison juice would wash off her coat. After many drenchings Sam came clean..

Crispin spoke up. "Speaking of sticks, we were planning to introduce you to a snipe hunt when conditions seemed just right. It being cool and getting dark, we may as well proceed."

"What do sticks have to do with a snipe hunt?" asked Olivia.

"They are the essential element, that and being able to make a call as similar to that of a snipe as possible. Oh, and having a gunny sack to catch the bird in," Crispin said.

Trevor Shaw joined in. "There used to be a market for snipe, they're such a delicious bird. Back in the sixties, I sold several hundred birds a week. But they were over-hunted and one hardly ever hears of them nowadays."

I took the bait. "Then why bother hunting them? There are plenty of other wild fowl such as grouse, partridge, quail, ducks, geese. Not to mention deer, bear, turkey, and rabbits."

"One reason, Jamie, is that you can catch them in the dark. And if you know how to simulate the mating call, they come to you," Dan added."Not many can say they ever caught one." Crispin snickered but Trevor hushed him.

"What does a snipe look like? I've heard of them in the Wye Valley, but never saw any."

Trevor thought for a minute, "They are about the size and shape as a seagull but they have a longer bill and more brown feathers than white."

"How come you have all seen them, but I haven't? And why do you care if we go snipe hunting? It sounds like you're pulling my leg," I said.

Nobody said anything until Crispin relented, "Alright. Forget it. We just thought that, being new in the colonies, you might like to try it. Trevor taught me and I thought it was a lot of fun."

Crispin was almost desperate to have me engage in a snipe hunt. When I finally agreed and he had five gunny sacks, sticks, and small lanterns at the ready, there was no question that that was the plan of everybody from the start.

Olivia looked at Crispin and then at me, "Are you boys really going to play at this child's game?" I felt silly but I had relented so I could not disappoint them. And I was curious as to how far they would expect the hunt to go, and what part each would play.

Crispin had me go through the awkward motions of hoisting the empty sack and beating the sticks together like a drummer without a drum. Then he said, "Stop and listen for a response—so you know if a snipe has heard you and is coming your way."

I stopped and listened. Nothing. "Keep beating," Crispin insisted, and I did, this time accompanied by Trevor, Dan, and Crispin. I stopped. So did they. I thought I heard a squawk ahead and saw some movement in the almost dark night. Olivia laughed but was squelched.

I told her it was her turn next but she did not answer—nor did I expect her to.

Hulking bodies sounded to the side and behind me though I could no longer identify them. A quick shuffling in the bushes seemed that it might be a bona fide capture of a snipe but ended in confusion and the sound of someone running.

I called out for Olivia—no answer. A light briefly glowed by Fort Shanppanack. A door slammed. I might as well have been in a closet crowded with people who could not speak.

I yelled to Crispin, " Where's Olivia? Is she with you?" He yelled back, "Something hit me." After I called for Olivia, so did Trevor and Crispin. Dan was up ahead, thrashing through the brush and calling for Olivia.

We looked half the night. There was no sign of her—no note, shred of clothing, or other indication as to what had happened. Finally we all went to bed, but I couldn't sleep for worrying what had happened to her. Episodes of violence to Olivia kept recurring in my mind, or was I dreaming, and I had no rest to see me through the following day because of the nightmares.

Early the next morning there was scratching at the door. It was Sam. When I opened the door, she came in but went right out again and looked back to see if I would follow. She went to the field where we had conducted the snipe hunt and then up the Old Mine Road to the knoll where old Fort Shappanack was. Sam whined a few times and circled the ramshackle cabin.

I thought that this definitive trail would lead us to a useful clue. A young unkempt man, by way of introduction, threw an old boot at Sam from inside the cabin. Thank god Olivia had not been held captive among this reeking refuse. In contrast to the dinginess of the place, someone had left a sprig of ginseng. Was this a sign that Olivia had been here? We decided it was.

Impatiently, Sam whined again and I gladly rushed from the festering flies to follow Sam south down the old road. I soon encountered Pegg and Dick on the side of the road, presumably looking for more ginseng, and asked if they had seen Miss Olivia. "She came by earlier, Mister Jamie, with Mister Cyrus. She seemed sick and he was helping her along."

"Where were they going?"I pleaded.

"Maybe they were going to the mine. There ain't nothing else down that way," said Pegg.

"How far is it? Is there a house there?"

"It's about five miles. There's a small rest cabin there for shelter from the rain."

"Who is Cyrus? Does he work for Mr. Van Campen?" I knew only one Cyrus and I didn't expect him to be in the mountains.

"No, he just came here with the horse buyers about a month ago."

What could this Cyrus fellow have to do with Olivia, I wondered. Was she hurt? This couldn't be the same Cyrus who keeps cropping up with Mochter, could it? I continued to follow Sam. After a while I began to wonder if Crispin had something to do with Olivia's absence. His much-desired snipe hunt coincided with her disappearance. It would upset me and add to the joke laid on me with the snipe hunt. But no, the others wouldn't let the joke go that far or serious. Crispin had been a good friend going back to early childhood. He wouldn't perpetrate such a horrid act on me, not even as a joke.

I sat down on a boulder to rest. In a few minutes, I noticed that Crispin had been following and checking the undergrowth on the other side of the road. I resumed the hunt.

Together we covered several acres but detected no footprints, scrap of clothing, or any other clue. We sought the help of Dan and Trevor; surely they had seen her.

The four of us fanned out along the valley, searching out paths that occasionally intersected but they led to nothing. Then the road turned away from the river and behind a hill to a flat plain that stretched at least a mile in which grazed thousands of horses. To the near side were several sheds made of freshly-sawn wood. The only visible sign of human activity was smoke from the smoke stack of the nearest shed. I proceeded with caution.

Olivia was inside resting on a cot near the stove in the jacket she had been wearing during the snipe hunt. I put my finger to my mouth to signal her to make no sound and crossed the room to inspect her bindings. Her hands were swollen and rough as was her brow. "Are you alright? How long have you been here? Have you been mistreated?" I whispered. She answered softly, "I've been here only since sunrise; they haven't mistreated me. What you see is the result of the poisin ivy."

"Oh. Who is they?"

"Just one person, a young man about eighteen or twenty. He seemed harmless and was only doing what someone had told him. He had on a British army uniform. I'm alright."

I offered her some Johnny cake which she wolfed down having not eaten since last night.

She was unharmed, but frightened and was chained to an iron ring bolted to a sturdy wallplank. I had nothing I could use as a wrench but there was a box of horseshoes in which lay a pair of farrier's pliers. The hardware was new so the bolt turned in the nut, but the chain was still attached to Olivia's wrist and was heavy and abrading her skin. Her hands were badly chafed.

The shed was windowless. It was claustrophobic and it was not possible to see if anyone was nearby or coming to arrest our escape attempt except by leaving the door open which would announce my presence. Fortunately, a knot had shrunk and loosened in the plank wall next to the stove. A light push and the knot fell away giving us some view outside. I told Olivia to keep her eye at the hole and to tell me of any activity nearby while I tried to free her from the chain.

I was able to find a farrier's course file and nippers. I began to file the chain but each stroke seemed outrageously loud. I stopped, fearful that somebody could hear. After a minute she signaled me to resume filing. I stopped several times in the hope that the link was thin enough for the nippers to quietly cut through. Finally it did but the heavy chain fell to the work bench making a racket like drum taps on a sounding board. Olivia signaled violently and all went quiet.

The door of the shed was opened and there appeared Cyrus, my breakfast benefactor and survivor of the shark five months ago. His hands were blistered and he continually scratched them.

"Why Mr. Claveraque, Mr. Mochter said that we would probably be seeing you! Congratulations on having such a lovely lady," Cyrus beamed.

I was flabbergasted. So capturing my wife was for the purpose of baiting a trap to catch me. "But how did you know that we would be here?" I said.

"We didn't. We came up here to acquire as many horses as we could for General Howe's New York campaign. Horses have a terrible survival rate crossing the Atlantic. They take up too much space aboard ship—they and their forage—and many suffer broken legs during storms causing the need to discard them overboard. So Mochter was certain there would be a handsome market to sell them to the British army when it arrives with a deficit of horses. Why are you here?"

"We *were* here to enjoy the country. We had no concern where you would go after you left Philadelphia. But why should Mochter want to catch me? I can do him no harm or good."

"You'll have to convince him of that. He plans to see you at dinner tonight. I'm here merely to entertain you till then. Maybe you can tell me of select estates for me to claim when we have defeated your army."

"I can think of one at Simsbury, Connecticut, that you could occupy, Cyrus."

It's just as well that he didn't understand that I was referring to Simsbury Mines. But he chained me to the stove and tied Olivia's hands. He left me alone in the shed and put a lock on the clasp before removing Olivia to another shed nearby. Though I couldn't see him do this I heard the shed door squeak as it opened and closed.

When one of one's senses is diminished it's true that other senses are intensified. I like the smell of wood shavings and sawdust, but the smell of fresh-sawn hemlock can sometimes smell like rotten garbage and I was becoming overwhelmed by it. Claustrophobia also set in. My hearing must have become more acute, also, when my vision became limited.

There were several other knots in the hemlock wall planks that might be pushed out for wider observation—one on the side facing Olivia's shed and others on the side facing the road. The boards had shrunk and the knots were loose enough to be pushed open. To alert Crispin and the others, I removed a brilliant red sock that they had ridiculed me for wearing and crammed it in the knot hole in hopes that it would draw their attention.

Time passed slowly waiting for my friends to come by but I managed to disengaged myself from the eye bolt and the chain. The chain was long enough to serve as a weapon to do severe damage to anyone opposing me. So too, the horseshoes were a supply of missiles to hurl. I squinted through the several knotholes to spot either my friends or jailors.

Soon, I heard the tread of someone approaching and moved to the nearest knothole. There was Crispin, just outside about to pull the sock away, and Trevor with a rifle at the ready.

"Is that you, Jamie, it looks like your sock," he said. What a relief it was to hear his voice! "Yes. Please get me out of here. Olivia is in the next shed. Keep low and keep quiet. My jailor is not that far away."

"We'll have to shoot the lock off," said Trevor.

"No, no. We don't want to alert our jailor. I have a file in here. I'll pass it out under the wall on your side. It should cut through quickly. But hurry. And no shooting. We only wish to leave here with Olivia safe and unharmed."

Within two minutes Trevor had the door open and was inside filing the chain securing me to the stove. Crispin had gone to the other shed and was talking in subdued tones to Olivia. "What happened to your hands? We'll get you out of here in a jiffy," I heard him say.

My friends worked fast and the cool outside air energized me. I could see something going on at the far side of this large pasture. Dan had anticipated trouble and was rounding up horses for our escape. He seemed ready, even eager, to use his new rifle for more than target shooting.

We had no idea how many men Mochter had gathered to help him amass and manage what must be over a thousand horses. A shot ringing out over the landscape could bring his men to Mochter's assistance in a short time. I hoped that firearms would not be used but Dan may not have a choice and we should know the enemy's strength soon. Dust clouds from several points of the pasture told of horsemen coming our way. We watched closely and happily verified that there were only four to contend with. At least at the moment.

Dan shouted, "Everybody mount up!" At the same time, he raised his rifle.

"Don't shoot, Dan. They may only want to parley," I yelled.

"I won't shoot yet, but firing this gun will likely cause their herd to stampede. The confusion will give us time to get away. They won't relish having to round up strays all over the countryside. Trevor, don't fire your piece. One shot should be enough to scatter their horses. We'll need to keep your fire as a reserve should it become necessary.

When Dan saw that Olivia and I were mounted, he fired a shot in the air and spurred his horse towards the herd of crowded, confused animals and the four horsemen charging our way. Having started the stampede, he waved us to follow him to the margin of the field where thick groves of rhododendron grew amidst scattered pines.

At the first trail in the scrub we turned off and followed Dan in a single file. As we entered, I turned for a last look at our situation on our hastily acquired mounts running fom Mochter's men hot on our tail. As I turned forward, Dan was busy reloading his rifle as he walked his mount along the narrow path.

The trail was a footpath only, too narrow to negotiate on horseback faster than a walk. Even so, the heavy waxy leaves constantly beat against us leaving bugs and spider webs plastered on our faces. Occasional branches snagged our equipment so that we had to back up to free ourselves and allow the offending branch to return to its natural position without swatting those behind.

We had gone about a mile through this tangle when we intercepted Flatbrook with a sense of relief. After resting the horses and ourselves we cautiously went upstream where we had left our gear. We decided to abort this fishing expedition which had become a nightmare.

# chapter 35

OLIVIA WAS UNHARMED and no one else was injured. When we reached Van Campen's house, we were shocked to find Mochter and four of his hands already there. We should have known that he would have expected our return here. His hands and face were red and blistered..

"I was expecting you for dinner and you didn't disappoint me," he gloated. "I'm happy to meet and entertain your friends," he added.

I felt that I had to say something, "I can pay for it with some of your phony pound notes."

Mochter ignored this and smiled as if he were among dear old friends. "I have a haunch of some field-dressed venison as well as some dry Riesling. Please allow Cyrus to serve as much as suits your fancies," he declared.

Compared to Mochter's usual acidic comments, this was uncommonly kind, especially at the end of this long day. It began the previous night with an innocent snipe hunt and evolved into a second captivity though more civil this time. My friends were determined to make the most of Mochter's rare attempt at generosity. They concentrated on savoring his offerings, or, more likely, what was really from Van Campen's cellar. But we were just buying time for an opportunity to flee. The venison and wine were equal to that served by the finest New York hostelries. Conversation suffered however much as Mochter wished to be considered a gracious and interesting host.

"I trust that Cyrus treated Olivia with respect during her enforced session as our house guest," he said as he glanced in Olivia's direction.

"As much as his abilities and employment allowed, I'm sure," she shot back.

"If he caused you any injury or discomfort, he shall pay for it."

"Why did you think it necessary to take me prisoner, or was I your guest, however involuntary" she asked.

"I had no intention of taking you prisoner, a harsh term for you to call it. I merely wished to question Jamie on why he is following me across the Atlantic to New York, Philadelphia, and finally to even Walpack Center, of all places. After all, he did cause me injury in Herefordshire, but denied it, and then made an adventure of following me to the American colonies."

"You accused me of stealing something from your property but I acquired it before you bought the property. Then you sold that beautiful section of land and water to the army whom you knew full well would trash it worse than if they trashed it by artillery barrage. You also made it possible to cozen your neighbors out of their homes, held by families for generations, by tempting them to borrow more than you knew they could afford to pay back.

"But that had nothing to do with our crossing the ocean. My uncle, who owns a plantation in New Jersey invited me to a tour of the colonies. Despite the imminent conflict, Olivia and I decided to accept such a rare opportunity. It is we who suspect you of hounding us. Wherever we went you were there making mischief."

Mochter had paid careful attention and his eyebrows lifted and his mouth turned down in a scowl. "Yes, someone accused me of counterfeiting US currency because a signature was signed with green ink, rather than black, and violated the terms of the printing contract.. It turned out that both my clerk and I are slightly color blind and neither of us could distinguish the difference. Things are not always what they seem, Jamie."

I ignored this as a distraction. "I was baffled by information that you sold a shipload of gunpowder to Washington rather than to the British. Is that true?"

"The ship was consigned to the British army, but General Howe had evacuated Boston by the time we arrived off that coast. We could have either been overcome by American privateers or sold the cargo to Washington who was desperate for ammunition. As a businessman, I preferred to sell it for cash to a ready buyer. But I gather that you thought that I was a British agent? You should know that I am accumulating all these horses to sell to Washington."

"You do surprise me.. You are close friends with high officers in the ministry, maybe even the king and those who, from the start, insisted on provoking a contest with the Americans. Yet you favored doing business with the Americans as a matter of convenience not to mention profit.

"Lords North and Germaine, Lord Mansfield, Dartmouth, and Sandwich, all would have you strung up if they knew, or even suspected, you of such acts."

"These men are not close friends. I am on a speaking basis with them, but only enough to recommend such as your wife's landscaping service to them. Speaking of friends., I know Trevor Shaw but I do not know these other gentlemen—the one in deerskins and the one with a beard."

I introduced Dan but as I was about to introduce Crispin, I found that he had ducked out.

Mochter ignored this, saying "You might say that Mr. Shaw and I are in similar businesses only he sells standard merchandise like shovels and staples from his store while I have no store and sell information. We both sell to patriots and Loyalists alike, but we are not accused of spying.

"What happened to your other friend? Oh well, he can't get far. Cyrus, I need you."

Cyrus was in the next room, eager to answer the call of his master. He appeared instantly with a pistol at the ready. "What do you want me to do, Mr. Mochter? He can't be far."

As if in answer, ominous thunder echoed along the Kittatinny ridge, our first sign that the weather was turning foul. The morning dryness had quickly been replaced by moist air from the southwest and dark, formidable clouds appeared on the horizon.

Mochter's train of thought had been thrown off by Crispin's sudden flight and the change in the weather. He seemed frightened and panicky.

"Get Clyde to help you. Also Bob at the sawmill and as many wranglers not rounding up horses. We can't let Claveraque or any of his friends get away."

This alerted us. As one we rose from our chairs, threw over the table and rushed out of the house making as much confusion as possible. Mochter's crew had contemptuously thrown our gear from the house. We salvaged it on the run as best we could, miraculously including our rifles and side arms which still hung from our saddles.

"Make towards the sawmill, " called Dan and we clattered off to the mill which we could hear laboriously slicing timber over the splash of the waterwheel. "At least three of them will be at the mill where we can keep an eye on them," Dan said."We'll figure out what to do once we know what we're up against. I think Crispin may head there, too. It's the only other building to get out of the weather and to use as a fort. Besides, Mochter has chosen to center his men there. I think the fourth man may be the ranger we met when we first arrived here. I doubt he'll side with Mochter."

We rode the quarter mile to the mill amidst pouring rain and frightening, continuous lightning and thunder, like tympanists gone amuck. It had turned cool and dark as twilight.

"Over here!" Crispin whispered. He had thrown the handle disengaging the saw blades from the waterwheel gear to avoid an accident and trussed up the sawyer to a post. We thought we would only have four, including Mochter, opposing the five of us, including Olivia.

The mill was protected by the bend of the stream on two sides, with the other two sides open about a hundred yards with a good field of view. It was sturdily built with hefty post and beam construction, mostly white oak, and sided with inch-thick hemlock planks.

We unloaded our gear and Dan carefully dumped the contents of a large canvas sack on the floor. Iron balls, the size of apples with spikes on them, clattered out.

"Quickly," he said, "scatter these on the ground fifty yards out. They'll discourage any surprise attack. They're called caltrops. You can see that they always lie with a spike facing up to pierce a trespasser's foot. But first, leave a narrow corridor free of them so we know where to step safely. And don't forget to remember where the safe path is."

We spread the wicked-looking objects and devotedly hoped for their effectiveness.

I turned to Crispin. "Did your prisoner give you any trouble?"

"No. I just wanted to keep him out of harm's way to avoid his making any mischief."

"Is your name Bob? Do you work for Mochter?"I said to the prisoner.

"Yes, I'm Bob. I really work for Mr. Van Campen until Mochter took over and put all of us to work for him, under protest."

"Does he pay you?"

"He forced us to work but hasn't paid us yet after more than a month. But where else can we go up here? We have no real choice."

"How long does he plan to stay here? Mr. Van Campen will probably return soon."

"Mochter plans to drive the horses to Staten Island when he knows that the British have arrived at New York."

"So he does plan to sell the horses to General Howe?"

"Oh yes, He says he'll be able to pay us all handsomely then. But he's been such a bastard nobody believes him."

"How many people did Mochter bring with him and are they armed?"

"I think only about a half dozen. They're toughs, lay-abouts mostly, some deserters from the loyalist's in Westchester County north of the city. Those last call themselves cowboys. They do have arms, but haven't used them except to round up the herd and shoot some game."

Crispin started untying Bob. "We came up here just to fish for a few days and have a good time but we ran into Mochter whom we have known long enough to know that he has no scruples. We don't want these horses to be lost to American forces and even less to have them fall into the hands of General Howe. We would like to divert the herd to General Washington and his troops and that's when you will get paid. Will you be willing to oppose Mochter and help us attain that?"

Bob jumped at the prospect. "Most, if not all, of us are anxious to escape from Mochter. All we need is some money to get started. I think Cyrus will stay with him. He thinks Mochter will give him an estate, like Van Campen's, when the horses are delivered."

"We can handle Cyrus," I asserted. "Get a message to your pals so we can assure them of no bloodshed and of escape from Mochter. We'll work out a plan…watch out for the caltrops."

Dan drew a sketch showing the layout of the mill protected by the bend of the stream and the open field to the south covered with brambles and witch hobble.. He explained his plan to us. "Our upstream side is vulnerable. Someone could come downstream either wading or in a small boat and we wouldn't know it. We need something to alert us to that eventuality."

Crispin found some twine and some sleigh bells. He tied the string to trees on both sides of the stream and waded the stream to fasten the bells in the middle. "When that rings, we'll know it."

Pleased with this, Dan turned to Olivia. "Olivia, how good is your night vision/"

"I could spot someone coming down stream. But I'd be reluctant to shoot him," she said.

"What if they took a shot at you?"

"That would be a different story." she said firmly.

"Good. I'll post you here. If you hear firing, stay here unless we call for you. All right?"

We all settled down to await an attack. The woods were at peace and the mill pond was dimpled. The trout were active. Shortly the dimples stopped—something had spooked them.

Complete darkness came on quickly without any afterglow in the western sky. The somnolent night whisper was shattered by shrieks shattering the mountain fastness. Our caltrops had begun to do their work. Creatures of all kinds knew the significance of that awful cry and the woods became intensely quiet after our besiegers retreated to lick their wounds. This brief activity revealed as many as ten men getting ready to rush us.

Crispin then whispered, "Look, two people are coming with a white flag to parley."

"Hold your fire," I called to our group. The two were Dick and Pegg.

"We heard the commotion and realized that you were being attacked by Mochter's men. We want to help." These boys couldn't be any older than twelve.

"This isn't your fight. Why do you want to help?" I asked.

"Those two soldiers, the ones in uniform, are bullies. They have been ordering us around for several days. Yesterday they stole our ginseng. We want to get back at 'em."

"That's very nice of you. Can you fire a gun?"

"No," said Pegg. But we can load for you. It'll increase your firepower. We know others who would like to take a shot at Mochter and his gang. We can probably get half a dozen Indians who would love to fire at white men. They figure they do not have many chances to do this legally. Shall we get them? They're nearby and armed."

I explained our position and where the enemy was.

"We know, Mister Jamie. There are more than you may think. Some of the men who went to round up the horses are back now and Mochter has bullied them to join him and Cyrus to fight you. We couldn't let this happen. They're waiting until daylight to attack again."

"We need any assistance we can get. Sure, tell them we appreciate they're help. Tell them where we scattered some spiked iron balls. Send them in and we'll tell them where we need them."

They relished this chance for revenge and ran off to bring their friends to our relief.

For the second time in two months I was going to be engaged in a fight that could be fatal for me, Olivia, and my friends. Back on the Schuylkill when I was alone, events happened so fast that I was able to fight back spontaneously as I was not even thinking of fighting in anger, but just to survive. And that was all over in less than fifteen minutes.

Now I have the time and anger to think about the coming danger not only to myself but to dear friends and to become fearful. But with the spirit and assistance of the others, fright can be laid aside in favor of planning our strategy. Dick and Pegg's help and any Indians they recruit for us lessened my concern.

We waited in silence for Mochter to attack us in the mill house. Sounds ordinarily ignored gained our attention: water splashing over the mill dam, the slow rumble of the water wheel turning in the current, wind shimmering the new leaves on the trees, and occasionally, one of the enemy shouting a challenge to muster his courage and that of his fellows. We were primed like hair-triggers for the faintest sign of movement.

"Ho, Mister Jamie!" a voice whispered and we jumped.

"No, It's Pegg with some friends. Dick will be here soon with some others. He has a plan he thinks will work." Pegg quickly announced.

They came in quietly and suggested a pow-wow. Two Stars was the tallest and stood more erect in the manner of one who is used to commanding others. He could have passed for white, his coloring was so light in the dusk, but there was no doubt that he was a warrior of the Lenni-Lenape. His hair was shiny black and in two braids down to his shoulders. Two eagle wing feathers stood up, tucked into the hair bun on the back of his head, showing he had rank. His large curved nose and the feathers were his defining features.

The other six Indians listened as Two Stars gave his greeting and opinion.. "We are happy to be able to offer our warriors to your people who fight the kind of whites who have caused our tribe grief and misery for many years. My men have staid here in our father's hunting grounds to assert our ownership just as you opposed the king on the other side of the big water."

Dan shook Two Stars hand as he grasped his left elbow to signify firm friendship. "I am pleased to have the power of the mighty Minisink strengthen our forces and defeat these exploiters and thieves. We welcome your brave warriors to our defense."

With these formalities over, Two Stars and Dan began discussing strategy. Dan explained our position and showed him where we had sowed the caltrops. Two Stars wasted no time. "There are about twenty men led by two soldiers in uniform against you. They show no skill with arms or the military arts. Each of my men is an able warrior and a good shot.

"I will give you two men to strengthen your fire power here and will use the others and myself to surround your besiegers and pick them off as we can. If we can cut down the two men in uniform, their leaders, the others will probably abandon their assault and leave. Do you agree?"

Dan agreed. "It's a good plan that we can carry out only with your band's help. How do we avoid mistaking your men for theirs? We don't want to be shooting at you."

Two Stars smiled. "They know that they must keep out of sight of the mill as well as the enemy. We are not worried by this."

When Dan nodded, Two Stars signaled two braves, Red Turtle and Gray Eagle, to stay with us. With the other four he disappeared into the dark of the woods without a sound.

'Did you notice their old muskets?" Trevor whispered. "Too bad they don't have modern guns, and rifles instead of muskets"

Dan offered, "Don't worry about them. They move so deftly in the woods that they can get close to their targets without being detected. Most Indian victories are the result of ambushes."

No one spoke for several minutes after Two Stars left. Then I turned to Dan,"Even though your rifle is accurate for several hundred yards, do you think it wise to target one so far distant?"

If you have a good shot, word will get around and the enemy will keep out of range of not just your rifle but all of us. It would have the effect of disarming us—none of us would get a shot."

"Well, if they did that, they wouldn't get a shot at us for the same reason, so I don't think it will be a problem. But, I agree, we should let them get within range of all of us before we start firing. I might feel different though if I see a clear shot at one of the leaders even at a long distance. Taking down Mochter would probably end the whole shebang."

It had been a busy and exhausting day for all of us. We made sure all our rifles were loaded including the two that Dick and Pegg had added. Red Turtle and Gray Eagle announced that they would circle our position to make sure no one had scurried up close in the dark to blindside us.

I decided to go for a swim to wash off a week's grime before going on the first watch with Trevor Shaw. After arguing with the others who had tried to dissuade me, I crept down to the pool and slipped out of my clothes. The water was far colder than I had thought it would be and I almost changed my mind as I shivered while trying to firm my resolve. Determination won out. I slithered into the pool behind the dam and made as little disturbance as possible and kept behind some bushes to avoid becoming a target even at such a long range.

This was the first time I had gone swimming since that fateful tryst with Ancie last summer. I almost felt disloyal to Olivia even thinking about it. Thank God I broke that relationship. And just in time to meet Olivia at the Guy Fawkes dance. Fortune had certainly been with me. I was emboldened thinking of how many occasions luck had been with me.

I swam along the shore avoiding logs, boulders, and debris that had washed down-stream. I was not careful enough because, of all things, I bumped into the bloated carcass of a dog snagged on a log. It must have died recently for there was little smell. But the thought of being in the water with a dead animal was repulsive and I climbed out straight away with it's body in tow.

"Look what I bumped into in the pool," I said.

"Whose dog is it? Do you boys know?" asked Trevor.

"Let's get him over to some light," I suggested. Trevor lit a candle away from the window.

"It looks like Sam," I was sorry to say. But, on closer inspection, I saw that it was not Sam.

It was a medium-sized animal, about the same size and color as Sam, but a different breed, one that I was not familiar with. The idea of being refreshed by a swim had been swiftly dampened. Now, I was fully awakened and alert for whatever was to happen during my watch. Dan and Crispin turned in and Trevor and I stood watch along with Red Turtle and Gray Eagle who had returned from their circuit of the enemy's perimeter.

As the false dawn brought a soft grey light to the mountains Dick and Pegg woke.

"That dog belonged to the nice lady friend of Mister Cyrus." declared Pegg. "She lives in the caretaker's house. The dog looks like it was shot, probably earlier today, Mister Jamie. I hope the lady isn't in trouble."

Annie McLauren. I had forgotten all about her. Or was she still playing Betty Ann Button, who was Cyrus' "companion" and working for the patriot's intelligence agency.

Trevor knew who Cyrus' companion was but kept mum.She was supposed to rport to him but he had heard nothing since her report from Philadelphia. Obviously, she was still keeping an eye on Mochter. But Trevor revealed nothing about Annie McLauren and her dangerous orders. He was sworn to secrecy.

Crispin realized Pegg may have been talking about his new-found girl friend."Is he talking about Annie McLauren? Is she the lady in the caretaker's house? By God, they may have harmed her. I'd better go find out if she's alright." he said, and was about to rush off in the dark.

"Crispin, we need you here. It will be hard enough to hold off Mochter and his thugs even with you here. Don't leave us and don't take any of our guns," I yelled.

"My gun firing at them from the woods will be just as effective as if I fire it from here. And I may need it to free Annie." He ran off after snatching a small bore pistol and powder and ball.

Dan noted, "At least, if he fires that gun, we'll recognize the sound and know where he is."

We were all wide awake now—it didn't make any difference about who was supposed to be on watch. All was silent, no bird sang, cricket droned, or spring peeper serenaded to enchant the night. Clouds obscured the stars, nor was their any moon light. It was ominously dark and quiet.

After half an hour we heard a shot from the hill. "That's Crispin's pistol," said Dan.

"How do you know,?" asked Trevor.

"The small bore makes a higher pitch and it's not as loud."

"Well, we won't know what's happened to Crispin or his girlfriend until we thrash this out with the thugs and that won't be until dawn, most likely." Trevor said.

I questioned, "Why do men fight for another man they hardly know and where they could be killed or badly injured? They have nothing to gain and much to lose. It's not like they were defending a principal, home, family, business or farm.. Maybe some increase in pay. But, other than that, there is no sensible reason."

Dan was surprised at my query. "Half the men probably turned down the proposition to fight and walked away. The others either don't want to be considered cowards, or they enjoy the excitement of fighting. You're right, though, it's not a reasoned response."

"I hope they change their minds," I said.

The night dragged on and nothing happened. Then, since our eyes were accustomed to the dark, we could discern a haze of light on the eastern horizon—the false dawn. An owl hooted.

Fifteen minutes later it became noticeably light, I could make out Gray Eagles outline where he crouched. Birds began hesitantly to warble and another day began to unfold.

Then, one of the enemy yelled, "Let's get 'em boys" and a dozen shots shattered the morning tranquillity. I called to see if Olivia was alright, no answer. I left the mill house and crept the few feet to her station—she was washing her hair!.She towled her head and grabbed her musket. "What happened? Am I too late? Has someone come down the stream?" she queried.

"They're attacking us. Is your gun loaded? They probably won't come this way but keep an eye open. If they do, give me a call and I'll come out. I'll send Pegg out to reload for you. I have to get back." I returned to the mill and made sure my piece was loaded, too.

One of Mochter's men appeared barely obscured by the witch hobble. Trevor took a shot at him and missed. The man shot back at me, and missed. I leveled my gun on him and took careful aim, even planning to shoot through the bush where he was hiding. I got him in his shooting arm! He dropped his rifle and ran off yelling. That was the first time I ever shot a man. Thank God, I didn't kill him. I felt elated and guilty at the same time.

Another attacker became visible on the right, sheltered behind a large tulip tree. He took a shot at Dan, a hapless selection. He had the satisfaction of shattering the window frame where Dan was kneeling. Dan fired back and winged him out of the action.

A number a Mochter's men began to run for it. Three shots rang out from the their rear. Dan called out, "That must be Mochter firing at his men to turn and fight us. Let's keep up the pressure. This won't last much longer. We'll be having breakfast before the sun is an hour higher."

We heard Crispin's pistol fire again and then shots that Dan thought came from Two Stars and his men.

We had only fleeting glimpses of Cyrus or Mochter. They were in British army officer's uniforms, though I think neither qualified, waving pistols to threaten their men who were fleeing. The men ignored them knowing that they were being shot at by unseen men in the underbrush. The siege was close to being over and Mochter and Cyrus were probably with the retiring throng.

I suggested to the others that we leave the mill and attack the enemy. "We should fire a flurry of shots to let Two Stars and his men know we are closing in on Mochter." They agreed and checked their arms.

Olivia called, "I'm coming with you. I'm as ready as you are!"

"Let's go," I yelled to start us across the crest of the dam and surge across the bushy field. We all yelled blood-curdling threats to scare the demons of hell. The half dozen of the enemy beat away out of the woods. I saw none falter, but our goal was not to wound or kill but to make them abandon Mochter's attack. Olivia kept pace with me. Brave girl.

When Crispin left, I said a prayer as I watched him disappear in the bushes through the gray mist of dawn. He made his way, skirting the scattered caltrops, but picked one up which he placed in his ditty bag, probably for hand-to-hand fighting. He held the leather ditty bag at arm's length to prevent the sharp point from stabbing him.

As he entered the woods and we followed, we could see the witch hobble and brambles thinned out, reducing his cover. But he could move faster without the cloying branches obstructing his way. Dodging between boulders and ancient tree trunks was his main protection.

He had to pick his way carefully to avoid ground clutter and fallen branches which could slow his progress. Crispin spotted Two Stars who had intentionally made his presence known to avoid friendly fire. Two Stars signaled by hand for Crispin to move to the left and forward for a safer path. Only one of Mochter's men confronted him during the half-hour it took him to travel to the edge of the clearing by the housekeeper's cottage. He waved to the man and kept still, pretending to be one of Mochter's goons, and then side-stepped as if approaching the mill, before resuming his advance to the clearing.

Just after that was when we started firing in earnest. They fired back, one of them became visible and Crispin took a shot at him, wounding him in the shoulder. Within a minute, Crispin arrived at the edge of the clearing surrounding the old fort.

Lying in the open on the grass were the bodies of Mochter and Cyrus in their scarlet and white uniforms. Crispin thought the fight was over. With the leader and his lackey out of the action, there was no reason for his men to continue fighting, Crispin reasoned. But something was amiss, something Crispin could not identify. He hastened to cross the clearing along a line of large elms to the left. This enabled him to approach the housekeeper's cottage from the chimney side where there were no windows. He stopped and listened for conversation against the wall. It was deaf-dumb quiet.

He knelt down turning the corner to the front of the house Then he heard commotion from inside and looked up to an open window where a hand suddenly thrust a pistol pointing straight out.

He reached up and grabbed the pistol just as it was fired. The concussion visibly shook him and he suffered some mild powder burns to his hand. He jammed the spent pistol under his belt and took in hand his own gun before he thrust open the door and rushed in.

"Hands up," Crispin demanded. He was startled to see Mochter and Cyrus alive and well, standing by the fireplace. Mochter had made two of his men act as decoys, probably tried to make them feel rewarded by letting them wear his officer's uniforms, he thought. He saw that Mochter's hands were not only red, but severely blistered.

But Mochter's decoy plan backfired. When his men saw what they thought were Mochter's and Cyrus' dead bodies, they stopped fighting. Mochter was hoist by his own petard.

Mochter and Cyrus raised their hands in submission, and Crispin scanned the room, desperate for rope to tie them. It was then he became aware that he had fired both pistols and not reloaded them.

He would have to carry off a big bluff. Mochter realized that one of the pistols had been his and that Crispin had not had time to reload it. But Crispin trained the two guns on him and Mochter knew the other might be loaded, ready to put a lead ball in his belly.

Cyrus did not have the wit to question the readiness of Crispin's pistols and was easily bluffed. He cringed, alert to any demand, to any craven chance to save himself.

Mochter tried his own bluff. "So you're the one who abandoned my well-intentioned dinner yesterday. That was very rude, and now you have the audacity to challenge me and my aide with two guns, only one of which is loaded." .

"If only one is loaded, you can count on it that it is aimed at you, Mochter. Cyrus will not be the one shot," retorted Crispin.

Just then, Trevor, Dan, Olivia, our Indian friends and I arrived at the two bodies on the clearing in front of the cottage. We shouted in joy at our victory. This distraction allowed Mochter to pull his pistol from his belt, risking that Crispin would not fire.

Crispin quickly confronted him, "Don't try it, Mochter. If you shoot me, you'll be cut down by my comrades within seconds. Better to put the guns down and surrender."

By this time, Crispin realized that Mochter knew that both his guns were most likely harmless. His bluff was not going to work.

Crispin offered his guns to Mochter, but suddenly thrust them on the man to confuse him. At the same time he grabbed the leather bag from his shoulder and threw it at Cyrus, hitting him in the chest. Cyrus fired as he fell to the floor and the shot went wild. Mochter tried to fire but his hand was too swollen with poison ivy blisters to manipulate his trigger finger. Crispin then threw himself at Mochter and knocked him breathless and crushed him to the floor.

The tackle jarred Mochter's pistol to the floor. Crispin retrieved it and sat down in the Windsor chair. He was exhausted and exhilarated, and shouted, "The game's over, boys. One more move and one of you gets shot. It would be a pleasure. Any takers?"

Just then, the rest of us surged into the cottage. All of us had guns drawn and Crispin had no further need to deal with Mochter and

Cyrus. He ran into the back room where he found Ann Mclauren tied to a chair.

"Annie, did they hurt you? I'll kill the bastards if they did."

"No. They didn't harm me. Don't hurt them. I want to question them as soon as I can compose myself from this ordeal. I consider it poetic justice that you can tie them up with the rope they used on me."

We were all pleased that we had won with a minimum of bloodshed. We were even glad that Mochter and Cyrus were not shot. It was not any humane feeling we had for the pair of them, we wanted to know what brought them up here to the woods and why they had kidnapped me and then Annie McLauren. Just then, Dick and Pegg came into the room and were delighted to see that Mochter and Cyrrus had taken the bait as evidenced by their swollen hands

In a surprisingly stentorian voice Annie stood and said, "I claim the right to question them first before you all do—and in private. Now tie Mochter up and move him to the back room where I can interview him. This is official business."

They did as she had asked and then turned on Cyrus with questions.

I blurted, "I think you should save the questions for Annie to ask. She's been on this case for months and our intrusion may interfere with her success in bringing these two to justice."

There were a few embers smouldering in the fireplace and Dan threw o few spruce splints on them to bring the fire to life. There were rashers of bacon and a bowl full of eggs on the table.

"We must have interrupted their breakfast. How about it, everybody, bacon and eggs?" he asked. Everyone agreed as he reached for the iron skillet hanging from the overhead beam. Fifteen minutes later, Dan began to serve breakfast and the door to the back room opened. "You can come get Mochter and bring Cyrus in now," called Annie.

Mochter was seated, offered breakfast, and was bombarded with questions about our little battle, who were the dead men in uniform, was he rounding up horses for Howe, what were Cyrus' duties, *ad infinitum*. Crispin reached into the fireplace for a small splint of wood and sharpened the charred end on the rough stone of the hearth.

"You stood me up for your portrait sitting in New York. See what trouble you've put me to to arrange a second appointment," Crispin said with a cynical smile to Mochter and grabbed a linen dish towel

"So you're the painter with the grand reputation! I was disappointed to have to skip that sitting. Go ahead and sketch, but isn't that a dirty cloth to use for a canvas?"

Mochter's character appeared on the cloth early on. "Yes, it will suit your likeness perfectly," Crispin said.

"You're a friend of Claveraque's then, eh?"

"We've been good friends a long time."

"Then, I have probably met you someplace. Your voice is vaguely familiar. You will come to regret assisting him and opposing me."

"I don't think so, not where you're going. Have you heard of Simsbury Mines?"

Mochter shook his head.

"It's the only real estate in this country you'll earn. You will probably come to be very familiar with it."

With that, Crispin turned from Mochter and we all departed, hoping never to see him again.

Made in the USA
Charleston, SC
21 December 2010